THE WOUNDS

WE CARRIED HOME

THE WOUNDS WE CARRIED HOME

SUNIL SETHY

NU VOICE PRESS

First published by NU VOICE PRESS 2026
An imprint of Hubhawks Pvt. Ltd
www.nuvoicepress.com

ISBN: 978-81-995376-5-1

Typeset by: Pooja Sharma

Published by: Nu Voice Press
Printed at Manipal Technologies Limited, Manipal

To Rita

In your strength I abide

“A circle of light always gives me a sense of security. It leaves a soft blanket of darkness around it. I can hide in the darkness but still be comforted by the light.”

C.H. Zhu, *Descent*

“Still, you should know when a man’s heart wakes and his body, too, they can be bent this way or that, as the wind bends a sapling. But after a while the sapling stiffens and grows hard as a tree. Then it cannot be bent anymore, but grows to its own shape. The proper way for a man to grow is toward a woman — not toward a *femmenella.*”

Morris West, *The Devil’s Advocate*

Disclaimer

The Wounds We Carried Home contains mature themes and depicts traumatic events that may be distressing for some readers. The story includes portrayals of childhood sexual abuse, sexual assault, family dysfunction, grief and loss, miscarriage, identity struggles, emotional and physical betrayal, discussions of trauma, and references to wrongful accusations. It also touches on themes related to mental health, sexuality, and complex family dynamics across generations.

Reader discretion is strongly advised.

Author's Note

Life is full of twists, turns, and occasional clear paths. It would be a mistake, then, for the narrator of a story to believe that he can fully understand his characters, as they weave their way through the pages of a book and behave as portrayed, as if they had mysteriously stepped out into the real world. The author can, at best, establish a deep bond with his characters and, as they come alive in his artful hands, collaborate with them in determining their destinies.

Contents

Part I – Present Day

Chapter 1
Husna

Husna wakes with a start, and her hand strikes out in panic. It hits the Ikea table, and the Persian lamp starts a slow slide but stops, changing its position as the table rights itself. The darkness around her is a silky shroud; her slowly waking eyes pierce through its rich fabric to find the glimmer of light from the streetlamps outside her mother's house. She lies prone in her bed, her heart resonating with the dream—the unknown—trying to find its rhythm. As she gulps in air, a shadowy image lingers in her mind.

Unbidden, this image trespasses into her quiet sleep, bringing with it echoes of a past hidden in the mists of time. His long, pale hands, with their tapering fingers, slim wrists, and wiry black hair peeping shyly from under his sleeve, slowly smooth her brow, and she feels safe in the crook of his other arm as he hums her back to sleep. Who is this man whose presence in her dream leaves her forlorn and lost on awakening? Could it be her father, whom she hasn't seen since she was a baby?

After he disappeared from her life at an early age, and for as long as she can clearly remember, there wasn't a dominant male figure in her life, surrounded as she was by her mother and her grandmother. Immediately, Husna thinks of Adam, whom she loves with a single-minded passion that scares and consumes her. He is her present, her lover. They met in graduate school at the University of Wisconsin-Madison six months ago and have been together since. She wants him next to her now: his tender kisses would console her. Her body hungers for his firm strength, the passionate surrender, and then the cosy nestling against him. An image of him floats into her mind, his tousled head, soft brown hair cascading down to his sparkling blue eyes, and his large, awkward limbs. She shivers in anticipation, imagining his arms around her, holding her, caressing her.

Husna is majoring in Economics and Adam in Psychology; he wants to be a counsellor, as her mother, Kalpana, once was. Just the thought of her mother brings her emotions, held in check since the cremation, lunge chokingly up in her throat, forcing her to make unearthly guttural sounds as she dissolves into violent tears.

As the sky outside lightens and her sobs slowly subside, Husna looks back into her memories to find some clue about the shadowy image in her mind. She has always known that she was adopted as a baby by Kalpana, a few years before she left India with Husna to initially live with her mother, Urvashi, in New York. About her early life in India, Husna remembers nothing, except for a few vague shadows that occasionally pass through her mind, punctuated with occasional sensory signals—acrid cooking smells and notes of melancholy music—all buried deep somewhere in the recesses of her mind. At times, she senses thunder, lightning, and dark clouds outside large windows. She also remembers love and someone reading to her when she was very small, but try as she might, she just cannot recall this person's face. She struggles to clean the hazy windows of her mind, but still, there is nothing. She remembers the face of her kind grandfather, Urvashi's estranged husband, who died some years after they came to New York. She distinctly remembers his visit in Chicago when her mother moved here within a year of arriving in New York. Other male figures who had passed in and out of her childhood were her grandmother Urvashi's boyfriends, fascinated by this Indian heiress who taught yoga and who, even in middle age, looked stunning. But none of the men had left any lasting impression on Husna.

No, this man in her dreams was someone else. A manifestation of her intense longing for a father would be Adam's quick assessment if she had told him. And why is this dream repeating itself now, so soon after Kalpana and Urvashi have disappeared into the void? Once again, she chokes at this thought, but continues to deliberate rationally. Is there something about the accident that has triggered these dreams? Yes, that must be it! But the answer evades her. A voice from the past is trying to push its way into her memory; she searches her brain, but no face appears. Confused, she climbs out of bed and stands at the window, blindly staring at the street lights flickering in the distance, then turns away and lies down again.

"What happened to my father?" she had asked her mother when she realised that all families had one.

"Your father left us. I have told you that you were adopted," her mother had replied quickly, looking away from her hopeful face evasively. "You must, of course, have had a biological father and a mother, but now I am your only parent." Kalpana looked directly at her then, her face betraying nothing, no doubt nor deception.

"Tell me why he left us?" Husna had asked when she was older and understood that a father cannot just get up one day and walk out of one's life.

"I have no idea why he did it," Kalpana replied, but Husna's piercing gaze caught the pursed lips of her mother and the veil dropping over her grandmother's eyes. *They are hiding something, I know it!* She had thought to herself.

"Tell me, Mama! Tell me, Nana, please tell me!" She had pleaded again and again, but as always, they remained silent and unmoved.

By now, Husna's tears were falling unchecked; she lay back on her pillow and wept and wished Adam were with her.

"I feel so alone," she sobbed. "Why did you leave me, Mama… Nana, why?"

Twenty days earlier, before Husna's life had been overturned by this traumatic event, Kalpana and Urvashi had been working on a list of friends to call for the small get-together they had planned for her homecoming. She had just graduated. Urvashi had come down from New York, where she lived, and, on the spur of the moment, Kalpana and Urvashi decided to hold a little celebration at an Italian restaurant in downtown Chicago.

It had been a long time since Kalpana had openly talked to her mother about the pain she felt, her sense of being cheated in life, time and again, whether it was by Urvashi herself, who had never been part of Kalpana's childhood, or by her unfaithful and lying husband, Sudhir. Even the gods had decided to punish her by preventing her from having children. But then Husna came to fill her world with joy and happiness, though this was later overshadowed by Sudhir's treacherous betrayal. He had left her alone to bear the burden of keeping a secret from her own child. Husna's pleas to know more about her father made her break inside, the turmoil twisting her guts till she wanted to scream out in grief. Kalpana knew that one day she would tell her daughter about Sudhir, and it would have come to pass if only another cheating husband, besotted with a younger male companion, had not violently ended Kalpana's and Urvashi's lives on Lakeshore Drive.

***

Stewart, the cheating husband, should have been on the flight out from Midway that day if the notorious Chicago winds and unstable weather had not grounded the incoming flight at Minneapolis.

"We have transferred you to tomorrow's early morning flight to Pittsburgh," the bored ground staff had told him when his flight had been finally cancelled after a series of changing estimated times of departure. He had checked into an airport hotel and, after hiring a car, had driven to a bar that he normally frequented in downtown Chicago. He had called Marie, who was grumpily preparing their overactive twin boys for sleep before the babysitter arrived, to tell her that he would see her the next day. She sounded relieved; she had a dinner planned with her ex-beau back from his Afghanistan tour of duty and was happy that the guilt, which had been consuming her the whole day, could momentarily be put aside. A shadow crossed Stewart's mind after he got off the call; Marie had been socialising a lot lately, without him, he thought. But then he, too, had not been all that attentive, refusing to bring to his mind forbidden desires which had been plaguing him. *I can blame this on my solitary evenings in bars, in so many cities and towns,* he said to himself. In bars full of single men. He still wasn't ready to face up to the fact that he chose seedy bars mostly frequented by men, with the occasional desperate woman hoping to be picked by one of them. Fooling himself in denial, he wouldn't frequent gay bars.

Stewart was on his third drink when the just emptied barstool next to him was occupied by a young man. He could smell fresh soap and lime, and when he turned to look at the new occupant, he realised that he had seen him on the other side of the bar, drinking alone and occasionally running his gaze across the space between them, his eyes stopping a little bit longer on Stewart's face before moving, unseeingly, over other faces. Stewart, living within his own deceit, had been doing absolutely the same thing from his side of the bar.

"Hey! I'm Grant," said the young man. They shook hands, and he mumbled "Stewart" in return.

He is so young, fresh out of college, Stewart thought as he appraised Grant's fair skin and blond hair, broad pink lips, eyes the colour of cornflowers, upturned nose. There was a knowing smile in his innocent and direct look.

"I could do with some conversation tonight. Caught you looking and saw an opportunity when the dude sitting next to you went to the restroom. You look like you've had a rough day. You outta town?" he drawled.

Stewart felt the excitement in his loins and somehow knew that he had struck it good this time; this guy was going to lead him to places that he had denied himself. All thoughts of Marie and the twins swung conveniently away as he felt a stir of anticipation. They ordered another drink. Grant was "experimenting", trying to find himself. He had seen the look in Stewart's eyes, seen the want, the denial, the wedding band glinting, and it excited him. He had said he liked older men who were married, not revealing that closeted married men were so much hungrier and more passionate when they had an opportunity to lie with a man; not mentioning that they were far more generous with their gifts, even if sometimes it needed to be forced out of them using the right kind of persuasion.

After a few more drinks, they left the bar and headed for Stewart's airport hotel. In the parking lot, Grant kissed him deeply on his mouth. By the time Stewart drove off, Grant had pulled himself out and was struggling with the zipper of Stewart's trousers. Stewart stroked Grant while he steered with the other hand, and by the time they hit Lakeshore Drive, Grant had pulled him out and started stroking him, making him moan in ecstasy. He wanted him to stop, but it had been so long. They were so lost in their hedonistic pursuit that they ignored the beeps of the car reminding them to put their seatbelts on.

By the time the police reached the wrecks of the cars, three people had died: the two unlucky women in the Audi, smashed to their death when the hired car had swung into their path on the high-speed expressway, and Grant, whose neck had snapped when it hit the steering wheel, just as Stewart was about to come. Stewart, in the throes of release, was thrown clear, just as the Audi ploughed into his car. When he regained consciousness at the hospital, he was alone, suffering from a mild concussion, broken ribs, and facing a marriage in ruins, and a couple of years in jail for manslaughter.

***

Chapter 2
Adam

The Day before the Accident—

Adam is visiting his mother, Adina, in Winona County.

"How serious are you about your girlfriend, Adam? What did you say her name was? Husna?" she grills him as they walk into 'Signatures', Adam's favourite restaurant.

"Yes, Husna," Adam smiles. "It means beautiful in Arabic. And as for serious, I'd marry her today if she would have me. I love her, Eema."

Adam's mother is still handsome, given the fact that this is her fiftieth birthday. She is quite used to admiring glances, such as the ones she receives from some of the men and even the women, as the *maître d'* guides them to their table. Her naturally curly black hair frames her high cheekbones, and she has a slender, pointed nose. Adam often wonders how he ever got his button-shaped, slightly upturned nose. Adina's Jewish heritage lends her a Mediterranean exoticism, with her sharp features, hazel eyes, and tanned complexion. She gazes lovingly at her son while he busily devours a shrimp and crab-stuffed walleye.

"I wonder where all that food goes! Not an ounce of fat on you, while I am forever watching my weight," she says, looking approvingly at him, while picking at her sparse green salad dotted with egg slices and chicken strips.

"Eema, you will love her once you get to know her better," continues Adam, bringing the subject back to Husna. "If only you had spent more time with her when you visited Madison. She was shy and quite intimidated by your regal manner. I hope to bring her home at Thanksgiving so that you can spend more time with her."

Adam looks at his mother gently. "You know, she reminds me of you. Large black eyes, an enigmatic and mysterious smile... and she is the kindest and most sensitive person I have ever known. Now that I think of it, when I first laid my eyes on her at the UW's library, something drew me to her. I believe I saw something of you in her. And, no, I don't have an Oedipus complex!" he quickly adds when he sees Adina arching her eyebrows, the hint of a smile spreading over her striking features.

"But she is a gentile!" Adina continues, ignoring Adam's attempts to win her support by bracketing their beauty. "How will you bring up your children if you marry her? You have always been a good Jew, often visiting the synagogue, though not as many times as I would like. Would she allow your son's Bar Mitzvah? You said she is Hindu and adopted. I have no issue with her being adopted, but I am sure your father would never approve of marriage, if he were alive, given her religion! And when I met her, even though she looked self-assured, there was... it was just... just," Adina struggles to voice what she wants to say, "that somehow, I felt she was hiding behind a wall of immense sadness. She seems very vulnerable, and without intending to, of course, you or someone else could hurt her very much someday."

"Oh, Eema! Why bring *Abba* into this conversation!" Adam sighs, ignoring the comment on Husna's vulnerability, although knowing it to be true. "Jewish tradition clearly states that the child's religion is based on the mother's religion. My being a Jew does not mean that my child will have to be a Jew. And, Eema, you have always found our religion stifling. Abba had to force you to go to Israel to live on a kibbutz with him, and it had nothing to do with my being only two years old. If that sniper's bullet had not killed him, you would still be living in Israel, perhaps unhappily. You came to Winona, and thank god, I grew up in America, where I can be whatever I want to be. I visit the synagogue because you want me to, and I do it to assuage your guilt of deserting Israel and Abba's vision of living a true Jewish life out there."

Adina looks away, and Adam stops, realising that he has gone too far. He has touched on a sore and emotional point, and now he feels awful as he watches her struggling to hold back her tears. He puts his hand out to cover hers and says, "I apologise. That really was not kosher. Forgive me. I know how much you loved Abba. I came home to celebrate your special day, your fiftieth birthday; I wanted this to be our weekend, Eema."

Adam signals the waiter, who fills their glasses with more champagne, and then Adam raises a toast, "Happy birthday, my charming mother. I love you and always will."

They leave soon after. Adam is leaving early next morning for Madison, in time for classes, and Adina has her teaching job at Winona High School. They drive to the town of Goodview, where Adina's parents had settled after leaving Germany to escape persecution during the Second World War. This was where her brother, Amos, had come back from New York to die. Adam has grown up here, except for the one year that he spent in the kibbutz in Israel, and he knew every lake, creek, and forest of this beautiful county. As the landscape slips past his window, Adam thinks of his early life in Goodview, the anguish when his beloved Uncle Amos had died of

AIDS; he was openly gay at a time when homosexuality was met with ostracism, even in liberal cities like New York and San Francisco. When it was discovered that he was HIV positive, his lover deserted him; Amos had no one else to turn to, so he came home to his sister, her eight-year-old son, and a father who did not want to see his face, let alone allow him to live under the same roof. It was Adina who pleaded on his behalf and allowed him the dignity of breathing his last among loved ones. In the early days of the disease, when Amos was still healthy, Adam and his uncle spent glorious days cycling and hiking in the hills surrounding the small lakes in this area of Minnesota. They used to swim in the cold waters and fish for walleye. Later, after they had roasted and enjoyed the fish, they would lie down on the picnic blanket and, as they lazily sunned themselves, Amos would tell Adam about his exciting life as an actor on Broadway in New York.

But in a small town like Goodview, tongues wagged even faster than dogs' tails, and the family were treated like lepers. Luckily, Adam's school did not hold Adina responsible for her brother's "deviant" behaviour, but Adam still had to suffer the cruelty of the young. He was hounded by cries of "faggot" or "homo," and the boys would give him a wide berth if he passed them in the corridor. Girls, too, would pull their boyfriends closer when he passed them, calling out, "Hands off, he's mine!"

At Amos's funeral, there weren't enough mourners to form the *Shura,* but some members of the community did provide the first meal for the family to sit *Shiva* for the departed soul.

After Amos's death, Adam sought refuge within himself. He had loved his uncle, and his death had left a giant hole in Adam's heart, but, if nothing else, his death brought an end to the incessant bullying. Snide remarks were made occasionally, when some idiot would giggle and look at Adam knowingly when someone's sexual orientation was being debated. However, he was largely left alone from then on.

Adam learned early on not to show his feelings. His childhood friend, John, a Roman Catholic whose parents had emigrated from Poland, stood by him throughout this period, but the feeling of being a victim stayed with him for a long time. In high school, Adam dated as many girls as he could, just to prove his sexuality, earning himself a dubious reputation. He saw women as sexual objects and wasn't ready to form a committed relationship. It was only when his prom date got pregnant and they had to go through a messy abortion (the girl was Catholic) that he came to his senses. Adina gave Adam the money to pay for the abortion, but punished him by grounding him for months after that. The ensuing period of introspection gave Adam a deep understanding of his motivations and also inspired him to read more about the human mind and its continuous war with itself. Long before he passed high school, Adam had decided to study psychology, which became his major at Madison. He wanted to be a psychological counsellor and help others, mainly the young, who saw themselves as, or were, victims.

"You are deep in thought, Adam." His mother's voice brings him back to the present.

Adam looks away from the window and smiles, "I was thinking of Uncle Amos and how much he would have loved Husna."

"Have you told her about him?" Adina asks sharply.

"No, we haven't talked about him yet," Adam lies. He does not want to tell his mother about Husna's horrified look when he had told her that Amos had been gay. Her reaction had baffled him and made him uneasy.

They drive on in silence until they can make out the glow of the lights of Goodview in the distance. Adam looks at his watch; it is nearing 11 pm, and he is looking forward to sleeping in his old bedroom, his sanctuary during all those years of growing up and even more so during the traumatic year of his uncle's illness. Adam loves the red maple tree outside his bedroom window; it was his escape route on the days he was grounded after the abortion. He wants to bring Husna to this room and show her all his childhood memories. He would drive her around the picturesque and quaint county with its lakes and Sioux history.

"Adam, I can hear your cell phone buzzing. You seem to be lost?" Adina says as they turn into the driveway and she punches the garage button. Adam pulls out his cell, Husna's name flashing, and happily puts the phone to his ear.

"Hello?" It is Kathy's voice, Husna's roommate at their apartment. "Adam, there's been a terrible accident." Adam's heart starts racing. *Why wasn't Husna on the phone?* "It's Husna's mother and grandmother... their car was in a collision in Chicago, and they are in a serious condition at the hospital. We're both heading for Chicago now... wait, wait, Husna wants to talk to you."

Husna's frightened, sobbing voice comes on the line.

"Adam, oh my god! I know they are both dead, Adam, I am sure of it, though the patrol officer didn't say so, but I could hear it in his voice. I know, I *just* know it, I'm an orphan now..."

Adam can hear her struggling to hold herself together, and all he can say is, "Hush, baby, everything will be fine, it will be fine."

Kathy takes the phone back.

"Kathy," Adam says, his voice tight, "who is driving?"

"Husna! She insisted on it, told me that she would go mad if she had nothing to do, and clearly, she knows the route better than I do. Don't worry, I am not going to take my eyes off the road, even for a moment."

"Thank you, Kathy. Thank you for being there for Husna. I'm just dropping my mom home and will head for Chicago as soon as I can. I will see you at the hospital. Just text me the name and address. Shouldn't take me more than five hours to be with you."

Adina, looking shocked, quickly helps Adam put all his stuff into his backpack—there isn't much to pack anyway—and hugs him tight. Jumping back into his car, Adam's soon driving down Interstate I-94E, headed towards Milwaukee, and then on to Chicago.

Husna, Husna... hold on, honey. I'm coming, he whispers to himself. *Oh god, just let them not die!*

***

Chapter 3
Adam

As Adam drives towards Chicago, images of Husna, from her moods and laughter to her intense belief in justice, flicker in front of him like a kaleidoscope. He marvels at what she has come to mean to him in just a few months.

It was just like any other day that Adam, looking for solitude in the library, had spotted a table with only a single occupant. He had hardly looked at the girl who was sitting there, lost in her book. He was soon lost in Dr Stephen Everson's treatise on ancient concepts of the nature of the psyche and the dualism of Plato and Plotinus, when he heard the unmistakable sound of a mobile phone vibrating somewhere close by. The girl seemed completely oblivious to the irritating buzz that was clearly emitting from her bag and grating on Adam's nerves. He looked angrily at her bent head just as she raised hers and gave his hostile stare a 'what's your beef?' look in response. When he pointedly looked at her bag, she sheepishly realised the source of his irritation. Shamefaced, she jumped up from her chair (making even more noise than her phone), grabbed her bag, and raced out of the library, presumably to take the call, leaving her book open on the table.

Never one to believe in the cliché of being struck by lightning, Adam shocked himself with what he did next. Glancing furtively at the door, he quickly peeked at her book, titled *Peace and Conflict: The South Asian Experience*. Then he spied her student ID card, which she had forgotten on the table, and was about to take a peek at her name, when he saw her coming back, and quickly began making a big show of hunting for a lost pen under her book.

"My name is Husna, and I am an Indian American, just to satisfy your curiosity," she said, standing with her hands on her hips, "and I definitely do not appreciate your jiggery-pokery!" With that, she picked up her book and card and moved to another table, leaving Adam red-faced. *Jiggery-pokery indeed! Damn the Brits and the ridiculous expressions they had left behind after the Raj*, Adam swore to himself.

But by then, Adam had been swept away on a tide which was never going to ebb. Something had shifted deep inside him. At that moment, when Husna had raised her head and looked at him with such charming irritability, his heart was lost. Long eyelashes sweeping over a perfect dusky face of beautiful proportions, a delicate jaw anchoring an oval face, and dark eyes angrily looking at him. He was completely captivated. Adam knew, *just knew*, at that very moment, that this was the girl he had been waiting for all these years.

Before that day in the library, Adam had never sought a long-term relationship. In high school, he was busy proving his machismo. If any relationship looked like it was going to go beyond the physical—a girl wanting to know more about what went around his head, or about his early life, or why he was such a bastard—Adam just disappeared into himself. He built zones around himself, and entry was strictly monitored. When the abortion happened, it opened Adam's eyes to what he was. It made him sick: his selfishness, the bizarre need to prove his 'straightness', and his weakness in trying to blame his gay uncle for his own insecurities. Later, in college, Adam stayed away from any serious relationships and hung around in nerdy groups, where the main pastimes were discussions of the Freudian theory of the ego and superego, or the parallels with Kant's moral reason and inner sense, or Hegel's thought, or everyone's favourite: Nietzsche, the anti-Christ and anti-Semite.

During the early months of his master's, Adam had started going out with Nancy, a young sophomore he had met at one of the socials. Impressed with his pretentious ideas, Nancy started following Adam around, or so he felt. He kept meeting her at every bar or party he went to. One day, Adam cornered her and asked if she was stalking him. She replied, "Yes," with such seriousness that Adam's expression twisted in shock. Her brashness and his reaction prompted them both to start laughing. After that, they discovered that they had a lot in common: she was from a small town near Colorado and, like Adam, wanted to escape the small-town provincial attitudes. Plus, she had a weakness for brainy dudes. They met many times after that, and Adam basked in her admiration, but when she wanted to make their relationship more serious, he backed off.

Until the day he spoke to Husna at the library, Adam was satisfied with his single status. During his studies, he discovered that the trauma of his past could find salvation in Eastern Philosophy. He found a young yoga teacher who gave him twice-weekly lessons in various yogic exercises and encouraged him to visit the Shambhala Meditation Centre for meditation sessions; he had yet to sign up for the classes.

Adam saw Husna a few days later, on a Saturday, while hiking on the Lakeshore Path towards Picnic Point. He had planned a solitary hike with a swim after. The path wound through the woods, and he could hear the sounds of birds warning other feathered friends about this human interloper, one of possibly many others, as it was a popular hiking trail. But today, surprisingly, Adam didn't meet another hiker. He was happily enjoying the meditative silence and sunlight as it gently caressed the soft green trees when suddenly, he heard a crash and a cry of distress on one of the trails ahead of him. He pushed forward quickly down the trail to find Husna, her name vivid in his memory, seemingly in great pain and supported by a very handsome young man, whose origins could have been from any part of Central Asia. A bicycle was lying twisted on the side of the trail, and there was another (presumably the handsome guy's) propped against a tree.

"Hey," the man said, waving at Adam, "good to see you, we sure need some help!"

Husna, recognising Adam, spoke through teeth gritted in pain.

"Oh, shucks! The last person I would have ever asked for help."

The man looked at Husna, surprised.

"You know each other?" he asked.

"No!" Adam and Husna both replied in unison.

Adam quickly moved forward to support Husna from the other side, but she shooed him off. He looked at Husna and her companion questioningly, and by way of explanation, the man told him that they had been bird watching. Adam noticed the binoculars around their necks as the man continued. In the excitement of chasing a male indigo bunting, which was flying close to the ground in front of their bikes, Husna missed a protruding root and came crashing down, twisting her bike and ankle.

"By the way, I am Feroz and this is..."

"Husna," Adam interjected.

"So, you do know each other?" Feroz replied in confusion.

"No!" Adam and Husna both said together again, and despite her pain, Husna laughed.

"I'm Adam," said Adam, with a little smile.

Adam held on to Husna's twisted bike along with his own while Feroz made her sit on his bike. The trio walked together back to the university hospital to have Husna's ankle checked.

"I just hope that it's a sprain and not a fracture," Feroz said, at which Husna grimaced.

On the way, Husna, now a little friendlier towards Adam, told him that she had been an avid bird watcher for many years. She had dragged Feroz with her, explaining, "he hardly knows nature, considering he is a city boy from Lahore. It is in Pakistan by the way, which I am sure you wouldn't know." *Indian Americans believing all white Americans are ignorant*, Adam thought, but kept quiet and let her have her say. Husna continued, "…to catch birds, with our binoculars." They had left very early in the morning, before the crowds scared the birds away from their natural habitat.

"But your countries are always at war, aren't they?" Adam asked, which got him a withering look from Husna.

"Ah, but Indian girls love handsome Punjabi men from Pakistan," replied Feroz, which got him a good pounding on the side of his head.

Adam's heart sank; they definitely seemed sweet on each other. With his spirits sagging, he wanted to leave as soon as they reached the hospital. However, Feroz suggested that they exchange mobile numbers, so that he could let Adam know how Husna fared.

A week later, Adam texted Feroz and asked about Husna's ankle.

"We had it strapped that day, and I suppose she is hobbling around these days," was his answering text.

That means they don't see each other every day, Adam exulted.

He went on Facebook to look for her, and although he did come across two profiles with the same name, both turned out to be from Pakistan. He couldn't find her, which he found extremely surprising. A few days later, Feroz invited Adam to The Terrace for a talk by a prominent Lord of Indian descent, from the House of Lords in the UK, on the Indo-Pak Friendship Forum. He guessed that the reason Feroz invited him was because of his ill-timed remarks on the relationship between the two countries. The talk was part of a Friendship Series, normally held by various student bodies, between politically warring countries. These talks were normally chaired by a prominent member of one of the countries and delved into the centuries-old bonds shared between the citizens of both countries.

Adam went in the hope that he would meet Husna, and he wasn't disappointed. She was there, standing with a large group of students. What surprised Adam, though, was the interactive talk between the Lord of Indian descent, a Parsi (descendants of the Pharisees from Iran who came to live in India in the eighth century to escape persecution) and the audience. They talked about the shared history, art, music, dance, food, and language that bound the people of the Indian sub-continent until politics and the British arrogantly decided that India would not be able to govern itself without splitting the subcontinent into two countries.

Husna told Adam later that his understanding of it being a matter of different religions was very simplistic and that the issue was far more complex, covering territorial greed and tense military standoffs. She had understood this from intense discussions between her mother and grandmother.

During the talk, Husna had somehow manoeuvred to take the seat next to Adam and whispered, "The politicians may fight, but the common folk want friendship. You Americans are so ignorant of what goes on beyond your borders."

"And what are you, if not an American?" Adam whispered back.

"I'm not sure who or what I am," she said matter-of-factly.

Adam was taken aback. He felt that there was a lot left unsaid behind those words, and he was surprised that she had so easily confided in him.

After the session finished, Adam and Husna just naturally walked away without reaching out to Feroz and their other friends. She asked him to join her for dinner at 'Maharani', an Indian restaurant nearby. Adam was secretly thrilled that it was only the two of them. At the restaurant, Husna told him that she had asked Feroz to call him for the talk.

"And why was that?" Adam asked, trying to suppress a grin.

"I could easily tell you that it was because of your ignorance," replied Husna, "but, no, I wanted to see you and get to know the nosy guy who was poking his head in my books at the library."

She smiled so sweetly when she said this that Adam had to fight the urge to take her into his arms right then and there. Before ordering, she asked him whether he only ate kosher, saying, "I have no idea how they kill their meat here."

Adam laughed and told her that he was fine with any food.

"But what made you think that I am a Jew?" he asked.

"From your name, Shimon," Husna shrugged, and Adam was surprised that she had found out his last name, as he had introduced himself only by his first name at Lakeshore Path. He told her that he had to Google 'jiggery-pokery' to find out what it really meant, though it was quite clear at the library what she wanted to say.

"How come you used such a British phrase even though you are an American?" he asked.

She told him that her mother had lived and studied in Indian schools, which were more British than schools in England.

"Not the Indians, though. They speak the Queen's English and are crazily proud of it," she added.

"I tried to find you on Facebook and was completely taken aback when I couldn't," Adam said, as they were walking back to her apartment from the restaurant.

"I've never been on social media, nor do I plan on it," Husna explained. "I learnt this from my mother, who is a very private person. I am actually very shy, and I can't imagine sharing my personal life with all and sundry. I find it so difficult to understand how people can share so much information about themselves. Nope, it's not for me."

Over the next few days, then weeks, and then months, Adam and Husna discovered each other. They became inseparable. Each day was new as they explored the different lives the other had lived till then. Husna told Adam vaguely about her Indian roots, about her American-ness always being shadowed by a home country she had never been to but lived through the conversations of her mother and grandmother. She opened up about the deep longing she felt for her foster father, which was lodged inside her, and how sometimes she wondered whether he had ever existed. Then there were the mixed cultures, the subtle racism in school and her brand of ethics and moral behaviour, learned, no doubt, from the Anglo-Indian morality practised by her mother, which so often alienated her from her other school friends. Adam wanted her to tell him more about what this meant.

"Oh, things like not being allowed to hold hands on your first date, only kissing after the tenth date, and so on," Husna explained.

"And what does 'and so on' lead to?" Adam smirked, but she wouldn't be led and asked him to shut up.

She talked about her mother, who watched over her like a hawk, often stifling Husna with her intense love and attention. Adam told her about his dad, who had died in Israel, about the lonely life at the kibbutz and their return to his grandparents in America after his father's death. About his mom, whose bohemian behaviour when they lived in the kibbutz turned to orthodox Jewishness, supposedly out of guilt for having ignored his father's rigid adherence to Judaism when he was alive. He talked about the love he had for his uncle and the circumstances of his death. It was then that her mood changed; she became silent and looked away, pursing her lips. By now, Adam had figured out that meant disapproval, so he asked her what the problem was. She just said, "I don't like gays!" and wouldn't clarify further. Adam was about to tell her about the sneers and the taunts that he had to face when he was in high school, but decided to leave it for another day, even though he knew he would need to find the reasons for her antagonism to gays.

They would often go on double dates with Husna's roommate, Kathy and her boyfriend, Colin. Once, during the intermission at Overture, where they had gone to see the musical *Chicago*, Colin pointed out a famous but ageing playwright in the audience with a beautiful man, young enough to be his son. Later at dinner, Colin regaled them with stories of the young man, Trevor, as being the arm candy of many ageing but famous gay men, a fact that he had picked up from the gossip columns of the tabloids that he loved to read.

Throughout the conversation, Husna looked appalled and finally blurted out, "I think it is disgusting that gays flaunt their relationships in public. What is worse is how they seem to be so polygamous, jumping from one relationship to another!"

"Hey, baby," Adam said, trying to calm her down, "you can't generalise like that; homosexual relationships are the same as heterosexual ones and they are, more often than not, monogamous." Husna just shrugged her shoulders disbelievingly, and Kathy changed the subject.

Kathy and Husna were childhood friends, both from Chicago. After high school, they both chose to apply to Madison University so they could stay together. While Husna was an introvert, sitting with her nose in a book most days, Kathy was diametrically opposite. Vivacious and loud, the beautiful blonde loved making shocking remarks in company. Even Husna, who preferred serious conversation and did not normally enjoy trivialities, laughed happily at her jokes and smart comments. With them, it was clearly the case of opposites attract. Kathy looked out for Husna like a big sister, and Husna adored Kathy, warning Adam early in their relationship that any criticism of Kathy was absolutely taboo. Luckily, Kathy and Adam hit it off from the word go, precisely for the same reasons that Husna loved her. She was a great balance and foil to both their 'no laughing matter' blinkered vision of life and the world. Kathy once told Adam that she would "fucking hunt him down" if he hurt Husna, ever. That was her way of warning him off if he wasn't serious about his relationship with Husna.

Adam and Husna realised by their second meeting that they were crazily in love with each other. They met most of the time, and if on any day they were away from each other, they would be on the phone at least twice. They did have their share of disagreements, but it never pushed them away from each other. Once, Husna walked out of a restaurant in anger over a trivial argument about Colin's habit of gossiping about famous people, which became too personal. But when they met the next day, the look that Husna gave Adam from under her lashes made him forget the anger that he had felt when she had left him in the lurch the previous day.

Surprisingly, it was Husna who first kissed him after an evening together. After the dinner at the Indian restaurant, Adam asked her out the next day. When he was dropping her back at her apartment, she turned towards him and, before he could make a move, held his face in her hands and kissed him fully on the lips.

"I have been wanting to do that the whole evening, maybe even earlier," she said. By then, Adam had taken her into his arms and was fervently returning her kiss, his body curving into hers as every nerve in his awakened, razor-sharp. He didn't want to rush her, but a few days later, he invited her for dinner at his studio apartment.

Adam had taken great pains with the menu; there was seared salmon with lentil salad, followed by spaghetti aglio e olio with veggies, topped off with a triple chocolate mousse, which he had picked up from a neighbouring patisserie. A bottle of Edna Valley Chardonnay was chilling in the bottle cooler. They were going to eat at the kitchen counter itself, and Adam had set it up for two with a large bottle-candle in the centre.

Husna arrived by cab; Adam had offered to pick her up, but she wanted to come by herself. She put a bottle of Pinot Grigio on the counter and walked straight into his arms. Adam held her tenderly and kissed her softly. They clung to each other; Adam heard her sigh in his arms, then she put her hand on his face and traced the outline of his lips. Adam felt a deep contentment just holding her to himself, and as they looked into each other's eyes, they knew that this was a love that was going to last forever. Nothing needed to be said. Soft and seductive jazz streamed out of Adam's Bose speakers as Husna walked around his apartment, commenting on the décor and the Van Gogh prints on the walls.

"Thank god, I didn't bring you to my place; it's a hovel in comparison to this tastefully done-up apartment," she said.

They were sipping glasses of crisp wine on the sofa after dinner when Adam got up and held out his hand to Husna. They walked together to his bedroom. She kicked off her shoes while Adam removed his, and they both lay facing each other on the bed. The glow of a single table lamp shone on Husna's angelic face in the dimly lit room. Her full lips were wet where she had licked them. With a small cry, Adam enveloped her mouth with his, passionately kissing her, filling her with his love and himself.

"I love you," he said, "and will love you forever."

"Don't let me go," Husna breathed into his neck.

Adam's mouth slowly moved from her lips to her ears, her eyes, down to her neckline. He tenderly removed her top and bra and put his mouth on her, making her gasp in anticipation. Desperately, they removed their clothes, and then she was naked in his arms, her dusky beauty waiting as Adam melted into her body. Husna's hands moved tightly around him as he entered her. She was ready and waiting, and as they moved in unison, she moaned and gave out soft cries of pleasure; Adam could feel her nails digging into his back as she became taut and, with a shudder, started to come. He couldn't wait any longer, and as his thrusts grew faster, he came inside her. For a long time afterwards, they held onto each other with their lips playing over each other's faces, and then lay back, spent and in complete harmony...

The deep buzz of Adam's phone pulls him out of his reverie; he has almost forgotten he is still on the freeway. It is Kathy.

"Adam, terrible news, both Husna's mother and grandmother have died. Their injuries were too severe. Husna is in shock, and the doctor has given her a sedative. We are both in the Double Tree, not too far from the North-western Memorial Hospital. I've put Husna to bed. She will need to handle all the arrangements tomorrow, so I thought it best she gets some sleep. I'll wait up for you. How far are you from us?"

Adam looks at the GPS; it shows he is about half an hour from the hospital.

"I'll be there in thirty minutes. Book me a room, too?"

Kathy hugs Adam at the hotel reception. They grab a coffee from the counter, and she tells him about the heartrending scene when they got to the hospital. When the cops told Husna the details and the nature of the accident, she kept crying and calling the other men in the other car "animals and deviants," even though one of them had also died instantly at the scene.

"The guys weren't up to any good, for sure, given the state of their partial nakedness," says Kathy. "The cops are sure that it was because of what they were doing that they lost control and caused the crash." Kathy looks as shocked as Adam when she tells him this. Whatever the reasons are for Husna's hatred of gays, this accident will ironically legitimise her animosity.

***

Chapter 4
Husna

It has been two weeks since Adam left Husna at her mother's house in Chicago. He had stayed with Husna throughout the paperwork with the hospital and the interviews with the cops. Husna had quietly cremated her mother and grandmother with only Adam and Kathy present. It was as if suddenly she had matured. She was calm and collected throughout the Hindu service and the various rituals that followed, meant to ensure that the souls reached the afterlife, as the priest intoned Sanskrit verses that none of them, including Husna, understood. The priest, however, spoke fluent English and translated some of the texts as he read them, explaining the need for each ritual and how its practice nourished the soul on its journey, roaming through the sacred Hindu sites before it was ready for rebirth. The only time Adam saw Husna letting her emotions get the better of her was when the bodies of her mother and grandmother were consigned to the electric furnace of the crematorium. She held his hand tightly as he heard sharp sobs rack her body, but she held on. After that, they leave for New York to pack and store her grandmother's possessions till Husna makes up her mind about what to do with them and the house, which has been bequeathed to her mother and, in the event of her death, Husna.

When they return to Chicago, Husna, who has been up and running like a demon, tells Adam that she wants to be alone with her mother's memories in the house before she tackles her possessions. Adam wants to stay with her, but she is firm that she needs the time alone and that, in any case, "you need to submit your dissertation to the university, so please go."

Adam is just wrapping up his dissertation when Husna calls. She seems excited; there is an unexpected lift to her voice.

"Adam, I've just found a manuscript; there is a note with it, and it mentions me."

"A manuscript? What are you talking about, Husna? What manuscript?" he replies.

"I was going through my mother's cupboard, removing her dresses and packing them away, and hidden right behind all the dresses was this manuscript. There is a note. Shall I read it to you?"

She continues without waiting for his answer.

I am sending this manuscript to you through your Mom, as she refuses to give me your address.

Maybe someday you will let Husna read it... when she is older. It may help her to understand.

"The note is unsigned, but it comes with a painting. Can you come back to Chicago?"

"Now?" Adam asks, worried about having to finish his dissertation.

"Yes, now, if you have finished your project," Husna replies. "I want to read the manuscript with you. I am apprehensive about what it will reveal. Why is this manuscript with my mother? Who wrote it? I just feel sure it will tell me something about my father. The painting, too, is very strange."

"What do you mean strange?"

"It's of a young boy sitting... but there's something odd about his appearance. His hands are large and calloused, and he has an angelic face, but there is a slightly malevolent, almost knowing, look about him. He frightens yet attracts at the same time..." she tails off.

"Whoa, okay," Adam replies gently, "you're obviously disturbed. I should be there tomorrow; I just need to hand over the project, all printed and tied up, by today."

The next day, Adam drives to Chicago and to Naperville, where Husna's mother's beautiful home is. It is a typical Craftsman double-storeyed house on a wide, tree-lined avenue, with a covered porch, a lovely lawn in the backyard, and a tiny brook running just behind the property. After hugging Husna, Adam heads for the guest room downstairs, where he stayed when he visited, but Husna takes him upstairs to her room instead, situated just next to her mother's. Husna's room is spacious with a writing table that holds her laptop. The writing table is placed just below casement windows, which look out to the front of the house. Branches from the beautiful oak tree outside tap lightly against her window, and a splash of bright sunlight falls on the cashmere bedspread, giving the room a rich, golden glow.

"There it is," she says, pointing to a manuscript, its edges curled slightly, lying on the table. Adam can make out the title, *The Wounds We Carried Home*, on the first page, but there is no clue about the author. Next to the manuscript is a painting. It is of a fourteen or fifteen-year-old boy who is looking unwaveringly out at the observer. His hands, as Husna described, are too large for his body, which is clothed in a blousy white shirt and brown trousers that merge into the background of the painting. The boy has sharp features and a narrow mouth, and the look on his face isn't malevolent exactly, but his eyes look as if they had seen all the tragedies of the world. It is a sweet face, but it is also damaged. Yes, that is the word—damaged—not malevolent. Adam suddenly feels sad looking at it.

He asks to see the note that came with the manuscript. It is handwritten, though the manuscript itself is a printed document, and is slightly yellowed with age. It looks like it had lain in Husna's mother's cupboard for many years.

Knowing that Husna wants to dig deep into the manuscript, they settle down on her bed and start reading together.

***

Part II – Manuscript

Prologue

"Speak to me, Sush!" I nervously shout at Sushmita, who has turned pale and looks as if she is ready to throw up. I shake her firmly as she tries to get a hold on herself to speak, but the words seem to be choking her. I look around helplessly; maybe the doorbell will ring or Ramu the cook will break another dish or the cooker will blow its whistle, anything but this. I now wish I had seen the letter beforehand. Then I would have kept this to myself. I would have been deceitful, as always, and let certain truths be forever locked inside me. *I can feel the panic building up inside me, but I push it away, desperately looking for a way out.*

It was a morning like any other, grey and dreary, with the monsoon just a whisper away from arriving in Bombay. I looked out the large ornate windows and was elated to see that the roads outside were wet, but even though the clouds looked threatening, the weather forecast did not predict showers, so they would disappoint once again. The hazy sun played peek-a-boo with the patches of dark cloud floating over the horizon beyond the sea. It was humid, still, and overcast, just the kind of day to receive gloomy news. I came to the end of my morning walk, smiling at other irritable-looking walkers, who probably wondered what reason there was to smile given the oppressive atmosphere, but forced a perfunctory smile in return.

That morning, Sushmita walked into the large sitting room as I sat down with my morning cuppa and the newspapers. She looked annoyed, but that was normal; she hated waking up to the world, and she hated my cheeriness in the mornings. I, on the other hand, loved to rise early. Sometimes, I would enjoy a round of golf if I wasn't taking a brisk walk along the tree-lined pathways around our condominium, as I had that morning. Sushmita was busiest in the evenings and wasn't usually at home when I returned from work on the few days that I was in Bombay. Most days, she would return from her late yoga or frenzied fitness workouts after I had showered and settled down in the sitting room with a large scotch and jazz streaming through the Bluetooth speaker. Our daughter would be in her evening bath, splashing water in the tub with the nanny.

That day, at work, it was the usual routine—meetings and more meetings. Stella, my secretary and all-time lifesaver, was dousing a verbal onslaught from someone on the phone who had been persistently seeking an appointment for the past month. Between meetings, some IT guys bustled around my office trying to connect my desktop PC, imported from Taiwan. They finally left, promising to demonstrate the system for my benefit the next day. Office hours had ended, but I stayed to deal with a pile of letters in my in-tray. Finally, with relief, I turned my attention to the unopened 'private and personal' mail folder kept aside by Stella, which contained two letters, one from the hotel where I normally stayed in Delhi and the other from Clive.

Letters from Clive were always a joy to read; they were full of hope, love, and friendship. I saved them like a child saving the best sweet for last. I sat back and opened Clive's letter, looking forward to reading his news; instead, I couldn't believe what he had to say. Clara, his wife, had gone through our private mail and believed that we were in a relationship. She was planning to use our letters to petition for a divorce. *How could Clara read his private mail?* My mind raced. Was this all an overreaction on his part, given that his marriage was already on rocky terrain? We both know we are innocent of Clara's accusations; clearly, in thought and deed, Clive is innocent here. *Am I, too, in thought?*

With everything swirling through my mind, I forgot all about the other letter from the hotel, which I carried home and had carelessly tossed on the dining table. Sushmita, thinking the letter would contain more of the freebies that the hotel often gave us, opened it and called through to me in the sitting room, "Let's hope they are planning to give us a free weekend in Goa, considering how many times you have stayed in that hotel chain."

After that, there was silence for a few moments, and then I heard her let out an anguished cry. She walked into the sitting room, looking absolutely flabbergasted and gave me the letter accusingly without saying a word before sitting down heavily on the sofa. I looked at her, then opened the letter. Inside was an envelope labelled 'private and confidential', containing another letter, the one which had been opened by Sushmita. With a feeling of dread, I saw that it was from Karl and even before reading it, I knew what it would contain. I was in serious trouble. I knew that I would be sucked into the vortex created by this tsunami from where it would be impossible for me to swim back to the shore.

A series of troubled thoughts runs through my mind as I wait for Sushmita to say something.

I can see that she has pulled herself together and is now looking at me as if seeing me for the first time. Angry and perplexed, everything is suddenly falling into place. I am so absorbed with the raging battle between my thoughts and the kaleidoscopic emotions flitting across her face that I witness her outburst as if watching a movie.

"Tell me, Arvind, you deceiving bastard, tell me that you aren't... that you are not a..." She gulps and swallows, her words choked by her great, heaving sobs.

I know that there is no way out for me, except to come clean to Sushmita. I had to tell her about my life and all the secrets that I had kept hidden from her.

***

Chapter 1
Tillotama – 1947

There is complete chaos at the station. Throngs of people are pushing inside, and the few who want to leave are being pushed back onto the platform. A great sea of humanity moves towards the platforms where trains are leaving Lahore for destinations across the now-partitioned India. But they are full, with no room either inside or on the top of the trains, not even on the curved roof of the steam engine. In the background, some distance away, the call of the muezzin echoes over the rooftops, a grim reminder to many of the reason for their flight. Manmohan is desperately looking around for his friend Abdul, who has promised to get them seats on the train on his unreserved tickets to Amritsar. His old mother, in her thick-lensed, soda-bottle-sized glasses, is peering around with interest. She nudges his wife, Tillotama, whose pregnancy is just starting to show, to point at a small boy shyly eyeing them from his mother's lap.

"Tillotama, look! Look at that little boy, tempt him to your lap, and you will have a son."

Tillotama is weary and frightened; having a son is far from her thoughts. She looks at every bearded *Mussulman* passing by, as if she is in danger of getting raped right then and there. She cannot forget the last terrible month in Lahore, so soon after she had married Manmohan; her waking hours and even her dreams are haunted by the trauma of those days. The cries of, "kill the bastard Hindustanis!" rising from the old Muslim Quarter, the rush of Hindu men to the *mohalla* screaming, "the *Mussulmans* are coming, the *Mussulmans* are coming!"

the scrambling of the women to the roof terraces of the houses intending to throw themselves off rather than be taken should their men downstairs, armed with knives, swords and kitchen implements, be overcome. Thinking about it makes Tillotama shiver, and the hair on her arms stands on end.

Focusing on the chatter of her garrulous mother-in-law, *Bheji,* Tillotama finds some semblance of calm and thinks back to the days before she married Manmohan. She recalls her childhood, first in Srinagar and later, as she grew up, in Rawalpindi. She thinks of her friend, Maya, somewhere in Kashmir, her other friend, Waheeda, in Rawalpindi, and her wonderful brother, Randhir, who is already in India. He left Rawalpindi for Old Delhi earlier in the year along with their younger brothers, Shiv and Trilok, and her parents. Her father had already exchanged his lands in Rawalpindi with a friend who owned property near Kashmiri Gate in Delhi. Manmohan had sneered at this, telling her that after Partition, the new governments of India and Pakistan would not recognise the changed ownership deeds. However, she had shown no interest in his ever-present antagonism towards her family.

From the time she was just over a year old until she was six, Tillotama was sent to live with her grandmother in Kashmir. A few months after her birth, her mother had found out that she was pregnant again and therefore sent Tillotama, a mere toddler, to her own mother, as she couldn't take care of both her and the new baby. Tillotama was brought back home to join her brothers, Randhir and Shiv, five years later.

She remembers how much she loved going on family vacations to Srinagar and coming back with rosy apple cheeks. For months afterwards, she'd miss the myriad colours of the chinar tree, whose leaves turned from green to yellow to fiery orange, carpeting the roads of Kashmir, and the cold and woody air that descended from the hills. Her mind wanders to Maya, her childhood friend from her grandmother's neighbouring Pandit family, whom she loves like a younger sister. She still lives in Kashmir and is already a mother to a son. In her last letter, she was full of hope that Kashmir would remain a part of India and that they would see each other soon, "*Insha'Allah.*"

Screams and shouts bring Tillotama out of her reverie. She feels Manmohan's strong grip on her arm, pulling her from the bench and pushing her towards the train, which has started moving slowly. There is sheer terror in his voice as he urges her and his mother to jump into the unreserved women's compartment. As he presses the tickets into her hand and pushes out of the compartment, *Bheji's* shout of, "Where are you going?" gets drowned in the *chug-chug* of the train as it moves away from the station. A crowd of Muslim men with drawn swords charge threateningly towards the train, which fortunately has gathered speed. Tillotama looks out of the window and, as the train curves out of the station, sees her husband clamber onto the roof of the train. Later, his fair face blackened with soot, Manmohan tells her that he managed to stay on the train only by crawling all the way to the engine.

Tillotama is being constantly pushed and jostled in the unreserved compartment. A young woman, seeing her pregnant state, gives up her hard-won seat for her, and she finds herself next to a woman whose face has horror written all over it. The woman tells the people in the compartment that the Ambala-Lahore train has just steamed into the station and that most of the Muslims on it were massacred by Hindus and Sikhs before it left the borders of the new India.

"Pray, pray, everyone, that the same fate does not befall us before we reach Amritsar! Did you not see the bloodied eyes of those men rushing towards our train when they realised what had happened?" the woman cried out to the shocked passengers.

Tillotama is shaking. *God, when is this going to end?* Why did she refuse to go with Randhir when he asked her to join them earlier this year? All because Manmohan would not accept that the partition would actually happen. At that moment, she hates Manmohan. All of her as-yet nascent love for her handsome husband melts away when confronted with the fear of the unknown.

"Stop it, woman!" another woman nearby shouts. "Can't you see that you are scaring this poor girl?"

"She may miscarry, you fool!" cries a stout woman sitting next to *Bheji,* who is quietly counting her prayer beads.

Slowly, the passengers settle into the rhythm of the train, and Tillotama tries to sleep. Thank god her first trimester is over and the violent retching and vomiting are now a thing of the past.

Life hasn't been smooth for Tillotama, with her displaced childhood and confused adolescence, filled with strange longings that she couldn't fathom. Her dream and desire to continue studying after she matriculated was overturned by the occasion of her marriage just some seven months earlier. Her mother, ever the domineering matriarch, had put her foot down when her father, who could never refuse his beloved daughter, tried to convince his wife to allow Tillotama to continue studying and graduate.

"I will hear of no such thing," her mother had said, decisively. "It's time that we found a boy for her to settle down with."

Bauji, her father, who had always stood by her, became a turncoat overnight in Tillotama's mind when his brother told him of a handsome boy from a well-known family of 'modest' circumstances.

"The boy is a graduate and lives with his mother, his brother having left for Bombay to seek his fortune. Two of his sisters are happily married in Punjab. He has a good marketing job in a British company in Lahore," said the uncle in his pitch to her father.

Tillotama was unhappy at the decision but quickly changed her mind when they showed her the boy's studio photograph. He was tall and very handsome, like something out of those posters of the *Angrezi* movies. He was wearing a sola *topi,* and his thin lips and sharp nose gave him a truly aristocratic look. Manmohan told her later, after their wedding, that he had first seen her at a cousin's wedding and that he was the one who had subtly initiated the move for their marriage. However, as was the convention, Manmohan and Tillotama were not allowed to meet until the wedding and were obliged to leave all the decisions concerning their future to their parents. Tillotama's father acquiesced to her mother's absolute authority in this, in spite of his liberal tendencies. So it happened that Tillotama, a petite and shy young woman, married Manmohan without ever having met him.

Once she was married, Tillotama realised that 'modest' circumstances had been a very generous term to describe Manmohan's financial situation. Keeping the home fires burning on Manmohan's meagre salary as a salesman was a struggle. Nevertheless, her mother-in-law loved her dearly, and *Bheji's* presence helped her to cope with her changed fortunes.

At night, in their small bedroom close to *Bheji's* room, and in the arms of her husband, the stress of her chores and the daily grind was forgotten. When Manmohan first held her, she was afraid, fuelled by a gaggle of aunts who had painted a painful picture of what these 'dirty' men did after they married you. Manmohan, though, was gentle and experienced, and after the first few nights when she remained frozen in fright, she found that her body responded eagerly to his. At times, she wanted more, but did not know how to go about it. Thinking of this, Tillotama blushes and looks around shyly at the other passengers in the train, as if they can guess what she is thinking about.

During the day, however, Manmohan was a different man. Right from the beginning of their life together, he had been critical of her family. He was jealous of Randhir's success and was brusque with her younger brothers. Often, Tillotama saw Trilok, the youngest, flinch with hurt whenever her husband threw a barbed comment at him about his clothes or his posture, though the boy was only ten years old. Manmohan's aristocratic lips could utter cruel words, and his bright brown eyes flashed with venom whenever he was angry, which was often. He was obstinate, arrogant, and brooked no dissent. Even as Tillotama is harsh in her thoughts about him, she also knows that she delights in his touch when he holds her at night.

A sudden jerk of the train as it passes over the criss-crossing tracks at a station breaks the tumble of her thoughts, and Tillotama sees that they are reaching their destination. Hungry and weary, but safe, she and *Bheji* step down from the train at Amritsar and reunite with Manmohan, who has climbed down from the engine. Refugees from a divided Punjab—leaving behind their hopes and aspirations and dispossessed of their lands and many of their belongings—joined the masses spilling out of the trains to face an uncertain future.

The British Raj now vanquished; Gandhi, Nehru and Jinnah have set in motion a chain of individual events that will reverberate for their families for decades to come; the plight of these displaced, rootless people was never foreseen in their scheme of Partition.

***

Chapter 2
Randhir – 1951

"Have you heard from Tillotama?" *Bauji* asks Randhir. They are sitting in their spacious house on Alipur Road in the Civil Lines neighbourhood of Old Delhi, having their morning cup of tea, a daily ritual. The family has acquired Kohli Mansion, as it is now called, from Wajid Akram, *Bauji's* friend and business associate, who now lives in their abandoned palatial house in Rawalpindi. *Bauji* is astute, thinks Randhir, without considering his own role in making this barter, as it were, happen. But that is Randhir, modest as ever. *If only he would marry soon*, *Bauji* thinks wistfully, looking proudly at his son.

"If you are thinking about my marriage," says Randhir, reading his father's look, "forget it for now, *Bauji*. Let us settle our business interests first in this new city..."

After a pause, Randhir continues, "Tillotama is obviously very unhappy in Ludhiana. Even at the wedding, Manmohan's elder sister behaved obnoxiously, minutely examining Tillotama's dowry. I can imagine how difficult it must be living with this woman. You know, she once wanted to get rid of her own husband's sister, Guddi, by marrying her to Manmohan. It doesn't help that Guddi is still a spinster and Tillotama has to bear her malicious taunts."

"We could ask Manmohan, Tillotama and their little daughter, Meena, to come and make a life in Delhi," proposes Randhir. "If only Manmohan were less judgmental, I could learn to like him, and of course, you cannot say anything to Tillotama, for she always jumps to his defence, even though he treats her so badly."

Randhir continues to tell his father how Tillotama had been accused of stealing the milk that Manmohan's sister had kept aside for her son, and Manmohan had just stood there without defending her.

"Who have you been talking to, the maid or the driver?" asks *Bauji* in an exasperated tone. He loathes petty talk and chooses not to heed insinuations of this nature. "Instead of listening to gossip, why don't you visit her in Ludhiana? And while you are there, you could call on my childhood friend, Madan. The last time I heard from him, he was so excited that his daughter had graduated with distinction."

"I'll go and meet Tillotama and Manmohan, but don't think you can lure me into meeting another suitable girl. I am just not ready for marriage," Randhir retorts, a little stung by his father's words.

Randhir finishes his tea and then goes to his room, which overlooks the huge garden. It is March, and the borders are full of phlox, pansies and nasturtiums, with sweet peas and hollyhocks standing as sentinels behind the beds. He can see bees merrily buzzing around, collecting nectar. The faintly scented air comes wafting through the window, blowing the floral curtains into the room. The old Muslim gardener, who has loved and nurtured the garden for decades, refused to migrate to Pakistan and is now their responsibility. Randhir, by nature reclusive, enjoys his solitude. Sitting at his window, looking at the beautifully arranged garden with jamun, neem and anjan trees shading it, he gives himself over to nostalgia.

He fixes a 78 RPM record on his gramophone, his most precious possession. K. L. Saigal's deep and gravelly voice fills the room, carrying the burden of his pain in *Jab Dil Hi Toot Gaya, Hum Jee Ke Kya Karenge* (when my heart is broken, what is the point of living?). Randhir allows the music to seep into him, invoking pain from the depths of his being. His thoughts travel back to Rawalpindi and Waheeda, Tillotama's childhood friend, whom he loved from afar, never finding the courage to tell her about his feelings. The fact that he is a Hindu and she a Muslim, and that any interaction is impossible, had never entered his mind. He thinks only of her laughter as she played hopscotch with Tillotama and of how her curly ringlets swung and swirled around her face as she hopped. He had to be content with watching her quietly from his room above. His mother would rush the girls into Tillotama's room if he or his brothers came down into the courtyard, as if the bodies of these girls, fully clothed, would corrupt their innocent minds.

I wonder where in Pakistan she is now. I will ask Tillotama when we meet, he thinks.

Randhir's dreams are rudely interrupted by the sound of footsteps rushing along the hall; it must be his youngest brother returning from school. Sure enough, Trilok bursts into the room in a flurry of excitement.

"I scored a goal in the football match!" he gasps. "Our house won the championships!"

Trilok's eyes are bright, he is breathing heavily, and his body exudes the acrid smell of a young buck sweating on a spring day. Randhir hugs him and affectionately ruffles his hair. Trilok is the family favourite and gets his way in everything. He has the hardy, swarthy look of a typical young lad from Northern Punjab, though his appealing features are partially marred by remnant smallpox scars from which he nearly died as a child. He has thick red, sensual lips, which are slowly turning brown as a result of the cigarettes he smokes surreptitiously with the servants behind the gardener's shed. Nearly fifteen years old, Trilok is turning into a rebel, and there is a slyness to his movements that worries Randhir.

"Would you like to come to Ludhiana to meet Tillotama Didi?" he suddenly asks him.

"Not if *Jeejaji* is going to be there," says Trilok with a frown, referring to Manmohan. "He always picks on me, and I get so mad at him. You also forget that I have tuition to attend if I'm going to pass Senior Cambridge next year. I don't understand why *Bauji* wants me to continue in the science stream. Shiv is so lucky to be studying law, to be able to shake off physics and maths from his life."

Randhir thinks of his brother. Born four years after him, Shiv, at twenty, is awkward, shy and lacking in self-confidence, often stammering when agitated. *Bauji* generally considers him a fool. Even during the terrible days of the Partition, when the family were so closely bonded through trauma, he never took him into his confidence. It was always Randhir that he turned to for his counsel. As for their mother, *Bhabiji,* she also relies on her strong son Randhir for every major decision. She considers Shiv to be weak. Trilok, as the youngest, is her absolute favourite. Thanks to the attitude of his parents, Shiv—feeling more and more discriminated against—withdraws into his little, insecure world. By the time Randhir realises this, it is too late. And for Shiv, resentment towards his older brother has already taken deep root. He barely tolerates Randhir, steering clear of him whenever possible, and immersing himself in his law books.

The Kohli family is insular and conservative. *Bhabiji* is contemptuous of her husband, even though the family lives in comfort due to his business acumen. His worldly wisdom, liberal views and deep understanding of philosophy do not impress her at all. To her, his gentle ways with everyone, including his children, show him as a weak person. *Bhabiji* is a handsome but uneducated woman, believing that real power comes from a singular ruthlessness in making sure that the laws laid down by her are followed. This ensures her control over the household; she knows that her husband, wary of her pettiness, will not step into her domain so long as there is no serious rebellion. She is proud that her sons obey her laws, which include not entertaining male friends and having to look away in the presence of a young woman, without demur. She discourages any socialising with young women, asserting that any interaction with them will only be possible after marriage.

Randhir, as the eldest brother at twenty-four years, is fully aware of his responsibilities towards his middle-aged parents and his siblings. Although he understands that his mother is rigid in her approach and is scornful about his father's softness, he refuses to take sides. In fact, he acts as a balance between his parents' opposing views. Even in the case of Tillotama, *Bhabiji* would prefer to leave her to her fate, while *Bauji* would want him to find ways and means to rescue Tillotama and her daughter from the vicious behaviour of her sister-in-law. The security of his elder sister and her husband, who is callous at times, is uppermost in his mind.

***

Chapter 3
Tillotama – 1951

Three-year-old Meena sits quietly next to her mother, Tillotama, who is weeping pitifully into her *pallu*. Meena is frightened; there is a change in the sound of her mother's crying today, and though she is too young to put words to it, she senses the desperation in Tillotama's suppressed sobs. Meena has learnt, probably by instinct, and quite early in her life, that calling to her father will only worsen matters. The only friend she can count on in the household is Ganesh, the chauffeur, but he is out shopping for her aunt. Meena pulls at her mother's *sari*, puts her thumb into her mouth, and waits for the crying to cease.

Meena was so excited that morning when her mother told her that Randhir *Mamu* was coming to visit from Delhi. She does not know that this very news was the cause of the quarrel between her parents. Her mother's sobs are slowly subsiding, which stops Meena from whining, something she often does to bring her mother out of these crying fits.

Tillotama can't understand why Manmohan vents his frustrations at her; in time, she will realise that, with Manmohan's suppressed rage against all and sundry, she is the perfect punching bag, given that she meekly accepts his continuous rants. Like nomads, they travelled from Lahore to Amritsar and then to Bombay, before finally, after many disappointments and conflicts, settling in Manmohan's sister's house in Ludhiana. Manmohan's personality has undergone a complete change. He has little time for her now, and their once-passionate nights are a distant dream.

Tillotama thinks of how, within a month of their arrival in Bombay, Manmohan had sent her to her parents' house in Delhi for Meena's birth, even though she did not want to burden her mother. He insisted that, as per his family's social norms, the first child must be born in the maternal home. Tillotama's mother does not take kindly to the invasion, but she forgets that she had, after all, nursed Tillotama for only six months before sending her away to her own mother's house for five years to focus on her precious sons. Adding to the awkwardness of the situation, Manmohan sent *Bheji* with her to Delhi, just another reason for her mother's 'sensitive' hackles to rise.

Dear *Bheji,* ever smiling, even as she is tossed from place to place like unwanted baggage. When Meena was born, it was *Bheji* who sat through Tillotama's difficult labour, wiped her face and forehead, and allowed her to grip her hands tightly when the contractions got the better of her. It was *Bheji* who made the sign of *Om* with honey in Meena's mouth while *Bhabiji* kept her distance, her stiff posture silently voicing her disappointment at the birth of a granddaughter. Manmohan came, refused to hold his daughter, and left soon after.

This, then, is the fate of Tillotama: she is adored by her father and mother-in-law, but feels unloved and unwanted by Manmohan and her mother, and is therefore cloaked in bitterness. She thinks back to when Randhir told her that her own mother abandoned her to her grandmother when she was only six months old. Without her mother's milk, she had to make do with buffalo's milk, fed to her from a glass bottle with a rubber nipple. She would never really know if missing the comfort and nourishment of her mother's milk affected her, but she remembers being a lonely child. At her grandmother's house in Srinagar, her aunts and uncles were married and lived elsewhere except for one uncle, who was a confirmed bachelor and lived with his old mother. He was amused by his little niece but had little time for her, spending it—and the money he inherited from his father—in the clubs of Lahore and Delhi. But Tillotama was devoted to her *Nani-ma,* who was so unlike her draconian mother. Even after she returned to her mother in Rawalpindi, she visited her *Nani-ma* every vacation.

During her vacations in Srinagar, Tillotama met Maya, the daughter of the Pandit family who had moved into a house in her grandmother's neighbourhood. Maya was high-spirited and ebullient, and a complete foil to Tillotama's shyness. In her repertoire, Maya told many stories from the film world, which she had deliciously absorbed from her relatives when travelling with her parents to Bombay, home of Hindi cinema. Sohrab Modi, Leela Chitnis, Fearless Nadia, Ashok Kumar and Devika Rani were all actors living in Bombay. Maya described their colourful lives, imagined or otherwise, to a rapt Tillotama. She was completely captivated. Back home in Rawalpindi, she savoured these stories, keeping them to herself as she couldn't talk about them to her brothers, lest her disapproving mother hear of them. Popular film songs, gossip and movies were taboo in their home. The children could only listen to music (unless it was classical) surreptitiously on Randhir's radio. He loves K. L. Saigal's songs; he later mutinies and buys his own gramophone.

In Rawalpindi, before she was married, Tillotama's school friend was Waheeda. During her vacations to Srinagar, she and Maya were inseparable, but in Rawalpindi, Maya was replaced by Waheeda. Tillotama wanted to study beyond matriculation and go to college, but Waheeda was content to get married even before finishing school. It was Waheeda's uncle, a scholar, who insisted that she should complete school, as did her brothers. Her father would have married her off at the age of fifteen to one of her mother's cousins otherwise.

Once, in Rawalpindi, when Tillotama and Waheeda were having a sleepover. Waheeda saw Randhir pass by the window to Tillotama's room and touched her nipples with a sigh of longing. Tillotama saw the small buds rising from Waheeda's chest and was excited by them. Waheeda then took off her blouse and showed her the brown areola, and Tillotama put her mouth to them. In the thrill of this illicit action, she wanted to sink her hand into her own *shalwar* but held herself back. Later that night, she had guiltily rubbed herself, feeling her heart racing, and had to stop when strange moans threatened to come out of her mouth.

In Ludhiana that morning, Manmohan can't keep his temper in check when he asks her, a tinge of guilt in his voice, "Why is Randhir coming? What have you been telling your family, you wretched woman?"

Tillotama knows that silence is best; any reply will rile him even more. Manmohan is frustrated, bitter and angry, running from pillar to post in search of a job to match his ambitions. This is what has led them from Bombay to Ludhiana, where he feels he is more likely to find work. Manmohan's envy of the Kohli family makes the bile rise higher in his throat until it nearly chokes him.

When he made the phone call, Randhir confided in Tillotama that he was visiting to convince Manmohan to move to Delhi, where all the economic action was taking place in newly independent India.

Tillotama starts reminiscing again, this time about the days when they first arrived in Amritsar from Lahore to stay with Manmohan's friend, Deepak, who had got married only recently. After a few days, Deepak suggested that they move to the refugee camps, never saying anything directly but letting the tension between him and his wife speak for itself. Tillotama felt ashamed when she heard Deepak's wife meaningfully describing the shortages of wheat and sugar, and the difficulties she was having feeding so many. Tillotama had then pushed Manmohan to consider the camps. With Amritsar in the throes of rioting and chaos, and even though Tillotama was six months pregnant, it made more sense for them to move with their few meagre belongings to Manmohan's brother's home. So, within a few days, they were on a train to Bombay. Randhir had come to the Old Delhi train station to meet them while they were waiting for the train to Bombay. Manmohan had arrogantly refused to stay overnight in Delhi with Tillotama's family.

"I will make it in Bombay!" Manmohan told Randhir. "*Bhapaji,* my brother, assures me that there are many opportunities for salespeople there."

"Will I get to see Devika Rani or Fearless Nadia in Bombay?" was Tillotama's innocent query.

"They don't walk around the streets like us," said Manmohan spitefully, "and if they do, they cover themselves up in a *burqa.* We are not going to Bombay for a holiday, stupid woman."

Bombay was teeming with refugees from Punjab, Sind and even some Parsis who had left Pakistan to make new lives. When the country was divided into three parts, the Sindhis who belonged to the State of Sind lost all their lands to West Pakistan. Punjab was split between India and West Pakistan, and in the East, Bengal was shared between India and East Pakistan. It was the Hindus from Sind who had left their homes in Karachi and escaped by sea to reach Bombay as stateless refugees. Though they had lost their land and property, their exodus from Pakistan was virtually bloodless, not like the Punjabis, most of whom had lost a family member or friend to the massacres, rapes and other horrors of Partition. Most of the Sindhis had resettled in the northeast of Bombay, in the Kalyan transit camp—an area later called Ulhasnagar, literally meaning 'city of joy'. The Sindhis then set about converting this colony of migrants into a successful business hub, eventually becoming adept at producing fakes of branded goods, which in turn attracted many underworld gangsters over the next two decades.

Fed on Maya's stories, Tillotama had romanticised Bombay and was appalled by its dirt and squalor. This 'city of seven islands', which had been given as a dowry by the Portuguese to King Charles II in 1661, was not what she had imagined. Manmohan's brother lived in a *chawl* near the Mahim Causeway. In the mornings, Tillotama could look out to the slums in Dharavi with their patched roofs and winding, dirty streets where garbage and puddles full of disease accumulated, and in which young urchins played, seemingly without a care in the world. Everything was saturated with the smell of fish. Tillotama had never eaten fish; the post-monsoon humidity and the smell of drying fish were overpowering. Even though she had passed those nauseous days in her pregnancy, she felt her stomach heave often; it took all her willpower to keep down the small meals she ate.

Manmohan's brother Bhupinder (or *Bhapaji*, as he was called) and his wife Bimla were in dire financial straits; definitely not the successful brother living in Bombay, as she had been told before the wedding. Bimla, thin and racked with a continuous cough, had just lost her third child to a miscarriage. *Bhapaji* should have taken her to the doctor, but he was never at home, and when he did return late at night, he was usually intoxicated. One day,

Manmohan went looking for him and found him in a dump of a bar drinking moonshine distilled in one of the shacks that littered the beach. *Bhapaji* lost his temper; in the ensuing fight, Bimla sided with her husband and threw Manmohan out of the house. Tillotama could only look on in disbelief. *What kind of a woman was this who could bear such rotten treatment from her husband and yet not recognise someone who was on her side?* Tillotama, protected all her life, was aghast and cowered with *Bheji* in the small room they shared. The next morning, Manmohan took Tillotama and *Bheji,* sent them back to *Bhabiji* in Delhi and then moved to a small room near Bombay Central Station. He started work as a ticket clerk at the Victoria Terminus; he seethed, waiting for the day that he would 'make it' and see the respect in the Kohli family's eyes.

The sudden death of Bimla in Bombay cast a shadow over Meena's birth. Manmohan had hastily left Tillotama and his newborn daughter and returned to his brother. By the time his brother, on one of his sober days, had finally taken Bimla to a lung doctor, it was too late. She had suffered from tuberculosis when she was young, a fact which had never been disclosed to him, and her youthful and slim look was just seen as a fashionable statement at the time. Subsequent pregnancies and miscarriages had taken their toll on her health, and when the tuberculosis recurred, it was not treatable by any of the drugs available. Bimla died, a sad, childless woman with a drunken husband and so little air in her lungs that the darkness which drowned her at the end was a welcome relief.

Manmohan had met his sister from Ludhiana during the mourning period. Few details of what transpired at this meeting were provided to Tillotama, who was recuperating at her mother's after Meena's difficult birth. What she did decipher from a confused letter her husband sent was that they were moving again, this time to Ludhiana, to live with his sister. Manmohan would work for her husband, a successful wool and cloth merchant. He asked her to pack her bags, and so, with the baby Meena and *Bheji* in tow, she met Manmohan at the railway station in Delhi and left with him for Ludhiana.

They have now been in Ludhiana for nearly three years. Tillotama spends little time with Manmohan, who is the odd-job man at his brother-in-law's shop. He keeps accounts, handles suppliers and runs errands, while his brother-in-law handles the main purchasing and dealing with large customers and collections. Manmohan is paid a measly fifty rupees a month and has a roof over his head. It doesn't seem to matter to him that his sister finds fault in everything Tillotama does, constantly haranguing her. He has a vision of launching his own cloth trading business, but he needs capital for it, to negotiate with the main suppliers and to meet the big customers. His sister's husband, though, is not going to encourage additional competition, and Manmohan is indispensable to his business. None of his other employees are as honest in their dealings as he is, nor as helpful to others when their work is finished. Manmohan would have been content, biding his time, except for Tillotama's emotional outbursts. She doesn't seem to realise her lowly position in the household, he often thinks.

Happily playing with the doll that her Randhir *Mamu* had brought for her that morning, Meena jumps up and runs towards the veranda from where she hears terrible shouts and her mother's shrieks of distress. Ganesh, who has just come in from the market, catches hold of her and takes her out to the garden to play. Meena can never resist her friend Ganesh; she takes one last look towards the veranda where her mother, father and *Mamu* are angrily gesticulating at each other.

On the veranda, some order has been restored, and a pale-looking Randhir is pleading with Manmohan.

"*Jeejaji,* I did not come here to create problems for your family, but I will not allow you to hit my sister. All she wants is a better life for you and Meena," he says, holding his hands out. "If you look back and remember, once *Bauji* was sure that Partition was definite, he made plans and asked you to consider a move to Delhi with us. At first, you wouldn't accept that Partition would happen; when it became a reality, you decided to join your friend in Amritsar. Then you moved in with your brother in Bombay, and once again to Ludhiana. We, too, are family, and *Bauji* looks upon you as his eldest son. We respect you and want you to make your life in Delhi. The house at Alipur Road has an annexe that I have furnished; you can use it till you settle down on your own. Tillotama *Didi* will have her own home..."

"Stop it! Stop it!" Manmohan cuts in angrily. "I do not want to live on the charity of my in-laws and be a *Ghar Jamai.*"

"Why do you believe that you will live on our charity? We just want you, *Bheji,* Tillotama *Didi* and Meena to have a home, for as long as you want," soothes Randhir. "Chamanlal, *Bauji's* friend and the owner of the largest clothes store in Chandni Chowk, is very impressed by your experience and wants you to work with him. You will replace his only son, who was unfortunately killed in the riots at Amritsar. He probably will set you up later in your own shop, since he wants to grow in other areas of Delhi, like Daryaganj, Connaught Place and Karol Bagh. If you feel an obligation while using the annexe, you can pay us a rent of ten rupees each month, once you start working."

Randhir is clearly deviating from the script that *Bauji* had planned, but he is sure he can convince *Bauji* that rent was necessary for Manmohan to keep some semblance of self-respect. Quite frankly, he couldn't care less for his brother-in-law's feelings; he heeds them only for his sister.

"And *Didi*," Randhir continues, "has said nothing about her life in Ludhiana. We heard from Chamanlal that his cousin Roshanlal, who is a yarn supplier, gossiped that you were unhappy working in the shadow of your brother-in-law, even though you are liked and trusted by the market. You must have realised by now that the wholesale cloth business in Punjab and Delhi shares common suppliers and associates and is also a very cohesive network?"

Randhir feels no shame in mouthing these untruths; he only needs to make sure that Chamanlal will not contradict him if Manmohan seeks confirmation. By now, Manmohan is mollified and is beginning to think about a move to Delhi. He knows that his sheer presence will be enough to intimidate the brothers; he knows that *Bauji* loves and respects him and that Tillotama's tough mother will be brought under control by his charm. Randhir, watching his face, realises that he has succeeded and looks over at his sister, who seems curiously detached. Tillotama sees herself as a single leaf blown off a tree, tossed around at the mercy of the wind, with no control over her fate.

Before leaving, Randhir asks Tillotama if she has any news of Waheeda. He is sickened to learn that she was raped and left for dead during the Partition riots and is now existing as a 'living corpse' with her mother; her father having committed suicide upon learning of his daughter's dishonour. Distressed and broken-hearted, Randhir vows never to marry.

***

Husna closes the manuscript, marking it with a bookmark, and turns to Adam in confusion.

"Who are all these people?" she asks. "My mother was born in Independent India, and her grandfather was an industrialist, not a trader." Husna searches her mind for a reason why this manuscript is in her mom's cupboard. Maybe a friend of hers, an author, sent it to her for her comments... No, it can't be that, Husna realises in frustration, I know of no author among her friends. No, it is more personal than that...

"The note wouldn't have said, 'you will let Husna read it'. This was meant for me," she says to Adam.

An Indian family, Partition, the perplexing norms of those times completely engulf Adam with the scope of what they have read so far. It appears to be a family saga, and even though it all seems so strange, they vividly feel the many characters' lives and emotions being played out on the pages of the manuscript. Some of the Indian words were difficult, but Husna had translated them for Adam.

"Manmohan seemed a real bastard, and Tillotama such a doormat. I can't believe that people were like that all those years ago. I can't imagine my grandmother ever taking such nonsense from a man," Husna says, seeming genuinely angry.

Adam is extremely worried for Husna. She has been under stress and still has to come to terms with her mother's and her grandmother's tragic deaths. What the manuscript might reveal, and how it could affect her, troubled Adam, but he sees he can't stop her from reading it. It could be her one chance to know more about all the people from her past, and of course, about her father. Adam understands that the only family members Husna has known are her mother, her grandmother and her grandfather, who was estranged from her grandmother. He knows he has to be there for her and to stand beside her as this story reveals its secrets.

Husna looks back into her memory for some semblance of familiarity—not just with the narrative, but the aura of those times—yet it all feels so alien to what she knows of her own background.

"Let's get ourselves some dinner and then sleep," Adam says, putting his hand around her shoulders. "We can continue reading tomorrow."

***

Chapter 4
The Chopra Family – 1951-1959

With their impending move to Delhi, Tillotama starts washing and ironing the extra sheets and pillow covers she will take, before packing them into steel trunks for the journey. She packs Meena's and her clothes in one suitcase, leaving only a few *shalwar kameezes* and frocks out for their last few days in Ludhiana. She helps *Bheji*, now tired of being shunted around, to stash her pitiful little mementoes and memories in the battered suitcase, which she has carried around with her on their endless moves.

Tillotama is excited. She visualises the tree-lined lawns that Randhir had described to her. She pictures savouring the freshness of the morning dew on the leaves of the bougainvillaea, the smell of the earth beneath her feet and all the joys of her future home. Manmohan, too, seems excited about this move. Tillotama's breezy happiness makes him laugh and tease her, showing improvement in his general demeanour towards her. He seems more considerate and spends more time with her while he wraps up his affairs in Ludhiana. Tillotama is full of hope for the future, and the taunts of her sister-in-law, calling Manmohan a *Ghar Jamai* behind his back, do not affect her at all.

Manmohan's brother-in-law feels grievously wronged when he discovers that he is joining a competitor in the wholesale cloth business, calling him a traitor. He wants to turn them out of the house immediately, but knows that he needs Manmohan to pass on his knowledge of the account books and other administrative work to the next gullible and needy relative, this time a cousin, who is called in urgently from the Jullundur office. For the first time since their marriage, Manmohan buys Tillotama a silk *sari*, hiding it behind his back as he carries it to their room to surprise her. Tillotama, whose love for him never diminished, is thrilled to see his ardour return. By the time they leave Ludhiana, Tillotama is pregnant again.

The little family stands outside Old Delhi station, their steel trunks, holdalls and military green suitcases piled before them, waiting for Randhir to pick them up. Tillotama, nauseous with the new child growing inside her, is worried about Randhir's lateness; looking at every vehicle that stops to drop off passengers. Manmohan—a stickler for time and hoping to find one more reason to torment his wife, especially when it concerns the Kohli family—is smugly negotiating with a *tongawallah* when Randhir turns up, late because of a procession.

Tillotama's first view of her new home is mixed. The main house on Alipur Road, with its beautifully manicured lawns, is, of course, delightful, but the annexe is small and barrack-like, just a row of contiguous rooms running next to each other. She likes the wraparound veranda, which has potted plants equidistantly placed along the edge. For Tillotama, this is her first independent home since Partition, and so she isn't going to complain. She soon settles down. Manmohan is initially grateful to his in-laws, but his dislike, born of years of envy at their continuing success, eventually shows its churlish face. In time, he grows more aggressive towards them, finding fault with everything.

During the days of the Raj, when the majestic house on Alipur Road had been built, the annexe had housed the many retainers that the English *memsahib* and *sahib* needed. No doubt, they had to be compensated for leaving their tiny three-bedroom terraced house with one toilet back in 'genteel' England to live among the 'heathens'. When Wajid Akram had purchased the house, he had used the annexe to store canned foods imported from England. Randhir imaginatively converted this storehouse into a little family home: one living room, three bedrooms, a pantry and a separate bath and toilet located behind the house. All the bedrooms opened onto a wraparound veranda encircling the house. There was no kitchen attached to the annexe as Randhir had created it for Shiv, who needed privacy for his college studies. The main house supplied cooked food, and the pantry was used for dining. Shiv is livid at being evicted from the annexe by his sister and her family, and as usual, feels victimised by Randhir.

Tillotama loves the annexe, the first place since her marriage that she can really call home. Although it takes her a considerable effort to walk along the path skirting the gardens to the main house to cook in the kitchen and then haul it all back to the annexe, she is happy. But this joy is short-lived. After a few months of good behaviour, Manmohan begins looking to create discord again. One day, he walks into their bedroom and declares in a self-righteous tone,

"Do you know who used these rooms before you?" he pauses here for full effect, before spitting with rage, "Servants! Yes, servants! This is what Randhir wants his sister to understand: that she has the status of a lowly staff member in this grand family of theirs."

Tillotama, sensing her feelings of happiness evaporating, hisses back, "Why do you create hostility wherever you go? Shiv was using these rooms before us, and that is all that I want to know. If you don't like it here, find us another place to live. I don't particularly enjoy listening to my mother grumble every day about my pots and pans cluttering up her kitchen."

This makes Manmohan even more furious, and he fires all his pent-up venom at her, citing various perceived insults that he has received from her parents and brothers, being the ungrateful wretch that he is.

Manmohan starts work with Chamanlal and is quickly drawn into the inner coterie that surrounds him. There is Chamanlal's younger brother, Kishorinath, his son, Bittu, and his accountant, Kasturi, who is Mrs Chamanlal's brother and exerts a strong influence on the family. Chamanlal is aware that, as his son is dead, he needs, in addition to Kasturi, another balancing factor against the wiles of his brother and nephew. Manmohan, well known for his honest dealings, is just the foil against any tricky moves this duo might pull. He will suffice until Chamanlal's daughter, Swarna, who is still in college, marries and joins the business with her husband. She is already promised to the son of the largest cloth merchant in the fast-growing area of Karol Bagh. Before the merger of both these businesses, Chamanlal plans to buy out his brother and leave his daughter and future son-in-law with a strong legacy.

This suits Manmohan. He is getting the opportunity to learn all he can from spinning to cloth and from buying to selling, so that he can set up his own business one day and service newer places in the south of Delhi, like Jangpura, Lajpat Nagar and South Extension. The richer refugees here from Punjab are slowly buying up land and property at throwaway prices. This is where they are setting up markets to feed the growing population of less fortunate refugees, pouring into Delhi, the 'city of opportunity'. The problem Manmohan does not foresee is that his employer leaves control of the wages to Kasturi, who does not like this handsome new upstart. Manmohan is too arrogant to plead his case with Chamanlal directly, so he has to be content with what Kasturi decides is his worth.

Tillotama finds herself in an unfortunate position again. Manmohan grudgingly gives her a pittance to run the home. She stretches the household budget to such an extent that at times, she has to secretly take money from Randhir after promising to return it. She is caught in a huge dilemma. If Manmohan ever finds out that she is taking money from her brother, he will be outraged, but she has no choice; asking for money from Manmohan is like asking a tiger to give up his kill.

As time goes by, Tillotama's miseries accumulate. The move from Ludhiana, the dashing of her hopes that the positive change in Manmohan will be lasting, the tiny slights meted out to her in her mother's kitchen, the shame of being a married daughter living in her parents' home, all take a toll on Tillotama's health. Arvind was born in 1952, a full month before his time, and an arrival that should have been a joy to the family hungry for a boy, is anything but. Tillotama suffers from post-natal depression, and her premature son is weak and continuously fretful.

Arvind takes a long time to say his first few words and to walk independently of his mother's support. By the time Arvind is six years old, he and Meena are used to the constant strife in the house, but as long as their father's anger is not directed at them, they feel safe. If Tillotama, pushed to the end of her tether, retaliates with unkind words to the constant mental stress brought on by her husband, he disappears from home for days until, guilty and sick with worry, she is ready to do whatever he wants. His return is always triumphant, and peace reigns for a few days. Arvind is terrified of his father and looks to Meena for support, but she doesn't want to be a nursemaid to her brother, whom she sees as the usurper of her mother's attention. Instead, she spends all her time with Dev, who was born in 1954, just under two years after Arvind.

The early years of the children's lives, spent in the gardens at Alipur Road, are full of fun, especially on the days when their father is travelling, or has left home on one of his make-my-wife-guilty trips. They have the run of the gardens, and on most Sundays, one of their uncles joins their games in the garden. Randhir loves the innocence and laughter of the children and happily plays hide and seek with them. The garden is huge, with many trees and large bushes. There are plenty of secret places to hide or trees to climb, with large leaves to use as a cover, from where they excitedly watch the futile attempts of the den in the game of hide-and-seek to try and find them. Randhir hangs a swing made out of a thick rope from a tall Jamun tree, and in the summer holidays, Meena spends the mornings rocking contentedly on the swing with Dev in her lap, while Arvind sulks on the branches of the buttercup tree growing nearby.

At six years old, Arvind is turning into a beautiful boy; he has cupid's bow lips, like his mother, and a fair complexion, with his father's chin and nose. Dev looks exactly like Manmohan and is very dear to Tillotama. Meena, at eleven, has her mother's looks but her father's height, making her posture awkward; she shows early signs of a hunched back in her attempts to fit in with her shorter friends. By fifteen, with the right tips, she will turn into a beauty, but at the moment, Meena hates her height and her mother's broad, sensual lips and swarthy features, which she believes make her look wanton.

The highlights of Arvind's childhood are the trips he makes with *Bauji* early in the morning to Ridge Road near Roshanara Club, where his grandfather meets his cronies in a park. The early morning cold, the hot mug of tea, which allows him to warm his hands, and the smell of the morning dew-soaked earth stay with him and provide a balm to his suffering in later years. The quietness of the forest encircling the park allows Arvind to imagine and create all sorts of adventures. When he comes across an anthill with holes on all sides, he conjures up a vision of snakes slithering out of the holes. The rustling of the trees and bushes, he is convinced, are sounds made by a panther seen often by bus drivers on the ridge.

Arvind, when he was nearly four years of age, was transferred to Meena's school after a terrifying year where he had been bullied by his teacher. Meena's school is co-educational and Protestant, run by a trust made up of Anglo-Indians who do not want to stay in independent India but are not welcome in England.

In the first week at the new school, Arvind goes looking for Meena to get his pencil sharpened, like she does for him at home. The laughter rippling through the senior class and Meena's murderous look mean that he will never do this again. He quickly settles down, however, and his winsome ways and sharp mind make him the teacher's pet. He looks forward to school each day.

Manmohan needs to travel often to the markets of Punjab. Chamanlal needs someone to mentor his daughter, Swarna, a wilful and stubborn girl, who often bullies the other members of her family. He chooses Manmohan, the outsider, to be Swarna's mentor. So, when Manmohan is in Delhi, he spends extra hours in the office teaching Swarna the ropes of the business after she returns from college; this means long absences from his home and family.

In the annexe, these are days of peace. In the evenings, with the domestic grind behind them, Tillotama and *Bheji* captivate the children with stories from the *Mahabharata* and the *Ramayana*, the great Hindu epics. Arvind is fascinated by Rama, prince of Ayodhya, who is sent into exile when his step-mother, in order to make her own son king, forces his father to send him and his wife Sita away for fourteen years. When Ravana, the King of Lanka, kidnaps Sita, Arvind dreams of chasing him, killing him with a sword and uniting Sita and Rama. Meena's heroine is Draupadi, a strong and independent woman. Arrogant and worldly, Draupadi can handle five husbands, and when she is humiliated, she causes a major war and the annihilation of her husband's cousins on the fields of Kurekshetra.

Deepavali, the Hindu festival of lights which celebrates the return of Rama with Sita to Ayodhya after his exile, is celebrated with firecrackers, a *puja* and a feast of delicious sweetmeats from the fat *halwai* in Chandni Chowk. It is the family's favourite festival. Tillotama loves *jalebis*, a crispy, deep-fried sweet shaped like a pretzel, made from the batter of fine wheat and dipped in orange sugar syrup. *Bheji* loves *gulab jamun*, soft fried balls of fine wheat, dipped in transparent sugar syrup. The children love everything and gorge on all the sweets until they are nauseated. The highlight of the festival is the burning of the firecrackers, and on this day, even their father is in a good mood. The children carry their crackers to the main house to join their uncles, who add more firecrackers to their pile. They have strict instructions to burn only the sparklers while the many servants burn the noisy 'bombs' and *anars* ('flower pot' fire crackers). When the firecrackers are lit, the children squeal with delight, covering their ears and running madly away from the loud bangs and cracks. Oh, how the excitement thrills them!

This year, on *Deepavali*, Arvind wakes up quivering with anticipation. Randhir *Mamu* has promised him a toy gun, and he is looking forward to shooting all the Lankan warriors. Seven years old now, he is the protector of his younger brother Dev, who follows him everywhere, and the chief irritant of his sister, Meena, who is trying her best to convince her mother that young boys are better off at boarding school. Their father has left the house early for the *puja* at Chamanlal's shops in Chandni Chowk and Connaught Place. The children are all dressed up in their new clothes and have escaped outside to run around the house and gardens with their cousins, who have arrived from other parts of Delhi to join the festivities. When Arvind is given his toy gun by his *Mamu,* he happily tries it out, to the envy of his cousins.

As the light of day slowly ebbs, giving way to the deep orange of dusk, festive lights flicker on and brighten up the neighbourhood. Tillotama is waiting for Manmohan and is worried. He has not called, and this is very unlike him on an auspicious day like *Deepavali*. Meena, as is a tradition for the daughter of the house, has lit the first *diya* lamp in the annexe. Tillotama returns from the main house having lit the lamp there. She sends the boys and Meena to the main house to start burning the firecrackers, which, according to tradition, are meant to herald the arrival of Lord Rama at Ayodhya after his exile. Tillotama's 'Lord', however, is missing, and she is at her wits' end.

Manmohan slips out of Chamanlal's house from the side door, which leads down from the woman's quarters. He surreptitiously looks around and then moves into the shadows. Inside Chamanlal's house, the *puja* has commenced in the front room, and Chamanlal and his family are religiously chanting the Hindu rituals to enhance their already burgeoning wealth. His wife impatiently glances towards the door from where her brother had exited some time ago to call Swarna, who retired exhausted to her rooms after returning from their shop in Connaught Place.

Manmohan sits on his motorcycle and roars off towards home, knowing full well that Tillotama will be pacing the house, waiting for him, and that the children will have forgotten him in the excitement of the celebrations at the main house. If he feels any guilt about his activities over the last two months, it does not show in his behaviour. He sweeps into the driveway and shouts for Rawat, the young cook and odd-job man from *Tehri Garhwal,* to call the children to attend the *puja* at the annexe. He brushes past Tillotama, who is standing in the doorway, without any explanation for his lateness, changes into a white *kurta pyjama* and sits down. Tillotama has already laid out the photographs of Rama and Sita, the sweetmeats, the incense and *dhoop* for the *puja*. The children come rushing back; they know any delays will be met with swift punishment. They also know that they can return to the main house after these rituals, as dinner on *Deepavali* is always eaten there.

Soon after the *puja*, Manmohan excuses himself while Tillotama and *Bheji* leave with the children for the feast, promising to send back food for him. *Bauji* and Randhir are annoyed at Manmohan's lack of filial duties, but keep quiet. Tillotama's mother, on the other hand, is relieved that she does not have to sit through an evening of being civil to her 'charming' son-in-law.

On this day, most families play cards in which cash stakes are involved, as winning is considered auspicious, a sign of prosperity in the coming year. The games are either *teen patti* (flush), in which three cards are dealt, or rummy, where thirteen cards are dealt. The Kohli family is extremely conservative and plays rummy; they consider *teen patti* to be a more extreme form of gambling.

When the Kohli grandparents retire to their separate rooms, Tillotama, Randhir, Shiv, and Trilok decide to play, while the children peer over their uncles' shoulders to look at the dealt cards. Arvind prefers to sit behind Randhir, but this time Meena beats him to it, and he finds himself behind Shiv instead. From time to time, his uncle lets him pick a card from the pile or throw the card that is discarded. Shiv starts winning, and every time he wins, he hugs Arvind and calls him his lucky mascot. Arvind is thrilled and hugs his uncle back, making up for the hugs that he misses from his father. Tillotama is happy, bathed in a warm glow of love for her brothers and her children. The game continues. *Bheji,* Meena and Dev retire for the night, but Shiv holds Arvind back until, exhausted, he falls asleep. At midnight, Tillotama leaves to go back to the annexe, hoping that her husband is asleep and that her pleasant evening will not be spoiled by his mocking. Shiv insists that Arvind should not be disturbed and that he can sleep in his room in the main house and return to the annexe in the morning.

The rooster's hoarse morning call makes Tillotama jump out of bed with a start. "I wish I could strangle that old cock," she mutters to herself as she walks groggily to her bedroom door to start her morning. "Why can't the haze of yesterday's fireworks block the morning light, just once, so that I can get some more sleep?" she continues talking to herself, as she lights the *hammam* in which the water is heated for their baths. There is a chill in the air on this late October morning, but she shivers, not from the chill, but from a strange sense of foreboding. Manmohan, an early riser, is normally out of bed at this time, but he has not woken up, which is surprising.

Rawat is nowhere to be seen; *he over-indulged himself last night*, she thinks.

As she is preparing to leave for the main house to get breakfast ready, Tillotama hears the footsteps of someone running towards the annexe. Arvind comes hurtling out of the morning haze and mist with his unruly hair falling all over his face. Out of breath, he looks at her fiercely and then hugs her tightly without saying a word.

"Hey, Kaku [his pet name], that's a lot of love for a morning! Run along and take a shower while I get your breakfast ready."

Arvind clings to his mother, then abruptly lets go and heads towards the room he shares with Dev. He sees his father disappear towards the bathroom at the back of the house, so he quickly slips into his parents' room and gets into their bed, needing its warmth and familiar smell to protect him from the horrible confusion, guilt and shame that have overtaken his whole being. Slowly, he slips into a restless sleep, where demons are chasing him and making him do terrible things. He pulls his legs up towards his chest in a foetal position and mutters in his sleep.

"Arvind, what are you doing in my bed? Wake up, you fool!"

He feels the thick blanket being pulled off his body and his father's harsh voice shouting for Tillotama. "Where have you gone, woman?"

When Manmohan gets closer to pull Arvind out of bed, he growls as he first smells the urine and then sees the wet sheets. The demons from his dream disappear, and Arvind jumps out of bed, his drowsiness violently dispelled, and cowers in the corner of the room waiting for blows to rain down on his head. He is saved by the sound of a loud voice coming from the veranda outside and recognises it as his grandfather, who is urgently seeking his father. Tillotama comes rushing into the room and pulls him out without saying a word, while *Bauji* enters and shuts himself in the room with his father. His mother, who seems to be under great stress, notices that his pyjamas are wet with urine and pushes him hard towards the bathroom, where Rawat has left hot water for the bath. She pulls off his clothes and then suddenly leaves him to his own devices. Arvind groggily climbs into the bath.

"I don't care how and why it happened. You are the mature one here, yet you have been an absolute cad towards your employer. You have cheated on your wife and children! On all of us! I want you to get out of this house. Tillotama and the kids can stay, but I do not want to see your face around here again!"

Tillotama, who is listening at the door, cannot believe her ears when she hears her soft-hearted father berating her husband with such harsh words. *What has Manmohan done? Cheating? He is an honest person, but why is he not saying anything to defend himself?* She curses silently that she missed the earlier part of the one-sided conversation due to being preoccupied with Arvind. She quickly moves away from the door when she hears her father storm out of the house. He looks pityingly at her as he passes, but leaves without saying a word. Tillotama rushes back to the room.

"What has happened, Manmohan? Why is *Bauji* so angry?"

"Ask him yourself!" is Manmohan's angry retort. He looks shaken, his face is crimson, and his sharp features are contorted, displaying an emotion she cannot define.

"You and your family, so holier than thou! I shouldn't have come to stay in this house. The *Ghar Jamai*, that's what everyone calls me behind my back. Your brother Randhir, with his sweet tongue... your brothers are more precious to you than me or your children. Live with them now, I am out of here. I will let the world know how your father threw me out of this house and took my children away from me!"

"Manmohan, please!" Tillotama gasps, clutching at his sleeve. "I have no idea what has happened! Why would my gentle father be so angry? Why did he look at me with such pity? Why are you so angry with my brothers, and what has Chamanlal got to do with this? I am not going to leave you and nor will our children be without their father." With these words, Tillotama rushes out of the annexe and hurries to the main house, ignoring Manmohan's call to stay back.

When Arvind comes out after his bath, he sees Meena and Dev silently watching their father throw his clothes into a battered suitcase.

"I will show them. I will show this bastard Kohli family what it means to mess with me," he mutters darkly.

***

Chapter 5
Arvind – 1959

I wake up with a start. Something does not feel right. My eyelids push open, and I see unfamiliar walls. It is night. I can feel someone lying next to me, and it is not Dev. This person is bigger, and the hand lying on my thigh is heavy. I look up and see that it is Uncle Shiv. He is reading a book, holding it with one hand in the light of the bedside lamp. I am still in that drowsy state between waking and sleep, but the game of cards from the night before floats into my mind. I must have dozed off in my uncle's bed. I have to pee, so I slowly slide out of bed.

"Where are you going, Kaku?" my uncle asks, looking up from his book.

"To the toilet to pee," I say, raising my pinkie finger, like I do in school. As I pass by the dressing table, I see my uncle watching me in the mirror. He has a look that I cannot understand, like a hawk watching its prey, and it makes me uncomfortable. Then he smiles at me, and I feel fine.

When I come back to bed, the table light is switched off. There is only one bed in my uncle's Spartan room, so I slip under the covers next to him. There is a shadow looming at the back of my mind, possibly because of his strange look, but I am too sleepy to heed it. I settle against the warmth of my uncle's back, surrendering to its sturdiness and strength. A little while later, I feel him turn towards me. Then his lips move all over my face, finally stopping at my lips, as he holds me in a tight embrace. I feel his warm breath on my face, and then he pushes his tongue to open my lips. I can feel the hard stubble on his face and chin scratching my skin.

I do not know what this means, and I do not resist him. I have my teeth clamped down, but I feel his tongue slowly push my teeth open and enter my mouth. I gasp then, whether in shock or in pain, I don't know, and he slows down and takes his mouth away from my lips. But then he does not stop. I feel his hand push into my new pyjamas and hold me there, which now behaves a little strangely, the way it does when I sometimes secretly touch myself. His other hand is moving fast in his own pyjamas, and after some time, I feel his lips fiercely crushing mine. He shudders and then becomes still.

There is complete silence except for the sounds of the crickets in the garden. The sound of the silence is broken by him saying, "I am sorry, I am sorry, I could not help myself," and I think that he may start crying. He holds me close to him, and although I am confused, I feel that this was meant to happen.

When I open my eyes in the morning, it seems peaceful, but what happened the night before comes roaring into my mind. My uncle is nowhere to be seen. In the morning light, I feel ashamed, dirty and scared. I run my tongue over my hurting lips and try to understand the meaning of what happened. So many emotions rush through me; I feel like I have been smothered, like I have done something really bad, and it makes me sick and frightened. I know that I cannot tell this to anyone; it has to be my secret. I cannot tell this to Meena, and definitely not to my mother. She will tell my father, and he will kill me. I run back to my home, which is my sanctuary, and straight into my mother's petticoats.

Later, in a daze, I wake from a terrible dream, and I hear, as if from afar, my father shouting at me, shaking me awake. *Oh my god, he knows*! I feel my heart drop down to my feet; I am so afraid that I feel a warmth running down my legs, and I know I have made things even worse. After that, I am pulled out of bed, and there is nothing but shouting. My father, my mother and–I cannot believe it–even my grandfather is shouting. Then my mother quickly takes me by my hand and pushes me to the bathroom to change my pyjamas.

***

Husna stops reading. She is breathing heavily.

"This is terrible! He was just a child!" she cries. "Isn't this the same Arvind that we read about in the Prologue, where his wife suspects he is having an affair? Oh god, I cannot read any further. Who are Arvind and Sushmita? What is their connection to me?" she asks desperately.

Husna rushes out of the house and down to the lawn. Adam follows her.

"I can't breathe," she says, gulping in air. "I cannot stop thinking about that boy. Oh no..."

She gradually makes the connection between the young boy Arvind and the painting of the older boy, which was with the manuscript.

"No wonder that painting is so disturbing, does it show the effect of the corruption of that boy?" she whispers, almost in pain.

A memory from middle school comes to her mind. Rumours had floated through the classrooms about a coach's excessive interest in some of the boys. One day, the cops came and arrested him. They said that he had molested... no, he had sexually abused a boy repeatedly at a school camp she had also attended. Husna was not friends with that boy but had sometimes shared a table at lunch with him when other children were present. The boy had been removed from school and sent to another private school. Later, when she was finishing high school, she had learnt that while undergoing treatment for depression, he had shot himself with his father's gun. The memory makes her shiver.

Adam and Husna walk for some time around the lawn, both silent, trying to get some semblance of equanimity. Adam, too, is terribly shaken by what he has just read. Arvind had an abusive and overbearing father, and now this—his childhood destroyed by knowing adults. In his studies, Adam has read of acts of evil, but this being somehow connected to Husna and the fact that it was done to a small child by a knowing adult shocks him to his core.

"There are many people that populate this narrative," says Husna, turning to face Adam, "and yet I don't know or recognise any of them. I was so sure that something I would read would trigger a memory lost in my subconscious, but so far, all of it seems so strange to me. Why did the author, whoever he is, want me to read this manuscript? Why?"

***

Chapter 6
Tillotama – 1959

Tillotama is raging as she storms towards the main house. *How can her father insult her husband in this way? How dare he? How could he look at her as if she were nothing but a beggar? Does he really think that she can stay here, in his house, after such insults?*

"My place is with my husband!" she thunders as she enters her father's sparsely decorated office, lined with books on Hindu philosophy.

Her mother, who seldom enters her father's domain, is there with him, speaking vehemently. As Tillotama enters, she reins in her tongue, though not fast enough; Tillotama hears her mother berating her husband for assuming another's responsibility. Realising that her daughter has heard her, she clenches her hands and looks away. Her father, who has his head in his hands, looks up and sighs.

With great anguish, he whispers, "Go away, my daughter, stay with your kids and hold your anger. I don't want to speak anymore; I am taking a vow of silence, do you understand?"

Tillotama is shocked. How can her father take a vow of silence at such a time, when she so desperately needs him to speak?

"I don't care," she replies, her voice shaking. "Speak to me, tell me how you can throw my husband, my lord, the father of my children, out of our home? How can you? And why did you look at me in such a pitiable way?" Then her tears flow, her sobs filling the room, but nothing can persuade her father to speak a word. Her mother glares at him but says nothing. Tillotama's sobs are wasted, her anger is spent, and she feels the ground coming up to meet her.

When Tillotama opens her eyes, she sees that she is in Randhir's room. The sun is shining brightly through the windows by now; it must be late morning. Randhir is making her sip water with a teaspoon, but most of it flows down her chin and onto her neck. She holds on to Randhir's hand, and he looks away. She tries to get up but feels faint again, then, with a great effort, she forces herself to stand.

"Please, Randhir, please tell me what's going on," she pleads. He turns towards her, his eyes betraying a sadness and the same look of pity that she saw on her father's face. By now, she cannot ignore that something shameful has occurred, and that it has to do with her husband, and somehow also with Chamanlal. Before Randhir can say anything, Tillotama's deep-buried suspicions, which have been threatening to take root due to Manmohan's furtive and strange behaviour over these last few months, make her blurt out, "Is it Swarna?"

Her voice is so faint that Randhir can barely hear her. "Has he behaved shamefully with her?" As soon as Tillotama speaks these words, she instantly rejects them. Swarna's handsome but equine looks would never attract him. But in the next moment, Randhir lowers his eyes. He doesn't have to say a word. *It is to do with Swarna, oh my god!*

"Randhir, what is it? For heaven's sake, don't go silent on me like *Bauji!*" Tillotama is trembling by now, imagining the worst. *Oh, the scandal! Could he have molested her?* Even now, the truth is too hard to face.

"Tillotama, I really don't know the exact details because Chamanlal has only talked to *Bauji* directly. *Bauji* is very angry, so much so that while he related the details to me, he uttered some dreadful slurs against *Jeejaji*." Randhir stops and looks away from Tillotama again.

"You can't just stop there. Tell me! I am strong enough to hear whatever Manmohan has done," Tillotama cried.

"Tillotama, don't say I didn't warn you. You will hate me for what I am going to tell you. Please hear it from someone else."

"Oh, stop it, Randhir! This anxiety is killing me, and I need to go back to my children," she replies irritably.

"Alright then," Randhir sighs. "Yesterday evening, when the *puja* started in Chamanlal's house, Kasturi was sent up to Swarna's room to call her down, and he saw her kissing *Jeejaji* passionately, who had his hand... no forget it, I can't say it." Kasturi was too shocked to react immediately, and before he could call the family, *Jeejaji* had left. Thereafter, the scenes in their house were very ugly. The menfolk wanted to come here and drag *Jeejaji* out and thrash him to an inch of his life. Chamanlal stopped them; he wants to put a lid on this, knowing that such a scandal will spoil all chances of Swarna marrying the boy he had chosen for her from a family in Karol Bagh. Swarna has been shunted off to a relative in Kanpur today."

All of a sudden, Randhir's tone changes, and he shouts, "How could your husband bring this on the family? We have done so much for him! He is a cad, a good-for-nothing..." A quick, hard slap from Tillotama stops Randhir's tirade. Before he can say anything else, she leaves his room.

Tillotama reaches the annexe, keeping her head down so that the children cannot see the state she is in and shuts herself in her room. She slides down the closed door and, holding her head in her hands, weeps quietly, muffling her sobs and ignoring the worried calls of her children and *Bheji*. She feels betrayed by her husband, father and brother. She also feels hopeless in the face of her inability to become financially independent. Wallowing in self-pity, she sinks even lower in her own estimation. Finally, after her tears are spent, she rises, wipes her face with her *pallu* and opens the door. She gathers Meena and Arvind and holds them tightly. They have been waiting for her, hungry and apprehensive, while *Bheji* soothes Dev in her arms. After the previous day of festivities and the morning of shouting adults, they are anxious and confused. Dev bursts out crying, and Meena is quickly dispatched to the main house for some toast, butter and jam, while Arvind clings tearfully to his mother.

Tillotama decides that the time for passivity is over. In spite of Manmohan's betrayal, she has to think about the future of her children. Although her husband has been a cad, she and the children need him. She needs to protect her family, including her errant husband. To do that, she needs to make some bold decisions, even if they are morally wrong. She knows that never again will she allow herself to be discarded like a leaf, floating aimlessly from one situation to another. She will create her own destiny, and for that, she needs to get her husband back. She will never forgive him, nor will she forget this day, but she needs to keep her family together. She straightens her back and knows exactly what she has to do.

***

Chapter 7
Arvind – 1960

I am waiting for the last bell of the day to ring so that I can go home. I feel like a misfit, alienated from the other children, and school feels daunting even though nothing has changed, except me. I look at my classmates, the 'normal' boys and girls, and envy their happiness. I wonder, as I do each day, what they would think of my shameful behaviour. Can I tell any of them that I look forward to visits to my uncle's place with both dread and anticipation, wanting his hugs, yet dreading what comes after, which makes me feel filthy and guilty? Even thinking these thoughts makes me nervous. My fingers steal into my mouth, and I involuntarily start chewing my already badly bitten nails.

"Arvind, lost again? And stop that filthy habit, you leper! Go and stand outside the classroom this very minute." Miss Howard's shrill voice makes me jump. "I will need to speak to your father if you continue this way in class. Now, go to the door and wait."

I move quickly, my face red with embarrassment, as Miss Howard moves threateningly towards me with a raised ruler. Miss Howard is a complete dictator; she feels no compassion and clearly revels in humiliating us children. I remember Malti's face turning red as a tomato when Miss Howard raised her skirt to deliver six quick hits to her buttocks with a ruler, or another time, when she nearly broke Manoj's nose with the duster she threw at his face. I am eagerly waiting for winter vacation, after which we move up to the fifth standard, the start of middle school. Miss Howard can gladly have the next bunch of kids to bully, thank the lord!

My neighbour and closest friend, Rishi, is waiting for me at the gate as I stumble out of school to walk the two miles to our houses, which face each other across the street. Rishi is a heavy-set boy and is looking forward to boxing, which is introduced in the fifth standard. His movements are awkward, except when he is on the sports field. There, he can move as gracefully as a ballet dancer. He never backs away from a fight and has long been my protection from the bullies in the neighbourhood. Today, he is looking grim and angry.

"Why don't you pay attention in class, Arvind?" he shouts at me. "The last few months, your marks have been falling. What if they keep you back in this class? You don't want to fail, do you?"

I can't believe my ears.

"Are you joking, Rishi? I've fallen behind in some subjects, but being kept back? That only happens to the real duds," I shout back, too loudly to be convincing. "My dad will murder me if I fail… tell me, what should I do? I just can't seem to keep my mind on my books. I don't understand what's happening to me."

"Just study, Kaku," was his reply. Rishi seldom calls me Kaku. Clearly, he is very concerned.

We had moved to this house on Court Road after *Deepavali*, about a year ago. I was thrilled that the bungalow, which my father had rented, was right opposite the apartment building where Rishi lived with his mother and two older brothers. Rishi's mother is a sturdy and imposing woman who rules the household with an iron fist. Rishi does not talk about his father, who died soon after his birth, but his mother and brothers seem to manage fine. Irrespective of the season, Rishi wakes up early every morning and walks to a nearby dairy farm to pick up fresh, buttery milk, while his brothers help his mother with kitchen chores and get the lunch ready to take to school. Rishi is always on time, waiting outside my gate to walk with me to school, his lunch in his satchel, while my hot lunch is delivered to school by the *chowkidar* from my father's office. Rishi is serious, quiet and confident of both his physical strength and intelligence, quite unlike me. He is not a teacher's pet and is highly respected; Miss Howard seldom raises her voice at him. He is the Junior School Captain and is involved in all school activities. In the absence of a teacher, he is invariably made the class monitor, and none of his classmates challenge him. He is fair in his monitoring but is especially hard on me if I step out of line, just to prove that he doesn't play favourites. Rishi cares for me like a brother, and we talk about everything—the tension at my home, his fear of his tough but loving mother, the problems they face if his father's state pension is late. I cannot, however, ever talk to him about my dirty secret.

A few weeks after Miss Howard sent me out of the classroom, just before the winter break, our report cards got distributed. I am horrified; the worst has happened. I am the only person to be kept back in the fourth standard. My heart sinks, and I am terrified of what my father will say. How will I show my face at home? Rishi has left school early because he needs to catch a train to visit his grandparents, who live in Rampur, a town close to the hills of Kumaon. He is only coming back in the last week of the vacation, but I really need his support today. Crazy thoughts of running away from home run through my head, but I would rather be beaten up by my father than become a beggar on the streets of Bombay or Calcutta, as so many children do. Fortunately, my father is travelling to Poona to meet some suppliers for his new motor parts business, which he started in Kashmiri Gate, but I still have Meena and my mother to contend with.

My mother has just returned from her parents' house and is busy in the kitchen. Instead of changing from my school uniform to go out to play with the neighbouring kids, I go to *Bheji's* room and pretend to listen to her recital of the day's events, surreptitiously watching the doorway for my mother's arrival. I can't see Meena; she has probably left to play with a friend. What should have been the joyful start of my vacation is turning into a nightmare. Listening to *Bheji's* chatter while my mind is elsewhere does not quieten my sense of panic. I rudely leave her in mid-sentence and walk to the kitchen.

"I failed to move up to the next standard, Mummy," I say softly. She looks at me in shock, but before she can say anything, I burst into tears.

"I cannot believe that you are such an idiot! How will I ever face my friends in school when they know that my stupid brother has failed?" I hadn't seen Meena in the kitchen, drinking water from the tap.

"Send him away to boarding school, Mum! They will beat him into shape. Stop sniffling, you sissy!" she snaps at me. "Save your tears for when you really need them: when Daddy gets his hands on you." The terror of hearing that dreaded word 'Daddy' makes me cry even more.

"Stop it, Meena," says Mummy. "Let me do the talking. You were doing so well till last year, son. Have you found the lessons very difficult this year, or is it Miss Howard who scares you, *beta*? I grasp at this lifeline she has thrown at me and nod in assent. Meena looks at me contemptuously and leaves the kitchen with an angry shrug. Mummy rebukes me gently as she reads my report and later saves me from the wrath of my father by putting the blame on Miss Howard.

During most of the winter vacation, I am schooled at home by my mother and Meena. I'm given a respite for a few hours in the late afternoon to go out and play. Rishi comes back from his vacation eventually, and we spend a few desultory hours together, finding little to say to each other.

"What did you do during the vacation?" he asks.

"Nothing much, morning walks with our neighbours, studied with Meena most of the time and went a couple of times with Mummy to my grandparents' place on Alipur Road." That we will not be classmates is sitting heavily, like a huge weight, between us.

When Rishi goes back to his house that day, my mind wanders back to my visits to Alipur Road during the vacation. Invariably, I would leave my Mummy with her parents and go looking for Uncle Shiv, or he would send his manservant Thapa from the annexe to ask me to visit him. I knew that this was terribly wrong, but I needed those hugs, those long kisses, and the love he gave me. I also knew he would make me do those other things that made him moan and gasp. I was always scared that Thapa or Uncle Trilok would walk in and see me doing those awful things. Afterwards, I would return home, confused and guilty, and promise myself that I would never go back to Uncle Shiv. They were promises I would always forget the next time I visited.

After the vacation, I return shamefully to the same class. Miss Howard is not returning, we are told. She has left India to go to a young country called Australia. Our new teacher is Miss Gupta, who is young, pretty and has a perpetual smile on her face. I know most of the faces in class, after all, they were the kids who looked up at us, the seniors of the junior school. I am not made junior school captain for obvious reasons, but I become a house prefect. I hide my face in my sleeve when I climb onto the stage during assembly to have the badge pinned on me. Tuck time is humiliating; my new classmates stick together while my previous classmates jeer at me if I join their activities. Rishi often leaves his classmates to sit with me, and his loyalty moves me to tears.

Thankfully, my studies during the vacation pay off, and I am well ahead of the class in the first monthly tests. Even during lessons, I can answer all the questions before the others even raise their hands. Miss Gupta convinces the junior school principal that I should be moved up to the fifth standard and, to my joy, into the section with my previous classmates. Rishi cannot stop smiling when the class teacher of fifth standard welcomes me, and I quickly forget that many of my classmates had once jeered at me. I happily relinquish my junior school prefect badge.

***

Chapter 8
Tillotama – 1961

The debate regarding Shiv's demand to marry continues to rage at her parents' house. Tillotama finds herself at Alipur Road on most days, hurrying back to Court Road in the late afternoon to have meals ready for the children and Manmohan. Shiv wants to get married, now that he is twenty-nine; he is restless but continues to hide himself away in the annexe. Instead of spending time working the family business, he keeps studying to add to his qualifications: a Bachelor of Arts, a Law degree, and then a Master's in Political Science, hoping that it will make him a more respected man than his brother.

"So let Shiv marry!" is Tillotama's angry retort to her mother, who thinks otherwise.

"The younger brothers can marry only after Randhir," she insists, fully aware that Randhir refuses to even consider a marriage proposal. At thirty-four, he is way past the customary age of marriage. He has ignored all pleas in the past, citing preoccupation with the business as the reason, which is partially true now that *Bauji* spends most of his time with his books on philosophy. Tillotama understands that Randhir's angst is largely to do with Waheeda's terrible fate and wants the family to back off and look for a bride for Shiv instead, but she is shot down by her mother.

The stalemate continues, day in and day out, everyone's energy wasted going over the same arguments. Shiv, Randhir, Tillotama and their mother are in the sitting room, arguing.

"What will the community say?" is an oft-repeated refrain from their mother.

"Community means what, Mother?" Tillotama says. "Is it the *Punjabi Sabha* or the *Khukhrain Biradari*? Who, exactly, are you talking about?"

"Hush, you stupid girl," Tillotama's mother, forgetting that she is a mother of three. "I cannot have an unmarried son hanging around the wife of his younger brother."

Shocked at her insinuation, Tillotama and Randhir retire to another room. Shiv walks off in disgust and shouts angrily at them all, "All your life you have never cared about me, none of you!"

Finally, Randhir gives in to the pressure, and the Kohli family begins merrily searching not for one but two brides for the not-so-eligible bachelors. They strut around from family to family, virtually prodding and nitpicking at brides-to-be as if they are part of a village cattle exhibition. Randhir wants Tillotama with him when he 'inspects' any potential bride, while Shiv does not want anyone to have a say in his choice. There are night and day runs to Jullundur and then to Rohtak. Next, it is Ambala, Ludhiana and Dehradun. Ultimately, Randhir chooses Anchal from Jagadhri. She is pretty and plump, ten years younger than Randhir, with a keen sense of humour. She is considered 'homely', which means she knows the art of keeping a good house, a great virtue in 'good Punjabi brides'. After a few meetings with Anchal, Randhir declares that he has fallen in love.

Shiv insists on looking for a postgraduate, and after some deep introspection, affirms his willingness to marry Reena, the principal of one of the largest government-run schools in Jullundur. She is haughty and knows her mind; she has a fair complexion and flat features, but sharp eyes that absorb everything around her.

"Not very demure, is she?" is Trilok's cheeky comment when he meets her at the engagement party.

The marriages are fixed within two weeks of each other, with Randhir getting the privilege of taking the *baraat* to Jagadhri first.

Tillotama steps out of Randhir's car at Court Road and lets out a sigh of relief now that all is settled and she can go back to her life. She looks at her house, thinks of her children and *Bheji* inside, and then inexplicably stops in the veranda at the entrance to the house. The memories of that fateful *Deepavali* day, and what came after, suddenly wash over her.

After confronting her father, she had left the children with *Bheji* and gone to see Chamanlal. He was shocked when she arrived; she was the last person he expected to come to his door. Tillotama and Chamanlal shut themselves away, with Kasturi in close attendance. After the meeting, she left both men with a sense of grudging admiration towards her. She then went looking for Manmohan, whom she knew would be with one of his associates from the Punjabi Sabha, and told him of what she had done. Shocked by his usually timid wife's audacity, Manmohan understood quickly that he needed to get his act together or he would lose his wife and children. He had immediately started searching for another home for his family. After finding a small bungalow with a large garden on Court Road, he pledged lifelong loyalty to Tillotama and his children. With the help of some of his loyal friends, he set up a business in motor parts at Kashmiri Gate, catering mainly to Chevrolet, Dodge and other American cars. He never spoke of why he chose this business, even though his true expertise lay in the merchandising of cloth.

Tillotama loves her house at Court Road, which she feels is now truly her own, even though it is rented. She doesn't doubt that in time, she will possess it as an owner. She casts aside any inner conflicts and pours all her sense of beauty and love into the house, making it a home for herself and her family. Now content, she is ready to forgive her parents and brothers for what had transpired at *Deepavali*. She starts visiting Alipur Road again, unknowingly becoming the cause of her son's long fight with the demons that will overtake his life.

Manmohan, after a year of good behaviour, proves once again that a leopard does not change its spots.

***

Chapter 9
Arvind – 1962

I am shaking as my father drags me towards the coal and wood shed. At times like these, when he has built himself into a frothing monster, no one can stand in his path. My mother and Meena have averted their faces, and Dev is probably hiding under the bed. I am breathing heavily, and I can hear my heart beating wildly. I know that I have to bear this punishment; I only wish my father would beat me instead of shutting me in the shed. Every time I am locked in, I panic; I can feel the walls moving hungrily towards me from all sides, and then I find myself struggling to breathe. When I'm in the shed, thoughts of my terrible shame come rushing to my mind. I want to weep, but I will not give him the satisfaction of seeing my tears. *But how do I escape all this?* My mother teaches me to pray to Rama; my school teaches me to pray to Jesus, but nothing can help me. I feel as though I am damned!

Just a few hours ago, I was happily playing *pittu* with the neighbourhood kids. I love this game, which involves two teams, seven stones and a battered tennis ball. I have to explain to Dev, who always wants to play with us, how the game works. A pyramid of flat stones is built, with the largest stone on the bottom, followed by smaller stones being placed on top until there are seven in the pyramid. Each team gets a chance to throw the ball to break the pyramid and then has to rebuild it. As they do so, they keep shouting "*pittu, pittu!*" while dodging the ball thrown by the attacking team. The members of the defending team are allowed to push the ball away with their closed fists. If the ball touches any other part of the defending player, he has to drop out of the game. If all the players of the defending team are eliminated without the pyramid being rebuilt, then the game is won by the attacking team, who get the next chance to break and rebuild the pyramid. At nine years old, I was the youngest and the weakest player. As usual, I am the last to be picked by any of the teams.

On this particular day, I am doing extremely well; I am the only player left to put the seventh stone on the pyramid and am about to win it for my team when I hear the sound of my father's Enfield coming down the street. I freeze for a second and then sprint down the pebbled driveway into the house, just making it before my father swings the bike into it. I know that if he catches me playing instead of studying, I will be in a world of trouble. I don't have the time to pull out my books, so I slip under the bed, agitated and out of breath, hoping my father will call for my mother or Meena before looking for me.

I am appalled when I look down and see that I have only one slipper on; in the rush, I must have dropped the other somewhere on the way. I know I will be dead if my father finds it. I shiver at the thought, but stay under the bed, sure that my father will hear the sound of my heart, which is drumming so loudly in my ears. I hear my father enter the house, but he moves towards the kitchen where my mother is cooking dinner on a coal fire. This isn't what he usually does, but I don't think anything of it as I move from my hiding place to join Meena and angelic Dev at the study table and quickly pull my homework out. Meena, who has just become a teenager and is unbothered by anything, including my agitation, scrunches up her nose as if to say "you stink" and kicks me under the table before going back to her books. We hear our parents heading towards the dining room where we are studying. The next moment, my father is twisting my left ear with one hand and with the other, he swings the lost slipper across my face.

"You think that you're smart?" he snarls. "I could see from the guilty faces of your friends that you had run away from the game when you heard my bike. And then what do I find? This filthy slipper of yours, lying as useful evidence."

His voice rises in terrible anger, and I squirm in pain.

"What happens to your studies while you play?" he yells. "I am wasting my hard-earned money on your stupidity, aren't I? I should pull you out of school and let you fend for yourself on the streets, you moron."

I have always been mortally afraid of my father, possibly from the day I was born, if I can remember that far back. My early memories are all fear and dread. It wasn't that he beat me or was physically abusive. It was far more psychological than that. When he shut me up in the shed, I wished he would just hit me instead. The one severe beating that he gave me was at the age of three, when I wanted to stay home from school with Meena, who was feverish and had been allowed to stay. My mistake, I realised later, was the lie I acted out to miss school. Lies were like a crimson cloth to my bullish father. I pretended to have a stomach-ache and called out in pain. But my terrible hamming at playing sick was rudely interrupted by the back of my father's palm. A slap so hard it made my ears ring; he ended up dragging me from one room to another, hitting me as he did so.

I was warned that if I ever told a lie again, I would be thrashed worse than that. God! Even if I had told him the truth about why I wanted to miss school that day, he would never have believed me. He would have thrashed me all the same. How could I have told him that my teacher locked me in a small room each and every day because I wanted my mother and wept all the time? How could I tell him that I hated that school, that I am frightened, that I see ghostly figures in the darkness? That I hurt and keep hurting? He would never believe me.

My mother does not have any say in these matters. Matters of study and discipline are not her domain. Her responsibility ends within the home, never outside the four walls of the house. Dad is temperamental and angry, shouting at the least transgression, so we have learnt to keep out of his way at all times or as much as possible. How many times have I wished that he could be like other dads who come to school to watch their children in sports or on stage, who hug them when they win a trophy and proudly introduce them to their friends? These dads play cricket with their sons and take them on holidays.

As we grew older, we preferred to communicate with our father through our mother. School books, shoes, broken laces, new hockey sticks, and new clothes as the old ones shrink, pocket money, and money for school fetes; whatever we need, we go to our Mum. She has to face his ire, his refusal to pay for what he thinks is frivolous, like school fete and new clothes, despite the fact that we have grown so fast. He is consumed only by anger, money worries, Mummy's relatives and, as we learn later, other women.

Chapter 10
Arvind – 1963

The fever rages. It feels like buckets of water are crashing on my head. I am suffocating, I am dying! I am nauseous; I throw up in a tray that my mother holds to my mouth. I am sweating, then I feel a cold compress on my forehead, and I feel cool and calm. I hear voices.

"I think his fever is going to break now, it's down to a hundred degrees."

I hear my mother's voice, pleading, "I hope he will be fine. He keeps calling for his father, and then he shouts, 'Leave me alone!' Doctor, what is happening? Has his mind been affected by the fever?"

"Hush, Mrs Chopra. His fever was so high that he was just hallucinating. Stop worrying. Loving care and these pills will help him. He will be fine."

I slip back into a deep dream…

I am travelling in a car. Uncle Trilok is driving, and Uncle Shiv is sitting with me in the back. He is kissing me and forcing his tongue into my mouth. He takes my hand and puts it on his crotch, then opens his fly and pushes it inside his trousers and makes me stroke it. He moans and makes funny gagging sounds when he spurts out the sticky liquid onto a handkerchief, which he has pushed into my hand. Later, he lovingly strokes my face and then falls asleep. I look at the scenery passing by outside the car window. Sugarcane fields, as far as the eye can see. I can see a well with a pulley operated by oxen, which continuously pushes the water through channels to flow into a field. I feel like them. Nowhere to go, nowhere to run, just tethered to a wheel that turns round and round. After some time, the car stops. Uncle Shiv takes the wheel, and Uncle Trilok slips into the seat he has vacated. Then he starts on me. He kisses me and bites my lips, and then, like Uncle Shiv, opens his fly. However, he puts his hand on my head and pushes my lips on it. I take it in till all of it is in my mouth, and I know I am going to choke. I scream and wake up. I am alone in my room, my clothes smell of cold sweat, and I am breathing heavily. Meena comes running into my room. I look up at the tenderness in her eyes and the concern on her face makes me break down in tears, but my secret stays with me.

Uncle Trilok targeted me in Jagadhri, where we had taken the *baraat* for Uncle Shiv's wedding. I had gone back to the room I shared with Meena and Dev in the guest house where we were staying, and was surprised when he barged into the room after me. It seemed he had been watching me and had taken advantage of my being alone. He had a sly look on his face, and as he sat on my bed, he started stroking himself.

"I know what you have been up to, you sexy thing. I have often seen you go to my brother's room in the annexe. The window at the back provided me with a view of the long kisses you gave him and the other playful things you did. Looking at you, I couldn't stop beating my own meat. I have wasted so much of my load outside that window, watching you." He stopped and looked meaningfully at me.

"You are going to be lonely now, my boy. Now that my brother is getting married, those bee-stung lips will remain hungry."

I moved away in horror. "No, no, leave me alone!" I didn't like the look on his face and the way he was holding me.

"What? You want me to tell your father about all I have seen? I would love to see that bastard's face when I tell him. Do you think he won't believe me?"

I froze. I knew that I had to do what he asked. Listlessly, I let him do all those dirty things to me. It was much, *much* worse than with Uncle Shiv, who would lovingly hug and kiss me and, only near the end, make me stroke him till his juice came out. Uncle Trilok was rough. He pushed my head down and made me take him in my mouth. When he pushed his lips on mine, it was like he would devour me. All the time, he talked about Meena's budding breasts, thighs and legs in her school uniform, while he stroked himself or made me do it. I was so sick of myself. I knew that I was lost forever.

When we return from the wedding, the abuse continues whenever an opportunity is presented, either at my grandparents' house, where I have to go at least once a week with my mother, or at our own home if I am alone. I do not protest, except when he turns me over and wants to push himself inside me. Then I shove him away and am ready to hit him, telling him he can tell the world about me, but I will not permit him to violate me in that way. It is never brought up again, though he continues seeking and receiving other forms of sexual gratification from me. When he wants to turn his attentions to Dev, I make it stop. I had just entered my teens, and I was ready to face the consequences of my actions. During those years of abuse, my uncle had called me a 'bitch', 'cocksucker', 'Satan the tempter' and other names whenever I refused to allow him to touch me. I deserve those names. There are times when I enjoyed my control over him, to have made him slobber while I held back.

When I became older, I read a line from Pat O'Brien's book *Angels with Dirty Faces* that said, "Let's go say a prayer for a boy who couldn't run as fast as I could." Looking back at those days of shame and torment, I try to figure out whether I was the boy who couldn't run fast enough or the boy who did not want to run.

For most of my life since then, I have been trying to find this out.

***

Husna flings the manuscript down in a rage.

"Now you know why I hate gays. They have no scruples and target young kids for their own satisfaction."

Adam looks at her passionate face and has to correct her.

"Husna, these men are evil, but not necessarily gay. Shiv and Trilok are 'pedos' and are clearly getting their rocks off on this kid. The society that they lived in didn't allow them to mix with women and, in fact, from what I have read so far, they were not even allowed to look at women or admire them, let alone have a friendship or any form of intimacy. That came only after marriage." Adam watches the anger drain a little from Husna's face and decides to continue.

"You know, these were the societal norms in many Asian countries. They possibly still exist in the region now. It's a little like Catholic priests in the Western world. Devoid of any contact with women, they pick on the most vulnerable, young boys, and get away with it. The Catholic Church is like a traditional Indian family; they are ostriches. They don't see what they don't want to see. Often, people who prey on kids have themselves been victims in their childhood. Paedophiles also target young girls, too, so why focus only on gay men? Arvind's uncles will have married and lived like model husbands,

without a thought for the young life they destroyed for their sexual gratification."

Adam can see that he is getting through to Husna, but her animosity towards gay men is deep-rooted. Somehow, for Amos's sake, Adam needs to find out why.

***

Chapter 11

Tillotama – 1963

Tillotama paces the veranda, back and forth, back and forth.

"I wonder why your father is late," she sighs worriedly. "He left Ambala after lunch, more than eight hours ago, and he hasn't arrived home. I hope nothing has happened to the car; why hasn't he called?"

"Mummy, sit down. You are making me dizzy with all your walking," says Meena.

"I hope he has had an accident and is dead," is hardly out of Arvind's mouth when Tillotama smacks his face with her open hand.

"How dare you speak such inauspicious words? Go wash your mouth or I'll put red chillies in it, you wicked boy!"

There is a tremor in Tillotama's voice, and she shivers; her fears articulated in Arvind's words.

Much later, she hears the car being parked in the garage and the sound of Manmohan's footsteps as he walks to the front door, which she has left unlatched. Anger flares in her, even though there is also a feeling of relief. She feigns sleep. Manmohan walks into the bedroom and roughly shakes her awake.

"Is there anything to eat, you lazy woman? I have been working and on the road all day, and you are sleeping? Get up and serve me dinner!"

"Have you seen the time, Manmohan?" Tillotama fires back. "I have been sick with worry; the children fell asleep, having hoped to eat with you, and now you barge in at midnight asking for food? You left Ambala ten hours ago, so where were you?"

"You *kulta*! What makes you ask such a stupid question? I told you. I have been on the road! Instead of serving me dinner, you ask these questions?" Manmohan's hand flies up as if he is about to hit her, but he thinks better of it. Tillotama catches his arm and screams.

"Go on, hit me! Hit me! Why did you stop? That's all you are capable of. There are unpaid bills everywhere; Arvind and Meena were sent home today because their school fees have not been paid, the grocer has stopped further credit till his bills are paid, and you come home at midnight demanding food?"

Manmohan cannot believe that his supposedly dutiful wife is speaking to him like this. He drags her out of the bedroom, into the living room, and shouts for the children. Meena and Arvind come running in with wide eyes; they were awake anyway. They stand aghast as their father pushes their mother onto the carpet, nearly stepping on her, before storming out of the house. Meena breaks down and holds her crying mother, while Arvind looks with hatred at the figure of his father as he noisily pulls up the garage shutters and slams the car door before driving off into the night.

Manmohan does not come home for a week after that night, leaving Tillotama in a frenzy of guilt. The poor woman never realises how she is manipulated by this emotional blackmail.

That night, Arvind rages, angry at his own impotence. *I hope you die, I hope you die*, he mutters over and over again through clenched teeth. He thinks of the reasons for wishing his father dead. Is it to do with his mother's suffering, or is it his thwarted love for this man? He loves his father with an obsession that scares him. He is ready to do his bidding and make him proud, just so he would hug him, hold him, make him feel whole and warm, and be more aware of his existence. The poor child doesn't realise that his father feels that he has fulfilled his duty by giving them a good education in an English school, providing them with shoes, books, satchels, uniforms and the occasional treat from Bengali Sweet Mart, many of which were denied to him when he was young. He has little time for emotions; to show love will only make his children weak and dependent. He is ignorant of his daughter, her feelings, her awkwardness, her awakening young body, the hormones flowing freely, leaving acne scars in their wake and giant upheavals within. He is ignorant of the anguished love his son feels for him, which drowns him in shame as he seeks another man's embrace, a man who uses Arvind's innocent hunger to feed his own sexual release. Manmohan abuses Tillotama's love in his own selfish way and spends those days away from home feeding her guilt, in the arms of another woman, enamoured of his looks and virility, even though she is promised to another: a young man defending the country's borders, counting the months when he can return home to marry his young, adulterous lass.

Later, these transgressions will lead to the collapse of Manmohan's business; his 'trusted' employees, who are robbing him blind while collecting evidence of his many travesties, end up blackmailing him.

When Manmohan's ardour and anger are spent, he returns to Tillotama, who is ready to serve him. He generously forgives her for her justifiable anger. Tillotama thinks back to how shocked she had been in Mumbai when her sister-in-law, Bimla, had turned against them to protect her errant husband. Now, she realises that in her blind love for her husband, she has sunk to depths far, *far* below what poor Bimla had ever sunk to. She thinks of how she has cheated and lied and fought for her husband for so long. Drowning in self-pity, she lets the tears flow. Arvind walks in at that moment and, without saying a word, holds Tillotama with understanding until she manages to pull herself together. Something beautiful is communicated between them, their anguish flowing from the same source. Tillotama sees a tear trickle down his face and quickly wipes it away with her finger. These strong feelings of empathy flow strongly in that room for a brief moment, and it's as if no force on earth can break its magic.

Tillotama has another worry. Her father's health is failing; his lungs had filled with fluid, and the doctors had found no apparent cause. There were no indications of any cancerous growth in his body, although he kept losing weight and was looking more skeletal as the days went by. Tillotama's mother is now spending more time with him, having conceded defeat in the kitchen and accepted Anchal's superior cooking skills. She also leaves the running of the house to both her daughters-in-law, Reena and Anchal. But trouble is brewing at Alipur Road.

Just the other day, when Tillotama visited, she found Trilok and Reena whispering to each other in the dining room, but when they saw her, they shut their mouths quickly. She then found Anchal in the kitchen, looking very tense and disturbed.

"Anchal, is everything all right? You seem very upset. Is everything fine between you and Randhir?"

"Oh, *Bhabi*, it's not Randhir but Shiv and Reena. Shiv is harassing *Bauji* to give him his share of the property; he doesn't give a damn that *Bauji* is suffering. Randhir lost his temper with Shiv... I agree he shouldn't have, and it nearly ended in a fist fight. When *Bhabiji* and *Bauji* intervened, Shiv went ballistic. He said some terribly nasty things to them and accused them of treating him like a step-son. Instead of calming him down, Reena has been poisoning his mind against all of us." Anchal barely drew breath before she continued tearfully.

"And then there is Trilok. He will tell me some mean things about Reena and Shiv and then fill their ears about me and Randhir. The other day, I innocently remarked to him that we should call you in to mediate between the brothers, given that you are the eldest in the family. I don't know what Trilok said to Shiv, but Reena was livid and shouted at me that everyone knows how biased you are towards Randhir and that this was my ploy of grabbing all the property."

Tillotama had been extremely worried when she heard this. She always knew that one day the deep-rooted animosity Shiv had long felt for Randhir would raise its head. *Bauji's* sickness has now become the catalyst for a power tussle within the family's wholesale grain and dried fruit business, its mainstay for many generations. She is also worried that small problems between manipulative Reena and Anchal could blow up into a full-blown war, pitting the family against each other. She realises that Trilok, in his typically sly way, is playing the role that suits him best—sitting on the fence so that he can jump over to the winning side at the last moment.

When Randhir calls Tillotama a few days later and tells her that the doctors have finally discovered malignant lesions in *Bauji's* liver—already at an advanced stage, giving him only a few months to live—Tillotama is not at all surprised. She breaks down on hearing the news, and for once, Manmohan is solicitous, rushing with her to Alipur Road.

***

Chapter 12
Arvind – 1963

There is a ripple of excitement among the girls in class when Rishi and I walk in on the first day of seventh standard. Before we can figure out what the cause of the twittering is, Mrs Sen—my favourite teacher, who teaches us English Literature—walks in and announces that she is going to be our class teacher this year. We are sitting in our usual fashion, boys on one side and the girls on the other, with Rishi sitting at the desk next to me. To our surprise, Mrs Sen immediately shuffles us, which means that most of us are now sitting next to a girl. The boys are shocked, and since there are more boys, they try to hang on to each other. There is a collective gasp in the class; this has never been done before, and some of us are squirming. Who wants a silly girl next to him?

Mrs Sen looks pointedly at me.

"Stop looking like you've swallowed a frog, Arvind. And that goes for the other boys, too. Most of you will enter your teens in a year, so it's time you learnt how to deal with girls and treat them as your equals. Make friends and learn how to be comfortable with them!"

"But ma'am, Mrs Sharma, the Hindi teacher, is not going to allow it," said one of the boys.

"What are our parents going to say?" someone else piped up.

"You boys have sisters or cousins at home, don't you?" said Mrs Sen, unfazed. "Deal with your classmates the same way and don't worry about your parents or Mrs Sharma; I will handle them. As a starter, I will send a letter home with each of you explaining the reasons for this change. It surprises me that only the boys are objecting to this?"

"Ma'am, these guys need to grow up," Renu says loftily. "They are so juvenile."

"Boys, Renu, not guys," Mrs Sen replies archly. "Though I agree with your sentiments. They do need to grow up."

The novelty soon wears off. Mrs Sharma accepts the change with pursed lips, although the school grapevine is alive with chatter about angry arguments in the staff room. There are complaints about how Mrs Sen is encouraging boys and girls to sit together so that they can get up to 'reprehensible' and 'immoral' things.

A few days after the shuffle, Renu, who now has the desk next to me, tells me something with suppressed excitement.

"Have you seen the new PT teacher? He is young and very handsome; the girls just can't wait for the next PT class. His name is Mr Jones, but he wants us to call him Gregory."

"That means he's an Anglo. I thought they were all leaving for Australia? They hate us, you know," I said, thinking back to my problems with Mrs Howard.

"Stop calling them Anglos! They are Indians, and they don't hate us. In any case, Gregory is a dreamboat," Renu sighs. I raise my eyebrows.

Our class meets Mr Jones the next day, when we have our PT class. He is waiting in the gym and is wearing white shorts, shoes and a t-shirt. He has curly blonde-brown hair that is a trifle too long, and a sharp, slender nose. He is also young; he looks fresh out of senior school, and you can tell that he spends his time out in the sun. He is tanned, but there are flashes of pale skin showing under the edge of his shorts and the short sleeves of his t-shirt. I notice all this within the first few seconds and am surprised to realise that I, too, had been eagerly looking forward to meeting him. My face flushes at the thought.

Mr Jones talks about himself; he has a nice sing-song twang in his voice. He tells us that he completed school at a hill station, Mussoorie, the previous year, after which he worked in his father's farm in eastern Uttar Pradesh, which did not pay him enough. He decided to teach us so that he could save his earnings to pay for college. I notice that he has nice blue-green eyes, and he looks kind. There is an aura of toughness about him, even though he isn't really tall or muscled, and he exudes warmth. By the end of our first PT session, I had developed a crush on Gregory. I want him to be my friend, my confidante. I start looking forward to the PT and games periods, where I will be able to see him.

A few weeks later, during a hockey game, Mr Jones calls me aside.

"Chopra, on the double here, what was all that about? You are meant to go into the ball, not away from the ball. Are you scared that your opponent's stick will hit you? This is no way to dribble," he lectures in his sing-song, irresistible twang.

"Sorry, sir. No, sir. I am not scared, sir," I reply, a little breathlessly.

I look down at my feet. I do not want to look at his face so as not to betray my feelings. All I want to do is to tell him that I am always scared of boxing, horse-work in the gym, fast balls on the cricket pitch. I have panic attacks, and I do not like touch games. I want to run away from the other boys, and I have too many secrets. I love athletics, long jump, the arts, and drama. I want to share all of this with him, and I want him to tell me that he understands and will look after me. All this time, I am hoping that the bell for the next period will ring, so that I can move away and breathe again.

On another day, when I am walking home after school, Mr Jones passes me on his bicycle.

"Hey Chopra, we meet again! Going my way? What happened to your cycle? Hop on, I'll take you as far as I go. You can walk the rest of the way."

I jump up on the bar in front, and we cycle towards the family he lodges with, which is on my way home. I can smell his peppermint breath on my face as he tells me about the family he lives with and their cats.

"Give me dogs any day; I have two of them on the farm, a German Shepherd and a Golden Retriever, and I miss them. Do you have dogs at home?"

"No, sir."

"Call me 'Gregory' when we are out of school, will you?"

"Right, sir! Sorry, sir. Err... *Gregory*," I whisper his name. My eyes go to his hands on the handles of the bicycle: white, with long tapering fingers, not the hands of a farmhand.

Just before dropping me off outside the house where he lives, he says, "Chopra, meet me after school tomorrow. I want to try you out for the cricket team, both batting and bowling."

I walk home in a daze, savouring the experience of his nearness, the sweet smell of his breath, his kind blue eyes on my face and his elegant hands. I fall asleep thinking of him.

Cricket practice comes a cropper; Mr Jones just can't get me to do anything right. I am scared of the red ball hitting me. My slouch does not help my stance facing the ball, and my height, which should have been to my advantage, does not help my bowling.

"You are hopeless, Chopra," is Mr Jones's parting shot when I am getting on my bicycle to go home. "Don't come to practice tomorrow."

I can hear my heart breaking into pieces as I move away.

Some days later, there is a hockey match in school and Mr Jones is playing for Brown House. It is a rough game, and most of the school is out in the field watching the match. Mr Jones is a bundle of energy. All the girls are chanting, "Go, Mr Jones! Go, go, go!" and Mr Jones, loving the adulation, does not disappoint. I have to finish an English composition, so I leave the match at halftime.

I finish my work when school is over and head to the staff room to hand it over to the teacher, who generally works late. My path takes me past Mr Jones's office, and I spot some of the girls peeking through the small window at the side of the office. They shush me as I pass, but curious, I push them aside and look in. Mr Jones is with an older, married junior school teacher. She is sitting on his lap, and they are kissing—tongues and all—oblivious to the spies outside the window. Mr Jones has taken off his shoes and socks, and my eyes are riveted on his bare feet; they are white, with smooth pinkish nails on bony toes, long like his fingers. There is a roaring in my ears, and my heart starts racing. Then I just run… run and run and run, in confusion and disgust. *God, what is wrong with me? Help me! Help me!*

It is a bleak day when Rishi tells me that he is leaving school at the end of the mid-term to join a military school in Dehradun, where they train to compete for a military career as commissioned officers. Rishi is very keen to do this; his father had started his profession as a non-commissioned soldier but rose through the ranks to become an officer before he died. When he leaves, before the summer vacation, I will feel terribly alone.

Mr Jones starts riding back with me on his bicycle on most days after Rishi leaves school. Some days, he stays back for special practice, so I ride alone. Mr Jones is about seven years older than me. He finished his high school studies in a boarding school, where his mother was a teacher. His father lives alone on the farm and ekes out a difficult existence, since his holdings are small. Mr Jones's holidays are spent with both his parents at the farm, his mother's earnings being reinvested in additional land that they are trying to acquire around their holdings. His tough childhood does not take away the cheer on his face; his open smile is captivating, and at times, I cannot help but stare at him.

I know he notices how I look at him and how I blush if he playfully boxes me or twists my arm. These moments of intimacy are a constant source of anguish for me, and I cannot concentrate on my studies at home, especially on the days when I cycle back with him. Yet I never think of avoiding him; the pain of being close to him is worth the time I spend with him. He never asks me to his room, and I never ask him to join us for a meal at our house, even though he lives a few blocks away. At school, he is the tough PT teacher, popular with the boys and girls and a lapdog to that older, married teacher.

Then, one day, the inevitable happens; he is caught romancing the married teacher in school with his fly open and her bouncing tits in his mouth. They are asked to leave immediately. The next day, he comes to my house to give me some house plants that he has nurtured and wants me to look after. He doesn't want to leave; it seems he is hesitating about something. He suddenly asks me to go for a walk with him. We don't say anything until we reach a park in the neighbourhood. It is early afternoon, so there are a few people around. A soft breeze ruffles the branches of the trees and, with Mr Jones next to me, it's as if I can hear music in the air.

We find a bench, and then he looks at me and says kindly, "Arvind, isn't there something that you want to say to me that you have been wanting to for a long time? I have seen it in your eyes, but I want to hear it from you."

My heart starts beating fast. I am not sure what Mr Jones means. Is he returning my love for him (just the thought makes all the blood rush to my head), or is he just satisfying his curiosity?

I blush and look away. Without looking at him, I blurt, "I am terribly confused about my feelings for you. I am scared all the time, and you make me feel safe. Sometimes I want to... I want to..." and then I stop. I just can't tell him I am crazy about him, that I want him to hold me and hug me; make the terrible things that have happened to me go away.

Mr Jones turns me around and looks me straight in the eye.

"Whatever is troubling you, please tell me so that I can help you. I obviously cannot do so in the way that I believe you want me to because my feelings for you are brotherly, as they should be. My Christian teachings tell me that we are brought into the world to procreate, and for that, you must lie only with a woman. I am sure even the Hindu religion will tell you that the only way for a man is to grow towards a woman; any other way is abnormal and against the laws of nature."

My heart is breaking, but I cry out in desperation, "I really don't know what is normal and what is not. My uncles have made sure that I will remain confused forever." Tears swim in my eyes, and I feel as if I will break.

Mr Jones looks shocked.

"What is this about your uncles? What have they been doing to you?" he thunders, grabbing my arm.

That's when I tell him about my uncles and what they have done to me since I was young. How one of my uncles continues to molest me even now. I tell him that, initially, I wanted the hugs and the kisses, but when they shamed me to do other things, I felt dirty, guilty and used. Now, I wasn't sure if this was what led me to have such confused feelings for him.

While I am telling him all this, I can see Mr Jones's face getting very, very angry. When I finish, he says that he will go to my dad and tell him to bring a stop to such abominations. I beg him not to, saying my father will blame me and will never understand. Finally, he agrees, after extracting a promise that I will never allow my uncles to touch me again. I promise, and he holds me close to him, as an older brother would, and lets me weep until my eyes have no more tears to offer. I feel relieved that I have shared my troubles with him. At this moment, I would go away with him if he asked. Oh, how much I want to feel safe!

After the term ends, Mr Jones leaves for his farm, and I never see him again. I did hear much later that he joined the Indian Air Force, like many daredevil Anglo-Indians did at that time. In the 1971 war with Pakistan, his Hunter crashed somewhere over West Pakistan. He left behind a wife and a young son whom I never tried to locate.

Rishi disappeared from my life, too. After he joined the military school in the Doon Valley, some 150 miles away from Delhi, his family moved as well. We never wrote to each other, and all I have left are the fading memories of our friendship.

***

Chapter 13
Meena – 1964

Tillotama enters the gates of Alipur Road and looks around; the huge bungalows in the neighbourhood are decked up for *Deepavali*. Most of the houses are using traditional *diyas* and candles to light up the façades, but recently, she has noticed ugly multi-coloured electric bulbs replacing the traditional low-flame lights. With her keen sense of customs, Tillotama frowns over such modernisation. It does not matter to her that the residue of melted wax and oil stains needs to be scrubbed afterwards; she would still prefer to take on the extra work than have these garish artificial lights glaring outside her windows.

This year, there are no decorations at her parents' house. Everyone is in mourning for her father, who had passed away some six months back. Her mother still wants the Laxmi *puja* to take place, however. So, as is tradition, she has come to light the first *diya*, which is then placed at the altar of the Goddess Laxmi in the temple created in the house. Tillotama considers this a great honour, and she has made sure that Meena also gets the privilege to light the first *diya* at her home in Court Road.

Anchal opens the door of Alipur Road and hugs Tillotama. The traditional *thali* to the goddess is ready, and with the Kohli family in attendance, Tillotama lights the big oil *diya*. In the shadows thrown up by the light, she feels *Bauji*'s presence. She is not to know that this will be the last time this family will gather in such an atmosphere of peace.

Meena, a few months over fifteen years old, waits for her mother to come back so that she can light up the *diya* in their house. Meena has turned into a teenager in full bloom, having gradually lost the awkwardness of her earlier years. She has full lips and huge almond-shaped eyes, but her bushy eyebrows and wisps of rogue blonde hair on her chin and cheeks betray her mother's lack of awareness; she could have been groomed to be even more stunning. She may even have been more beautiful than the reigning queen of Bombay's film world, Asha Parekh. Fed on the romantic novels of Denise Robins and Hermina Black, Meena waits for the ideal 'chocolate hero' to sweep her off her feet and carry her into the sunset, away from this unhappy home.

When Meena and her family lived in the annexe of Alipur Road, she grew into adolescence under the gaze of her uncles. She was fully aware, judging by the awkward glances of her Uncle Shiv and the lusty looks of her Uncle Trilok, that her slowly blooming body garnered men's attention. This gave her an odd sense of power. She imagined that Draupadi, heroine of the *Mahabharata* and of her childhood, would avenge her honour against these men. Hermina Black's strong female protagonists also shaped Meena's attitude towards young men as she entered her teenage years.

It would have been a brave boy in her school who would dare to challenge her haughtiness. Her closest friend in class, Namrata—a mousy little girl—was probably the only one who knew the insecurities that existed within Meena and how they manifested in her character. Meena adored her younger brother Dev, sheltering him as a mother hen would, proudly watching him grow into a confident young boy. Arvind, on the other hand, disturbed her; he was mostly aloof, preferring the company of his friend Rishi or no one at all. She was afraid for him and of his dreams, which on some nights made him shout and scream. When she tried to shake him out of these nightmares, he would look at her in terror as if she were some stranger out to kill him. A couple of times, she saw him sleepwalk to the door of the house and try to unlatch it. Their mother had to install a double lock so that he wouldn't walk out of the house in his sleep. Once, Arvind woke up from what seemed like a very frightening dream. He wanted to say something to her, but before the words formed, his eyes glazed over, and he dropped back onto the pillows.

In his waking hours, Arvind was the irritating younger brother, often bothering her and Namrata, especially when they were sharing some smutty magazine that Namrata had sneaked from her father's cupboard.

Deep in her thoughts, Meena does not hear her father returning from his office after performing the Laxmi *puja* with his employees. She knows that both Arvind and Dev are playing some stupid game inside, disappointed with the parental diktat that there would be no celebrations this year. They had all argued with their mother, invoking *Bauji*, adamant in their belief that, looking down from heaven, he would be happy they were celebrating the life of Rama, his 'Master in Heaven'. Their mother ignored their smart logic. Meena's father comes and sits next to her on the veranda, and for some time, they sit in silence, watching celebratory rockets being fired in the air, listening to the initial hiss and then the loud explosions as they reach the star-studded skies.

"I remember *Deepavali* in Lahore when your grandfather, my father, was alive," begins Manmohan, "sometime in the thirties. I was eleven then, and during the day he would take all four of us—me, my brother and two sisters—to the Residency Hotel or the Lawrence Gardens while *Bheji* was preparing the sweets for the night. Those were wonderful days; everything was cooked at home, and the delicious smell of *jalebis* and *samosas* being fried enveloped the rooms in their rich aromas. *Bheji* would sometimes let us eat them as soon as they came out of the cooking dish, hot and fragrant. Ah!" Meena looks in surprise at her father's ecstatic expression. He is not usually this open with his memories or his emotions. Manmohan warms to his theme.

"Nothing was bought from the *Halwai* like it is today. *Lalaji* loved to set off the fire crackers, and he was as excited as us when evening approached. He would take all of us and some other kids from the *mohalla* to the terrace to shoot rockets from old kerosene bottles. Once, I knocked over a bottle in my haste to get away after lighting it, and the rocket chased many of us around the terrace. It was hilarious!" Manmohan laughs gleefully, as if he were a young boy again.

Meena has seldom seen her father smile, let alone laugh, and she does not want the mood to go away. She feels so happy that he has chosen her to reminisce about his childhood.

"What happened to *Lalaji?* You've never told us about him," Meena innocently asks.

Instantly, Manmohan's good mood disappears, and he crossly replies, "He lost all his money and died from the shame, leaving us near destitute. Luckily, this happened after my sisters had married. *Bhapaji* had left for Bombay, and I was left to look after your grandmother. I had to forego my studies to work and earn money as a salesman in a small firm in Lahore. You children don't realise how lucky you are: studying in good schools and having a future to look forward to. If Partition hadn't happened, I would probably have remained in that hole of an office in Lahore, and you kids would have been roaming the streets."

Tillotama arrives soon after this, and her father goes to shower before the *puja*. Meena sits alone, wishing she hadn't broken the magical mood by asking her question. *Stupid, stupid*, she berates herself. Her mind inexplicably wanders to her latest biology class and a lesson on crustaceans, how turtles and other creatures evolved with outer shells. If Meena were asked what mammal had the hardest shell, she would have named her father. Suddenly, she is engulfed with sadness as she tries to understand the loneliness of her father. Then she snaps out of it and is angry. *It was an innocent question, wasn't it? Why is he so secretive about everything? Why does he treat my mother with so much contempt? What right does he have to make us feel guilty for so many things, like wanting to see a movie or wanting a new dress? Why does he break our hearts again and again?*

Waiting for her husband to finish his shower so they can light their *diya*, Tillotama looks out of the window at her daughter on the veranda. Lost in her thoughts, Meena does not realise how her face mirrors the sadness of most of the members of this household, and her mother looks at her helplessly.

***

Chapter 14
Arvind – 1966–67

Coloured lights blink in flashes of eerie blue, green, red and dirty yellow; they sweep around the dance floor, which has been erected in the gym, making the dancers look ghoulish. The farewell dance for the eleventh-graders, the class taking the Indian School Certificate this year, is underway. Our class, the tenth standard, are the hosts. It is a formal dance, and the boys are looking nerdy in their father's suits or their elder brother's hand-me-downs. My mother borrowed Uncle Trilok's suit, and it is flapping around me like the wings of a bat. The tag dance is on, and most of the boys are trying to tag Latika's partner so that they can steal a dance with her, much to the chagrin of the other prettily-attired girls. I am dancing awkwardly with Renu, and even though the winter is slowly spreading its chilly shroud over the city, I notice that her hands are slippery with sweat. She keeps dabbing them with a small lacy hanky, which doesn't help at all.

Cliff Richard, with his mushy love numbers so popular with the girls, is singing *Evergreen Tree*, and I am attempting a foxtrot, stupidly looking down at my feet and softly mouthing the steps needed to complete a square. The music in the early part of the evening encourages vigorous body shaking, which has most of the boys on the floor behaving like spastics doing the Twist and Shake. The more intrepid couples swing along to the cha-cha and rock and roll with Chubby Checker. The girls have to drag the boys onto the floor for the slow dances—all except for Latika, who has a constant supply of suitors. The music changes to the Tennessee

Waltz, and I abruptly excuse myself from Renu. The foxtrot is fine, but a waltz is beyond me. Renu curses and then clamps her mouth shut as Mrs Sen, in the arms of the maths teacher, floats by.

I go and sit next to Mrs Sharma, the official wallflower, glowering at every student who has the temerity to meet her gaze.

"You seem to enjoy this kind of dancing, Arvind. I feel it is a dangerous trend to allow boys and girls in school to get so close to each other. We are asking for trouble," she says with a grimace. "All this is fine in England, but in India, we should think of our traditions, our cultural heritage!"

"What would you prefer, ma'am? All of us dancing like Shammi Kapoor and Asha Parekh, a twist here, a jerk there, moving our backsides all over the place?" Latika suddenly asks from behind me.

"Where did you spring from, Latika, you bold girl! I meant that we should appreciate our Indian dances like the *Kathak* or the *Bharatanatyam*."

Latika winks at me and then makes a funny face, bringing me into her orbit. Wow, it feels good!

"Where have you been hiding yourself? I saved two dances for you, but you were stuck to Renu," she says huskily, just out of Mrs Sharma's earshot.

I am tongue-tied, but then Latika always has this effect on me. She joined the school a year after Rishi left. She is different from the other girls, all of whom we have known since childhood; they are practically our sisters. Latika transferred to our school from a girls' boarding school, her parents believing that a day school and co-education would be a sobering experience for their bold, undisciplined tomboy. So, Latika swept into school and was soon very popular with the senior boys. While most of the other girls have long hair tied up into ponytails or pigtails, Latika has short curly hair that makes her look like a cute pixie. She has beautifully shaped lips, and her body has matured faster than most of the other girls. She is the talk of the school; the grapevine buzzes with stories of her making out with innumerable boys. Some days, the rumour mill churns out a story of how a teacher caught her kissing a boy under the staircase. Another time, during a school excursion, she had disappeared for an hour with another boy in the forests near the colony of Hauz Khaz. If any of these stories are true, Latika would have been expelled from school long ago. Most of the boys, of course, secretly hope that there is some truth in them.

I have made myself insignificant in school, preferring to stay away from cliques—the always-worshipped sportsmen, the academic superstars—and the various school clubs. I am self-conscious and terribly fearful of any attention being focused on me. My favourite class is English Literature, where I can escape and wallow with the characters in the books, hoping to be redeemed in the end. What I love even more is acting in school plays. At these times, I can live another person's life and act out with confidence what is pre-ordained by the story and the director, without having to figure out what and how to be, like I have to in real life. I revert to my naturally hunched, self-effacing state off the stage. Latika fascinates me with her apparent ease in dealing with the nasty stories about her love life and her self-assurance; I often surreptitiously steal glances at her in class when her attention is elsewhere.

After the farewell party is over, Latika, for reasons I cannot fathom, chooses to direct her full attention at me, taking full advantage of my tongue-tied fascination for her. To the amusement of the other boys and girls present, she climbs onto the saddle of my bicycle and holds on to me, making kissing noises in my ear as I flush red with embarrassment and beg her to let me get home.

A month later, Latika bags the role of Portia to my Antonio in *The Merchant of Venice*. Staying late for rehearsals means biking back to our homes together. She lives a mile or so from my house, on a street where the trees have formed a canopy across the road, and though my house comes first on the way from school, I ride on with her and see her to her door. As I get to know her better, I open up like a hardened chrysalis to her gentle urgings, feeling stupidly happy for the first time in my life. She is high-spirited and sweetly quirky. But I love her zaniness. Many of the other girls are mean to her, but she responds to all their envy-loaded ribbing with aplomb and laughter. Before she 'got her tentacles' (her words) into me, she used to hang around with a crowd which was considered to be *fast*, a nasty catchword for anyone who is daring. Ever since the play began, we have always been together, and I am often at her house, listening to the latest records that her father picks up from London. There is little chance of her coming to my home and relaxing in my room, which is still shared with Dev; both my parents are too old-fashioned to allow it. They would have been shocked and angry to know that Meena, studying in Hindu College, is madly enamoured with a sometime pro-Israel, sometime Marxist, thin-faced '*Jolawala*' (she revealed to me after I had snatched a handwritten, awfully-structured, prissy poem from her hands).

Latika and I are together on the sofa in her bedroom, listening to the new Beatles album *Rubber Soul*. I am marvelling at the use of the sitar in *Norwegian Wood*.

Michelle starts playing, and Latika becomes all dreamy and unlike her usual self.

"*I need to, I need to, I need to make you see...*" the lyrics float into the room and then, "*I want you, I want you, I want you...*" My ears are popping and my heart is beating, when suddenly our lips find each other. Latika quickly pushes me away and looks guiltily at me.

"This is awful! I know you must think that all the stories about me are true, but Arvind, you must believe me. You are the first boy I have kissed." She kisses me again, and I am about to push my tongue into her mouth, but I stop just in time.

I leave after a while, thanking my loose trousers for hiding my hardness. I feel the memory of her soft lips on mine and am elated. This is different. I want to do this right and not scare Latika away with my inappropriate expertise in French kissing. This self-control feels good, and I feel a wave of purity run through me. Mr Jones... *Gregory* would have been proud of me, I think, but this thought reminds me that I have not kept my promise to him, and I am ashamed.

I reach home but find that my mother is out, visiting her family in Alipur Road. Meena has just returned from college, and I can smell cigarettes on her; she glares at me in anger when I not-so-subtly sniff the air around her. Meena has had her own room since *Bheji* died. Thinking about my sweet grandmother makes a lump of sorrow form in my throat. She died quietly in her sleep; one morning, the house woke up to find that she had gone. No fuss, no noise, just as she had lived all her life, smiling and kissing all our pains away and keeping our spirits up with her continuous chatter, which had slowly quietened down a few months before her death.

Mummy comes home with Uncle Trilok. There must have been another major row at my grandmother's house. Mum often asks Trilok to join us for dinner when this happens, leaving the others at Alipur Road to sulk in their rooms. Today, even more so than usual, I am not thrilled with his presence, and he quickly senses it. In retaliation, he directs his attention to Dev throughout the evening.

"Dev, I hear you are playing footie in school, the new 'Pele of Delhi'!" or "You must be quite a heartthrob now with the gals, with those rosy cheeks and dreamy eyes," or "Does your brother have a girlfriend now?" eyeing me spitefully. He goes on and on with the inane questions that embarrass Dev and me. We are relieved when we can go to our rooms to do our homework and sleep, leaving Trilok with Mummy and Dad, where the conversation continues on the subject of events at Alipur Road.

I am dozing off to sleep when I hear my Mummy come in, wake Dev up, and hustle his sleepy form towards Meena's room. She looks at me, and my heart sinks when she says, "Your uncle is going to sleep in Dev's bed tonight; it's too late for him to go back home." I feel breathless and stressed. My mind and body are working at odds with each other. My mind is repulsed by him, while at the same time, I feel my body getting excited as the blood rushes towards my core. I have recently discovered the amazing zing in masturbating, and it takes little for my body to start tingling in anticipation. I know that I have to bring a stop to this madness, as my uncle will not. I hear him getting into Dev's bed; he waits for the sounds of the house to die down. I wait with bated breath, his nearness making me terribly anxious. When it becomes clear that everyone has gone to sleep, he climbs into my bed, putting his body close to me while pushing his lips against mine. His hand goes down to loosen my pyjama cord. Violently, I push him away. He is shocked.

"Why did you push me away, you beauty? Don't you want me anymore?"

"No. No! Please, leave me alone. I want you to stop this, please, I beg you." I can hardly believe I am saying this. His hand again goes down my pyjamas, and he fondles me through the cloth. I frantically push his hand away before my body betrays me.

"Ah! I get it now," he smirks. "Jealousy raising its head? Dev got the attention today, yes? Come on, I was just teasing you... Though your brother is really cute and ready for some action," he laughs. "Come on, kiss me and let's make up." He grabs hold of my shoulders and pulls me to him.

"Leave me, I said, leave me! I will kill you if you look at Dev in that manner, ever!" My voice rises in fury.

"You bitch, you've always wanted it, and now you want to play games with me? You damn cocksucker," he whispers ferociously. I jump out of bed, ready to confront Satan if need be.

"I don't care! I'm going to call my parents, and I will tell them everything if you do not stop, you bastard!"

Thankfully, he sees the madness in my eyes and stops. He gets back into Dev's bed, whispering, "I will get you one day."

I find it difficult to sleep after that, and though I can hear my uncle snoring in the darkness, I keep waking up with a jerk every time I nod off in exhaustion.

When I reach school the next day, Latika is nowhere to be seen, but I am unsure how to face her with the wretchedness in my mind. I am strung out like a kite, broken in spirit; much of what my uncle said the previous night is true. I let it all happen. I have lived in a world inhabited by evil beings swirling around in glee, with no morals, and the satisfaction of lust being their sole goal. But I have been complicit; I have given into this illicit pleasure. Latika can save me, I think, like rain on the parched earth, or like the morning light to my dark and scary nights. I am lost inside myself, grappling with black shadows, when I hear the teacher talking about Latika. I realise that I have missed something. I turn my brain off to listen to everyone wanting to know the name of the hospital and about visiting hours. I look up in a daze to hear the teacher say:

"She is in the intensive care unit; her parents will let us know when any of us can visit, so for the time being, just pray for her."

"What happened?" I whisper to Ramya, who is sitting, shocked, next to me.

"Didn't you hear? Latika got knocked over by a car when coming to school today; she has been unconscious since this morning."

I feel my insides flip sickeningly.

After school, I cycle to Latika's house, but I am told that the family is at Irwin Hospital. I rush to the hospital but get lost in the maze of corridors. I hang around for an hour or two near the car park and eventually see Latika's father walking towards the hospital. I run to him, and he holds me by the shoulders and hugs me.

"Arvind, what are you doing here? Why aren't you inside?" Without waiting for an answer, he takes me inside to where Latika's mother and some other family members are sitting.

"Thank god! She has regained consciousness, but the doctors want to keep her in the hospital for a few more days," her mother says, with deep relief in her voice. She looks at me kindly. "We have not been allowed to see her. I will call you when she can take visitors. Now go home, it is getting late."

The word 'home' makes me jump. I have completely forgotten about home. I realise that I am in deep trouble. No one at home knows my whereabouts. I had forgotten to tell Dev to go home on his own after school because I was so consumed with thoughts of Latika. Before leaving the hospital, I charm the receptionist into letting me use the phone to call home. Dad picks up.

"Where have you been, you idiot? Your mother is in tears, and the school has no idea where you are. Dev waited for you, then managed to get a ride home. I was called home from an important meeting. We have just called the police, you fool!" he rages at me.

"I am at the hospital," I reply, getting a real kick using the word hospital. For a moment, I wish that it were me in the ICU; I would have loved to see the shocked look on my father's face. In my gleeful imaginings, the fact that I wouldn't be conscious to actually see his face escaped me.

"Hospital?" my father shouts down the line. "You said hospital?" I hear a commotion in the background, but before it all gets out of control, I explain what has happened. "Get back home, you stupid nut!" he says, but I hear the relief in his voice. *So, the old man has a heart after all.*

Latika returns to school after three months, but since the doctors fear that her concussion may flare up again, she is advised to avoid stress at home and in class. Visitors are allowed, but 'no excitement, no noise' is her mother's continuous refrain. She protects her daughter like a vicious German Shepherd, and slowly, Latika's friends find other places to go. I visit her often after school, but she seems far away, and her mother hangs around, lingering in corners all the time. We are also busy studying for the tests the school makes us take for the Indian School Certificate. Added to that, I am taking extra classes in mathematics and physics. After a few months, Latika gets a clean bill of health and is cleared to take the examinations by her doctors.

It is with a sigh of relief that we finish the tests. We leave school for our eagerly-awaited six-month break, which also heralds the start of a life freed from daily parental constraints. Latika and I, and with a group of other friends, form an excursion group to cycle around various places in Delhi. New Delhi is in the process of being built, double and triple-storied houses are replacing the stately bungalows, and the forests around the city are getting pushed further south by greedy developers. For cycling enthusiasts like us, the historical red-stoned old buildings of Hamayun's Tomb, the Qutab Minar and Hauz Khaz, and the forests of Mehrauli are a major attraction. We often stop at the Lodhi Gardens and behave foolishly, role-playing star-crossed lovers from the film world, chasing each other around the trees. It is March, and there is a chill in the air as we cycle on the roads. On most days, Latika and I are together. Every day I wake up in anticipation, feeling the energy of youth with the heavy black clouds of my past temporarily abated, until my happiness is cruelly burst by my father.

Dinner is over. During the meal, I have the strange feeling that my father is waiting for something, like a hunter watching his prey. His eyes dart from the food to my face throughout the meal, and when I return his look, I see a challenge there. I am a little unnerved, though the intense fear of him I felt during my childhood has long been replaced by wariness. Meena has, after considerable interrogation, been allowed a rare night out with one of her friends. Dev is at an overnight camp with school. It is just me, my mother and father. As the plates are being removed by my mother, Dad looks directly at me and asks innocently, though his eyes say otherwise, about my friends and what we do during the day. I excitedly start telling him about my explorations of Delhi and the discovery of some forgotten historical monument, when he suddenly stops me and asks pointedly about Latika.

"Isn't she the only girl in your group?" Without waiting for an answer, obviously having reached a conclusion already, he pounces, "and hanging around Lodhi Gardens, fooling around on the benches and getting up to all sorts of...'

That's when I stop him.

"What are you trying to get at? It's all harmless fun," I say, my face red with guilt. I can smell the sweat in my armpits; someone has definitely spied on us and has told him about our role-playing, the fun we have at the gardens.

"Trilok has often seen you there, behaving like a hooligan and thank god..."

I never let him finish; I am in such a rage that I scream at him for the first time in my life.

"*Trilok*, that snake! You want me to be like him? Tell me, do you? Doing filthy things with innocent young boys. Oh, the things he did to me, that... that... scum!" I stutter. I just don't know how to continue. My mum rushes into the room then and looks at me in shock. "You have no idea what he has done to me," I scream. "I cannot speak about it!"

There is complete silence, and then my father laughs. Seeing Mum's terrible look, he just titters again and then sheepishly sidles off to his room. My mother does not follow him as she would usually do. She asks me softly, "Kaku, is this true, the things you are trying to say?" and then, "Who else knows?" I nod in response to her first question and then say, "No one."

"Oh, my dearest, Kaku. I am so sorry," she cries, pulling me into her arms. I can feel silent sobs rocking her body.

Later, she comes to my room. I am in a dangerous mood with my vengeful, black-hooded companion firmly sitting on my shoulder, its claws digging deep into me, preventing my escape.

She sits next to me on the bed, runs her cool hand over my forehead and begins to plead for her evil brother.

"Son, please don't speak about this to anyone. Your uncle is a sick man; he has caused a lot of trouble in your grandmother's house, pitting one brother against another. We have found a good girl for him, and in a few days, his engagement will be announced. If this gets out, it will not only destroy your grandmother but also other lives, too."

"Why did he laugh?" is all I can say in response, unable to get my father's inexplicable amusement out of my head. "Does he not know what this has done to me?"

***

"Even though I still have no clue about who all these people are, I feel I am slowly getting sucked into this family," says Husna. "It's horrifying that no one seemed to understand the effect this had on Arvind. Even his mom was more worried about the scandal than about the degradation of her son. Oh! I wish Arvind had someone

to talk to, like a school counsellor. On the other hand, guilt for his own mixed feelings could have stopped him from talking to someone. He could have tried talking to his doctor, maybe..." Husna's brow is furrowed with worry, and she pushes the manuscript away from her in disgust.

Adam thinks about what she says. "Look at it from Arvind's point of view," he says. "He must have been terrified about sharing all this with anyone, even with a counsellor, if such help was available in schools those days. Given that Arvind was mortally afraid of his father, he couldn't have talked to anyone without worrying that this would get back to him." But then Adam thinks of his own experience during school in the early nineties and realises that he never spoke a word about the terrible bullying he faced about his own uncle, to either his counsellor in school or to his mother.

"It is horribly sad that these criminals, for that is what they are, get away with such depravity. Their deeds did not affect their future lives, but the innocent Arvind is left to fight the demons unleashed by his own family by himself. I, too, wonder about how Arvind is connected to me. I know most of my family members except my mother's grandparents. I have no clue about my mysterious father and his family. Adam..." Husna continues, getting more animated, "...could this be the story of my father and his family?"

***

Chapter 15
Arvind – 1971

The upheavals in the Indian subcontinent in 1971 are mirrored in the experiences of the Kohli family. While East Pakistan is being painfully wrenched from West Pakistan, Uncle Shiv and his wife Reena physically break the Kohli estate into two, to be shared between themselves and Randhir. Uncle Trilok and his new wife receive financial 'compensation', with which he moves to Poona, where he already has a job as the marketing officer in a well-known automobile manufacturing company, and promptly buys a house.

A wall of division now stands between the brothers. My grandmother stays with Randhir *Mamu* but spends most of her time believing in a fraudulent *swami* who is more interested in her share of the wealth than her spiritual well-being. There is not much left of her wealth in any case. The squabbles between the warring brothers and their wives have taken a toll on the wholesale grain business, and certain speculative transactions by Uncle Shiv further erode the firm's capital, leaving it entirely on a knife-edge.

One night, a year after Uncle Trilok had married and left home, the silent hours are pierced by the shrill ringing of our house phone. I hear my mother muttering to herself as she picks up the phone, and then her voice hoarsely cries out, "What? When did it happen? Oh god, no! What, what?" Before she can collapse, I run to her side, holding onto her, before passing her to my father, who has also jumped out of bed. The phone slips from her hand, and I grab it. It is Randhir *Mamu*. He tells me how Uncle Trilok has died on the treacherous road between Bombay and Poona. His family will be taking an early morning flight to Bombay, from where they will travel to Poona for the last rites. My parents leave the next morning.

The whole day, I am beset with feelings. What am I to think? That I am free? That his death will give me solace? That the terrible dreams will leave me now, that the damage to my soul, my inner being, will be miraculously corrected? That his death will open a path of purity for me, strewn with white lilies, or that the panic attacks will cease? What am I to feel? Happy? Sad? Relieved?

I feel none of these things. Instead, I am depressed. Strangely, the fun days before Uncle Trilok started molesting me come to mind. The days when we played cricket together, or hung upside down from trees in the garden at Alipur Road. I say a prayer for Uncle Trilok and hope that his restless spirit will now find peace.

When my parents come back, I learn that he left Bombay after imbibing too many drinks at a bar, and that a young man travelling with him in his car had also been killed. Did he pick him up at the bar or on the road? Was he going to be one of his sexual conquests, a victim of his abuse, before death got in the way? Who was he? I never find out. My uncle's widow is blamed for bringing evil luck on her new husband and causing his death. Perhaps no one would be ready to accept that such a man might have brought this on himself due to his own evil deeds.

Uncle Trilok's wife leaves Poona after selling their house and moves back in with her father in Kanpur, carrying Trilok's child in her womb. After that, I completely lose touch with his family till I meet, or rather see, his son many years later at the wedding of an extended family member. No one introduces us; I am busy meeting uncles, aunts and cousins from various sections of the family when I spot a boy of about nineteen with long eyelashes standing all alone. There is something familiar in this young man's face, the same animal magnetism, the same sneer and sensual lips; it doesn't take me long to realise that this is my cousin, the son of my childhood nemesis. Dev, who is passing by, stops when he sees me looking at the young man, "Oh, that's Pramod, Uncle Trilok's son. You want to meet him? Come, I'll introduce you."

"No, I will go and introduce myself. You move along, Dev."

Of course, I do not introduce myself. What would I say to him? That his father was a sex fiend, a beast, a satyr who preyed on vulnerable kids? I know that I have already judged this boy and have saddled my own burden, as well as his father's crime, onto his young shoulders. I know then, as I have always known, that I will never forgive myself for the darkness that stains my childhood, and I am damned to remain flitting in the shadows forever.

Back to the present day, at Court Road, changes are coming. Rebellion has raised its head: my father is beset with problems of poor management and blackmail in his company, and his two oldest children will finally find the courage to break from the shackles that his toxic nature has bound them with for so long. We aren't yet fully aware, but this is going to be the start of the radical changes that will be wrought in my father's superior, patronising nature.

The first salvo is fired by Meena. It happens on the night before she decides to run away from home. She has a heated fight with our father at the dinner table. Dinner at our house is always a one-sided affair, with our father doing the talking and us kids nodding our heads. We wait for this one meal—where it is mandatory to be present—to end quickly, so that we can go to our respective rooms. Our mother is talking about Alipur Road and all the problems that had befallen her mother after my grandfather died. In his usual arrogant fashion, our father says, "Serves them right. Your Kohli family has always considered it their birthright to lord it over others. I hope they realise that this is the fruit of their karma."

He has hardly finished when Meena sarcastically fires back, "And what about your karma, father? Will it be any better?"

"Hush, girl! Apologise to your father at once!" is my mother's predictably one-sided response.

"Mother, I hate you. He treats you like dirt, he insists on saying 'your Kohli family' in such a derogatory way, yet you defend him. I hope I never become like you, ever!" Meena sits back, glaring at our mother, with fire in her eyes.

"Enough! Leave the table at once and go to your room, now!" shouts my enraged father, but Meena does not budge.

"I will stay here and finish my food, whether you like it or not," she says with steel in her voice.

Before anybody can stop him, our father stands up and tries to drag Meena off her chair. Dev's face has gone completely pale, and I am looking on helplessly when, suddenly, my mother flings herself at our father and pulls him away.

"It's all your fault, you harridan!" he screams at our mother and slaps her hard across her face. Meena, in the meantime, has started screaming like a banshee, and Dev is weeping. I walk around the table to put my arms around Mummy and then turn to face my father. My back is straight, and for the first time, my angry eyes look directly and without fear into his. He looks at me, shocked, understanding possibly for the first time that his days of bullying are over. Then, he just walks out of the house.

Mum walks up to Meena and shouts ferociously at her to stop her screaming, and then there is silence, punctuated only by Dev's soft crying. I take him to our bedroom, there is nothing else to do, and we both fall into a restless sleep.

I wake in the middle of the night and go to check on Meena; reassured by her soft breathing, broken by short gurgles, I slowly move towards my parents' room. The moon is shining through the window, and I see Mum sitting alone in the middle of her bed, staring into space. It looks like she has been crying; the planes of her face are crunched up in misery. I watch her for some time. She is not aware that I am standing at her door, and I feel like an intruder spying on someone's deep emotional trauma. In my mind, I etch her face, her posture, the moonlight seeping in from the window. It is an image that will remain with me forever. I slowly make my way back to my room and try to sleep with this image of absolute misery overshadowing my mind.

The next day, Dad has not returned. Evening comes, and there is no word from our father, which is hardly unusual. He normally sulks for days on end in one of the towns where he goes on marketing trips, returning when he thinks that the guilt will have eaten us up. There is no sign of Meena either. When she woke up this morning, she had said very little about what happened the night before and headed out to college as she usually did, except that this morning her leftist *Jolawala* chum had come to pick her up in an autorickshaw. My Mum,

Dev and Randhir *Mamu* (who has come immediately for support) are all thrown into a panic. I somehow know that she has run away with her boyfriend and feel like saying, "Good for you, Meena!" The Beatles' song *She's Leaving Home* keeps repeating itself in my head like a mantra.

"She (we gave her most of our lives)

Is leaving (sacrificed most of our lives)

Home (we gave her everything money could buy)

She's leaving home after living alone (bye-bye)..."

***

Chapter 16
Meena – 1972

As she steps into the portals of the Graduate School of Industrial Administration at Carnegie Mellon University, twenty-four-year-old Meena thanks whichever gods she can think of that she has finally rid herself of all the men in her life. Her bully of a father, her overly idealistic boyfriend and her yet-to-be-divorced, abusive husband of just a few months. But it is only when she steps off the plane in Pittsburgh that she feels she has truly escaped; the relief drives her to her knees as she re-lives the last horrifying eight months since the day she decided to run away with Kailash in Delhi.

Before the rest of the house is up, she steals to the telephone, which sits in the alcove next to her parents' room and calls Kailash. He is her knight in shining armour and has been pestering her to marry him and run off together into the hills of Uttar Pradesh, where he wants to spread his brand of social uprising. Encouraged by the Naxalite movement, which started in the sixties in West Bengal, Kailash is keen to carry on its leader, Charu Majumdar's ideologies to the rural villages in the Shivalik ranges of the upper reaches of Uttar Pradesh. He intends to do this without the violence that the movement had generated in the belly of West Bengal.

When Meena first met Kailash at University of Delhi, he had been trying to get as many students as possible to sign a petition for the Government of India to establish diplomatic relations with Israel, something that was being opposed by the government to appease their Palestinian friends in the non-aligned countries. She was fascinated with this Bengali man with his fashionable goatee and his ability to passionately defend what he believed in. Soon, like a groupie, she started hanging around him as much as she could. Later, he started preaching Marxism and Naxalism, though these philosophies directly contradicted his support of the capitalist Israeli state. But by this time, she was already in love with his mind and thought his smoke-tainted lips were the sexiest part of him. To be fair to Kailash, he wanted to do something for the downtrodden in this country, nearly a billion people, of whom at least two-thirds were very poor. Meena, with her stubborn and daring spirit, was exactly the kind of person that he wanted by his side as he battled the Establishment, and given her contempt for her mother's weakness and hatred for her father's bullying nature, she was willing to go with him wherever he wanted.

The morning after she calls Kailash, she sets out with a small bagful of clothes and her savings. They are going to stop for a night at Dehradun, where Kailash has friends. Then they are on their way to Mussoorie, where they plan to get married, before setting up home in either Uttarkashi or Tehri Garhwal—a decision they have yet to settle on.

By the time they are on the bus to Dehradun, she knows she has made a mistake with Kailash, who hadn't gambled on having to elope with her. Being an idealist, he wanted to ask her father for her hand and was sure it would have been granted, given that Kailash belonged to a rich and cultured Calcutta family. But Meena was adamant on eloping, and he had succumbed to her persuasions without realising the full implications of what they were doing. He is soon hyperventilating at the Delhi bus stand. He relaxes somewhat as the bus leaves the station, but cribs about everything in sight: the snot-filled kid in the arms of the woman in the seat across the aisle, who keeps making friendly overtures to him;

the bus conductor who jokingly asks him whether he is running away with a young *chokri,* given his nervousness. At stops, he refuses to get off the bus to go to the loo, quite sure that the police will be out looking for him. When it becomes unbearable, he stops the bus and jumps into the fields to relieve himself.

By the time they reach Dehradun, Meena is ready to hop on a bus back to Delhi, had it not been for the image of her gloating father playing on her mind. The first night, they spend restlessly in Kailash's friend's one-room apartment. He is quite fascinated by the fact that he is helping two young people to elope, a story he can hear himself repeating to his friends and family. The next morning, when they get to the bus stand, they walk straight into the arms of the police who are waiting for them. Standing with them is Randhir *Mamu*, who quickly pulls Meena to his side and lets Kailash be handcuffed. Kailash looks like he is going to the gallows and is ready to collapse when Randhir *Mamu* intervenes and manages to convince the cops that he is not a dangerous criminal. After that, everything happens quickly. Meena is released into the care of her uncle (after a humiliating medical check to ensure that Kailash has not raped her), and kidnapping charges are dropped against Kailash after she swears in front of a magistrate that she had gone with him of her own accord. Meena then is driven back to Delhi with her uncle while Kailash carries on with his journey to Uttarkashi. Meena never sees him again, though she did hear from her friend, Namrata, that when he returned to college, he was hailed a hero for trying to elope with the sexy Chopra girl.

When Meena gets home, her mother locks her in her room and refuses to let even her brothers talk to her. Manmohan returns that night, after frantic calls from Tillotama, to find that he wasn't needed after all and that his job has been carried out by Randhir. He refuses to see Meena and gives instructions that she should not be allowed out of the house except to be escorted to her final exams, and then proceeds to look for a boy for her to marry. Manmohan knows that he will never be able to control his daughter, so he takes the easiest way out, which is to transfer his 'burden' to another man. The only person who sees Meena during this time was Namrata, and she is sworn to secrecy about what her parents plan to do, lest Kailash create a fuss (something they needn't have worried about, as he was thanking his stars to have escaped with no harm done except to his over-inflated ego).

When Paddy, actual name Parminder, walks into their house, he has just stepped off the plane from Chicago. The jet lag causes him to elongate his vowels so they are even more pronounced than a 'Texan drawl'. For the first ten minutes or so, most of the people in the drawing room, which includes Meena's parents, Arvind and Dev and Paddy's parents, sit listening to his prattle. They nod their heads without actually understanding a word coming out of his mouth, when Dev perks up and tells Meena quite innocently that he hasn't understood a word of the conversation. Paddy then switches to Punjabi, and there is relief all around. Meena is aghast. Did her parents actually think that she would marry this smirking old man, who was a full seventeen years older than her? She can't believe that her aunt had actually proposed this man. Unbeknownst to her, the family was clear that the only way they could keep her attempted elopement hidden was to send her away to the UK or the USA. Luckily, the family, which originally came from Jullundur, are in a hurry to settle their son down with a well-educated young girl, knowing that an American visa will counteract the age difference. Paddy speaks a few words to Meena, who responds with no great enthusiasm, but it thrills both families, except for Tillotama. She is surprised that Manmohan expects her daughter to marry a much older man.

Meena protests. "I won't marry this man. I don't like him. He has a sly face, and he is too old for me." "You can't force me. I will go to Granny at Alipur Road and ask for her help." "I will run away from home again if you make me marry him." "Please Mum, please tell Dad not to do this to me, I cannot marry this man, I am frightened of him!" But all her protests matter little to her father and his sister, who stand steadfast together. Tillotama tries hard to convince Manmohan to look at another family who are expected to arrive from the UK a few months later, but it is to no avail. Social norms in the seventies in India were such that no force, including the police, would help a woman to get out of such a predicament. So, without too much fuss, Meena is forced to marry Paddy, and she resigns herself to it. At the very least, it gets her away from her bullying father.

On the first night of her marriage, Paddy tells her he was too tired to stay awake, so he turns off the light and falls asleep. Similar excuses are given night after night; either he had too much to drink with his friends, or he had developed a stomach flu. He finally leaves for Chicago five days after their wedding, with the plan that Meena will follow when she receives her visa. With her marriage unconsummated, Meena returns to her parents to wait for her visa to be sent from America. She does not say anything to her parents about what has happened with Paddy, just stays listlessly in her room waiting for her escape. She knows something is wrong with Paddy, but somehow, she feels confident that she will win him over when they are alone in Chicago, instead of the noisy house in Jullundur. What she wants more than anything is to leave her childhood home and never go back.

Her visa arrives a couple of months later, and she is soon on a flight to JFK, New York, from where she is to fly to Chicago. Immigration at the airport moves fast; her fluency in the English language is a great help. By the time she reaches Chicago and Paddy, she is exhausted. She carries with her the phone number and address of her cousin, the daughter of the aunt who arranged the union and also lives in Chicago.

Paddy has a modest apartment in Bridgeview, which, for a bachelor pad, is quite nicely done up.

"You must be tired after your trip; why don't you get some sleep while I quickly run into my office?" Paddy says. "I have bought enough groceries, and when I return, I will explain how to use the gadgets in the kitchen so that you can take charge." All Meena can do is nod. As he leaves the apartment, Paddy calls over his shoulder, "I am going to double padlock the front door; this is not a safe area."

Meena falls asleep and wakes up to the sound of the door opening and Paddy walking in with some pizzas.

"I was sure you'd be asleep, so I got these pizzas for tonight, but from tomorrow I want to eat home-cooked food," he says. "I have been surviving on takeaways for too long."

Later, they sit quietly eating their pizza, which is so new to her. There are a few formal questions thrown in about the welfare of each other's families. After the heated discussions she was used to having with Kailash on just about every subject, this was all very boring.

"Tell me about your life in America," she asks, hoping to invigorate the conversation. "When did you come here? When did you move to Chicago, and is it true that there are no poor people in this country?"

Paddy looks surprised at her questions. He thinks for a moment and says, "Look, I'm tired. I want to turn in. Let's talk tomorrow."

With that, he disappears into the bedroom. By the time she has cleared the table and washed the dishes (she has been warned that in America, there isn't any help for domestic chores), Paddy is snoring in bed. Meena changes into the negligee that she has purchased for her first night in Chicago and slips into bed. Due to the time difference, she stays awake for a long time listening to his snores and guttural grunts. During the night, she wakes up and looks out her window at the street far below and the cars zooming by.

The next morning, she wakes up late to find that Paddy has already left for his office. She sees that he had made himself coffee, eaten some cereal, spilt milk on the dining table, and left whatever dishes he had used piled up in the sink. She notices there is a dishwasher, but not knowing how to use it, she washes the dishes by hand. She manages to light the stove, praying she won't burn the place down, but thankfully, the instructions are clearly written out on the hob. She must make sure, she thinks, to ask Paddy how to use these gadgets that evening; most of them didn't even exist in India yet.

Paddy does not come home after work, though she has cooked an Indian meal for him. He walks in at ten that night, and she can see that he is drunk. She was alarmed during the day when she realised she had been locked in and couldn't find the keys to the main door anywhere. She was further distressed when she couldn't locate her passport where it was supposed to be. Even though she had no plans to leave the house, these two discoveries made her feel claustrophobic and trapped. She knows that she is alone and vulnerable in this vast country, so she asks him tentatively for the house keys.

"Why do you need the house keys when you don't have to leave the house?" he asks crossly. "I have told you that this is a dangerous area, and I do not want to expose you to any danger. On weekends, we can go out together."

She can't believe it.

"I looked out of the window and saw many women on the road, even Arab women in *burqas*," Meena protests. "All I need is to feel reassured that I can go out when I want to, and that I am not a prisoner in this house."

"Well, I need some assurances from you before I let you have the house keys and your passport, which you can see is not where you left it," Paddy replies coldly. "This whole marriage is a charade! I never wanted to marry you or anyone else from India. Why do you think I had not been married till such a late age?"

Meena is shocked by what he says next.

"I am in love with a woman from Pakistan who works in my office. She has managed to avoid being married off and has been living with me. If I ever tell my parents that I am in love with a Muslim woman, they will cut me out of my inheritance when my father dies and leave me without a penny. When I visited India this last time, they gave me an ultimatum. Either marry or lose the inheritance. They think I am *chakka* (homosexual), but they don't care if I am, so long as I marry and bring kids into this world. I have not touched you so far, because I wanted you to know all this before I slept with you."

Meena is stunned and can't believe that he expects her to be a conspirator in deceiving his parents. Before she can react, he continues.

"Once I have my inheritance, I will let you and the children born out of this 'understanding' go, and since the inheritance is substantial, I will give you enough so that you can live like a queen back in Delhi."

"And how long will that be? Your father is still young... or are you planning to put poison in his food the next time you are in his house?" she says, sarcasm hiding her fear.

"There is no way I am going to be a party to this charade," she continues. "If you have any decency, you will take me back to India and have this marriage annulled. Don't even dare think I will let you into my bed so you can show your prowess in bringing grandchildren for your parents. You are completely out..." She never sees the blow coming, and before she knows it, she is on the floor with blood dripping from her mouth.

"You stupid bitch," Paddy spits. "You will do exactly what I tell you; otherwise, you will disappear. I know how to do that." Then he drags her into their bedroom, tears off her clothes and rapes her.

Paddy leaves her afterwards and goes into his study, closing the door on her quiet sobs. This is where the only telephone in the house is kept, and it also has a sofa that can be conveniently converted into a bed.

Meena whimpers in pain; as she slips in and out of consciousness, she knows that she has to survive to escape. This is America, not some remote village in India; all she needs to do is keep her wits about her and not let him break her spirit. She also knows that her menstrual cycle is due in a day or two, so the chances of her getting pregnant are very low, at least at that moment.

The next morning, Paddy leaves for work and, as before, locks her in. She knows she has to get in touch with her cousin Meenakshi and her husband, but she can't enter the study where the phone is kept because it is locked as well. Meena looks at her face in the mirror and is horrified. Her lips are swollen and blood-stained, one of her canines is loose, and her eyes are red-rimmed. She thinks of calling attention to herself by starting a fire in the living room, but she gets scared that in the process, she might burn the house down and die a painful death. She is not ready to die, not by a long shot. She wants to kill her husband instead, she thought, and then, *no*—she will not sully her hands with his blood. She will alert the police and have him thrown in the slammer forever. *Think woman! Think!*

She goes over to the windows and tries to open them, but they won't budge. She summons all her strength and pushes one of the windows as hard as she can, but it won't open beyond a few inches. She is too high in the building to catch anyone's attention by waving. The only option is to throw a note out of the little chink in the window, hoping it will fall into someone's hands. She looks around for paper, but the bastard had thought of everything. There is no paper, no pens; then she remembers her eyebrow pencil in her bag. She runs to fetch her handbag, throws it open and sees it nestling there. *Thank god, thank god!* She knows she is hyperventilating, but she needs to do this fast. She finds some tissues in her bag, but they are too thin; then she looks on the kitchen counter and sees the paper towels. She tears one strip off and writes, "*Help me. I am a prisoner here, call Meenakshi on* ______" detailing her cousin's phone number, and ending it by giving her full name and the address of the apartment she is in. She rolls the paper around a teaspoon to give it weight and pushes it through the window, hoping it will land where it can be seen and picked up. She slowly closes the window, paranoid that Paddy will guess what she had been up to, hides the pencil inside the *saris* in the cupboard and waits.

That evening, when he comes back home, he is far more solicitous. He apologises for losing his temper and explains to her that she is now in America, the land of opportunities. All she needs to do is carry on with the pretence of being his wife, but allow him freedom with his lover. He will relieve her of this once his father dies. Meena says nothing and lays his meal out for him. Later, she tells him she needs time to think through what he had said. She then asks him if he plans to bring his mistress to live with them, too.

"She is not my mistress!" he roars at her. "In the eyes of my family and yours, maybe, but in my mind, she is and will always be my wife." He shuts himself in his study, and Meena becomes relieved.

The next day, she sends another message on a paper wrapped around a spoon through the chink in the window. She does the same the following day, and in the evenings, Paddy would once again ask her to agree to his proposal. She does not deny him when he comes to her at night, nor does she acquiesce. Then she starts her period, and when he comes to her room to push for his conjugal rights, he quickly leaves when he realises that she is 'unclean'. For the next few days, she gives up sending any more messages through the window.

Then the weekend comes, and Paddy decides to go away with his mistress to some motel out of town. Meena is securely locked in the apartment when she hears the phone ringing in the locked study. Hope raises its head. She hasn't called home, nor has she called her cousin, and her silence would definitely have been baffling to her family. What she did not know was that Paddy had already called her cousin, telling her that they were going away for a long-delayed honeymoon; he asked Meenakshi to pass this on to Meena's parents. She can't believe he expects her to go through with his plan.

She thinks of the many women in India who would have jumped at the chance to get away from their parents' home and live in America. It was very possible that they would have agreed to go along with such a charade.

The night before, he had even said, "Look, if you don't want us to have children that is fine with me. Just live like my wife until my father dies."

Meena had asked him, "What if I agree to do this, to live as your wife and have no kids, and then go back on my word and tell your parents everything?"

His face became grotesquely distorted, and he snarled, "Then I will kill you. I will find you and kill you; maybe that's what I should do now—drop you in a lake and make it look like an accident."

It was terrifying, the look and tone of his voice. She realises she is now his prisoner. She is sure that soon, he will make her call her parents and cousin Meenakshi and tell them that all is fine. Maybe he will never let her out of this apartment. *Maybe he will kill me first*, she thinks.

Meena is lost in her thoughts, miserably gazing out at the world moving outside her window; she feels completely hopeless. Her messages had surely been lost, *the spoons gracing some other person's table*, she thinks wryly. She is about to turn her head back towards the room when suddenly, she spies a slight movement outside her window. She had nearly missed it. There is a black man in a maintenance uniform sitting on a platform being hauled up and down the façade of the building by a pulley. He is cleaning windows. He waves at her and mouths a greeting as he goes down. Meena quickly springs up, shouting and waving her hands at him. She jumps and yells like a crazy woman—and, thank the lord, he stops, pulls himself up, and looks questioningly at her. Using hand gestures through the glass, she asks him to wait, runs into her room, writes the same message on the paper towel and pushes it towards him through the chink in the window. He says something then, and she shows him the cuts on her lips through the window, miming being beaten and asks him to read the note. Thankfully, he takes the paper and disappears from view.

A couple of hours later, she hears the phone ring and ring. This time, she knows it is Meenakshi calling, because the phone won't stop ringing, and once it stops, it starts again. After dozens of tries, there is silence. Meena prays that Meenakshi will come to the apartment quickly. She waits. In mid-afternoon, she hears Paddy come back to the apartment and pretends to be asleep. After some time, he calls out to her. She goes into the living room, and her eyes immediately glance at the window. She had forgotten to close the little chink. She is further terrified when she sees that she had left her eyebrow pencil on the kitchen counter. Paddy is sly and would put things together fast. He sees her looking at the pencil on the counter, and just as he was about to look where her gaze fell, the doorbell rings.

"Wait here. Who could this be? No, go to your room and wait," he says, flustered.

Meena goes to the bedroom, hears him walk to the door, unlock the padlock, and then she hears voices. She strains to hear, but the sounds are muffled. She can first make out a man's voice, and then a woman's. Then there are hysterical shouts and a loud banging on the door. By then, she is sure it is Meenakshi and her husband. She knows that Paddy will kill her. She has already locked herself in, but then she looks for something to block the door with. Meena begins dragging the bed to the door. She hears him running towards the door and finds a small cupboard, which she topples onto the bed, resting it against the door as well. Paddy is screaming obscenities outside, and she is screaming herself, "Run, Meenakshi! Run! Get the police, get the police!"

By the time the police arrive, Paddy has run away, leaving the apartment door open for them to just walk in. They have to break down the bedroom door, where they find Meena whimpering in a corner of the room in a state of shock. Meenakshi holds her for a few brief minutes before she is quickly taken away by the police and rushed to the hospital. There, she is given first aid and gallons of water to drink, which she promptly threw up. When she is feeling better, Meenakshi and her husband, Ravi, accompany Meena to the district station house where her statement is recorded. The police then hand her over to Meenakshi, who takes Meena to her home in a quiet suburb, where she sleeps soundly for the first time in weeks. She wakes up refreshed and ravenous. She knows what she wants to do.

The next few days are spent shuttling between the police, lawyers, an agency for victims of domestic violence and her cousin's home. Serious charges are being built against Paddy, which include assault and battery, rape and kidnapping, and the police are sure that they will find and arrest him soon. Meenakshi and her husband, weighed down with guilt at having been the matchmakers, provide both emotional and financial support to Meena during this period. They are with her throughout the ordeal, and though the agency is ready to help with money and temporary accommodation, she prefers their presence and counsel.

"Let me see if she will come to the phone," Meena hears her cousin speaking in the other room. Her parents have been calling every morning since her escape, but she refuses to talk to them. Meenakshi comes into her room and tells her that Arvind is on the phone. Meena, about to refuse, thinks better of it, so she walks to the other room and picks up the phone.

"Meena! How are you, my dearest sister?" his voice is disembodied, as if coming from the bowels of the earth, and sounds grave.

"Hello Arvind, I am fine now," is all she can say.

"Sis, why aren't you talking to Mum and Dad? They are completely sick with worry."

Meena can hear the accusation in his voice and is about to put the phone down when her mother's sobbing voice comes on the line, "My darling daughter, we are so, so sorry. Please, do not put down the phone. Talk to us. Your father is shattered. Please, please..."

"What do you want me to say to you, Mum?" Meena says, her voice filled with pain. "You stood by while my father gave me away to a beast. *Thank you very much*, is that what you want to hear?" Meena wants to hurt her parents and is about to add some more barbed comments, but then gives up and starts weeping.

"My baby, we are sending you your return ticket. We want you to return to us," her mother sobs on the line.

"No!" Meena shrieks. "I am not coming back! I will never return to my father's house again; you will just be wasting your money. Now listen, Mum," she says coldly, preventing her from saying anything else, "if you care about my happiness, let me stay here. Get back whatever you gave to Paddy's parents as dowry and use that to pay for my education in this country. I promise you that after the first year's fees are paid, I will not ask for any more money from you. I will work to pay for my second year's tuition and accommodation. I am planning to take an admission test for a graduate business school and get into a management course for the semester, which starts in September. Until then, I am staying with Meenakshi, who is happy to have me."

Things happen pretty fast after that. Paddy is arrested and awaits trial. Meena's lawyer moves to fast-track the divorce, and she gets accepted at Carnegie Mellon in Pittsburgh after scoring brilliantly on the Graduate Management Admission Test.

***

Chapter 17

Arvind – 1972

I am flying over small hills and over dark green forests with rivers glistening under the foliage. There are waterfalls and tiny fish jumping in the brooks, and the sunlight shimmers on the rippling water, breaking it into diamonds. I glide without a care in the world, and then, all of a sudden, a huge waterfall comes in front of me; angry foam rises from far below, and I am climbing and climbing, but the waterfall doesn't seem to have an end. I crash straight into the waterfall and wake up with a start. I am sweating profusely. I look at my roommate sleeping peacefully, the moonlight accentuating his sharp features, fair skin, thin lips and straight nose. I see the soft rise and fall of his chest under the sheet and his narrow, perfectly pedicured feet peeking out from beneath the covers. He sleeps soundly, and I walk to the long balcony outside our rooms to look down at the quadrangle below. The crickets are chattering merrily, and the frogs have started their mating calls; besides the sounds of nature, the silence is absolute and strangely comforting. I look in the distance at the lit clock in the centre of the administrative block, beyond which our classes are held, and it shows 2 am. It has been a week since I joined this prestigious business management institute, and I am slowly getting my bearings.

I left home without any remorse; I couldn't wait to get out of that house. Later, I felt a twinge of regret at leaving my mother; I missed her after a few weeks at the institute, but at that time, it was with ungrateful pangs of relief. My parents had decided to leave Delhi; my father was selling off his business and the house on Court Road.

They were moving to Dehradun, a beautiful valley in the foothills of the Himalayan ranges, 150 miles from Delhi. The ivy-walled cottage that they had found in Rajpur, a picturesque area in the shadow of the Shivalik ranges, was a fraction of the sale proceeds in Delhi, so for once, they had enough to live on. My father took the counsel of a wealth advisor, who helped him to invest the surplus wisely. His business had suffered greatly, largely due to the fraudulent transactions of his officers and staff, who had been robbing him blind by substituting genuine motor parts with poor copies from unauthorised garages situated in the northern outskirts of Delhi. For some reason, he did not press charges, even though this had destroyed his business. Dev told me much later that there were rumours about Dad being blackmailed by the same staff members over his many romantic dalliances, and he had just decided to cut his losses and move on.

We had all been terribly upset by what had happened to Meena. No one spoke about our father's role in forcing her to marry Paddy, but this, combined with the collapse of his business, had left him completely adrift; our mother was his only anchor. Dev was starting college at a leading engineering institute in Bombay and, like me, was exhilarated to be leaving home. At times, I felt disloyal to my parents, but I quickly pushed such thoughts away. None of us gave a damn about our father's feelings, but Mum became an unwitting victim of our apathy.

When I was at college in Delhi, in the three years before I joined the management institute, I was truly happy—perhaps for the first time in my life. To a large extent, the clouds that had hung around my head for so long dispersed in the company of the wonderful friends that I made in college. It was here, too, that I met Mala and enjoyed a sexual experience with a person of the opposite sex. But then there was Tanvir!

I had entered college as a traumatised adolescent, and even though my uncles were out of my life, the scars inside me had manifested themselves in many ways. I often dreamt about drowning, had anxiety attacks, and unreasonable fears crept up on me a lot. A private library where books could be borrowed became my salvation during those difficult days. I used most of my pocket money to literally devour every book that I could lay my hands on. Morris West, Ayn Rand, Daphne du Maurier, Arthur Conan Doyle, James A. Michener, Thomas Eugene Robbins and a host of other authors became my dearest friends. I imagined that Howard Roark, Nevada Smith and Sherlock Holmes were my alter egos. Dagny Taggart from Ayn Rand's *Atlas Shrugged* became my ideal woman. I lived more and more in a fictional world, running away from reality as much as I could. In my literary escapes, I travelled from Hawaii to Israel, Paris and London, from small Tuscan towns in Italy to exotic places in China and Japan. I felt agony for the Jews of Europe, hearing the accordion play as they were killed, or the cries of the passengers of ships that crashed against the rocks in Jamaica Inn. And then there was poetry: Oscar Wilde, John Milton, Robert Frost, Edgar Allan Poe and a host of others taking me through meadows, dark forests or sunlit woods and along singing brooks. There was also Morris West with *The Devil's Advocate* and E.M. Forster with *Maurice*. Often, I could be found lost in a book, reading and sobbing at the same time over a plethora of plots and themes, like the death of a character or unrequited love.

When I began college, I was full of fear and confusion. I found the sudden break from the daily routine of school—and the freedom to be what one wanted—daunting. I often woke up at night in a panic, with dark shadows chasing me. I was fearful of death, driving, and learning how to swim. My anxiety increased whenever a social situation developed around me or if I saw a group of young men standing together. I was scared of speaking in a crowd because I was sure I would say something that would give my dark secrets away or that I would humiliate myself.

The knot that had built up in my stomach in the days before I had to go to college to pay my admission fee was still twisted inside me like a coiled snake. Much later, I would look back on this day as the turning point of my life. It was also the day I met Tanvir.

That day, at a college in the North Campus of the University of Delhi, there was a long queue outside the office for the payment of fees. I approached the line of students waiting with great trepidation. I took my place at the end of the line, which quickly started filling up behind me. The young man standing behind me kept pushing against me because of the pressure from the restless students behind him. He was so close to me that I could smell the distinctive freshness of Old Spice on him. A little later, due to the jostling of more students joining the line, we were all pushed forward. Already pretty nervous in the crowd, I lost my balance and my arm hit a burly Sikh, just ahead of me, on his turbaned head. Although his turban remained intact, it came off his head, which is a great insult for a Sikh. He turned around and grabbed me by the collar.

"*Sala*, you have no shame! Insulting a Sikh by pushing off his turban, huh? I should bash your head in," he said, shaking his fist in my face.

He continued to throw the choicest abuses at me while I stood quaking in my shoes, when suddenly this tough-looking young man behind me took the Sikh's hand in his and said, "Forgive me, *Sardarji*. It was my fault, not his." He looked at me after he said this.

The furious Sikh put his turban back on and snarled, "I'll let both of you off this time, but stay away from me in the future if you value your skin." A bunch of cronies who were hanging around him winked at us and laughed. After I paid my fee, I waited for my saviour. I introduced myself shyly and thanked him for saving my hide.

"I'm Tanvir. That could have turned nasty," he said, his grey-green eyes resting on mine. I felt a familiar tug in my heart and found it hard to stop looking at his handsome face.

The Sikh and his friends were waiting for us as we walked away. At first, we thought they were spoiling for a fight, but they were smiling. We all shook hands at the end, and then the five of us went to the college canteen for samosas and tea. Over time, we became the 'Goddamn Five', infamous among students and faculty for our outrageous but harmless escapades. We stayed a tight-knit group for the next three years, until graduation.

The burly *Sardarji* was called Devinder, and he could not have been more different from the initial impression he gave me. He was a gentle and kind person; he just enjoyed using his awesome bulk to scare the shit out of some people, as he did with me. Devinder had studied at the Modern School in Delhi, and his parents were affluent. The second guy was Prabjot, and he was the brain; cynical, sarcastic and argumentative, he also loved the sound of his own voice. He was thin as a ramrod, but a tough cookie and extremely gutsy. He was related to Devinder and had come from a small town in northern India to study in Delhi. He secretly trimmed his beard (something Sikhs were not meant to do) and was waiting to graduate so that he could cut his long hair, which he later did, although he continued to wear a turban when he went home. He kept it a secret from his family for nearly five years. Prabjot lived in the residential hostel, and it was to his room that we all sojourned when we wanted to smoke, with Prabjot and Devinder joining in even though it was against their religion. The third guy was Raman, a friend of Devinder's from Modern School. Though he wasn't a Sikh, Raman kept a beard, presumably to hide the acne he suffered from. He had a horsy laugh and was generally amused with everything. He was the only boy in his family and had two beautiful sisters; we often went to his house in hopes of scoring the younger sister. He lived in an upcoming South Delhi Colony, so he had to make the longest commute. Finally, there was Tanvir. Good-looking, clean-shaven with sharp features, he was the son of a colonel in the Indian army. His ancestors came from the hilly region of Kumaon in northern India. When I first saw him, he reminded me of the young Al Pacino straight out of *The Godfather*. He had studied in Sherwood College, a boarding school in Nainital, a hill station in Uttar Pradesh.

***

Latika scored extremely high in her Cambridge examinations and was quickly admitted to one of the best colleges in Delhi. We lost touch after she moved into her college hostel, as she only came home on the weekends. I heard on the grapevine that Latika had many beaus swooning over her and scandalous stories of her escapades filtered through to me. But by then, I was too busy with my new friends to give it much thought. As it seems to happen in many Punjabi families, Latika's parents—worried about her waywardness—married her off to a businessman before she could finish college, and she ended up settling in London.

My new friends soon realised that I had lived a monastic life under my father's thumb all those years in school. One day, Devinder and Prabjot said they wanted to go for a late-night screening of *Pakeezah*. They were amazed when I declared that I had never gone to a late-night movie in my life and had only been allowed to attend matinee screenings, with a strict 6 pm curfew.

"Are you crazy? Who sets these rules in your house?" Devinder asked incredulously. "I hope you realise that you are over eighteen years old."

"It's my dad, stupid. I am shit-scared of him."

"Hey, we have to get this sissy out for a late-night movie. I have an idea," said Devinder. His idea was to get me to stay over at his house for a fictitious test on a subject that I was having difficulty with. Dad had no idea I was bull-shitting him, and we managed to get to the cinema, but I hardly saw the movie. I was so scared he would somehow discover my deception. I drove my friends mad with my paranoia, making us enter the cinema before time, then swivelling my head looking for Dad or one of his friends hiding in every nook and cranny.

On another day, just outside my house, I nearly got caught smoking.

"Shit! Just hang on to my cigarette, I can see Dad leaving the house!"

"Throw it away, you know that I can't smoke in public," replied Prabjot.

"Damn it! He's heading this way, and he will see me throw it! Just hold it, you don't have to smoke it!"

Later that evening, my father called me to his room and told me to stay away from Prabjot.

"Why?" I asked innocently.

"He's a Sikh, and yet he smokes. I don't want him to influence you," he replied.

A year later, I told my father that I smoked. He was furious.

"Why did you take up such a horrible habit? Have you ever seen me smoke, or even drink for that matter?" he raged at me.

"Precisely! All the more reason to smoke and drink—so I can be as unlike you as possible," I retorted.

I shocked him and loved the feeling of power it gave me.

These were the days when hordes of hippies were passing through Delhi on their way to Goa or Kerala. We were obviously fascinated by their anti-establishment philosophy and confidence. Devinder, being the wealthiest, had a mean music system, and we often hung out at his place listening to Jimi Hendrix, Joe Cocker, Janis Joplin, Arlo Guthrie and all the Woodstock gang. Once Prabjot managed to sneak in some hash when Devinder's parents were away, and we all learnt how to burn the 'shit' and stuff it into a cigarette before smoking it. I loved the kick, the sense of floating, and most of all, watching myself as an observer while I did some pretty crazy things. After that, whenever we got an opportunity, one of us headed to the *paan* shop on Hanuman Road to buy the stuff. Tanvir was never with us during these times; he was too straitlaced. Thank god for that! My desire for him wouldn't have remained a secret during those pot-suffused hours when all my inhibitions fell away. Tanvir attracted me in the same way Gregory had. What I once thought was merely a juvenile crush with Gregory grew, with Tanvir, into a suppressed obsession that scared me with its intensity.

And then Mala happened! I had skipped college on the day I met her; I had missed my bus and would have missed most of my classes if I had waited for the next one, so I decided to play hooky. I headed out to Connaught Place to hang around at the United Coffee House. Midway there, I changed my mind and decided to watch a movie at the local Odeon cinema. There wasn't much of a crowd, it being a weekday, and I had a row all to myself. The movie was hilarious in parts, and I was having a good laugh until a woman wearing a soft floral scent sat down next to me. I was surprised, given that so many other seats were empty, so I stole a look towards her. She was looking at the screen, and from what I could make out from her profile, she seemed elegant and sophisticated. Sensing my gaze, she turned around to look at me, appraising me openly and then spoke in a husky voice, "I seemed to have missed quite a bit of the beginning; can you fill me in?"

"Oh, sure," I replied, and then proceeded to tell her about all the characters who had filled the screen so far, chuckling away as I described some of the situations.

During the interval, I got a good look at Mala; to my inexperienced eye, she was an amalgam of Gina Lollobrigida and Sophia Loren: large, sensual lips, big dark eyes and the largest pair of tits I had seen in my life. She was wearing a *sari* made of some diaphanous material that clung to her shapely waistline. She smelt heavenly (she whispered to me later that it was Chanel, bought from a smuggler). Throughout the movie, her hands accidentally brushed mine, resting on the arms of the chair. Once, she nearly touched my thighs, but quickly pulled back. I think I heard her mutter "sorry," but I was in too much of a daze to react.

We left the movie together, and Mala invited me for coffee at Rambles, an open-air cafe in Connaught Place. She told me she was married to an officer in the Indian Army who was posted somewhere in Northeast India, where she had lived with him for a while. Tiring of barracks life, she had returned to her father in Delhi, who had retired from the Air Force a few years back. She was hoping that her husband would get a posting to a livelier and safer place, so that she could join him. She stopped and then asked me how old I was.

"Eighteen, going on nineteen," I said, hoping she wouldn't think me too young.

"Oh! I thought you were older. There is something about your face and eyes..." she trails off. "How old do you think I am?"

"Twenty-five, twenty-six?" I lied.

"You've made my day, you cutie, considering that I am in my mid-thirties. Do you have a girlfriend? Someone special?" she asked.

Was she flirting with me? I wondered.

"I did, but we've lost touch. I've met another girl now," I lied again, wanting to come across as a player.

"Tell me about her; she must be pretty to have bagged such a handsome man," she said, smiling.

I knew I had to come up with something fast, so I described Raman's younger sister. As my fiction grew bolder, I made her sound very desirable and hot.

"Have you kissed her yet?" Mala whispered.

"Many times," I replied, blushing.

"Like in Hollywood movies?"

"No," I said, "I'd be slapped if I tried that."

"Would you like to?"

"Oh yes."

"Well! We'll have to do something about that."

After the movie, she left to meet her father, who she said was leaving for Kashmir the next day, which was where she was born. We exchanged telephone numbers, and she said she would be in touch.

She called me the next day. She said she had just dropped her father off at the railway station and then gave me her address in Defence Colony, inviting me over. I took the luxury of an autorickshaw to get there as fast as I could. Apprehensive yet excited, my heart beat in rhythm with the *tuk-tuk* sound of the autorickshaw. An anticipatory knot tightened in my stomach the closer I got to her house.

She was waiting for me in a small gazebo that was in the corner of the small walled garden in front of the house. It was November, so there was a little chill in the air, but the sun's rays had warmed up the gazebo. We were served tea here. We talked about politics, especially the Prime Minister. It seemed Mala had a special fascination for Indira Gandhi. I talked about the books I had read. Mala wore trousers and a full-sleeved woollen top, and I found it difficult to stop staring at the outline of her breasts and the points of her nipples. She saw me looking and gave me an enigmatic smile. The light was fading, and the woman who had served us tea came out to tell Mala she was leaving for the day. After that, we were alone.

"Would you like a drink now that it's seven in the evening?" Mala asked me. "I never have a drink till dusk is upon us. I remember being in Paris in the summer a few years back, and I couldn't have a drink until nine in the evening because the sun was still shining at this time."

Beguiled by her worldliness, I did not tell her that the strongest drink I had so far in my life was a beer.

We moved into the sitting room, and she poured me a glass of Peter Scot. I drank it slowly with lots of soda so that I could keep my wits about me. Mala had hers on the rocks. She got up, put on some soft music, switched on the side lamps, switched off the central chandelier and pulled the curtains together, bathing the room in a soft glow. She poured herself a second drink and slowly started swaying to the strains of *Unchained Melody*, a haunting song whose lyrics always awoke powerful emotions in me.

It wasn't long before we were pressed together in an embrace; I could feel her nipples hardening against my chest, and she must have felt me stirring against her belly as she held me more strongly with her thighs. I looked for her mouth, tasting the whisky on her lips, then, from years of practice, my mouth moved over her full lips first and then held on to her upper lip, moving to her lower lip while my tongue pushed deeper into her mouth. She gasped then and looked at me in surprise, but continued responding to my moves. By now, we were both breathing hard, and my heart was thumping loudly. She slowly pushed me away and asked if I was carrying a condom, which I wasn't.

"Next time, be more prepared," she whispered. Then, she pushed my head down to her nipples while she pulled a handkerchief from my pocket and made me come. I left soon after, and we agreed to meet a few days later, before her father returned from Srinagar. My feet were light as I took a long walk from her house to Oberoi Hotel, where I managed to thumb a lift to Minto Bridge, and then caught a bus to Civil Lines.

When I left school, I had read as many books as I could find about homosexuals coming to terms with themselves. The more I read about homosexuality, the more I understood that it was natural—contrary to what

I had been brought up to believe. Even though it was a crime in India, I did not see gay people as freaks or 'sissy' characters, as they were so crudely depicted in many Indian films. Yet I was terribly confused about my own sexuality and mortally afraid of being gay. I was obsessed with trying to understand myself. I knew that I had been sexually abused, and it had definitely scarred me. I realised I was attracted to some men—usually a little older than me, invariably heterosexual, exuding tremendous confidence, warmth and kindness; good looking, and, most of all, men who made me feel safe. It was only much later that I understood I was looking for a father in all of them.

I was terribly inexperienced with women; I had flirted with them, enjoyed their company, loved their beauty, and kissing Latika made me feel whole and guilt-free. So, I was really looking forward to my next visit with Mala.

A few days after our tryst at her house, she called to tell me that her father was going to be playing golf that day and would be out of the house for a couple of hours, returning only after lunch at his club. She told me to come at 11 am sharp; she was sending her maid to the market to shop, a task expected to take her at least one hour.

"And please be prepared this time," were her last words before she put the phone down.

I was at Mala's at 11 am, this time with a condom in my pocket. Luckily, before I reached the gate, I saw the maid leave and walk off in the opposite direction from me. But the neighbour on the parallel balcony was looking down at me as I rang the bell at the gate. Defence Colony houses are close to each other and generally have two or three floors; Mala's father's house was at one end of the row of houses. She came to the gate wearing a caftan and quickly bundled me in, ignoring her neighbour, who continued looking down at us. She wasn't too perturbed; they had possibly seen other young men coming to Mala's house, I surmised. I was not foolish enough to think that this was serious. In fact, it was perfect for both of us.

What happened as soon as I reached her bedroom was mind-blowing. I lost my virginity that day, but with it, gained a sense of my lost masculinity—or so I thought. Any doubts that I had about my performance being affected by my childhood experiences were put to rest.

We went straight to her bedroom.

"We don't have too much time before the maid comes back..." she started to say, but I had already grabbed her and started kissing her all over her mouth. There was no delicacy in our movements. My years of expertise in kissing guided me. I lightly touched her mouth first and then slowly started sucking her lips till my tongue pushed deep into her mouth. She took my hand and pulled up her caftan; she wasn't wearing anything underneath. She guided my fingers towards her body. Soon, Mala was moaning and pulling my hair. She pushed me back on the bed and pulled her caftan off. I threw off my shirt while she tugged at my belt to remove my trousers, which got stuck on my shoes. I quickly took them all off. Mala brought her hand down to hold me, but I couldn't bear it for more than a second. I told her that I needed to enter her quickly, unsure how long I could hold myself back. Mala's superior experience then came to play. She slowed down, pushed my mouth down on her breasts and allowed my fingers to explore her. I remembered that the condom was in my pocket. I tried to move back to pick up my trousers, but she picked them up instead and pulled out the condom, pushing it on me and whispering, "There you are, big boy!" I entered her soon after, and we moved in rhythm, both of us gasping and moaning. Surprisingly, she climaxed before I did.

I returned from Mala's house, happily whistling a tune with the remembrance and taste of her, her voluptuous body and hands on me. That night, I slept like a baby, without a care in the world.

The next morning, I awoke to see my mother weeping on the sofa and my father looking dumbstruck next to her. Randhir *Mamu* was also there, talking to someone on the telephone.

"Where is she now?" I heard him whisper down the phone, and my ears picked up the word police from the other side. "Let her sleep some more, and when you are back from the police station tomorrow, call us no matter what the time is in Delhi."

"Are you talking about Meena?" I asked, "I thought she was on her honeymoon with Paddy."

"It's all bullshit!" Randhir fumed. "He has been ill-treating her and holding her as a prisoner. Meenakshi has just rescued her with the help of the cops." Then he told me about everything that had happened. Mum was inconsolable, blaming herself for everything, while my father just sat there looking like he had swallowed a huge toad.

The next few days were spent trying to talk to Meena, who refused to come to the phone. Then came a big showdown with Paddy's parents, who had come down from Jullundur to plead with my parents to persuade Meena to drop the charges against their delinquent son, a request my parents firmly resisted. Mala called me twice during these days, then gave up when she realised I was caught in the middle of a family crisis. When it was all over, I called her, but she was very cold; I assumed that she had picked up another young man.

My mates were very excited when I told them about my short experience with Mala. Filled with happiness at my prowess, I unashamedly talked about the glorious details of our coupling; uncharitably justifying that Mala was a nympho and did not deserve the treatment that was due to a good woman.

I was surprised when Prabjot said to me separately, "Well, well, now we can stop wondering about you..." I asked him what he meant by this. He replied, "You know... whether you are gay or not. The longing looks and coy glances that you give Tanvir worried both Raman and me. I wonder if you realised how uncomfortable it made Tanvir as well."

I was mortified, but I couldn't tell Prabjot what Tanvir made me feel, longings that I wasn't even ready to share with myself. All I knew was that whenever he went home at the end of the day, I felt bereft and became happy again when I saw him the next day. I was continuously aware of his presence, the fragrance of Old Spice, his light hazel eyes and tender lips, but the glances I gave him were returned only with mocking indulgence. Nevertheless, his mere presence made me feel safe and happy. Mala had enabled my abused body to be familiar with a woman's body, and if my longing for Tanvir made me weak and guilty, the lust that I felt for Mala gave me immense power and filled me with wonder.

How uncomfortable I was making Tanvir feel only surfaced one day when I visited him in his house in the Cantonment area. He had been running a fever and was absent from college for a few days, so I decided to visit him. He met me very warmly, but my happiness in seeing him got the better of me. Later in his room, I started horsing around; he kept pushing me away, and I tried to get him in a chin lock, which brought our bodies in contact and our lips close to each other. He shouted, "Stop it, man! You make me sick!" I left after that, and when we met in college a few days later, I made sure to be more circumspect with him. No mention was ever made about the incident.

***

After college, we all chose different paths. Raman joined his father's business, Devinder got a job at a bank, Tanvir chose the armed forces, Prabjot studied for a Master's in Economics, and I decided to study Business Management.

At the institute, my roommate was Gautam, a Saraswat Brahman. On the first day, he told me about the Saraswati River and how his ancestors had become fish-eaters, probably migrated from Bengal to the Konkan regions of Goa, Maharashtra and Karnataka. He describes the mysteries surrounding the river that disappeared underground. He is a likeable person, if a bit of a drip. He immerses himself in his books most of the time and is deeply interested in delving into the origins of his tribe. He is very fair and good-looking in a pretty way. We have both taken the same subjects, with a specialisation in Finance. Gautam wants to become a banker and ultimately work with the World Bank. I was ambivalent about what I want to do, though the industry attracts me far more than banking. We believe we are the cream of the students who had graduated from college that year; entry to this institution is competitive, and only the best make it. Competition is fierce among the students, and no one takes the faculty and their studies lightly.

Gautam is the one who drives me to push myself and study hard. I would never get my projects done without him. Most of the time, we work through the night, with me smoking up the room, which he hates. We stay clear-eyed with our submissions the next morning, but crash in our beds as soon as we make it back to the room. Gautam has no other interests except his studies and his books on the Saraswats. I, on the other hand, love campus life, playing a game of squash at least three times a week, hitting the ball late at night, and then on weekends, joining surreptitious parties rife with weed and booze in the forest near the campus. It takes all my effort to drag Gautam to these parties, and he sometimes reluctantly comes along and stares in an exasperated way at the fun and madness around him.

The campus is full of diverse personalities. Over time, cliques have formed, and they hang out with each other all the time. You can walk around the mess or the club and hear an argument in progress about 'going nuclear', or a debate on socialism versus capitalism. I am not part of any group; I just join in whatever interests me at that time. My squash partner, Praveen, is part of a group that still lives as if they are in the sixties, and I join them often at their so-called 'pot' parties. This is how I met Sushmita, who I realised later was Praveen's girlfriend since their teens.

Praveen had been asking me to join these parties, which were held near the lake close to the campus. It was an overstatement to call them parties, though; they were usually just a couple of boys and girls sitting around a circle, passing a chillum around the circle while somebody strummed a guitar. We were sure the college knew about them but did nothing about it, so long as the parties didn't interfere with our studies. Although I had tried hash and weed on several occasions and was enamoured with the high it gave me, I preferred alcohol's kick better.

On this particular evening, I walk to the gathering of zonked creatures a little late and sit down next to Praveen. As the chillum heads towards me, this girl sitting next to him says, "Not him, he looks like the enemy," so I am bypassed.

"Now, now, Sush. This is Arvind, my friend," Praveen lightly rebukes her.

Sushmita giggles and says, "I know who he is; he was a friend of Latika."

"You know Latika?" I blurt out, amazed at what she has said.

"I must say, your ability to state the obvious is astounding, kid," she laughs.

I look over at her and see a beautiful, dusky girl with a nose ring, wide almond-shaped eyes that are mischievously bright, and lips made for kissing.

"Like what you see, *Orvi*? Ogle away," she teases, rolling her eyes.

"No one has ever called me 'Orvi', but how do you know Latika?" I ask her.

"I'll tell you some day, big time kisser."

Shit, Latika has told her about me. Latika, how could you? I think.

"Hey Arvind, don't mind her. She's been wanting to meet you for days," shouts Praveen as I trudged back to my room.

I bump into Sushmita the next day at the library; she cheekily pouts at me and laughingly walks away. I go for a game of squash with Praveen and another couple of guys in the evening, and she comes to cheer Praveen on… or bug me further, I think. The other team wins, and as we walk off the court, Sushmita shouts:

"Were you nervous, Orvi? You called many of their outs as ins."

"Hey, stop calling me Orvi. That's not my name," is my lame response.

A few days later, when I arrive at a party without Gautam, she asks, "Where's your nerdy friend?"

"He's not nerdy, you drip."

"Getting hot under the collar, I see! Are you in love with his pretty face?" she taunts.

"Yes, I am! You have a problem with that?"

"Touché! Now he wants to compete with me."

She is beautiful and damning, fascinating me with her easy repartee. She and Praveen love poetry and, at times, finish verses from poems started by the other. Praveen picks a verse and recites some lines like:

"*Drink to me only with thine eyes,*

And I will pledge with mine;

Or leave a kiss, but in the *cup*

And I'll not look for wine."

And Sushmita would finish it for him,

"*The thirst that from the soul doth rise*

Doth ask a drink divine;

But might I of Jove's nectar sup,

I would not change for thine."

I realise that this argumentative, fascinating and unsettling woman, my squash partner's girl, is getting under my skin, in my head and making me lose my sense of balance.

***

Chapter 18
Tillotama – 1972

As the Old Delhi Railway Station comes into view, she feels a tug at her heart. This old stone building, so close to the Red Fort, has been a monumental part of her nomadic life since she moved from Lahore; just the sight of it stirs tumultuous emotions inside her and makes her anxious. It is crowded as usual, being the largest junction for travellers from all over India. Manmohan insisted on dropping her with her small bag at platform four, from where she was to catch her train to Jammu. He then headed for their home of more than fifteen years on Court Road, which was waiting to be handed over to the new owners.

Tillotama is travelling to Jammu to be with Maya, whom she is going to meet for the first time since India's independence. She is very excited, though a little nervous. From Jammu, they will take a car to Katra and then both of them, with Maya's youngest daughter, are going to walk to Mata Vaishno Devi's shrine. Manmohan will travel to their new home in Dehradun while she is away, and she will join him there after this pilgrimage.

She boards the train and finds her berth, and while the other passengers are settling down, she tries to sleep. Tossing and turning and listening to the snores of her co-passengers, Tillotama finds it difficult to drift off. So many images are running around her head; so much has happened that she feels ancient in both body and spirit. She thinks of Meena: what her daughter is going through because she did not fight for her. She thinks of how vulnerable Arvind is because of his deep, although unrequited, love for his father, and she pictures the relief in Dev's eyes as he leaves to join his college in Mumbai. Tillotama knows that she has failed all her children for Manmohan's sake, but nothing can take away the intense love she still feels for her husband, the reason for her absolutely out-of-character actions when she went to meet Chamanlal on that fateful day many years before.

When Chamanlal agreed to meet her again yesterday at his huge house, he hadn't forgotten a bit of what happened that day. He was much older now, about seventy-five, and carried himself with great dignity. Next to him, his brother-in-law, Kasturi, looked much older, though he was probably a few years younger. They politely talked about Chamanlal's wife's death due to cancer, about his daughter, Swarna and her children, and how she was running his business now. They drank tea from a floral tea-set, saved from the days of the Raj when a British *memsahib* would have daintily held the same cup in her delicate white hands.

No one would have thought that the demure woman sitting opposite Chamanlal had blackmailed him and his brother-in-law so effectively.

"So, what brings you to my door after so many years, Tillotama? I haven't forgotten how you took advantage of a father's feelings for his daughter that day," said Chamanlal, sounding bemused.

"*Sethji,* I am sorry for what I did that day," Tillotama said, her voice breaking a little before she controlled herself. "I have suffered for it when it came to my own daughter. I can't make amends for that day, but I hope you understand what I did was for the survival of my family." With that, Tillotama opened her handbag and quickly pulled out a bank draft for one lakh rupees and gave it to Chamanlal.

Chamanlal shook his head gently. "No, I can't take this money, *beti*. I always knew that your intentions were noble that day, and even if I had refused to give you the money, I knew you wouldn't have carried out the threat of exposing my daughter's complicity in that sordid affair with your husband."

Kasturi, who was listening to this conversation, saw the amount of the draft and piped in, "But the money we gave you was only thirty thousand rupees."

Tillotama's mind did not register Kasturi's words immediately, as she was shocked when she heard what Chamanlal said. She couldn't believe that he had always known that she wouldn't carry out the threat of blackening his family name, and yet he had given her the money anyway. She pushed ahead with the task that she needed to carry out to lessen the burden of what she had done.

"*Sethji,* please. I need to do this. Tomorrow, I leave to pray to *Mata* at Vaishno Devi, and she will never let me enter her sanctum if I do not repay my debt. We have now sold the business, which, as I promised, was not in the wholesale cloth trade and which my husband set up using your money as capital. I am returning it with your share of the profits. Please accept this, so that I can die in peace after I have received the blessings of the Devi."

Tillotama then bent down, touched Chamanlal's feet, folded her hands in *namaste* to Kasturi and left the house. She did not notice that both Chamanlal and Kasturi, usually so tough, were wiping tears from their eyes.

Tillotama is awake before the train reaches Jammu the next morning, refreshed and waiting to hold her dearest friend in her arms once more. She feels at peace and looks forward to the walk up from Katra, the small town from where believers start their pilgrimage to the shrine. She eagerly searches for Maya's face in the crowd as the train steams into the station. There are so many relatives and friends waiting with expectant faces for their loved ones. She realises it will be difficult for her to spot Maya among them.

She steps off the train and is walking towards the exit when she hears a shriek and is suddenly enveloped in a huge hug by a matronly woman from behind.

"Maya? Is this really you, Maya?" Tillotama gasps as they hold each other. She looks into the lovely face of her friend, grown plump over the years but still retaining the same warm kindness in her eyes. Dangling from a piercing in her upper ear cartilage is the *dejhoor*, the traditional jewellery of a married woman, and she is dressed simply in the classic Punjabi *salwar-kameez*, which is what Tillotama is also wearing. Standing behind Maya is a studious-looking man with a hooked nose, long face, dark eyes and hair that is just starting to grey. He is about to introduce himself when Tillotama smilingly says, "And you must be Ajay, Maya's heartthrob! All her letters are full of you. I seem to know you far better than my friend. Oh, you must be Raveena," she adds, turning towards an absolutely enchanting young girl of about twenty years.

Ajay drives his Nissan Jonga from the station towards Katra, which he says will take about two hours to reach, given the state of the roads. It is hilly terrain, but the jeep is powerful, with high clearance, and can take the climb and bumpy roads extremely well. On the back seat, Maya and Tillotama giggle like schoolgirls upon remembering their childhood escapades, and by the time they reach Katra, they have caught up entirely with their lives. At times during the journey, they hold hands, laugh out loud, or just hug each other with happiness, and Ajay and Raveena feel that they are the interlopers watching the intimacy of strangers.

Maya has done this pilgrimage many times and knows that the track from Katra to the shrine is unpaved and treacherous in parts and will take about five hours. They had set out at eleven in the morning, the *darshan* at the shrine would take another three hours, which meant they would return by around midnight to Katra. Ajay was driving back to Jammu, but would be back later that night to take them home there. Tillotama was going to stay for a few days with Maya as Ajay returned to Srinagar, where he worked as a successful dry fruit merchant.

Tillotama, who is going on this pilgrimage for the first time, finds the voyage difficult on the first section of the track. Sharp stones are protruding on the path, and a false step could be disastrous, so she focuses hard. She is taken aback by the number of devotees who are walking barefoot on such a path without showing any discomfort. This is real devotion! Within an hour, she gets used to the rhythm of the walk, the calls of "*Jai Mata Di*" from other devotees and the appearance of ponies along the path. She had refused a pony for herself, choosing to walk with both Maya and Raveena. There is a great sense of community among the walkers, and the air is refreshingly pure most of the way, so unlike Delhi, except when they pass small villages and settlements where roadside stalls are selling soft drinks, hot *pakodas* and other savouries for the hungry pilgrims.

Tillotama is worried, and as she gets closer to the shrine, her anxiety grows even more. She can't tell Maya that her anxiety is to do with the entrance to the cave where the inner sanctum with the three *pindies* of the holy trinity of the goddesses Parvati, Laxmi and Saraswati is situated. She knows that everyone has to enter the cave through a mouth that is very narrow and full of rocks and water. Legend has it that a true devotee, even if very fat, can easily slip through this opening, but that a sinner who has not repented will not pass through, even if they are as thin as a rake. Tillotama, pure at heart but troubled by her one major deception, is overcome with doubt. Maya sees the troubled expression on the face of her friend and holds her hand, telling her to just "have faith," as if she knows what Tillotama is thinking about. This simple gesture from her friend is enough to quieten her fears.

There are many pilgrims near the mouth of the cave, and Maya easily crawls into it, followed by Tillotama and then Raveena. Though the rocks are slippery and many pilgrims are exiting from the same opening, Tillotama feels a great peace descend on her as she crawls and wades through the water to reach the inner sanctum sanctorum. Tears of joy stream down her face, and she is swept up in a wave of extreme emotion as she approaches the priests. These men are guarding the rock formations, which are the manifestations of goddesses. They had combined their powers to become the spiritually advanced Vaishnavi, who waited to be merged with her Lord Vishnu and granted boons to her disciples. Seeing the look of joy on Tillotama's face, the priests let her stay longer than is normally allowed to pray in the sanctum. So overcome is she with emotion that she forgets to ask anything of the goddess.

As they walk down to meet Ajay at Katra, Tillotama is finally at peace, free from the many demons that have been floating around her for years. She looks affectionately at her friend and her friend's daughter, who have made this beautiful pilgrimage with her, and she thinks what a lovely wife Raveena would make for

Arvind. She decides to broach this subject with Maya when they return to Jammu.

***

Chapter 19
Sushmita – 1973

Sushmita is waiting in the lobby of the Oberoi near Nizamuddin in Delhi for her mother to show up. She is exasperated with her; her mother always ends up in India unannounced and expects her daughter to leave everything and move in with her at the hotel. This time, Sushmita has decided she will have a showdown with her mother and get some answers to the questions that have plagued her over the years.

Her mother, Anjali, is looking as beautiful as ever. She is swathed in an expensive satin silk *sari* in turquoise blue, clinging to her shapely figure, the *pallu* just about covering her sizeable cleavage. Her face is delicately done up in soft tones, lipstick accentuating her full mouth, a far cry from the painted faces that adorn Delhi's upper-class women. Anjali is wearing diamonds in her ears and around her neck. She walks up to Sushmita, gives her a quick hug, making sure that her *sari* remains unruffled, and then looks around her.

"Where is your bag, Sush? Have you already sent it up to the room?" and before Sushmita can answer, continues, "and what the hell are you wearing? Isn't Rakesh giving you enough pocket money to buy a good wardrobe? What have you done to your face? You know we are meeting my friends for lunch!"

"Anjali, I am not staying with you this time," says Sushmita defiantly. "I've just got in from college for a short vacation, and Dad hasn't seen me for the last four months. You just can't fly to India and expect me to drop everything for you!" Sushmita has been calling her mother by her first name for quite a few years now.

"I refuse to get dragged into another round of mother-bashing, so let's leave it for now," replied Anjali, delicately raising her eyebrows. She walks quickly towards the restaurant to join her friends, with Sushmita reluctantly following in her wake.

Sushmita's mother's friends are already comfortably seated around the table. She knows all of them from her mother's earlier visits. They all belonged to the same ilk: bored housewives wearing too much make-up, living off their husbands' wealth, dressed in expensive clothes and contemptuous of women who have to work for a living. Her mother is a successful businesswoman based in New York. She has been divorced from her father, Rakesh, for many years and lives with her current boyfriend, Richard. Although the lives of these women are completely different, childhood friendship and belonging to the same class of old Delhi wealth bind them together.

Sushmita obviously does not belong and feels like a fish out of water. She hates these lunches. The women all look at her and her utter disregard for convention, judgmentally firing sly glances at her worn-out pants or denims, the silver ring in her nose, at her lips browning from smoking and her smouldering black eyes, a legacy from her handsome Bengali father. She bears all this for her mother's sake and looks forward to the evening when she will regale her father with some of the inane conversations at lunch. Why her smart mother would want to spend so much time with this bunch of morons is beyond Sushmita.

Sushmita lives with her father in a small apartment in Kaka Nagar. When Rakesh started his career at the age of twenty-two, he worked as a junior engineer in a factory making agricultural motors and pumps. Rakesh completed his mechanical engineering degree at Banaras Hindu University and was lucky to have landed a job with the largest industrial group in northern India. Though his parents were Bengali, his father worked as a civil servant with the Indian government, and Rakesh had grown up in Rabinder Nagar in South Delhi. When Rakesh was fifteen, his father bought this house in Kaka Nagar, which he transferred to Rakesh after his retirement. He moved to Calcutta with Rakesh's mother to be closer to their own community and its culture, putting as much distance from what they felt was the boorishness of the *Delhi-wallahs*.

Rakesh has music in his blood; he can sing both classical and Hindi film songs in a deep voice that reminds people of Talat Mahmood. His rendition of *Robindro Songit* (Tagore Songs) is haunting and romantic at the same time. He plays the sitar as a hobby and is in great demand whenever his company organises entertainment programmes for its employees. His fame has spread throughout the company to such an extent that when visitors from America were invited for dinner at the chairman's house, Rakesh was often requested to play for the evening's entertainment.

Rakesh and Anjali met at one such function. On that particular evening, he had dressed in his best kurta and pyjama with a small jacket, which made him look nothing less than princely. Rakesh was classically handsome, with deep, dark eyes and long pianist's fingers, perfect for playing the sitar. He was nervous that evening because he was going to meet the Chairman for the first time, but felt reassured when he was met by the Head of the factory, who showed him the place where he was to entertain the gathering of guests. The Chairman arrived with his two elder sons, one of them was the

Managing Director of the company, and the other was finishing business school in America. Also with them was the Chairman's only daughter, who was in college in Bombay. The Plant Manager whispered all these details to him as the guests found their seats, and then Rakesh started the one-hour recital he had worked out for the evening. As the strains of *Raga Bageshri* filled the room, there was utter silence; the audience was completely spellbound. He followed this with a romantic love song by Tagore, his sitar working its magic; later, he regaled the audience with Hindi film songs by Kishore Kumar, which he sang in his deep, melodious voice.

The Chairman's daughter could not take her eyes off this handsome young man, who played and sang with so much passion and emotion. She had also noticed that as the evening progressed, the singer had looked at her often; it seemed that the love songs were sung only for her, and he impressed her with his boldness. When the music ended, she insisted on being introduced to him. As Rakesh looked deep into her eyes, she felt like he could read her mind, uncover every detail of her thoughts, and she knew that she had to see him again. Her father was leaving the next day, but had insisted that Anjali and her brother stay for a week to understand the workings of the plant and the processes.

During that week, Anjali found ways to meet Rakesh. On the first day, she saw him at the officer's canteen. She went up to him under the pretence of congratulating him on his singing. That evening, she went to the club and watched him play badminton at the courts, then challenged him to a game. For the rest of the week, she played badminton with him, waylaid him on his morning runs and even managed to kiss him in the forest running parallel to the running track. By the end, they had fallen madly in love with each other, and she was sure he was the man she wanted to marry.

It was not long after Anjali left for her parents' home in Delhi that Rakesh was called in to the Personnel Manager's office and asked to hand over his resignation or face being fired. Nothing was said, no information was given, but both knew that the reason for the sacking had nothing to do with his performance, as he was one of the best junior engineers in the factory. Rakesh packed his bags, called Anjali to tell her what had happened and that he was heading for Calcutta, where his parents were living at present. He had to catch a train at New Delhi Station, and that is where they decided to meet.

Anjali fought bitterly with her parents and then left to meet Rakesh at the station to elope with him to Calcutta. A quick bribe for the ticket collector allowed them to share a berth in the sleeper coach, and the next day, they joined Rakesh's parents. They were initially taken aback by this development, but were soon beguiled by Anjali's vivaciousness and beauty. They kept them in separate rooms and then called Anjali's parents to come to Calcutta. Rakesh was made to promise (much against his wishes) to Anjali's father that he would join the top management of his industrial empire as befitted the son-in-law of the family. The marriage was solemnised in Calcutta, and the couple returned to Delhi, where a large reception was thrown in their honour and where politicians, industrialists and bureaucrats rubbed shoulders with the cream of the crop of Delhi's social set.

After they returned from their honeymoon, Anjali and Rakesh moved into a company house in Sunder Nagar, close to her parents' huge mansion. Rakesh was given an office on the same floor as his father-in-law and brother-in-law. As befitted his position, he was given a secretary and was often called in for meetings with the top management. Rakesh was a sensitive, culturally-aware individual, and he found the aggressive Punjabi approach that the company adopted extremely distasteful. He was just a junior engineer, untrained in the dynamics of senior management politics that Anjali's father and brother were so adept at. Senior management realised that he was a misfit and humoured him only because of his position in the family hierarchy. Rakesh was an operations guy; he only felt at home working with his people on the shop floor. Even at Anjali's family gatherings, he felt out of place in this glitzy world of fancy cars, foreign holidays and discussions on world business trends, so he kept to himself. The only time he felt comfortable with himself was at his parents' home in Kaka Nagar, when they came to visit. This led to constant battles with Anjali, who was by then unhappily pregnant.

One day, Rakesh went to meet one of his old friends from college, who was working with a relatively young group that had just set up a plant in the new industrial city of Faridabad. He returned from this visit with an appointment letter for the position of senior engineer at a salary which was about ten per cent of what he received at his father-in-law's company. After a very hostile meeting with his father-in-law, he and an angry Anjali left the company house and moved into his parents' house in Kaka Nagar. Anjali loved him and hoped that after some time, he would come to his senses and return to her father's company.

Anjali found fault with everything at Rakesh's parents' house, and though she did not defy his parents outright when they visited, she spent more time in her father's house, which was incidentally across the road from Kaka Nagar, separated not just by a road but by a huge difference in the wealth of the residents. Rakesh, meanwhile, started his new job and felt happy and comfortable being around his own kind. However, all was not well at home. He would often come back from work to find that Anjali was away, and his parents were hesitant to speak about the fact that they could not bond with their daughter-in-law. As Rakesh's resolve to stay away from his in-laws hardened, Anjali's resentment towards her stubborn husband grew until it felt like a millstone around her neck. If Anjali had been in an earlier stage of her pregnancy, she would have got rid of this new life growing in her body. She did not want to be tied to a life of nappies and babies without the comfort of nannies and governesses. She knew that she needed to convince Rakesh to come back to her father's wealthier hearth before the baby was born.

Sushmita came into the world in a rush, very quickly after Anjali's labour pains started and without giving too much discomfort to her mother. Anjali, who had not been able to convince Rakesh to return to her father's home, now used their daughter as the bait and decided to use all her powers of persuasion to make Rakesh return to the life of comfort she had always known. Within a few days of her daughter's birth, Anjali gave him an ultimatum to return to her father's company or lose their daughter. Rakesh told her that he would never rejoin his father-in-law and would fight to keep his daughter. Realising that her gambit had failed, she abandoned her child and, with help from her family, left India for America and a new life.

Rakesh was left with no option but to file for divorce on the grounds of desertion and happily take on custody of their daughter.

After eight years away, during which she had become a successful businesswoman, Anjali decided to return to India. She managed to convince the court that she should be allowed visitation rights with Sushmita. Rakesh did not bear any grudge towards Anjali, and though he seldom met her, he allowed Sushmita to spend time with her whenever she visited Delhi. When Sushmita was around ten, he allowed her to travel to New York during her summer vacation to be with her mother. While Sushmita was little, Rakesh's mother took on the role of being her mother, while Anjali became her 'aunt' whenever she visited. By the time she was ten, Sushmita knew that Anjali was her natural mother. As Sushmita became a teenager, the story behind the divorce, her mother's abandonment and her absent maternal grandparents was hidden behind a big wall. This made her extremely angry and insecure. Whenever she asked her father, he clammed up, and Anjali would mostly ignore her questions or give some convoluted explanation.

Praveen, who had been her friend from the age of about ten, was the son of one of her mother's closest school friends, and even he had only a sketchy knowledge of what had happened, although his mother told him that Anjali had made a big mistake by marrying beneath her. She also knew from Praveen that her grandparents lived in a huge mansion in Sunder Nagar. Once, when she was fourteen, she used a catapult to break one of their windows before running away from the *chowkidar* who had chased her. That was the only time her soft-hearted father had ever shouted at her; in fact, his hands shook as if he was holding himself back from hitting her.

Once, Sushmita found a sitar sitting in one of the cupboards in her father's room, but when she tried to string it, he walked into the room and snatched it from her, forbidding her to ever touch it again. She knew then that the sitar was somehow connected to her parents' story. Her earliest memories were of her father singing "*sleep my little princess, sleep*" while he patted her to bed, but as she grew up, she never heard him sing again.

Her grandmother once told her that her father had a beautiful voice; when Sushmita asked why he didn't sing now, her grandmother just burst into tears.

Sushmita grew into her teens, confused between the riches of her mother's life and the simplicity of her father's home. She also carried a huge sense of rejection due to the abandonment by her mother in the earlier years of her life and the continuing exclusion from her maternal grandparents' life. She had learnt to love her mother, but when compared to the values instilled in her by her father, she was contemptuous of the ostentatious lifestyle of her mother and her Indian cronies. Though her mother had insisted on applying and obtaining a green card for her to move to the USA, she refused to leave her father to study for her management course in an American university.

***

Adam has noticed for some time that Husna is getting agitated as she reads about Sushmita. All of a sudden, she stops reading. She gasps, her face frozen in shock.

"No, it cannot be. This cannot be!"

Adam quickly holds out his arms to her.

"What is it, baby? What has disturbed you so much?" he asks. He can see that she is trying to tell him something.

"This is my grandmother's history. Anjali in this manuscript is Urvashi in real life. My mother told me about her mother's rebellion, about her grandfather, who was an industrialist, about the elopement and her pregnancy... My God, that means Sushmita is my mother, Kalpana," she says breathlessly.

"Oh God," she says once again. "That means Arvind, or whatever his real name is, is my father!" Husna closes her eyes and says, almost to herself, "Yes, yes, now I know why my mother hated gay men, why she always spoke so negatively about them. She called them conniving and untrustworthy... She had warned me so many times that... I think she was afraid that I might find myself in the same position as she had. She warned me about them throughout my high school days. No wonder I hated them."

***

Chapter 20
Sushmita – 1973

It is very early in the morning, the day before Christmas Eve, and just a few days after their last meeting when Anjali calls.

"Sush, your grandparents are having a party tomorrow for Christmas Eve and want you to come and meet them."

"Why would I want to meet them when they have never shown any interest in meeting their only granddaughter?" replies Sushmita crossly. "No, I won't meet them."

"Sush, don't be difficult, please do it for me. My parents are very ashamed that they have ignored you all these years. My visit this time has given them an opportunity to make up for the past. My mother says that she wants to see you before she dies."

"So, is she dying?" is not a response that particularly humours her mother.

Sushmita has made up her mind that before she goes to *that* house, her mother will have to tell her everything about her past. She will use blackmail but will not back down this time.

Later that day, as usual, her mother and she are having yet another lunch with her mother's friends. Terribly bored, Sushmita suddenly spies Praveen in the distance; he is coming to drop his mother off, who couldn't make it for lunch earlier, but is now joining for coffee. With a sigh of relief, Sushmita jumps up and moves to head him off.

"Hi, Aunty! Hi, buddy," Sushmita says quickly, giving his mother a peck on the cheek and then pulling him away to the lobby.

"Let's buzz off out of here, Praveen. I've had it with that crowd," Sushmita says, holding onto his arm.

"I'll just go and meet your mum, Sush. She'll complain to my mother, and I'll get hell."

"Ok, but tell her we are heading out for coffee, to CP or wherever. You can pick up your mum later. They will spend ages gossiping about friends who aren't here."

Sushmita watches as Praveen disappears into the restaurant and knows he will be swamped by all the mothers. Nevertheless, it gives her time to have a quick smoke. Praveen has been getting at her to quit smoking and is getting more possessive about her. She wonders if it is because of Arvind, but then she drops the thought. Nothing, just nothing, has happened with Arvind; he is just one more person to join their group. She knows that, sooner or later, she will marry Praveen. They have been friends for so long that he is almost like a brother. *What an awful thought*, she grimaces.

It has been taken for granted by their families that they will marry. Her father likes Praveen and fully approves of him. In fact, Praveen will be at her grandparents' house tomorrow, and Anjali has been pressing for some kind of commitment from both of them so that she can share it with her parents. *Dear dependable Praveen...* Sushmita knows she should say yes when he pops the question tonight at dinner, as she suspects he will, yet she is hesitant. Once again, Arvind's face pushes itself into her thoughts; those cupid lips, the mystery in his deep eyes, so curiously out of place in his otherwise open face. She shivers and draws a long lungful of smoke, which results in a coughing fit.

"*Tut, tut*, little girls should not smoke. Such a terrible habit," Praveen teases, always on cue, and rubs her back. "Let's go."

"Hey, have you got in touch with Arvind?" Sushmita casually asks Praveen as they drive away from the Oberoi hotel. "He mentioned that he was stopping over in Delhi with some of his friends for Christmas before heading to his parents in Dehradun."

"Yep, I'm meeting him for lunch tomorrow. Would you like to join us?" Praveen asks. "Just don't bug him like you always do; he's harmless."

"I can't—shopping with Anjali and then dinner with the monster grandparents. Thank god, you are going to be there. But give me Arvind's number in Delhi? At least I can wish him a merry Christmas, even if I can't meet him.'

"In the meantime, are you ready to give our mums what they want from us?" Praveen asks her, changing the subject. Getting no response, he sighs. "Let's talk about it at dinner tonight, shall we?"

The next evening, in a cab driving the short distance from her father's house to the Oberoi hotel, Sushmita thinks of Praveen's face the night before when she asked for more time after he proposed to her.

"We both have to be sure, Praveen, before we commit to marriage."

"Sush, baby, how long do you think you need? I've always been sure that you are the girl for me, right from the day I met you wearing that ridiculous frock and pigtails. Our families wanted us to finish management school before making it official, remember? I always thought you were so sure, Sush?"

In the morning, she meets her mother to go shopping, and Anjali has been terribly upset when she hears that Sushmita has asked for more time from Praveen.

"It's my life, Anjali. If I need time, then that means I need it," Sushmita insisted.

"You are so headstrong. Is there someone else?" her mum glowers at her.

"Stop interrogating me. I hate it when you do that... there isn't... I just don't know, I need time and that's all there is to it," she angrily retorts.

"Praveen's parents can't wait for you forever. I want your answer tonight, before we go to dinner at your grandparents, whether you like it or not."

"Then you can have it now. No, I will not marry Praveen. There. Satisfied?"

By then, both of them are furious, and Sushmita refuses to buy anything that her mother wants her to from the upmarket stores at Connaught Place. Instead, she forces her to go to Janpath's bustling roadside stalls, where she picks up whatever bizarre outfit she can lay her hands on, without burning a hole in her mother's pocket.

Now, as she enters the hotel, Sushmita realises that she isn't too pumped about meeting her grandparents this evening. Without calling up from the concierge desk, she goes straight up to her mother's room. As she walks in, her mother, still in her petticoat, looks at her outfit and shouts in displeasure, "Couldn't you wear something more sedate today, now that you are meeting your grandparents for the first time?"

"Why, what's wrong with this outfit? You bought it for me from England last winter. It's just a tartan skirt, woollen at that, and woollen stockings—again, what's wrong with them? In any case, I'm not sure I want to go to your parents' house at all."

"Rakesh has put you up to this; he always hated my father!" Anjali replies angrily.

"Stop dragging Dad into this. He is very happy that finally I am going to meet my grandparents," Sushmita fires back. "He has wanted it for a long time; you have always been the one who has hesitated, not that I cared. Just stop talking about Dad in this manner. He was the one who sang to me, cared for me and looked out for me after you abandoned me! How did it feel when you walked out on me? Tell me! Was I so ugly? All kids are, you know, when they are just born. Tell me straight, what happened? Why did you leave Dad? I want to know, now!"

Sushmita suddenly chokes on her words, and her voice drops. Anjali looks at her, shocked at her daughter's outburst.

"I did not mean to abandon you, Sush. I was too young. The pregnancy was all wrong; it happened too quickly, your father was so difficult, so stubborn, and all I wanted was for us to live in comfort. My father had given him such a good job, and yet he... he was one who abandoned *me*. He dragged me to his small house, and his parents came to live with us and wouldn't let me breathe. I was so sick with you in my body, but he would happily go away to his job, which hardly paid enough. I loved him, but I got to the point where I just couldn't take any more. Then, when I left him, my parents weren't ready to take me back if you came along... Oh no! What am I saying?" she gasps, clamping her manicured hand to her mouth.

Sushmita has heard enough. She rushes out of the room, Anjali's voice ringing in her ears, "But... but I came back, didn't I? Didn't I?"

Sushmita doesn't know where she is going. She doesn't wait for the lift, just stumbles down the stairs, runs outside to the pool, a floor below the lobby, and then rushes back to the lobby in confusion. She is breathing heavily; all she knows is that she has to leave the hotel before Anjali comes out looking for her. She tries to calm herself down, to think. Praveen won't be home; he was planning to come directly to Sundar Nagar from the Chelmsford Club. She could call him there. *No, not him.* She walks unsteadily to the reception desk, gives them a number to dial.

"Hello," an unfamiliar voice crackles over the line. "Hello, who's this?"

"Can I speak to Arvind, please?"

"Sure, he's here. Is that Sushmita?"

"Yes... But how do you know me?" Sushmita's voice quivers with nerves.

"I'm Prabjot. Devinder and Raman are here too; we're all friends of Arvind. All he has done this visit is yap about..."

The line goes quiet as the phone is pulled out of Prabjot's hand, and Arvind comes on the line.

"Hi! Sushmita, ignore these morons. I was hoping you would call when Praveen told me that he gave you my number. Weren't you off to a special dinner this evening?"

She is so relieved to hear his voice.

"Listen, Arvind, I need to meet you... now... No, alone! I'll meet your friends later. I am at the Oberoi, but I don't want to meet you here... Yeah, it's close by, I'll take a cab from here to the Ambassador Hotel... it will be a hotel cab, so it will be safe, stop worrying. It's just eight in the evening. See you soon," her words and plan come out in an unexpected rush.

Sushmita reaches the Ambassador and waits for him at the coffee shop. As it is Christmas Eve, early revellers are hanging around the bar, just around the corner from the coffee shop, but they leave her alone. Arvind walks in a few minutes later, smart in a blazer, worsted trousers and a turtleneck jumper. He is tall and so good-looking that he overshadows everyone else in the restaurant. He has a serious look on his face, which breaks into a big smile as he reaches Sushmita. She holds out her hand, which he grasps as he sits down. Just seeing him there makes her far less agitated.

"No tricks up your sleeve, Sush?" he says with a mischievous smile that lights up his face. But looking more carefully at her face, which is clouded with worry, he instantly knows that something is wrong, and his eyes quickly change to reflect deep concern. He sits there and looks at Sushmita as if he has all the time in the world. There is something in his calmness and gaze that suggests that she can speak of anything in this world; she can say she had murdered someone, cheated, hated, but he would not judge her. So, she speaks and cries and tells him about Anjali and her childhood without a mother, about questions unanswered, and her sense of abandonment and self-loathing.

"My mother did not want me. Why did she give birth to me? Why not strangle me like they do to daughters in some villages in this country? My father could have told me. Why have they kept silent all this time? Was

I so tainted that my grandparents did not want to see me? I was not a bastard. I have been so confused all my life. Jumping from my mother's wealth, fine clothes, soft beds, foreign holidays and then back to my father's small home, warm and gentle..." she breaks off, covering her face with her hands.

"*Hush*," he whispers gently. "She herself was a child then; it's got nothing to do with you, and you are deeply loved by your father." He continues, "She came back, didn't she?" Arvind keeps interspersing her sad tirade with soft comments, and after some time, she grows quiet and still.

"Come, let's see the lights of this city on Christmas Eve. It should cheer you up. Let's take a cab to Connaught Place."

***

Chapter 21
Arvind – 1973

As soon as I order our coffee at Rambles in CP, I know that I have made the biggest mistake of my life in coming here this evening with Sushmita. There is not a single woman to be seen; most of the tables are occupied by men in various stages of intoxication. The restaurant is nearly full, it being Christmas Eve, and we are given a table that seats five. I am concentrating on the menu when four guys come over to our table and, without saying a word, sit on the vacant chairs, pulling another chair from a nearby table. They just stare at Sushmita, who is wonderfully dressed for a party, but in public, it is like a beacon for all these drunken sods. Without waiting for the order, we get up to leave, and as we walk off, there is a raucous yell from the table. We walk straight to a constable who is attempting to look threatening at the crowds of drunken young men sauntering around.

"Can you please help us?" I ask, "Just walk with us to the taxi stand outside Regal Cinema?"

"Sorry, sir. I cannot leave my post here," the constable replies. "Why don't you try my supervisor? He should be in that building over there." He points us to a spot which is even further away than the taxi stand.

"Let's walk, Sush," I say. "Just hang on to me and do exactly as I tell you."

As we walk, I see from the corner of my eye that the guys who had sat at our table are following us. Heading directly towards us, on the path to the taxi stand, is another group of men.

"Sush, don't sidestep these guys. Just hold tight onto my arm and keep walking. And look straight ahead, just don't look at them," I whisper. I am nervous, but don't want to pass my fear on to Sush, who seems quite cool.

We walk into the crowd without flinching, and the men part and let us through before joining the other guys behind us, who are throwing nasty catcalls at Sush. We reach the stand, jump into a taxi, lock the doors and tell the driver to move; all the calmness of the last few minutes replaced by sheer panic. As the taxi backs towards the exit, the men start dancing near the back fender. The vehicle brushes past one of the men, and he yells, "I've been hit!" Suddenly, the whole crowd of men are pushing themselves onto the taxi, hands are reaching through the front seats' open windows to try and unlock the rear doors. Sushmita screams and holds on to me, while I am pushing back hands from reaching the door handles. Suddenly, there are whistles, and some cops come racing towards the noise. In the confusion, our taxi driver drives us out of the melee.

Sushmita clings to me, and the driver of the cab curses me in Punjabi for my supposedly extreme stupidity. I just keep apologising to Sushmita.

"What an adventure! I can't wait to tell Praveen, I couldn't have asked for a more adrenaline-packed evening than this," she laughs nervously.

"Sush, I'm sorry for putting you in this situation. We are lucky. It could have been worse."

"Stop, Arvind. We got away, and I wasn't really scared. I had you with me."

The taxi drops us outside her house, and as she turns to get out of the cab, I put my hand on her shoulder and kiss her full on her lips. I feel her respond, but then she pulls back, opens her door and without another word, heads into her house.

The next morning, I leave for Dehradun. Dev comes to pick me up at the bus stand. It is late afternoon by the time I arrive, the sunlight slowly fading, and there is a sharp chill in the air as I take in my first sights of this town, where, during the British Raj, civil and military officers came after retirement. These settlers built quintessential English cottages with gardens and orchards. Dev, who had visited Dehradun earlier, pointed out the main British commercial buildings like the Astley Hall on Rajpur Road and the Irish Brothers School as we drove up to Rajpur, where our parents have bought an ivy-covered cottage complete with a lovely garden and fruit trees of lychee, mango, pear and plum. As we look towards the hills of Mussoorie, where the lights of the houses are shining down on the valley, the first stars of the evening are twinkling away in the sky. I hope so much that the tranquillity of this town has softened my father, especially in his attitude towards Mum.

It turns out that this isn't just wishful thinking; the man I meet this time is a far cry from the father I am used to. My mother continues to hang on his every word, but he talks *to* her now, not down to her. He takes time to explain his words to her and does not expect her to automatically understand his views and feelings as he had in the past. He enjoys their new garden, the friends he has made, and is now attempting to learn golf at the course owned by the Military Academy.

And yet, he continues to hold on to his old-fashioned ideas of how his children should be. On learning that Meena is seeing someone at her university in America, he sounds very peeved that she has taken it upon herself to choose her future husband this time. When I tell him that I will also find my own bride, he shows flashes of his past temperament, shouting that he will disown me if I do so. When I arrived, Mum hugged me tightly, but Dad did not. He just stood and waited for me to touch his feet in greeting; there were no hugs, not even a clasping of hands. Later, my Mum talks to me about Raveena, the daughter of her friend, Maya, and how they have both decided that even though it will mean marrying outside the community, it would be a fine merger for our families.

"Have you asked Dad?" I ask in response. "He only wants us to marry within our community. Anyway, no Mum. I will marry a person of my own choosing."

'We will see, son… when the time comes," is all she says. I want to tell her about Sushmita and my strong feelings for her, but I choose to keep quiet.

Dev talks to us all about his plans for the future. Although he still has another few years to qualify as an engineer, he is hell bent on reaching America when he completes his studies, and nothing will change his mind. Meena has decided that she will not come back, and, for reasons that I can't fathom, I know that I will never make any attempts to migrate to America.

I return to college, content that my mother seems so much happier now.

A few weeks after I return to college, Sushmita comes over to my room. Earlier in the day, I had met her with Praveen, and he seemed desperate and possessive of her. I could see that Sushmita wasn't happy about it, that his behaviour was just digging a grave for any love she may have felt for him. When she comes in, I am alone, and I guess she wants it that way since she immediately says:

"I know Gautam is going to be at the library for the next hour, so we will not be disturbed. I wanted to tell you what happened on the day you left for Dehradun."

I invite her to sit on my bed, and I take a seat in a chair opposite, remaining silent for her to continue.

"I was shocked to see Anjali at my house when I woke the next morning. She and Dad were drinking tea together in the sitting room when I walked in on them. For a moment, I thought it was some miracle, until they saw me and both stood up. Dad pulled me into a hug, while Anjali poured herself another cup of tea before she confessed that she was ashamed of what had happened yesterday. Then both of them confessed that their silence over the years had been completely unfair to me.

"My dad told me that he didn't speak to me about what happened because he didn't want me to be influenced by his hurt and anger when Anjali left him. He sounded sad when he said this. He explained that they were young, did not understand what they were getting into, but they both knew that I was the best thing that had happened to them. He told me that they love me and asked for my forgiveness.

"After that, they recounted the events from the time Anjali first set eyes on my dad to the moment when she left us. I was overwhelmed and ashamed, and tried very hard to understand. I need to tell you this, Arvind. I also need to tell you that you made all the difference for me that evening. I want to thank you for being such a good friend."

I look at her and then open my arms. She effortlessly slips into the warmth of my hug. I turn towards her, and we kiss as if it's the most natural thing in the world; we stay glued together.

"Sush, Sush… I—I think I am falling in love with you," I say, "and thank you, Sush… for sharing so much with me."

I also want to say much more: in a short time, she had taken over my soul, my mind, and I can't live without her. The moments that I have spent with her were very special, even when she bugged me. I dreamt about sweeping her off her feet like a young Lochinvar. Suddenly, Gautam chooses that moment to walk in, and we break apart.

After that, we see more of each other. It is mostly Sush, Pravin and me, but sometimes we are joined by Gautam. Pravin cannot recognise that he has lost Sushmita, continuing with a proprietary air. Since Sushmita does not make any moves to the contrary, I just wait for the day when I feel sure Sushmita will respond to my love for her.

Sushmita and I decided that when the recruiters come, we will try to opt for the same company. Praveen is joining his father's business in Delhi, while Gautam imploringly writes to the Ivy League colleges in America for admission and financial support. Interviews begin on the campus and, except for a few students like Praveen, who weren't looking for a job and Gautam, who wanted to study further, we present ourselves in our best clothes for the job market.

A week later, I leave Praveen and Sushmita at the college dining room and head for my room. I had hoped to meet Gautam for dinner, but none of us saw him that day. I had left early in the morning when he had just woken up, and after a cursory greeting, I had rushed from the room to get to the interviews I had lined up for that day.

I return to the room that evening, and the first thing I notice is that the lights are switched off. For Gautam, who stays awake till late, this is surprising. As I walk in, I can see Gautam's shape on his bed, and as I switch on the light, I hear a muffled shout to switch the light off. I can hear soft, silent sobbing from his bed. I sit on his bed and bend down.

"Gautam, what's happened? Have you received some bad news from home? Why didn't you come to me instead of lying this way in bed?" No answer. "Come along, tell me. What is it?" I say as I shake him.

"I wish I were dead, damn it! I was so sure that I would get a scholarship to Yale," he sobs.

"You got in, didn't you? So go," I reply, confused.

"My dad is not ready to spring for the money. He said he would pay my one-way passage, that's all. He's asking me to work here for a few years and then pay my own fees. Doesn't he know that I worked two years to pay for this course?"

"Then get a loan from a bank. Once you are in America, you can try for an apprenticeship."

"Who's going to give me a loan without a guarantee? My father has refused that too!" he cries.

Looking at his despair and sadness, I feel a strong protective emotion rise within me. I pull him up, hug him and say:

"Let's step outside and have a smoke," and as I am getting up, he pulls me down and says, "No, let's stay here. Just hold me tight."

I move towards him, and the next moment, we are in each other's arms. He is kissing me on my face, my lips, his salty tears mixing in our mouths, and I find myself responding to his need. I slip under his covers, and then we are both naked. Our mouths and hands are exploring, the moonlight being the only witness to our locked bodies, which are in complete harmony, until we both shudder and are still. Soon after, Gautam slips into a deep sleep. I climb out of his bed, pull on my pyjamas and go out into the night to smoke and think.

I know that what has happened could have been stopped by me. I know that I was in control this evening. I also know that today, I can't blame anyone else but myself. *Oh, why did I let it happen?* I also know that tomorrow will bring in its own set of problems and questions. Do I want this to happen again? Where do Gautam and I go from here? How do I face Sushmita, knowing I let this happen? I have these strong emotions for Sushmita; the jealousy I feel when Praveen still pretends like he owns her. *What am I?* Homosexual? Bisexual? Abused heterosexual? By the time I finally go to bed, I know that I need help and fast.

I wake up the next morning to Gautam's insistent shaking.

"Don't you need to head for the interview?" he says, tracing my lips with his fingers. "Get moving, and I will be waiting for you when you return. And, yes, I am now clear that I will work in India for a few years before I decide to apply to the US again. Let's talk later in the evening," he says with an innocent expression.

After my interview, I hurry to the medical doctor attached to the Institute and ask him if he can refer me to a psychiatrist or a counsellor. Asking no questions, he immediately sets up an appointment with one of the leading shrinks in the city and that evening, I present myself to a receptionist in an awfully crowded clinic. After waiting for half an hour, a good-looking man, not much older than me, asks me to follow him to a closed cubicle. He introduces himself as the assistant doctor and asks me to tell him about my reasons for requesting an appointment. This is the first time I have sought professional help, and I am unsure of how to start. I hum and haw initially, but the young doctor is very encouraging. I then describe all the incidents from my childhood. My sexual abuse, my fear of yet my intense love for my father, my other fears—of flying, death, crowds—my secret longings and unrequited love, my satisfying sexual experience with an older woman, my love for Sushmita and finally, last night's shame; all the dilemmas of my miserable existence.

He finally asks, "What made you want help? What kind of support are you looking for?"

"I really don't know myself," I say. "Am I gay, or am I straight? In my innocence, my uncles forced me into having sex with them and left me completely confused about my sexuality. Please, doctor! I really need to find myself so that I can live a normal life. I am so lost… so lost, please." By now, I am close to tears and struggling with the overwhelming emotions drowning me.

During all this period, he kept taking notes, and when I am emotionally spent, he sends me back to the waiting room, where I am to wait for a call from the senior doctor. An hour later, when I am wondering if I can make my escape, I am called in to the holy sanctum of the head doctor. Dr Mathur is huge and imposing, engrossed in the notes that the young doctor has taken. Then, he looks me in the eye and asks me without much ado:

"When you see a man and a woman in an advertisement, on hoardings or in a magazine such as here," he asks as he pushes a magazine where a handsome male model is preening in the latest fashions alongside an equally sexy female model, "then which crotch do your eyes first go to?"

I am amazed at this question. He thinks I'm a moron.

"To neither, doctor," I reply evenly, "I look at the clothes which are being advertised."

"Come along, I did not mean that in a literal sense. What attracts you more? The male or the female body?" he asks in an exasperated tone.

"I don't know... both, I would say? But that's why I am here," I say, looking accusingly at his assistant. *Why didn't he explain this to his boss?* I wonder. The doctor turns to his assistant and tells him to fix another appointment with me, where they will inject sodium pentothal and then ask questions. This sounds very ominous, so I ask the doctor to explain it to me.

"All we plan to do is to inject you with what is colloquially known as 'truth serum', and then ask you a series of questions. It will tell us everything about you, so that whatever treatment or advice I give you afterwards will be based on *true* facts and not ones coloured by bias or manufactured answers. I am also very interested in your relationship and feelings for your father. Since this will all be under medical observation, it is completely safe."

The last thing I want is for anyone to probe me more about my feelings for my father, but I say, "I thought that was achieved through psychoanalysis?" thinking about Freud from Irving Stone's *The Passions of the Mind*. Then add, "I am sorry, but I will not let you put chemicals in my brain."

At this, the doctor literally snarls at me. "I am dealing with issues of life and death, day in and day out. If you want me to treat you, I will use pentothal; otherwise, I have no time for psychoanalysis sessions."

With that, I am shown the door, and I know that I will have to look within myself for a solution.

I return to my room to find Gautam fast asleep; I am relieved, I couldn't have handled any more emotional baggage, but I know that soon I will have to address what has happened between us.

I needn't have worried. The next morning, Gautam is just as embarrassed as I am, and a few days later, we agree that we should just let the events of that night be forgotten, given that, according to Indian law, we had committed a crime and are liable to be thrown in jail if we had been caught in the act.

Too much is happening in our lives at this moment, so both of us focus on immediate issues like getting a job, living independently and rising above the burdens that we had shouldered as the sons of tough fathers.

This does not stop me from reflecting about my life, motivations, longings and future. I know that I am *different*, and I don't see myself as an ambitious man climbing the professional ladder with a trophy wife to be presented at corporate do's, having perfect children who would further brighten their father's name. All I want is love and harmony, a life that will make me feel safe and whole again. I look deeper into my motivations, my attraction for a certain type of man, mostly heterosexual, and the fact that I do not seek out gay men in seedy toilets or dark parks. I try to understand why Gautam's need for comfort degenerated into a sweaty encounter between the sheets, especially as I wasn't attracted to him. But I don't find any answers.

A couple of days after my appointment with the shrink, jobs are announced, and we all know where we are going. Gautam, registering late for the job fair, receives an offer with a multinational bank, and both Sushmita and I get offers with the same manufacturing company located in Bombay. She is joining the Marketing Department, while

I am to be posted in Finance. I am going home directly to Dehradun by train, and after the holidays, Sushmita and I have decided to leave Delhi together for Bombay to start our new jobs.

The sun is rising as the train shunts out of New Delhi Station, and the new day whispers of hope and happiness. As the landscape outside my windows moves from the front to the back of my vision and newer scenes merge with old, I feel peaceful, and it allows me to contemplate my feelings for Sushmita and seek answers to my muddled life. But the answers frustratingly keep evading me, and I have reached no conclusions as we pull into the station at Dehradun.

My father has driven to pick me up. Dev is in summer training with a factory in South India. As the train chugs in, I can see my father sitting on a bench in the quaint and extremely neat station. I feel an overwhelming love for him. When I get off the train, I spontaneously hug him after touching his feet. He is taken aback, but pats me on my shoulder, then holds me for a moment again. I feel happy that I have broken through his reserve, even though it is just for a short moment.

On the drive home, he tells me about the chrysanthemums, dahlias and roses that have bloomed all spring and the lychees and mangoes which will be ready for plucking later in summer. He seems younger, more vigorous and sprightlier, and I am looking forward to this vacation with him. It is only when we are nearing the house that he mentions Mum's ill-health; she is getting repeated asthma attacks, caused by either extreme changes in the weather or by other allergens which have not been identified.

Mum looks peaky, and her lovely smile cannot hide how drawn her face is. I hug her tightly, and she feels fragile in my arms; a painful sob pushes its way up my throat.

"Why didn't you write and tell me about this, Mum? Do Meena and Dev know that you have been so unwell?"

"I'm fine, my son. Every time I feel short of breath, your father panics. Dr Gupta is a fine doctor, and I can control it with medicines and inhalers. Some of the other patients are on steroids, you know."

Over the ensuing days, Sushmita and I speak on the phone often. The moment I hear her voice on the phone, I move out from the living room to the veranda so that I can get some privacy. My dad obviously notices this and asks about her. Before I say anything about her to my parents, I want to be sure. Not about my love for Sushmita, which I do not doubt, but more about my confused sexuality. I think of Sushmita continuously during the time I go on long walks, or when I am sitting alone in the shade in the garden. Innumerable questions swirl round and round in my head like a whirlwind. What is it that I want? Will my past come in the way of our relationship? How much should I tell Sushmita about my childhood? Will she marry me if I tell her about Gautam? *What do I feel, god? What do I feel?*

Then the answers start pouring in. I will not tell Sushmita about Gautam or about my past. What I want most is a normal family life, a loving wife whom I will treat as an equal, children who will live without fear and loads and loads of love, happiness and joy. I can feel my heart soar as I visualise Sushmita wiping away the terrible clouds of my childhood and confusion, making me secure in our love for each other. Not for a moment do I stop to think of her childhood experiences and how they might condition her future responses. All I think of is myself. So, I tell my father and my mother about

Sushmita and my love for her, and I plan to ask her to marry me once we are together in Bombay.

My father surprises me with the amount of interest he takes in Sushmita's family. He spends a long time asking about her background, her parents, her upbringing, noting that although she is the granddaughter of one of the richest industrialists in Delhi, she isn't acknowledged as such and is of mixed Indian parentage. Later, in his true manipulative style, he used her family's modernism to ensure that it would be Sushmita's parents who would object to this match.

***

Chapter 22
Sushmita – 1974

She looks around eagerly for Arvind. He had called as soon as he had arrived at the taxi stand in Delhi, and after shopping for some last-minute purchases in Connaught Place, he was to meet her at New Delhi Station to catch the Rajdhani Express to Bombay. It was an overnight journey, and they were travelling by chair car. She wasn't worried about the discomfort as long as they were together. She had missed him over the holidays; her dad had threatened to send him the telephone bill for all the calls she had made to Dehradun. A train comes to a stop on the platform, and Arvind pokes his head out of a window in the chair car compartment. She smiles; trust him to jump on the train at the railway yard to surprise her.

They have soon left Delhi behind, heading out to a new career, a new life. If he were to ask her to marry him now, she would readily give her assent. She curses the convention that does not allow her to ask for *his* hand. She laughs to herself as she visualises herself on a bent knee in front of him.

"What? Did I say something funny?"

She shakes her head and smiles at him. He had been telling her about his holiday and the seven-mile walk up to Mussoorie from his parents' cottage. She had been watching his earnest and beautiful face, and that's when she wanted to ask him to marry her.

"So, how is Praveen? Has he started work with his father?"

The mention of Praveen prompts Sushmita to ask the question that she needs to ask him.

"You went to a shrink during the last weeks of college? Praveen wasn't sure, but he heard that due to some trouble, you went to see a psychiatrist. Is that true?"

She sees his face flush and wonders what is wrong.

"Oh, yes, I did go. Nothing very important, just wanted to clear my head up a little bit. Too much stress, you know?"

She sees that he is not meeting her eyes, and then he laughs and says:

"He wanted to inject a truth serum..." and then he looks horrified.

"What?" asks Sushmita, incredulously. "Why did he want to do something like that? Hey, are you okay?"

She sees that he has turned pale and desperately wants to change the topic. Without saying another word, Arvind jumps up and heads for the restroom on the train.

He returns after a long time. Sushmita sees him standing alone near the train door after using the restroom; she was tempted to go to him, but decided to allow him his privacy. Her mind is in turmoil. She always felt that Arvind was mysterious, and that possibly, this was what excited her about him—that there were parts of him he just didn't share. He has secrets, she is sure of that, *but we all have them*, she consoles herself, *and whenever he is ready, he will tell me*, she thinks.

In Bombay, she is to stay with her father's brother in Worli until she finds suitable paying guest accommodation, while Arvind joins a chummery near Bombay Central. The first six months are a period of training, and for most of the week, they hardly see each other. Arvind is travelling to all the units of the company in the country, while Sushmita visits different markets in Bombay, Poona and Ahmedabad. The company is extra protective of women trainees and does not allow them to go to outstation offices alone. It makes Sushmita angry, and one day, she barges into the HR Manager's office and demands that she be treated like any other male trainee, not always having to take her trips with another colleague as a chaperone.

"I am quite capable of travelling in trains and cabs and living in hotels alone," she insists. Despite her objections, the company does not relent.

On weekends, when they have returned to Bombay from wherever they have been travelling, Sushmita and Arvind spend all their time together. They have their bun *maska* and *chai* at a quaint Iranian café, or roam around Jehangir Art Gallery, arguing about the artistic merits of the paintings, then finally ending up at Cafe Mondegar for beers and great music. Later in the evening, they hang around with the crowds at Chowpatty Beach or on the parapets of Marine Drive.

They soon become an item in the office and receive their share of good-natured ribbing from the seniors. Over the period of Christmas and New Year, they join others from the office and take a steamer to Goa, where they stay on Calangute Beach and party until the early hours of the morning. The evening before they are to leave for Bombay, Arvind and Sushmita decide to ditch the group and head to an obscure food shack at Bogmalo Beach. Arvind hires a motorbike, and they drive down dark roads fringed by palm trees until they find a narrow road leading to the beach. The silent sea is at low tide as they make their way to the end of the beach. They can hear loud music drifting out of a five-star hotel on the beach, but as they walk further away, the silence becomes enveloping and inviting. The shack is called Bar Anton, and it has a few straggly visitors, a surprise at this time of the year. Braganza, who ran the shack, explains that everyone is sleeping off the effects of the previous day's New Year's Eve party. There is a small group of young men at the bar who, judging by their close-cropped hair, are clearly from the naval base situated on a hill overlooking this shack. One of them is strumming away on a guitar. The whole atmosphere is surreal. They order their food, and while it is being prepared, they walk outside and onto the sand with their drinks as the strains of *When a Man Loves a Woman* drift in and out with the waves.

The atmosphere is soaked in romance. Arvind looks tenderly at Sushmita and tells her how much he loves her, then he asks her to marry him. Sushmita, who is expecting this, does not wait for a second before responding. She throws her arms around Arvind.

"Yes, yes, my love!"

By the time they return to Bombay, Sushmita is wearing a small diamond ring which Arvind had managed to buy in Panjim, and they have planned their wedding and entire future life together. They have yet to talk to their parents, but they don't expect any problems. Sushmita calls her father first, and he is on the next flight to Bombay. He has heard a lot about Arvind but is only now meeting him for the first time. Within the first hour, he is completely disarmed by Arvind's charm, and he makes plans to go to Dehradun to finalise the match with Arvind's parents.

Arvind immediately calls his father, who wants the meeting in Dehradun, as his mother is not well. She is now continuously on steroids and cannot, under any circumstances, travel to Delhi. Something in his voice makes Arvind uneasy, but he can't place his finger on it, putting it down to years of distrust towards his father. He tells his dad again that he loves Sushmita very much and pleads with him not to say anything that might come in the way of their marriage. Arvind's father assures him that he needn't worry, and he will take care of it all in a manner that he deems fit. This sounds even more ominous, but there is no option but to hope for the best, as Arvind cannot head out to Dehradun in the middle of his first year.

Anjali flies into Delhi to accompany Rakesh to the meeting with Arvind's parents, after which she will come to Bombay to meet him. Both Sushmita and Arvind know that this is not going to be easy; Anjali has always wanted Praveen to marry her daughter, as he was the son of her dearest friend. Already prejudiced, therefore, Anjali turned up her nose at Arvind's middle-class background, but she is waiting to see her daughter in person to voice her objections. Marriage for love in India is beset with many devious turns, which the young couple is soon to learn.

The visit to Dehradun is an unmitigated disaster. Tillotama has been breathless since morning, so she does not join Manmohan to greet the guests. Manmohan spends the first hour telling Sushmita's parents how he is dead against love marriages, that he belongs to the old school, and he expects his daughter-in-law to sit in *purdah* if he is around; he will not want her to follow a career after marriage to look after the home, hearth and kids. He spends the next hour talking about his precarious financial situation and how he expects his older son to financially look after them. His last trump card is to talk about a dowry, but before he can do so, Anjali gets up and tells him that she would be a madwoman to ever allow her daughter to get married into such a family, which so clearly belongs to the Middle Ages.

Arvind is waiting with Sushmita at her uncle's house when the phone rings. Her uncle picks it up in the other room, listens for some time and comes to the sitting room. He asks Arvind to leave the house, and tells Sushmita that her mother will call five minutes later, but she will not talk if Arvind is still in the house. Ashen-faced, Sushmita begs Arvind to leave, promising to call him at the chummery soon. Arvind sits next to the phone at the chummery for the entire evening, but there are no calls from Sushmita. He repeatedly calls her house, and her uncle picks up the phone but puts it down as soon as he hears Arvind's voice. On the fourth call, he tells him curtly that she is indisposed and cannot come to the phone. Arvind hesitates to call his father, but he needs to know what happened with Sushmita's parents. He finally calls him, and his father is nonchalant, saying that they came, they did not like what they saw and heard and then left. He divulges no further details except to tell Arvind that his mother continues to be in ill health.

The next day, Sushmita does not come to work. Arvind knows that he will not get past the door at her uncle's house, so he asks Lorna, who is in the Marketing team with Sushmita, to find out what has happened. Lorna cannot meet Sushmita, but she does tell Arvind that Sushmita's father has reached Bombay and is with her. She does not come the next day either, but Arvind sees her entering the office on the third day, and he is shocked. She is clearly completely distraught; her eyes are red-rimmed and swimming in sadness, and she carries a message for him. Her father wants to meet him after work at the club.

Rakesh is extremely kind to Arvind and, after telling him about the disastrous meeting at Dehradun, he says,

"Arvind, my daughter loves you, but you do see that I cannot ever let her, my most precious girl, rot in a family where the father has such old-fashioned ideas. Anjali doesn't even want to see you, though I told her that you are completely different from your father. You are so well read, so aware; I just did not foresee this, your father..." he stops himself from saying any further disagreeable things about his father. Then he makes a most surprising request:

"Arvind, you will have to convince Sushmita to give you up. The last few days have been terrible for all of us. Anjali gave Sushmita hell after the meeting; we both have been trying to convince her to forget you, but to no avail. So now I am asking you to help us."

"Are you serious, sir?" Arvind says, wounded. "I love Sushmita, and I plan to marry her, come what may." He shrugs his shoulders in exasperation, looks at Rakesh in defiance and then explains to him:

"My father definitely does not belong to the old school. I have never seen my mother in *purdah;* my sister studies in Pittsburgh and is currently dating a white American of Polish descent. I can understand why he did this. It is another form of control that he wants to wield over his wife, his daughter and now his son. I was worried that he would do something like this; in fact, I thought he would ask for a big dowry for me. He wants me to know that he is the real power in the house. But I am not going to let him get away with this. I *will* marry Sushmita."

***

Chapter 23
Arvind – 1974-75

"Hello, this is Sushmita..."

I hear the phone ringing as if from a great distance. *It must be at the neighbours' house*, I think, as I push myself further under the covers, feeling Sushmita's warmth next to me.

"Just a moment..." I mutter as she is shaking me awake.

"It's Dev," she says. I pick up the call.

"Dev, for god's sake, it's the middle of the night, couldn't you..."

"Listen, Arvind, it's Mum... she's gone. She passed away just a few minutes ago." I hear his voice break and a lump form in my throat. "Dad called me. I'm in Delhi, so I'm driving there immediately. How fast can you get there, Arvind? You are the eldest son; you have to perform the last rites."

I feel the ground spin away from me. My mother... She is no more.

"Oh my god, what happened? Tell me, Dev," I cry, tears flowing down my cheeks.

"It was a stroke. She was brain-dead before they got her to the hospital; it happened so fast. Just be strong, brother. Get to Doon as fast as you can; the cremation has to be done before sunset tomorrow."

He cuts the call before I can ask him about Dad. Sushmita holds me close as I let the tears overwhelm me.

I have not seen my mother or father since the argument. After I left Sushmita's father at the club, I went straight to a public phone booth and, for the next hour, exploded with rage at my father. I spat angry words that would be difficult to forget. I had broken off all relations with him and told him I would marry Sushmita without his blessing. My loving mother became the unintended victim of this rift.

Soon after this, I had convinced Sushmita that my father was a nasty man who had brought unhappiness to all of us—my mother, sister, brother, my mother's relatives and many others he had come in contact with over the years. We decided to get married in Bombay within the next month in an Arya Samaj Temple. Our witnesses were friends from the office, Sushmita's childhood friend, Neha, from Delhi, Prabjot and Tanvir, Dev, who came to the wedding in the middle of his studies, and, to the surprise of all of us, Sushmita's father, who fulfilled the Hindu ritual of handing the bride to me. Meena called me from Pittsburgh and told me that our mother sent her blessings and wished she could have been there. There was no word from my father.

After the wedding, Sushmita and I moved into a two-room apartment in Colaba. On one side, you could hear the traffic on the busy causeway and on the other, the noisy conversations of the neighbours. But we both loved it, and Sushmita teasingly flirted with the young son of the neighbours, who blushed whenever she passed him on the stairs or met him in the elevator.

We get on the first flight out of Bombay to Delhi that morning; a death in the family gives you a priority in getting seats on the only (government-owned) airline in India. From the airport, we head for the taxi stand at Ajmeri Gate and, by ten in the morning, are hurtling towards Dehradun. Sushmita and I are brooding and apprehensive as to how my father will react to us, but Dev had called after he reached Doon and told me he would fully support me and let me carry out the last rites. I am still worried about it, and all that anxiety does not give me the time to properly digest the fact that my mother is dead.

We are met by Randhir *Mamu* at the taxi stand in Dehradun. He is meeting Sushmita for the first time, and as we drive to my father's house, he explains to her that it is her duty to give her mother-in-law's body the ritual bath and get it ready for the cremation. Sushmita shudders; this is not what she ever imagined her first meeting with her mother-in-law would be.

There is a crowd of friends, relatives and onlookers outside the house as we turn into the gates. The house is bathed in afternoon sunlight, and my father's prize dahlias and chrysanthemums give it a festive look. It is in absolute contrast to the sombre atmosphere inside the house, where everyone is waiting for us to come and start the rituals that consign the body, now separated from the eternal soul, to fire, so that the soul can start its journey to its next abode. My legs feel weak as Sushmita and I walk to my mother's room, where her body is laid out on the floor in accordance with Hindu tradition. My emotions, which have been held in check throughout the journey home, overtake me, and my body is racked by sobs. An indefinable sadness sweeps through me, and each time I try to smother my tears, the grief breaks through like a giant tidal wave, dragging me down into the depths of despair. I will never see my mother again, feel her love, or hold her hands to feel safe. I will never again see the gentle look on her face as she exhorts me to understand my father and to love and care for him.

I did not see my father when I came into the house, but now I feel his hands on my shoulders as he lifts and holds me in his arms, saying in his practical voice, "Son, she has been waiting for you; now do your duty towards her." He looks at Sushmita for the first time, pats her on her head and tells her to go with the other ladies and dress my mother in the clothes of a bride and make her beautiful for her final journey.

Later, as the sun is progressing towards the horizon and its rays are fading, we watch the burning pyre together, the four of us—Dad, Sushmita, Dev and I—standing together. Meena is arriving tomorrow and will attend the *Rasam Pagri*, the ceremony carried out on the fourth day after the death, which signifies the transition of responsibility and the honour of the family from the parents to the eldest son. We are just leaving the cremation grounds when suddenly, an old man comes up to my father, who looks surprised at seeing him, and he offers his condolences. The man then turns to me, holds my hands tightly and says with tears glistening in his eyes, "I am so sorry, my son. Your mother was the bravest woman that I have ever met." Later, my dad tells me that the man is Kasturi, the brother-in-law of Chamanlal. That is when it all comes back to me, the story told to me by my mother of how she extracted capital to start my father's business.

The next day, we are driving to Hardwar to consign the ashes into the River Ganges, the holiest of the holy rivers for Hindus.

"I don't see any reason why Dad has to come to Hardwar with us. He could have rotted alone in the house for all I care," Meena says emphatically, her voice betraying a hint of an American twang. She had arrived on the night of the cremation and joined us in the morning to collect the ashes of my mother's body. We are in an Ambassador car for the voyage to Ganges, where we will immerse her remains.

"*Hush*, Meena, he may hear you. Can't you at least keep your voice down?" I say, simultaneously looking in the rear-view mirror at my father's sleeping form. I am driving, Meena is sitting next to me, and Dev and Sushmita are in the rear seats with Dad.

"It annoys me how easily you have forgotten how he treated all of us, especially Mum. I am raging inside, and I cannot find it in me to forgive him," she continues, ignoring me.

I see my father open his eyes while his whole body is slumped as if in pain. Before he closes his eyes again, he sees my look in the mirror. At that moment, I feel like gagging Meena, and the searing pain of the loss of our mother, who always knew how to protect our father, cuts to the bone.

Later, I ask Meena who she is really angry with.

"Not even once did you come home, not even during vacations," I say. "You preferred summer internships in America or spending Christmas and Thanksgiving with Meenakshi. I can understand why you blamed our mother for not standing up to Dad, but you need to eschew this hate now. You do realise that our father will also not live forever. Isn't it time?"

"What do you mean by that question, Arvind? Time for what?"

"I strongly feel that you are only angry with yourself. You find it difficult to forgive yourself for forgetting the existence of your parents. How long is this cycle going to continue, Meena? You did not find it in you to forgive them for what happened to you; now you are finding it difficult to forgive yourself. Just stop it! If you want to beat yourself up, do it, but don't keep bashing Dad." I find it hard to believe that I am defending my father.

The tension in the house is slowly diffused by Sushmita. She takes it on herself to sit with Meena and assuage her feelings, often holding her as she lets her grief flow. She helps Dad organise Mum's things, sitting quietly at his side when he breaks down while looking at some long-forgotten memento, and she takes on the organisation of the house now that our mother is gone. I feel so proud of her when I see her in conversation with Dad, or when Dev seeks her out to help sort out some issue. My heart beats crazily if she looks towards me, and all I want is to passionately love her.

Soon, it is time for all of us to leave. Dad has asked Rawat, who worked for us at Alipur Road in Delhi, to come and work for him in the house. He is sure that he will be fine on his own. He promises that once we have a bigger apartment, he will come and live with us in Bombay, at least during the cold Dehradun winters. Just before we leave, he calls Sushmita to his room and gives her the jewels that my mother had worn at her own wedding. His voice breaks down as he hands them to her:

"Even though I had forbidden it, she defied me and kept these aside for you."

***

Chapter 24
Arvind – 1976–80

"Can I help you?" the sister who answers the phone at Children of God Charity in Bombay says in a soft voice.

"We have started the paperwork for adoption, and we were wondering if we could come over and meet anyone who could help us find a young baby girl," Sushmita's voice sounds firm and unwavering.

When we returned to Bombay from my mother's funeral in Dehradun, we both settled back into our routine life. I had made the decision to leave the job, as it was forbidden for spouses to work in the same company. Sushmita and I had argued about who should look for another job, but given the sense of security the company gave to women employees, I chose to look elsewhere. It did not take me very long to find another job, except that it was in North Bombay, so I had a longer commute than Sushmita. After a few months, we moved to a bigger apartment in Bandra, which we rented for a steal, given that it had a brilliant view of the Arabian Sea.

Sushmita was impatient to start a family. Our lovemaking became more frantic, and Sushmita wanted me to stay longer inside her, even after we had climaxed, to make sure that the sperm did their work. Sushmita, like most Indian women in those days (and many men, too), was a virgin when we married. When she asked me if I was, I told her about Mala. That night, she was more aggressive in making love to me, from kissing and biting my lips until they were sore, to the more urgent exploration of my body with her hands and mouth, finally moving in rhythm to reach an explosive climax. My past, my misgivings about myself and confusions—all slipped away in the beauty and fervour of our lovemaking.

When Sushmita missed her period, she couldn't wait to find out if she was pregnant. When her pregnancy was confirmed, she was ecstatic. Even before I realised what this would mean for us as a couple, she had decided to call our daughter Husna, most beautiful. When I told her that it was a Muslim name, she looked at me with contempt, and when I asked her the obvious question—if it was a boy, would she call him Husna, too—she refused to consider such a possibility. I knew that deep down, she wanted to make up for the extreme trauma of being unwanted by her mother when she was a baby. She wanted to make amends for her mother's actions by bringing a precious girl into the world who would be cherished and loved. In turn, I wanted a son whom I would protect from the world. I saw him in my dreams growing up—at school on the stage, at the playing field, me in the crowd cheering him on and on...

In the ninth week of her pregnancy, Sushmita started complaining about lower back pain. We rushed to the doctor, who advised bed rest. When she started spotting, we pulled the panic alarm, and Sushmita was admitted to the hospital. By the time the doctor arrived to check her over, cramps had started, she had started bleeding heavily, and I was asked to leave the room. When the doctor came to find me later, his grave face told me what had happened. I went to Sushmita to find her sedated, and I sat helplessly holding her hands.

A few weeks later, we had studied enough about miscarriages to accept the explanation of our doctor. A foetus can spontaneously abort due to some possible abnormalities, and most miscarriages are a one-time occurrence. Though I wanted to wait for a few more months before trying again, dreading a recurrence, Sushmita insisted we start again immediately, and so we stopped using any birth control. This time, the pregnancy didn't last beyond the fifteenth week, and we were distraught. The doctor saved some of the tissue of the foetus and sent it for testing. There were no chromosomal abnormalities, and the doctor could not give us a satisfactory reason for the miscarriage this time. He just told us to give it more time.

The effect of the second miscarriage was severe on Sushmita. She often woke up crying out for Husna, and she was weighed down by a sense of unworthiness. No amount of reassurance helped, and although tests did not suggest that she could not bear children, she took the blame on herself. Her old insecurities of being an unwanted child have now converted to her being a failure as a woman.

"I wanted to be such a wonderful mother to Husna," she often cried bitterly. "I would have loved her, held her, never let her out of my sight... but Husna does not want a mother like me. I must be evil, a devil! An unwanted piece of shit!"

She soon began taking antidepressants until one day, by her own volition, she threw away the pills and started working like a woman possessed. All the energy that she had spent on self-pity was now channelled into her work. She had been passed over for a promotion, but now her zeal and energy were recognised. Thus, she started moving up in the corporate world. Her group in the marketing department won the highest sales award, and her bonus was even higher than my annual salary.

I, too, began making great strides in my job, and there was talk of promoting me to the head of the company's plant, which was situated close to Bombay. The company was novel in its approach and was keen that middle management moved both horizontally and vertically in different functions of the organisation, in order to build future leaders. I was singled out as one of those potential leaders. Luckily, the promotion meant that I did not have to move out of our rented accommodation in Bandra. It would just mean a longer commute for me, which meant less time with Sushmita. This led to continuous debates as to whether I should accept this promotion, but of course, ambition won over. I confirmed my willingness for the promotion.

Then our life took a drastic turn with the visit of a banker who, as we later learnt, held certain radical beliefs. Sushmita was leaving the office when I called to tell her that the new Head of Merchant Banking at the bank I was working with to raise funds for a new project would be joining us for dinner that evening. She was used to such corporate visitors; we generally maintained an open house, and our cook-cum-housekeeper would lay a third place most evenings without being asked. I liked Stephen considerably and had told Sushmita about him, how I was impressed by his wit and ability to talk about any subject thrown at him. I knew Sushmita enjoyed intense conversations and would look forward to meeting him that evening.

Our doorbell rang promptly at eight that evening, which augured well for the young man as Sushmita was a stickler for punctuality. Stephen was smart, articulate, and comfortingly left-of-centre, and soon the three of us were chatting as if we had known each other for years. It was when we began angrily arguing about Sanjay Gandhi's nefarious mass sterilisation programme during his mother's Emergency in 1975, which had seen the downfall of Indira Gandhi's Government, that the talk moved to population growth in India and the state of the country's many homeless children. Stephen, who was getting married a few months later, made a surprising revelation.

"My fiancée, Josephine and I have both discussed this and have agreed that we will not have any children of our own. There are too many children in orphanages due to unwed mothers or destitute parents."

Sushmita was shocked. "That's not going to make a difference. Will two or three more children make any difference to this country's population?"

"No, you didn't let me finish, that's not all. Depending on our ability to support children, we plan to adopt at least two, if not three, of these orphaned kids. If more people did this, it would be a win-win situation for the country."

We were both speechless for a moment. Stephen obviously did not know about the miscarriages, and his views immediately had a profound impact on Sushmita. After he left, she had already decided what she wanted. We argued about it daily.

"Ok, we don't believe in this idea as Stephen does, but look at it another way," Sushmita said a few days later, "We tried, and I am ready to try again for another child, but I don't think I can take another miscarriage, the sense of loss, self-hatred, my envy of any and all mothers. Arvind, only you and I can decide this. I don't plan to talk to my father, or yours, and definitely not to Anjali."

On another occasion, when I reminded her that adoption is for keeps, she was so angry that she refused to talk to me for a week.

Soon after, I gave in, and we met with social workers and a counsellor. Slowly, I became as enthusiastic as Sushmita, and I started looking forward, as much as she, to bringing 'Husna' home. This led us to the doors of the Children of God Charity in Andheri, Bombay. Sushmita had decided to stop working as soon as the adoption was over.

Adopting Husna was not easy. After we discovered all that was needed to be done, we made an official request to the sisters for a newborn girl. Sushmita wanted to be part of her upbringing from the earliest possible moment.

On the appointed day, we walk up to the old-style pink bungalow shaded with trees. We are met at the gate by the Catholic nun who deals with prospective parents. She seems very gentle and kind, and as we walk to the waiting room, she explains to us that, based on our requests, they will bring us a baby from the ones who have recently arrived from another state in India. They do not allow parents to 'shop' for babies, but considering our need, they have 'reserved' a baby girl of about three months, the child of an unwed mother. Soon, she comes out with the baby and, holding her long nun's skirt, is another young girl of about four years old.

"She's been very protective of this baby and wanted to meet you," the sister explains. The little girl is lovely and has a beguiling smile that melts my heart. I can feel a lump growing in my throat.

"Is she also up for adoption?" I ask quietly.

"Yes, we hope she will meet some good souls who will give her a home. She is very loving," replies the sister, smiling down at the little girl.

Sushmita is looking at the baby, and she lights up. The baby's eyes are open, and she seems to be looking for the little girl. Without consulting Sushmita, I ask if we can also adopt the little girl, seeing the immediate approval on Sushmita's face, but the sister says it is not possible. Even if they allow us another child, it has to be of the opposite sex of the first child.

The sisters allow us to take the baby home, though the formalities are yet to be finalised. That night, the baby cries constantly and keeps pulling up her legs as if she is in pain. Sushmita and I take turns carrying her on our shoulders and walking up and down with her, but as soon as we try to put her down, she starts howling. The next day, when we take her to the hospital for a check-up, the doctor realises that her liver enzymes are elevated. The most obvious reason is malnutrition, but it could be other reasons too, which won't be ascertained until proper nutrition is given to the baby over the course of some weeks. Knowing that we are in the process of adoption, he advises us to think hard about whether we want to keep her. Sushmita refuses to think of such an option.

"What if she were born out of my body? Would I have abandoned her?" is all she says as we take Husna home.

The rest all happens quickly—the paperwork, the visit by the social worker, the clearance from the court to enable Husna to become the most precious part of our family. A few weeks later, after Husna's liver enzyme report shows great improvement, we sigh with relief.

But after this, it is all downhill.

***

Adam and Husna have been reading the manuscript for some time now, but Husna has not spoken a word since her last interjection. Adam thought she would have been excited when the author chose to reveal her name in the manuscript, but surprisingly, there has been no response. He bookmarks their place in the manuscript and turns to Husna.

"Shall we give it a break and just go out and visit Eddie V's downtown?" he asks. "Let's make an evening of it, order some pricey wine and eat their great seafood. What do you say?"

Husna, deep in thought, does not respond immediately. After a while, she refocuses on Adam and says, "Yes, let's go and just get away from all this; I am completely overwhelmed with all this information. I can't believe that somewhere in India, or maybe right here in this country, I have a father, a grandfather, an aunt and an uncle, maybe even some cousins. I just can't get my mind around this. How could Mom keep all this information from me, knowing that I would have loved to have a brother or a sister?"

They call the restaurant as they drive to Rush Street and are told that they will have to wait at the bar before they can get a table. Luckily, the wait is not too long, and they move to the table with a just-opened bottle of Barolo, which both of them enjoy.

"It is interesting that Arvind chose to hide all the other names except mine," Husna says thoughtfully. "I wonder why? Do you think he knew that my mom would let me read it someday and wanted there to be no doubt about who he was talking about?"

"No, I don't think so. He just simply chose to use your name," said Adam gently. "Husna, there are details out in the open now; they must be troubling you. Please talk about them. Don't bottle them up."

"Are you talking about my supposed father, Arvind, or whatever his name is, taking up with his roommate while professing undying love for my mom?"

"Yes," replied Adam. "We have to try and understand Arvind. Remember when he was young, he was robbed of his natural right to discover his own sexuality in his own time? It must have been incredibly traumatic. Add to that his fearful yet intense love for his father. He must have been so confused. Let's not judge him."

"Adam, I don't understand what you are trying to say. All that is troubling me is the last sentence we read, about it all going downhill, which was after I came into their life. What is that supposed to mean? Was I the cause of whatever bad thing happened to them?"

***

Chapter 25

Arvind – 1981-1982

Rawat is waiting with the car at the station. Dad is at the golf course, so he sent him instead. I hug Rawat, noticing that he looks older and more rugged. He still has that toothy grin I remember from my childhood.

"It's good to see you, Rawat," I say, as he bends down to pick up my suitcase. "You were a godsend for Dad when you agreed to leave Delhi and look after him when Mum died."

"*Sahib* was the godsend," he replies, referring to Dad. "If it weren't for him, my son would have been a servant like me, not an ITI-trained crane operator with a big company in Delhi."

This is news to me. He also tells me that my father had paid for his son's education from school until he finished his training.

I have travelled to Dehradun just a few months after welcoming Husna into our hearts. Dad hasn't been feeling too well, and things are tense between Sushmita and me, so the best course was to take some time away from her—give her time, too, to think things over.

I am sitting with Dad in the garden a few days after my arrival when he begins talking about horoscopes. He tells me that, as a child, he was told that he had a terrible horoscope—that his destiny was to sow unhappiness wherever he went. I laugh and say that I can't believe that he would have such faith in destiny, considering he was a self-made man.

"What about Husna?" I say, turning my face to the warm sun, "We know nothing about her birth or her stars, except that she is the most loving and beautiful daughter one could wish for."

I look at my father's serious face. He begins speaking as if I had said nothing.

"A few years after I was born, my father lost most of his wealth. After I married your mother, her family lost their wealth, and deep divisions manifested themselves among them. Meena went through so much abuse at her husband's hands, and your mother died too early. When my horoscope was prepared, they foresaw all of this. Wherever I go, I spread discontent," he sighed.

"Was that why you were always angry with all of us? And why you wouldn't talk about your father? Haven't you thought that this guilt was pushing you to behave in a manner that made it a self-fulfilling prophecy?" I ask.

"Forget it, son," my father brushes my words away. "I am happy now. Despite my failings, all my children are prospering and successful. Meena's husband, Ivan, is a very good man; you will like him when you meet him. Dev got his Green Card when he married Teresa, and you taught me how to love again," he says, referring to our new closeness, as evidenced by the big bear hugs he gave me when we met this time.

Another day, he asks me, "Is everything fine between you and Sushmita? The last time I spoke to her on the phone, she seemed upset with you."

"No, it's nothing much. Husna comes first in everything, so I am sometimes given short thrift," I explain.

Obviously, it is not as simple as this. Both of us have loved Husna since the day she came into our lives. Except that Sushmita became obsessed with her, worrying constantly about her safety, health, and comfort, to the exclusion of all else. She had already given up her job, but slowly, she gave up entertaining her whole social life and directed all her energies to Husna. The days when we enjoyed the intimacy of each other's bodies seemed far away. Our lovemaking was seldom as breath-taking as before; Sushmita wanted to get it over and done with it quickly, until it felt like she was letting me have my way just so that I would leave her in peace for another one or two weeks. I felt that all the desire we once had for each other disappeared once Husna came into our lives. It was like Sushmita had needed me only for a child. Now I felt alone. The loss of intimacy was affecting me badly. I had become tense and insecure. It wasn't helping that my work was making me travel much more; I had been transferred back to the corporate office from the plant and was looking after planning and strategy, which involved acquisitions and joint ventures. Husna was now a toddler full of energy, and Sushmita and I had drifted apart. I wanted to believe it had nothing to do with me that Sushmita's devotion to Husna was so all-encompassing that she simply couldn't bear to be away from her even for a moment. On those rare occasions when we did manage to be together, while Husna was quietly sleeping, the talk would invariably centre on Husna. Normal, one would say, but with Sushmita, it was an obsession. If another couple was at the house for a drink or a meal, I had to steer the conversation away from our daughter, as Sushmita would not talk about anything else. Then she would sit in an ominous silence, later branding the conversation boring and commonplace.

We started having fights over mundane issues, like the volume of the music being played, even though the noise did not reach Husna's room, or my smoking, which was now only on the balcony. One day, when she was three years old, Husna picked up my lighter, which I had mistakenly left on the table, and Sushmita went ballistic. She grabbed my cigarettes and flushed them down the toilet, then hid my lighter. I stormed out of the house to buy fresh cigarettes, which I chain-smoked until I realised that I was acting like a fool. Resentments built up easily between us, and we found ways to hurt each other. I wanted to give up smoking; it wasn't helping my daily squash game one bit, but I did not want to give Sushmita the satisfaction. Often, without any reason, Sushmita would punish me with cold silences.

As these silences grew and her need for any intimacy with me disappeared, I started questioning myself again. I masturbated most days in the shower, and at times, the images to bring me to climax were mixed. Often, Gautam's face or body would find its way into my mind when I was thinking of Sushmita and her beautiful body. I began to question my feelings for Sushmita and whether I was relieved that I did not need to perform anymore. Feelings of guilt, as I had in my youth, came rushing back.

Though the growing distance between Sushmita and me was not influencing our love for Husna, it was building up into a mountain of bitterness between us. Initially, it was small, but the resentments kept festering, and where there had once been deep understanding, there was now only anger and recrimination. It is crazy how one's mind gets slowly poisoned. Where I once saw Sushmita as a caring, sensitive individual, I now saw her as someone totally self-centred. Everything had to be about her. Since she had always believed that her mother didn't want her, she became obsessed with herself. It was all about *her* hurt, *her* need, and *her* sanity. It was never about anyone else. It was all about what *she* wanted. My needs, hurts, and beliefs never really existed for her.

How could they when she was so consumed by herself? These feelings rotted inside me, and the disappearance of her arms around me, her hugs and her touch, completely shattered me.

In the midst of all this emotional turmoil, I was often travelling to Delhi for work. On one of these trips, I reached the hotel in central Delhi by 4 pm. I thought I would have enough time to head to the sauna at the health centre before my crucial meetings with potential partners in the evening, which was to be followed by dinner. I knew from my earlier visits that the sauna and steam rooms would be quiet and empty, giving me some peace before members and hotel guests come after 6 pm.

As I pushed through the door of the health club and headed to the register to enter my name and room number, I saw a towel-wrapped foreigner standing, talking on the internal phone. Something was exchanged in the glance between us as I passed on to the locker room. His voice sounded European, and I heard him say, "*Wie geht es dir?*" to someone on the phone; I guessed he was German. I dropped my clothes in the locker room and headed for the empty sauna. I stepped up to the upper wooden ledge, spread my towel and sat cross-legged, savouring the rising heat. I heard the door opening and, without looking, I knew it was the German. He stepped up onto the same ledge and sat next to me, letting his knee touch mine. This was the time to either walk off or tell him to move, but I sat and allowed an inner heat to rise and flood my being with anticipation. Once again, everything inside screamed silently for me to leave, to run, but I sat still until slowly the small finger of his hand wrapped around mine. I couldn't breathe. I stole a glance at his body and saw that he was erect, then felt the blood rushing to my loins. I knew that if I did not leave, then I would be lost. It took all my power to push myself out of that small, heated room, pull the towel over my own erection and cool myself off in the showers.

While I was getting dressed for my evening meeting, a note was slipped under my room door. It invited me, in halting English, to join 'Karl' for a drink in room number 612 later in the evening. I guessed he got my room number, which happened to be on the same floor, from the visitor record sheet at the health club's reception. I threw the note away and headed to my business. After the meeting and dinner with the Australian guests, who were in Delhi to negotiate a joint venture with my company, we all decided to go to the bar for a nightcap. Though the note from Karl had disturbed me for its many implications, I did not allow it to surface in my mind. I was sure as hell that I would go straight to my room after my work drink. Fifteen minutes later, I saw Karl peep into the bar and look meaningfully at me, before leaving again. After one more drink, we all left the bar, and I took the lift to the sixth floor. As I stepped out into the corridor, my eyes sought out 612. It was in the opposite corridor, but I strode purposefully towards my room. Halfway there, throwing all caution to the wind, I turned back, walked straight to 612 and knocked. Karl opened it, wrapped in a hotel towel. All he said was, "Oh, it's you," then I entered that room and lost the battle once again.

Karl turned out to be a gentle, sensitive man, and he held me close as if we were long-time lovers instead of just a one-night stand. He caressed me, kissed me and, knowing that I was nervous, made me comfortable in our lovemaking. He headed a tour agency in Munich and was shepherding tourists from Germany across India. When we parted, he told me he would be in Bombay later that week, and we decided to meet again.

In the early eighties, news was filtering into India from America about a new scourge that was affecting gay men. Word spread that it was the 'gay cancer'. Later, of course, it was found to be prevalent among intravenous drug users, heterosexuals, and, in India, amongst sex workers who had probably been infected by foreigners who came in contact with them in major port cities like Madras, Bombay and Calcutta. When I entered that hotel room in Bombay, I had a vague idea of AIDS. Since our lovemaking did not involve intercourse, it wasn't as risky. Years later, after reading more about the disease, I thought of my stupidity and the risk that I could have placed my family in by sharing my body fluids with a stranger.

The other implications of what happened between Karl and me were even more difficult to accept. A subconscious signal was passed undisputedly from me to him as soon as I entered the health club. He persisted even after I walked out of the sauna, which meant he saw me weakening. Karl was gay, and he could so easily read me, my darkest secret, as well as persuade me, which terrified me, especially as I always believed I would never indulge in that sort of encounter.

Some months later, a chance encounter on a flight from Singapore to Bombay showed me the philandering side of gay life. I met a man called Gerald on the flight. It was a full flight, but luckily, the seat next to me in business class was vacant. I had placed some of the documents I wanted to study here during the trip. Just before take-off, a man in his late twenties was guided by the air hostess to the vacant seat. He looked friendly, apologised for disturbing me and explained he had been upgraded at the last moment from economy. His accent was somewhere between British and Australian; I enjoyed guessing nationalities based on people's accents. Since I couldn't readily place this man, I asked him where he came from. He said he lived in England but was originally from Zimbabwe. He was an engineer, flying into Bombay to look at a project his company was bidding for. He had been in Singapore for a conference and was going back to London after finishing his work in Bombay. He had a sweet face, a little pretty, and his manner was fussy, bordering on prissiness. He clearly loved to talk, and we were soon deep in conversation. He spoke about his parents in Harare, who wanted to return to England, and he was telling me he was saving money to buy them a house in Hampshire. I asked him out of curiosity what his partner (assuming that he had one) would think about him looking out for his parents instead of their own future, when he said:

"That's not an issue as I'm gay," and then added, "I have a boyfriend, and we live together in a rented place outside London. The only people who know about this are my sister and my parents. The people I work with aren't aware of my sexual orientation."

I was surprised he had told me about himself, especially as I had told him earlier that I knew most of the people he was meeting in Bombay for his work.

"Considering that very few people know about you, how come you told me about yourself?" I asked.

"I felt very comfortable with you. Somehow, you don't look like a person who judges others, and I just felt like being open with you," he said.

I had never met someone who had accepted the fact that he was gay, so I was very interested to know more about him, hoping that in some way I might be able to understand myself better. He told me he had matured sexually very late; it was only in Cambridge, where he had gone to study on a scholarship, that he realised he was attracted to men. He had his first sexual experience on a trip to Bruges after his graduation. He had been seduced by the guy who had checked him into his room in the small hotel where he stayed. After that, he never looked back and has been living with his current partner for the last year.

Gerald came home for dinner on that trip and met Sushmita, who was very unlike herself and didn't take part in the conversation for most of the evening. She told me later that she was uncomfortable with Gerald and felt that something was not right. When I told her that he was gay, she said, "That must be the reason," and when I asked her if she was homophobic, she replied that she found "them" unnatural.

Gerald and I kept in touch, and a few months later, when I went to London, I met him and his new partner. I learnt that he did not like women; in fact, he referred to the English women in the small village where he lived as 'tarts'. He had broken up with his first partner, having become bored with him, and found his new partner in a gay sauna. Now he was planning to drop this partner too, since he had fallen out of love with him. It was only after getting to know Gerald that I realised that whatever may be wrong with me, I couldn't be gay or live the life of a gay man.

After I married Sushmita, I thought I had left my other self behind, hidden in the shadows; not repressed, just a second personality that sometimes stepped out to the light, possibly when I saw a face that reminded me of Tanvir or Gregory, or even just someone new with a charming smile. This 'alter ego' would cause me some heartache for hours or days, but it would soon be forgotten in Sushmita's arms. I loved this woman, her smell, her delicate skin, the rosettes on her breasts, the mystery in her dark eyes, and her generous mouth. I did not doubt, but being weak and morally ambivalent was also not in doubt after my tryst with Karl in Delhi.

***

Chapter 26
Arvind – 1983-84

Anjali's spacious and luxurious apartment in Manhattan, close to Columbus Circle, is the ideal place for us to stay after the hectic days spent with Meena and Ivan in Chicago and Dev and Teresa in LA. It is our first visit together with Husna, who, at three and a half years, is precocious. Central Park beckons us with its huge sunny spaces, and Anjali, Husna and Sushmita spend their mornings there while I walk to The Met to absorb the beauty of the Impressionists and post-Impressionists. The tortured lines of Van Gogh's paintings fascinate me; I become completely immersed in the strange, harsh lines of his self-portraits or the turbulence of Wheat Field with Crows, which had recently been lent to the museum. The poignancy of his life and his strange art is not lost on me. I have been writing poetry for some time now and strive to put into words my strange longings and despair with the mess that I have made of my supposedly ideal life. A life so perfect, made up of a beautiful daughter, an attractive wife and a job whose upper rungs continue to remain firmly in my grasp as I climb.

We had recently told Husna about her adoption, that she had not been born from Sushmita's tummy. She had looked at both of us and asked, "Does that change anything, Mom and Dad? Does it make me any different to you?"

We assured her that it made absolutely no difference, that we have loved her from the day she came to live with us and will always do so. Unfazed, she replied, "Then that's fine with me, too." We were relieved that it had gone so well.

One day, we take a cruise out to Ellis Island and the Statue of Liberty. As the ferry rounds the coast and the skyline of New York is pushed behind us, the majestic statue stands before us in all its beauty, looming in the foreground. The guide intones the words of The New Colossus, "Give me your tired, your poor, your huddled masses yearning to breathe free." Moved by the words I say to Sushmita that America is truly the country which not only gave homes to the Irish when the English oppressed them and the European Jews escaping from Nazi tyranny, but continues to do so to countless other individuals, like Meena escaping from an abusive husband and Anjali from...

"From what, Arvind?" Sushmita interrupts. "From the cries of a newborn baby? From her responsibilities? Say it!"

"Sorry, that was a mistake, I take it back," I hastily reply.

"No, you are right. She had her own reasons to do what she did. I can see it more clearly now." Then she looks at me with a hard glint in her eyes. "Have you ever wanted to escape from something in your life, Arvind? Have you?"

"Who, me?" I take my time answering, worried where this is heading. "No, not really."

She looks searchingly at my face.

"Sometimes, I don't understand you at all. I hope you will tell me more someday." She turns away to face the wind.

The next evening, Anjali arranges a dinner for us, and both mother and daughter seem to be in perfect harmony, Husna having healed all the wounds that these two women had inflicted on each other. Sushmita is more relaxed than I have seen her be for some time. At Meena's home, our first stop on this little tour of America, she constantly worried about Husna's and her diet, concerned that the excessive protein and too few accompanying vegetables would play havoc with her digestive system. At Dev's, she was more worried about the bohemian atmosphere and multi-faceted discussions between Teresa, Dev and me.

Anjali has invited a couple who live in Bombay for dinner. The husband is the son of her friend, who had first taken her in when she ran away from Rakesh to New York. We all plan to go to a nightclub afterwards, while Anjali babysits Husna.

They are a handsome couple. Kapil is an investment banker with Citibank in Bombay, and his wife, Mridula, is setting up a design house to showcase Indian fashion. As we have pre-dinner drinks, the conversation shifts to the latest Bollywood gossip, secret affairs between the reigning stars of the Indian silver screen, and tales of cuckolded husbands and cuckquean wives. Soon, as so often happens, the discussion becomes more personal. I suppose I start it when I say:

"One can always fall in love again. Why not come clean and let your spouse know if you fall in love with someone else? It's better than hiding and cheating."

"You mean to say that marriages are not for keeps?" says Sushmita, to which Mridula replies,

"I think that all Arvind is saying is that there is always a possibility that in your marriage, you may meet someone who will mean more to you than your spouse."

I interject here, "It happens all over the world. Why not in India?"

Sushmita looks angrily at me, possibly because Mridula seems to be in my corner, and says in a raised tone of voice, "Arvind, are you saying that if tomorrow you meet a more interesting woman, whom you fancy, you'll drop me like an old shoe?"

"Hey, Sush, this is a discussion; it's got nothing to do with us. We were talking about secret liaisons in Bollywood! Let me ask you, if I met someone else, would you prefer that I keep it dark, and carry on in secret?"

Kapil, trying very hard to get a word in, angrily speaks up, "An affair by a husband or wife outside a marriage is a big betrayal! Why did they get married in the first place? Marriage has to be for keeps."

"This is my view exactly! Kapil, you are right," says Sushmita. "It's always a possibility that one may meet someone who attracts you, but why should one have an affair? What about the vows of marriage? I cannot subscribe to these permissive views of Arvind and Mridula."

Anjali walks in to announce dinner, and the discussion peters out. At the club later, Sushmita seems irritated with me, avoiding my attempts to put my arm around her, and continues talking to Kapil. Mridula looks cool and amused, then takes me to the dance floor, where she dances with wild abandon. Whenever I look towards Sushmita, who is at the bar with Kapil, she turns her back to me, her shoulder blades straightening in disapproval. Mridula sees me look towards Sushmita and whispers in my ear, "She's beautiful. You sure are a lucky man."

When we leave the club, she says, "I hope I will see you in Bombay when we all return. There are great places to party there." We exchange phone numbers and agree to meet up in Bombay.

The next day, I am alone with Anjali, and she casually mentions the previous evening.

"Kapil seems a wonderful man and too good for Mridula, who seems to be such a flirt."

Though I disagree with her, I keep quiet. Then she comes to the point.

"I happened to hear parts of that crazy argument that had all of you in such a blather," she says, eyeing me severely. "Be careful with, Sush. Don't mock her. She loves you, but if Husna's happiness is threatened, she will fight like a tigress. Arvind, do not take her lightly. No secrets, be honest with her."

"I hope you realise that you have been the cause of a lot of her pain, Anjali. Pain in her most vulnerable years has left an indelible mark. I would like you to know that I have given her only happiness." I say with surprising venom.

"I'll be damned if I listen to such words from my son-in-law, who has no idea of my circumstances, to make such a comment," she replies angrily. "I wonder if you know that I never wanted to be divorced from Rakesh. I just wanted some time to myself when I left for America. I begged him not to file for divorce, but he was so angry that I had left Sush that he went ahead and did it. I never married again, hoping that someday we may have the courage to become companions again in our old age." Her tone softens as she reveals this poignant truth.

"I am sorry, Anjali. I was completely out of line to direct such comments at you," I reply, backing off.

The discussion with Mridula and Kapil is revived by Sushmita when she tells me that if she ever comes to know that I have slept with someone else, she will leave me without ever giving me a chance to explain.

She ends it by saying, "Just watch it, Arvind. There will never be any comeback." She says this to me after I had already slept with Mridula, six months after we returned to Bombay.

Though Sushmita is not at all fond of Mridula, she likes Kapil. We all started hanging out when we returned from America. Mridula called, and we met for dinner at the club; the next time, we enjoyed their hospitality at their tastefully done-up apartment in Malabar Hill. By then, Sushmita had warmed up to Mridula, which was fine with me as I liked her a lot.

The affair (more like a one-night stand) begins when one day, I receive a call from Mridula at the office. She sounds very distressed and asks if she can come over to our house to meet with both of us; she just wants to talk. I tell her that Sushmita and Husna are visiting her father in Delhi, but that she is welcome to visit, as long as she is ready for food to be called in, since our cook is on leave that day. I ask her about Kapil, and she says he wasn't in town and, in any case, she wasn't planning to bring him along even if he was.

Mridula's sadness is showing on her face. This is very unlike her, given her usually positive outlook on life. I pour both of us a whisky, and Mridula says, "Can you make mine a larger one? I need all my courage to be myself today." I don't give too much heed to her remark and add some more whisky to her glass and to mine as well.

"Sushmita had to go to see her father. He had a terrible bout of flu, so I told her that instead of fretting about him here in Bombay, she might as well spend a few days with him. It will allow her to cook for him and feed him some protein-laden soups," I chuckle as I say this.

I continue talking about my work, Husna's antics and the general political climate in India, but after some time, I notice that Mridula is answering dispiritedly in monosyllables.

"What's wrong, Mridula? This is not like you at all. You have hardly said a word. Are you missing Kapil?" I have hardly finished when Mridula lowers her head and starts sobbing.

"Hey, hey! Come along, nothing can be so bad. Just let it out," I say, and I leave my chair to sit next to her on the sofa and put my arm around her to console her.

"It's Kapil!" she sobs, "He's having an affair with my trainer, Iris. I am completely devastated," she cries. "How could he do this to me?"

"What?" I am stunned. "That doesn't sound like Kapil at all. Remember that argument we had in New York? He was dead against extramarital affairs. You must have got it wrong. How do you know it's true?"

"I caught them necking when they thought I had gone for a shower after I completed my training session. We had a terrible showdown after Iris scampered away, and he had the audacity to tell me that he had already slept with her several times, not because he loves her or anything like that. It's apparently just that she is far more 'adventurous' in bed."

This starts another bout of crying. I hold her closer to comfort her, but before we know it, we are in each other's arms. Soon we move to the bedroom and we make love. It seems so natural and inevitable, but later, when I take a saner view, it feels as if either I took advantage of her vulnerability, or she wanted to prove to herself that she was still attractive and sexy. The next day, she calls to tell me we shouldn't see each other for some time.

She sounds embarrassed, in spite of the fact that I felt the beautiful connection I had with her, had found its inevitable expression.

After Sushmita returns from Delhi, she starts contacting HR firms to plan a return to work. With Husna getting closer to four years old and safely enrolled in a play school, Sushmita wants to get back to work. Though she has kept herself abreast of the changing business scene, her lack of work experience means she is looking at a position far below her contemporaries. It is then that I suggest she should look at another career. She chooses psychological counselling and joins an intensive course with an NGO that is committed to providing support to disturbed individuals through helplines and direct interaction. Initially, she finds the process of self-actualising very daunting, leaving her in tears at the end of the day. As the course progresses, her self-discovery helps her empathise and understand how to support individuals to help themselves. When she finishes the course, she joins the organisation that provided her with the training.

As for myself, I am heading up the strategic alliances group in my company, which means travelling not just within India but across many continents. If I am in New York or Washington one month, I will be in Germany or France next, or Brisbane and Sydney. Travel means being away from home for long periods, living in luxurious hotels and developing friendships across the globe. I read voraciously, deepening my understanding of other cultures and norms; when visiting many of these countries, I often surprise and delight my hosts with my knowledge of their country. My reputation grows in the market. Trade and other associations start calling me to present papers at different forums or to become the main speaker and representative of more such alliances.

Sushmita watches my progress and rise in the business world with trepidation. She knows that I live in a make-believe world of success and achievement, which takes me further and further from the real world. She becomes ever more deeply involved with troubled people, listening to their heartfelt stories. She begins to shun materialism and is drawn towards a more Buddhist spiritualism. While I am indulging my senses in food and drink, she is reaching a higher plane of consciousness. While I come home jet-lagged and often with an unspoken disturbance of the spirit, she remains calm. She is the anchor for Husna, as well as her father and Dad, who depend more and more on her counsel.

Sushmita has come a long way in overcoming her inner demons with the strength of her spirit and indomitable approach to life. At the same time, I have lost my way in my personal life, letting my guilt, shame, insecurities and repressed passions take over many moments of my existence. It is not a hedonistic approach to pleasure, since I know that the physical act is not the earth-shaking event that others make it out to be. I am not naturally permissive, but the inner forces that cause such tsunamis of turbulence in my whole being become self-destructive. My torments, powerlessness and obsession with sensory pleasures begin to topple my world. I need to find a fulcrum to balance my life.

A few months after the night with Mridula, while I am packing up my work to rush off to catch a flight to London, the supply chain head walks into my office, very perturbed, and wanting five minutes of my time.

"What is it, Joe?" I ask.

Joe is one of our most valuable managers, as most of the company's factories are dependent on his skills to ensure that raw materials are available at the right cost and time.

"I just came to ask for your help with Clive," he says.

"Who's Clive? Ah, I remember, you aren't the first to have mentioned him. Some weeks back, the head of HR had some issues with him."

"Yes, that's right. He's the managing director of the company that controls our coal mines in Australia. He hasn't been responding to my emails on supplies of coal for our power plants. It's not that I am short of inventory, but he needs to be reminded that after the acquisition of his company, we run the show in Australia."

Joe is from the old school, believing in the hierarchical structure so prevalent in businesses in India.

"Joe, I remember Clive," I reply. "He is a reasonable young man and does not take kindly to being pushed around. We keep forgetting that the culture in other countries is very different to ours. These are professionals who do not take kindly to phrases like, 'I am the boss'. You have to respect his contribution to the group and his professionalism. I am sure he is aware of your inventory position and is sending the coal where he may be getting a better price. You forget that we have signed a preferred customer agreement, which gives us coal at lower prices than his other customers."

I had met Clive many times during the due diligence on his company, when he had given presentations to the team. He was young (early thirties), articulate and passionate about the business. Clive was a Yank who, after working in South Africa with an American company, was transferred to the company's holdings in Australia. His experience in the coal fields of South Africa had helped him rise to the position of MD. I met Clive again when he came over to Bombay after the acquisition, for the integration process with the Indian group. There were grumblings in various departments that Clive was being difficult with the integration.

Husna and Sushmita join me on the flight to London. After spending an evening together, they are heading to New York the next morning to spend some time with Anjali. Husna is now talking all the time. After dinner that evening, Sushmita and I went to a bar for a nightcap. While Sushmita orders a red wine, I ask for a malt whisky and we look at each other, realising that we haven't spent an evening alone like this for a long time.

Sushmita is looking radiant, though pensive.

"A penny for them," I say.

"Haven't heard that in a long time," she responds.

There is soft piano music playing in the background, and lights from the windows in the bar are highlighting Sushmita's full black hair. I remember the day when I first saw her at the management institute, passing the weed around.

"We've come a long way from the day we met," I say. "I wonder what happened to Praveen. Do you have any regrets, Sushmita?"

She looks unblinkingly at me.

"You were difficult to fathom then; you were a challenge, and in those days, I thrived on them. I needed to know you, but I still don't. Do I have regrets? No, you've been a good man, loved me, supported me, and allowed me to have Husna. No, I have no regrets. Sometimes you are very insensitive and I resent that you can run away from home using your work as a cover..."

"Sush, do you really believe I choose to travel to be away from you?" I ask, staring deep into her eyes.

That night, we make love. It is like all the years in between fall away, and we are still young and thirsty for each other.

"Sush, I do love you so much," I say to her again and again.

On my return to Bombay, there are frantic messages from Joe about Clive. I had forgotten to call him from London. I am heading for Shanghai at the end of that week to call Clive.

"Hello Clive, how have you been?" I say cheerfully. "I haven't seen you since you came to Bombay after the acquisition. That's been about six months now, hasn't it?"

His clear and pleasant voice comes over the line.

"Hey, mate! Yes, it's been more like eight months now, but I'll be in Delhi for the budget meetings in a month or two, so let's meet then."

"No, I need to meet you earlier than then. Could you fly to Singapore this Friday? I have a four-hour wait for my connection to Shanghai, so we could meet somewhere close to the airport."

"There is no flight that can get me to Singapore at that time," he says reluctantly. "The other option is to fly to Singapore the night before. But that seems quite a waste..."

So, all that I had heard of Clive being difficult is true, I think. I tell him that, at times, the urgency far outweighs cost consideration. I also assure that he could catch an afternoon flight back, so that he can be home for the weekend, even though I am working throughout them.

The meeting in Singapore is acrimonious, and Clive complains bitterly about the high-handedness of the individuals he deals with at the head office. It becomes my job to placate him. I know I need to be better prepared by studying his confidential files and the issues raised before meeting him again. We agree to meet in Sydney a fortnight later. I find myself studying him more closely than before, and though the meeting is not pleasant, his clear-eyed demeanour, passion for what he believes in and infectious smile when we part, leave a deep impression on me. I find myself looking forward to meeting him again.

As promised, I flew to Sydney a fortnight later.

"It's a very impressive operation that you run here," I tell Clive as he drives us back from the mines in New South Wales to Sydney. On the three-hour drive back, Clive brings me up to date on all the issues that have been cropping up between him and the head office. My reading of the coal supplies was right; to maximise profitability, Clive was sending his supplies to more lucrative markets, so long as he did not starve the Indian market. I have to counsel him to respond to his colleagues in Delhi, giving him a lesson in the hierarchical systems in India.

Clive invites me to dinner in the evening. I warned him that I wanted to get to know him and that there would be no talk about work. I am exhausted from my travels and looking forward to a stimulating evening with this man. We meet at a seafood restaurant on Circular Quay, which has a majestic view of the Sydney Bridge and the Opera House. As the evening progresses and we warm up to each other, we begin talking about ourselves, and I find I am sharing things about myself I have never shared with anyone, especially not with someone from work. Later, when we looked back at that evening, we realised that what we told each other was based on a feeling of immense trust in the other.

Clive was born in a poverty-stricken corner of Brooklyn in New York. His father deserted his mother when Clive was very young, and he grew up in a home where different men were always in and out of his mother's bed. His mother had loved his father, and the desertion hit her hard; she became depressed. She was a beautiful woman, but her depression led her to drink so that she could sleep at night, and then it started helping her to face the day. When she was sober, she got work, which could last up to a month, but on other days, they lived off welfare. When Clive was eight years old, his mother was beaten up by a boyfriend, and Clive went for him with a kitchen knife, but he managed to overpower him and thrash him too, which left Clive with hearing problems in his left ear. This episode changed his mother; she joined Alcoholics Anonymous, often taking Clive with her, needing his presence outside the hall so that she did not succumb to drink on her way back. By the time Clive was ten, she had stayed clean for two years and had married a colleague at work, then they moved to a better part of Brooklyn.

Clive enjoyed school even during the difficult days when his mother was too drunk to look after him, but with stability in his life, he began excelling. His stepfather was Roman Catholic, and they started attending Sunday sermons in the nearby parish. When he was twelve, he was molested by the parish priest while fulfilling his duties as an altar boy, something his stepfather insisted upon. When the abuse continued, he stopped going to church, which became a consternation for his stepfather. Clive kept his mouth shut as he did not want to pit himself against the priest, who was a close friend of his stepfather. He was happy that his stepfather had provided some much-needed security for his mother, and he did not want to 'rock the boat'.

In the process, he lost his faith in Christianity and other religions as well, for that matter. He decided to be an agnostic. It also made him look at his own body anew. He was riddled with guilt from letting the priest have his way with him. Clive did not delve more into this, except to say that it pushed him to seek out many women to clean him of the stigma of the priest's body on his. He met Clara when he started university, and they married before they both had finished college. Clara was of German descent; her family was from New Jersey, and she was interested in the arts. After they finished college, they moved to a tiny apartment in Manhattan. Clara would go to the Metropolitan Museum, where she worked, while Clive continued his Master's in Business Administration.

After Clive finished his Master's, he worked for a large American corporation which had interests in coal mines and other minerals in Canada, Mexico, South America, South Africa and Australia. He climbed the ladder quickly because he had no qualms about how much he worked or where he worked. Though Clara was not adaptable to living in other countries, Clive was intent on forgetting his early days of penury and hardship and was keen for postings outside America because of the potential increase in salary this work offered. His initial posting was in Ottawa, and Clara wasn't too perturbed as it was so close to home. But after a few years, they were posted to Cape Town, and Clara's insecurities surfaced. She wasn't keen on having children until they moved back to America. On his march to prosperity and the 'corner office', Clive chose to ignore Clara's silent reproaches and needs. Whenever she returned to America for a vacation, he was never sure that she would come back to him.

With the sale of the Australian assets, Clive realised that the American company did not give him an option to return to them. I had to tell him that his continuation was a key requirement of our purchase agreement. He felt forsaken by the previous owners, which was leading on him to take intractable stands with the current management in India.

When we parted that evening, we hugged each other in an entirely natural way. He says to me that he hasn't met a man like me before, with whom he can talk about himself without feeling it was not macho to do so. He is demonstrative in wanting to hug me and express his feelings of closeness without the inhibitions that he had been brought up with. I walk up to my hotel room, thinking about this wonderful man and the strong emotions he has invoked in me.

After I return to Bombay, we start communicating by mail and on the phone. On most Sundays, we end up on the phone with each other. Clara had returned from her latest trip back home to America, but is cold and complains most of the time. He shares his fears of feeling like a failure if Clara decides to leave him. I feel a swelling of love for him in his vulnerability. I become protective towards him, sometimes thinking of him as the son that I never had, though he is only a few years younger than me, or loving him like I would a younger brother. Sometimes, my thoughts move towards more physical feelings towards him, but this is a place I did not want to go to. He fills my mind and my waking hours. His platonic feelings towards me and my ambivalent ones for him are articulated in our letters to each other. We have also started ending our missives with 'love you, mate', which in hindsight does not sound as innocent as it really was.

We meet in London for a conference, along with other international arms of the group. It is in London that he tells me that he is planning to leave Australia to save his marriage. I hate losing a wonderful leader like him, but I agree to ensure that his break from the group will cause minimum disruption. It helps that he has already created a succession plan. That evening, we broke away from the main party after dinner and went to the same bar I had gone to on my previous trip with Sushmita. I noticed this time that there are many single women at the bar, looking at Clive with interest. He is a handsome man, and when he smiles, he seems vulnerable and very boyish. He has an open face, and as he looks around him, a woman walks up to him and starts a conversation, which Clive plunges right into. I soon realise that I am not ready to share him with another person, so I make him leave.

We walk back to our hotel, and he comes over to my room. We open a bottle of red wine and talk until the bottle is empty. We are all going back to our own cities the next morning, and when he leaves, I hold him tightly in an embrace, but he gently extricates himself, saying, 'Whoa, whoa! You okay, mate?"

Our mails continue: mine telling him how much I missed him after we parted, and his talking about how much I am helping him come to terms with his life, his past and what my friendship means to him. As usual, we end our emails with 'love you, mate'. Before he leaves the company, he visits Bombay, meets Sushmita, and tells me how much he adores her. He tells me that if Clara ever leaves him, he will marry an Indian girl who looks like Sushmita.

Clive returns to America. He and Clara settle in Philadelphia. Clara was close to her parents in Princeton, and Clive set up a company consulting on mining and minerals, with a focus on emerging markets like South Africa, India and China. He and Clara decided to seek help from a counsellor to save their marriage and deal with the anger and resentment Clara harbours towards Clive.

Clive is now a Phillies fan; I find it amusing how Americans change their loyalties in football and baseball depending on which city they live in. With the counselling helping both of them considerably, Clive's calls on Sundays are more upbeat, and he seems in harmony with his home, family and business. He is looking forward to bringing Clara on her first trip to India, and I am making an itinerary for the places they should visit. He is doing this in secret because he wants to surprise Clara.

Clara is worried about the constant Sunday calls Clive makes in his home office away from her ears, and about the fact that my name is often repeated in the household. For reasons that only Clara knows, she decides to go into Clive's study and go through my letters to him while he is travelling to the West Coast for work. The written word is always more damning than the spoken, and my 'loving' letters shock Clara.

When Clive returns, Clara accuses him of having an affair with me. She threatens divorce on the grounds of his sexual orientation, calling him gay and citing his molestation as a boy as the cause of his 'leanings'. He is very upset and keeps saying it was wrong of us to write 'love you, mate' as Clara considers this to be a declaration of love between us. He is devastated that all the understanding they have worked on for the last year has been destroyed.

***

Chapter 27
Arvind – 1984

I have been sitting opposite Sushmita most of the night, talking. I have told her about the parts of my life she never knew, trying to explain why I am the way I am and have done the things I've done. Her expression has not changed. I have drunk glasses and glasses of water, flushed out my urine and my secrets in equal measure, while she has sat without movement, little expression and without feeling. The letter from Karl is lying open in front of us.

Hi Avind (I hope I got your name correct)

I am asking the hotel where we met last year to send this letter to you. They are refusing to give me your address, but have agreed to send a sealed letter to you at your office address.

My letter will be short. I just want you to know that I waited for you last year at the Bombay hotel, but was sad when you did not call on the dates I told you I would be in your city. This year, too, I came from Germany with another group and hoped that we would meet. I am going to be there next weekend, 25th and 26th, and this time I must insist you see me. The time we met in Delhi was special, and there was a lot of love between us. I enjoyed your body so much, and your kisses were special. I hope to see you soon and halte dich wieder in meinen Armen... Let me hold you in my arms again.

Karl

"This thing with the German just happened at a time when I was most vulnerable," I say desperately. "You had moved away from me, and though I was not looking for an encounter with another man, it just happened. I never saw him again, which is why he wrote this note that you mistakenly opened. And Mridula… honestly, I was only consoling her. There was no premeditation; it just happened. Forgive me.

"You asked me whether I was gay; the answer is I don't know. What I learnt from Karl and Gerald was that they could never consider having sex with women. I love women, and I love you, Sush! Both physically and emotionally. Am I bisexual? I have wondered about this often. I know I have been attracted to some men with certain similar attributes: sharp aristocratic features, fair skin, thin lips, a strong personality, and a charming smile. Do you see the similarities to my father? He became a fixation for me, and as I grew older, it hid in my subconscious, I suppose. I missed his hugs, his strong hands holding mine to support me, to make me feel safe. My mother loved me, but she could not replace my father. I read somewhere that due to sexual abuse in childhood, there is a possibility that an abused person's inner ego and superego cannot stop what their id wants."

Sushmita continues to listen to me; I am speaking fast, and I want her to understand. Then, for the first time, she speaks:

"I am going to leave you, Arvind. I cannot stay in this house, and your presence is intolerable."

My heart sinks; a sense of dread bubbles up inside me.

"Sush, what are you saying?" I cry. "I can't live without you; you have been my strength. I have so often felt powerless, much as I felt when my uncles molested me. Even at work, I am afraid of confrontation; I bend to authority. You came into my life and made me whole, powerful and happy. With you next to me, I felt I could take on the world. But as we moved away from each other, my insecurities came back..."

I stopped and said more wearily, "I am weak, Sush, always looking... always searching for a hand that will guide me through this life and help me carry my cross. I have been honest with you, telling you about my love for Clive, too. He is just like a younger brother to me; nothing happened between us. He is completely straight; you've met him, he loved you."

I have started burbling now. *She can't mean this; she cannot leave me. I have to stop her, but how? What do I do?* I think frantically.

"Arvind, listen to me. Have you heard your own words? You have no morals; in fact, you are *immoral*, and don't give me shit about id and ego and superego. The fact is that you do not have a conscious. You slept with a stranger in a hotel while being married to me. What do you call him? Karl? Were you mad? Then you meet some floozy at my mother's house in New York, flirt with her outrageously in front of me and then the minute you get an opportunity, you jump into her bed back in Mumbai. And what crappy reasoning! You were consoling her because her husband was in bed with another woman?" Her rage intensifies with every word she utters. "What did that have to do with us? Wasn't I enough? I hate you, Arvind. And your so-called brotherly feelings for Clive? You are scum. No, I don't hate you... I feel *sorry* for you. You had a terrible time when you were young, I don't deny it, but find yourself a counsellor who can help you instead of coming up with these outdated Freudian theories. Damn it, I'm a counsellor! You could have talked to *me*. No, okay, I concede you couldn't have talked to me, but I could have referred you to a colleague, Arvind!"

"Don't do this to me, Sush. You are too involved to be dispassionate about this. I have no idea whether I would have been an immoral man if I had not been sexually abused when I was young, or if my father had been different and loved and nurtured me. Somewhere, deep down, I know that I am not immoral. I love deeply and just want love in return. I am not gay, I have never sought out men, and Karl would never have happened if my uncles had left me alone. I have always been pulled towards vulnerable people who have been hurt, like I was by my father, who withheld his love when I was young and defenceless. I extend my love, which quickly becomes physical. You and I had drifted apart when Mridula came to the scene. It happened only once. I never went back to her again. The guilt was killing me. Please stay, Sush. I will change, see a psychiatrist, and meet a counsellor, whatever you say."

Sushmita turns away from me furiously, but there are tears in her eyes.

"No, I need time to think, away from you. I obviously can't ask you to leave this house, as it's given by the company. I haven't seen my father for a long time. I will go and stay with him and then move to a rented house in Delhi."

And that is it. Within a few days, Sushmita left me. We decide we will give each other time and see how the separation goes; divorce is not mentioned. Husna is not to be told anything yet. Sushmita decides to let her father know that we are separating, and I tell her that I will let my father know too, but with minimal detail.

Soon after this, I have to travel to Germany for work. On the way back, I met Clive at Amsterdam airport. He tells me that Clara has agreed to hold off on filing for a divorce and that they have agreed to continue counselling. I tell him everything that has happened with me and Sushmita. He is shocked. At the same time, we also know that our friendship, as we once knew it, is now a thing of the past.

I have only been back in Mumbai for a few days when Rawat calls me from Dehradun. It seems that Dad had fallen in the bathroom and fractured some ribs. Rawat took him to the hospital, and they strapped up his chest, but kept him in hospital for observation as the doctors noticed a large bruise on the side of the head. They had performed some tests and asked Rawat to inform us as they believed his head injury could be serious.

I call the doctor attending to my father; he tells me that he has a concussion, that he has vomited twice and is complaining of double vision and disorientation. He also mentions that Dad is taking blood thinners and that this can cause an acute subdural hematoma. He wants me to come to Dehradun immediately.

I am on the next flight to Delhi. I call Dev and Meena and tell them to try to get to India as quickly as they can. I have a strong premonition that Dad is not going to make it. In Delhi, there is a connecting flight to Dehradun. I call Sushmita, but she does not pick up her phone, so I call her father and tell him what has happened.

Rawat is at the hospital with my father, so I take a taxi. By the time I reach the hospital, my father has fallen into a coma and his kidneys have stopped functioning. The doctor advises that there is not much he can do now; all his bodily functions will slowly cease over the next twenty-four hours. I ask him whether I can take him back home so that he can die in his room, where the windows overlook his beautiful and terraced garden, and the doctor agrees.

My father looks peaceful as the ambulance weaves its way to his cottage in Rajpur. I sit next to him and hold his hand. I whisper loving words to him, and I feel an answering pressure from him. When we get home, I prop him up on his bed, draw open the curtains and let the early afternoon sun stream in. I sit and quietly gaze at him, at his still-handsome face with a shadow of grey stubble and his full head of hair. He lies peacefully, but his breathing is shallow. I don't let go of his hand, fulfilling all those years of needing his strength to pass through to me. I weep and tell him again and again how much I love him. I want him to go peacefully, and I keep repeating, "Go, my father, my loving friend, go. Let's hope that we are reborn together as friends or as brothers so that I can love you freely without any fear."

Slowly, the room fills up with his friends and some of our relatives. I am oblivious. I notice someone has started reading the *shlokas* from the *Bhagavad Gita*, the teachings of Lord Krishna to Arjun on the battlefield of Kurukshetra. The holy words resound through the room and make us ready for the soul to depart from this world, leaving behind the body, which should not be grieved for.

My father breathed his last at about midnight. Most of the people had left by then. The doctor is called to confirm the passing away of my father's spirit, and I step out of the room for the first time, leaving the rest of the requirements to Rawat and his helpers. I walk out to my father's garden, which is alive with the scratching of crickets and the swish of bat wings, familiar sounds from my past. There is a full moon, and I can make out the lights of Mussoorie on the hills in the distance. I sit down on the bench in the garden and let the silence envelop me. After a while, I feel a presence, and I turn to see Sushmita standing next to me.

She sits down on the bench and says, "I left Delhi as soon as I could. No flight was available, so I drove down with my dad; I got here just before Daddy passed away."

With that, she breaks down in tears, and I let her cry. I know she loved my father with a love that was not tainted with a long history of rejection. I held her then, and we both cried in the moonlit darkness. We cry for the loss of my father, for the loss of promises not kept, and for the loss of her trust in me. We hold each other for a long time and cry for the strength that could be found to keep both of us together.

Sushmita and Husna move back to Mumbai as soon as the last rites are over. We know that we have a long way to go to reach the kind of trust and love that we enjoyed when we were first married, but both of us are ready for the long haul. I start going to a counsellor, who encourages me to speak about my childhood. As I remember and recount past traumatic events, it lessens their impact on me. It is as if the sheer recounting takes away the feelings of shame and anger and the terrible anxiety. Clinically, it is found that I have some deep-rooted fears, and the psychiatrist has prescribed anti-anxiety tablets, which help me to come to terms with myself. He promises that after a year, he will slowly wean me off them.

Slowly, we are healing. We haven't made love yet. Sushmita continues to hold back, but I am sure that it is just a matter of time. She is more relaxed, and I have learned to give more of myself, entrusting myself to Sushmita and knowing that ultimately, I will lose myself in her gentle and soft arms again.

I have not heard from Clive for quite some time now.

Then, out of the blue, another bolt strikes and changes our lives forever.

***

Chapter 28
Arvind – 1985

I have taken leave from work for a week. Sushmita is in the kitchen giving instructions for lunch, and Husna is sitting in my lap while I read the story of *Rip Van Winkle* for the hundredth time to her. Rip, meeting his grown-up daughter after sleeping for 20 years, gets Husna as excited as if this is the first time I am reading the story to her. Just then, I hear the doorbell ring; Ramu leaves the kitchen to answer it. He opens the door slightly, and I hear some voices. He then comes back and says that I need to sign for some registered post that has arrived. I am surprised to get a registered post, but go to the door, sign for the envelope, come back and start reading to Husna again.

Sushmita comes out of the kitchen, looks at the post quizzically and disappears again. After I've finished the story with Husna, I casually open the post, pull out a notice from my company's HR department and start reading it. By the time I read the first line, my knees become weak and I feel as if I have been struck in the chest by a bolt of lightning. My heart sinks further as I read the words before me… "…it has been alleged that you engaged in conduct that is inconsistent with our policy against sexual harassment. We are legally mandated to investigate…"

It went on to warn me not to engage in any discussions that could lead to the destruction of evidence. It gave me a date for when I was to present myself to the Internal Control Committee, where I would be allowed to defend myself against the charges attached to the sheet. Even before I looked at them, I knew who was behind them.

A further attachment indicated a temporary suspension order signed by my superior and the head of HR. The order was in force until the outcome of the hearings and all investigations was complete.

My head whirls. The first thing I do is to hide the letter from Sushmita, which, in hindsight, was the stupidest thing to do. The next was the lie that I gave her later. When she asks, I tell her that the letter is just a notice from a disgruntled shareholder of one of the companies, of which I was a director, and since it was also marked to the company secretary, I had destroyed my copy. In the complete chaos of my mind since opening the letter, I haven't stopped to think about how I will explain my absence from work after my week's leave is over. I vaguely assume that I will be able to resolve this issue before that even comes about.

The next thing I do is to call the HR head, Varun Sharma, when Sushmita leaves for the gym.

"Arvind, are you calling me about the notice you must have received today?" He literally barks at me.

"Yes, I just wanted to tell you that the charges are completely untrue and the fact is that Ankur has done this..."

"Stop, just stop. You know I can't talk about this. You will have your say at the hearings, so save your breath for then."

"Listen, Varun," I say in desperation. "I cannot wait till then, I haven't told Sushmita, and you know that things have been difficult between us lately; she has just come back to me and..."

"Arvind, you should have thought of this before you indulged in... whatever the allegations say you did. Once again, I must remind you, I cannot talk to you about this. I'm going to put the phone down..."

"Wait, Varun, please listen! I need some advice, dammit! How do I make sure these lies don't come out? My worry at the moment is just Sushmita, the rest can go to hell."

I am a nervous wreck by now and very close to breaking down.

"Arvind, even if the allegations are not true, I can't understand how you could make such errors of judgment, like approving First Class for him so that you could be together in the compartment... I've already said enough. My advice is you talk to Sushmita and tell her the truth; you owe it to her." And with that, he hung up.

I pick up the phone directory and throw it across the room. Luckily, Husna is with her nanny. I think of that snake, Ankur, and all that happened between us, leading to this.

A year ago, HR sent Ankur to me, a fresher just out of business school, to work with me as my executive assistant. He had a couple of years' experience before he went to business school, so he wasn't totally green. In fact, he was pretty smart, knew his job, and I think I subconsciously favoured him as he was also damn good looking. He was highly ambitious, which was the reason he was sent to me. I had a reputation as a hard taskmaster, but one who did not micromanage, giving executives lots of freedom.

Ankur quickly established himself. We built up a good rapport, and soon, we were spending a substantial amount of time together outside the office. We were also travelling out of Bombay together often, which brought us together in the evenings. I discovered that Ankur was a highly ambitious person, which in itself was a good quality, but what I did not fathom at the time was the extent to which he would go to attain his goals.

Coming back to our relationship, Ankur quickly caught on that I was a little enamoured by his looks and, though he wasn't coquettish, he started taking small liberties with me.One evening, I was entertaining business visitors from Sydney. Usually, Ankur did not join these dinners, but protocol this time required his presence, so I had asked him to come along. It was a wonderful, boisterous evening accompanied by some marvellous food and wine, and we were all in a great frame of mind. At the end of the evening, Ankur was about to call for a taxi to take him to Juhu, but I decided to drop him off, even though it was slightly out of my way. The valet brought my car, Ankur sat next to me in the front seat, and we drove off. On the way, we talked mostly about the Aussies. I hadn't realised it, but during the meal with the guests, I had glanced at Ankur several times because he looked very fetching in a dark blue shirt over denim jeans. So, in the car, as we were nearing his apartment, Ankur asked me why I had eyed him so much during the evening. As he asked me this, he put his hand on my thigh. I blushed and stuttered, but by then we had reached the building where he was staying. Ankur invited me up to the apartment for a nightcap, and he pressed his hand a little harder on my thigh. I looked at his face shining in the light of a nearby lamp, and I placed my hand on his hand. I remember saying that I would love to join him, but that it may not be appropriate, mumbling something like, "I am afraid of where it could lead." I surprised myself by firmly removing his hand from my thigh. After that, I gave him a wave and drove off.

But much worse was to happen some weeks later on an overnight train to Bangalore; we had to take it because no seats were available on the one evening flight. I was booked in first-class AC, while Ankur was in second-class one. He asked me if, as a special case, I would let him travel in first, as it was an overnight journey, and I agreed. I also asked the travel agent to book us together in a 'coupe', a train compartment for an overnight journey that allows only two passengers, one on the upper and the other on the lower berth. Given that there was now a sexual undercurrent in our relationship, travelling together in the same compartment was a recipe for disaster.

I landed at Bombay Central about five minutes before the departure of the train and made it to my compartment with moments to spare. Ankur had got there earlier and was watching the train attendant lay out his bed on the upper berth. We soon settled down, and after the train started, I pulled out a bottle of Chivas Regal from my bag. We had forgotten to buy any soda but settled for the water from the bottles the attendant had left for us. Soon, the conversation veered towards more personal matters.

"Sir, if you don't mind my asking, is everything fine with you and your wife?"

"Ankur, everything is fine. Now, why would you ask me a question like that?" I asked, then added, "Let's talk about you. Do you have a girl hidden away somewhere that we haven't heard of?"

"No. Actually, I've never had a girlfriend," he answered. "My parents might find a girl for me, and I'll marry whoever they choose."

"That's surprising in today's day and age, and considering that you are such a good-looking guy. I met my wife, Sushmita, in business school, and we married despite our parents' objections."

"Thanks, sir, but that's not likely to be the case with me. I am too focused on my job to think about girls. In any case, they don't interest me very much."

"Oh, does that mean you like guys?' I teased.

"Maybe," he replied, looking meaningfully at me. "Not guys really, I could go for older men... they attract me considerably, like you, for example."

His voice became deeper; he ran his tongue over his lips and stared directly at me.

All of a sudden, the whole atmosphere had become heavier, more laden with sexual overtones, and I could feel a stirring in my loins. I looked towards Ankur; he had changed into PJs, and I could see that he was excited. He saw me looking, then moved towards me. He was in my arms, and we started kissing. He quickly took off the top of his pyjama suit, and my lips moved towards his nipples, when he stopped and got up.

"Let me latch the door from inside, we don't want an attendant to walk in on us," he said, his face flushed, and I could see his excited member poking out of the buttons on his pyjamas as he walked towards the door.

In the little time that he had gotten up to latch the door, both Sushmita's and Husna's faces rushed into my mind. And that stopped me. By the time he turned towards the lower berth, I had got up and held out my hand.

"I'm sorry, Ankur. I can't do this. You are attractive, and I am greatly affected by you, but this is not right. I don't know what came over me. I love my wife and this... this..." I stopped saying anything more and put my head in my hands.

After a moment, I heard Ankur climb up to the upper berth.

Sometime after that, I switched off the light and tried to sleep.

I have no choice but to tell all of this to Sushmita, of course, withholding some of the more lurid details. I can't hide from her as to why I am not going into the office. Rumours have also started floating around, and I don't want her to pick anything up on the spouse's grapevine; it would have been humiliating for her.

"That is all that happened, Sushmita. I did not do anything else. These charges are all false. He says that I put my hands on his crotch and was insisting on going up to his apartment that first night, that I was drunk and tried to kiss him in the car. The charges from when we were on the train are much worse. He says I forced myself on him and told him that if he didn't let me get my way with him, it would affect his confidential appraisal."

Not a word came from Sushmita. So I continue, although I know I am getting nowhere and my words sound hollow and false.

"Sush, this happened some nine months back, before you left me; the only reason he is making a complaint now is because I didn't promote him at his appraisal. And it was not I who was seducing him; it was the other way round!"

"Stop it," she replies, her voice icy. "I am not interested in that man... Ankur, whatever his name is. All I want to tell you is that this time our marriage is over. I came back to you only because of Husna; I did not want her to grow up with only one parent like I did. But our marriage... it's a sham; it always was, and I didn't see it all this time. I cannot let your behaviour affect

Husna while she grows up. If it is not one thing, it will be another. These things are not going to stop Arvind. Ever. You are morally corrupt, a satyr, a devil. Don't ask me to feel sorry for you, you bastard. I only feel hatred towards you."

Angrily, she gets up to leave the room. I jump up and hold her arm, but it comes across roughly.

"Oh, now you want to manhandle me, you miserable shit of a man? I am not even sure whether you should be called a man. A freak, I should say, or should I call you a homo? What do you want from me? I am not staying, and that is final. And you will never get to see Husna. No visiting rights, nothing! Try going to court, and I will spill the beans on everything you have told me so far, and it will ruin your case at work. Remember that it was during work time that you had sex with that German. How will your boss like that information?"

I can't believe that Sushmita would go to such extremes.

"I am being framed, can't you see that?" I whisper, my voice cracking. "I haven't hidden anything from you. Once you came back, I vowed to myself that I would never stray from our marriage or look at another man or woman sexually again in my life. All of this happened before you came back to me. Please don't leave me and take Husna away from me. Please don't."

"Stop it, Arvind. I have made up my mind. I came back despite your sordid doings and now this. You need to find yourself, that is clear, but you do that as far away from us as possible."

Sushmita won't budge. She has always held a Green Card. Anjali had sponsored her much before our marriage, so she could easily live in the USA permanently. When we had temporarily separated, she had made an application for Husna, too, and was very sure that she would get the necessary approval.

This is when I start crying. I beg her not to do this to me. I can see my world disappearing in front of my eyes. No family, no friends, no job.

"Who will I live for, Sushmita, if you do this to me? Where will I go? I need your support to fight for my job, my survival, please, please don't leave me..."

***

Epilogue

I am alone now.

A few days ago, Sushmita left with Husna for New York, for a new life far away from me. She allowed me to meet Husna one last time, and I really tried to keep my emotions in check so as not to disturb my little girl. Despite that, Husna sensed there was something wrong, though she believed that they would be back in Bombay after a short holiday with her grandmother.

The hearing at work takes place, and ultimately, it is my word against his. Even if I am cleared of harassment, my truth is known to the committee. Though nothing happened, the intent was there. I suppose they will agree that I never used my position to compromise Ankur, but then I did use it to have him travel in the same compartment with me. My head is reeling with the consequences. I am worried that when the details of the hearing filter out to the rest of the company—which they definitely will—my reputation will be in shreds. Torn and devoured by all in the office, the gossip mongers. Will I ever be able to look anyone in the eye again?

I am shit scared now. All the demons of the past, and so many new ones, are slowly crowding around me, gleefully pushing me against the wall. I feel claustrophobic most of the time. I seem to be waiting for a disaster to strike, one that will obliterate me and pulverise my remains to a mist. My breath stops in my throat, and I choke. Strange sensations seem to be gripping the whole of my being. I have no one left.

In those moments, when I am not beset by anxiety attacks, I think rationally about my life. All I have ever wanted is to be loved, held tightly and made to feel secure. Everything that I ever did was to assuage this hunger in me: *to be loved*. But then there were pitfalls where I tripped a couple of times. I also saved myself a couple of times. I know I could have done better, and I have only myself to blame. Then I strike out at myself. *Drop this self-pity, you sissy*, I say. *You have damaged Sushmita's life and left an innocent girl without a father. What were their crimes? They loved you, but you mislaid your moral compass. Not once, but many times.*

I see no future in the dark and stormy sea that roils all around me. I wonder if I can take the easy way out. I know that Dad had a licensed revolver, which he used to carry with him in his car on his market tours for his safety. It's in Dehradun in his cupboard, which I have so far left untouched.

The thought of Dehradun calms me. *Yes, that is what I should do.* Go away to Dehradun. Live among the hills and the forests, with simple people as my company. Far away from the sharks in Bombay. Far away from my memories of Sushmita and Husna. Yes, that is where I will write my story, where I will draw and paint the boy whose innocence was lost and get all of this out of my system. One day, Husna will read about her father, and I might even get this published. It might help other abused young boys chart a life for themselves in truth and without the deviousness I fell prey to.

After this, I will decide what to do with this miserable life of mine, that is, if I cannot get Sushmita and Husna back. I know! I will go to Anjali in New York and state my case.

***

Part III – Present Day

Chapter 1
Trip to India

Adam and Husna finish the manuscript. Unshed tears glisten in Husna's eyes.

"I don't know what to make of my father," she whispers in a small voice. "First, the horror of his childhood, followed by redemption, the love of a beautiful wife and daughter, and then this terrible fall from grace. I don't feel hate; I feel sorrow for him and for myself. No one really thought of me. I was just condemned to a life without a father."

Adam puts his arm around her, everything within him wanting to salve her pain.

"At that time, your mother did what she thought was right for you," he says, trying to console. "Times have changed; more and more people are facing up to the ambiguities of their sexuality. In the eighties, with AIDS giving homosexuality a bad name everywhere, and in India with its extreme conservatism, same-sex relationships were completely taboo. And then your father cheated too..."

He stops as he can sense that Husna is too overwhelmed with all the information that has spilt out from the manuscript. She needs more time; Adam can see that she is buffeted by her feelings for her mother and her newfound feelings for the father she never knew.

"Tell me, Adam. What do you think Arvind was? Do you think he was bisexual and as promiscuous as he seems?"

"It's impossible to categorise people like that," Adam replies thoughtfully. "Though a larger proportion of the world population is heterosexual, there are, of course, many people who are attracted to those of the same sex. In my limited interactions with bisexual men, I have found that when such an ambiguity exists, one part of their sexuality is more dominant and only fully surfaces after the sexual fires of youth find a steadier rhythm and are no longer a significant controlling aspect in their life. We shouldn't forget that Arvind's childhood experiences would have accentuated this ambiguity dramatically. In any case, this is all so academic. Only Arvind has the answer as to his true nature."

"I don't even know whether he is alive or dead," says Husna. "He should be in his early fifties now, so there is no reason for him not to be living... unless he did something to himself with his dad's revolver?"

"No, he doesn't seem to be the suicidal type. Even during the abuse in his childhood, he kept his head above water and hoped for better times," Adam replies, hoping his words are true.

Husna looks expectantly at Adam, and he knows what she is going to ask.

"Will you come with me to India to look for my father?"

***

Chapter 2
Mumbai

"Ladies and gentlemen, we have just been cleared for landing at Mumbai. Please fasten your seat belts."

The air hostess on the United Airlines flight from O'Hare to Mumbai drones on. Adam shakes Husna awake as he fastens his seatbelt. Finally, after a long twenty-one hours, they are landing in Bombay, now named Mumbai. Husna wakes up, pushes her dishevelled hair back from her face and ties it into a messy knot, smiling weakly. Adam bends down to pick up the magazines that had dropped to the floor while they were napping.

Husna looks back at the past month, spent obtaining tourist visas and getting her affairs in order, mainly settling the legal aspects of her inheritance from her mother and grandmother, a small part of which went towards funding this trip. Adam managed to delay the date he was meant to join the hospital where he is going to intern in their psychiatry department as a counsellor; he has extended it by one month, though they plan to stay in India for about two weeks. Husna has great hopes that she will find her father during that time.

Initially, Adam had argued against what he saw as a foolhardy chase.

"We don't even know your father's name or his surname. Remember, you mentioned that Chatterjee was your mother's family name, and that she took her maiden name after she moved to America? So how do you expect to find someone whose real name is unknown? What about your mother's family? Do you know where they live in India?" Adam had persuasively argued.

"My mother has never known her maternal grandparents," Husna replied wearily. "Where my maternal grandmother is concerned, she was left substantial property by her father, due to which her two brothers went to court against her. She won the case, but her brothers never forgave her and broke away from her. My grandmother's family name was Bhasin, but that's not going to help finding my father."

"Is there anyone else you know? Your mother's father? Anyone in his family?"

"I have met my mother's father, but he died many years ago."

Husna thought for some time, her hands on her chin, then eventually said:

"Dehradun is mentioned in the manuscript. It seems to be the best place to start, but we won't get anywhere without knowing my father's real name." Then she excitedly added, "No, the best place for us to start is Bombay, where I was born. Okay, not literally, but it was my first home! The adoption agency! Remember, the manuscript says it was the Children of God Charity in Bombay. They should be able to trace my adoption and the name of my adoptive father. I will check all the details about the charity on Google, and then call them from here to find out if they are still operating from the same place."

By the next day, they had the address of the orphanage and a phone number, too. After a couple of tries, Husna spoke to Sister Agnes, who was initially hesitant but then agreed to help them once they got to Mumbai.

The plane taxies to the aerobridge, and Husna clutches Adam's hand tightly as they deboard. In the anxiety writ large on her face, Adam can also feel her exhilaration at finally coming back to the country where she was born and engaging in a mission which might reunite her with her father.

The airport is not very large by international standards, and there are short queues at the immigration counters. They learn later that most of the international flights land in India late at night and, with the huge number of flights disgorging tired travellers, immigration clearance can be unbearably slow. They are lucky, however, as their flight landed just before the big rush started; they are out of immigration in twenty minutes. There are customs officers everywhere, looking for contraband, and all passengers' luggage has to go through screening machines. Husna and Adam are carrying only two bags between themselves and move quickly through customs.

The first thing that hits them as they step out of the airport is the heat and humidity. It's the kind that cloyingly sticks to your body, seeping into your clothes, and before you know it, you have sweat running from your armpits down your arms, circling the back of your neck and slipping down your back, soaking your shirt and making it cling to your body. The second thing that hits them is the smell. The salt from the sea, combined with the smell of unwashed, sweating bodies and the metallic smell of gasoline, all mix to assail their senses. The third is the noise and the crowds. There are people everywhere, and the sounds of many vehicles blaring their horns, the calls of taxi drivers and hotel representatives exhorting and inviting, mingle in a cacophony. It is all so overwhelming, but surprisingly, Husna is exuberant and smiling. Adam hadn't seen her so happy in a long time.

"I have come home," is all she says as they sit in a cab, hired at the airport, taking them to the Novotel at Juhu Beach. As the cab speeds down the boulevard out of the airport, they are initially impressed by the trees and the broadness of the road. But soon, it narrows to a single path, and then they see the shanties that line it. Rows and rows of temporary structures covered with blue plastic sheets or aluminium roofs are all stuck to each other or wedged between the steel girders and mirrored glass of shiny, large buildings. These were the homes of millions of Indians who had moved to Mumbai to find jobs or start small businesses. Husna and Adam could only see them in the shadows, as they passed into streets with beautifully-lit, fashionable stores and more glass office buildings climbing up to the sky. Completely overcome by the contrasts, they mutely watch the city go by till they reach their hotel.

The next day, Sister Agnes asks them to come at 3 pm, but in their eagerness, they reach the orphanage a half hour earlier. They step out from the black and yellow cab and walk around the pink building. They do not enter and instead aimlessly wander until five minutes before the meeting. They walk through the gate to find a nun beckoning to them.

"You must be Husna from Chicago," she smiles. "I am Sister Agnes, and I have been talking to you on the phone these last few days." Sister Agnes looks to be in her forties, and her cheeks dimple when she smiles.

Husna has tears in her eyes as she looks up at the building and then blurts out, "Sister, this was my first home, and I am overcome..." Her voice gets choked with emotion as she enters the orphanage. "If it hadn't been for all of you, I wonder where I would be today. Forgive my weakness, Sister."

"And you are?" Sister Agnes says, looking at Adam.

"I'm Adam, a friend of Husna's. I am travelling with her and supporting her in her mission."

"And what is this mission, Husna?" she asks as she leads them into a Spartan room furnished only with a few chairs and a sofa.

"I am looking for my father and—" before she can complete her sentence, Sister Agnes interjects.

"But child, we do not help adoptees to find their biological parents. Apart from the fact that we may not have records, as a rule..."

"No, I am not looking for my biological parents," Husna replies, "I am looking for my foster father who left me and my mother when I was about four. My mother, for reasons that I am not aware of, never told me about him, and now that she is dead, the only place that I believe will help me to locate him is here. I don't even know his name, but I know I was born on the 30th June 1980 and that I was adopted from here when I was around three months old. I am sure you will have records from that time. All I want is his address in Mumbai."

"That is more than twenty-five years ago. Nowadays, we have all our records on a computer, but in those days, we maintained manual registers. Let me look for the register for the year 1980. I'll need some time, so please wait here."

After the sister leaves, Adam and Husna become aware of the sounds of the orphanage. They can hear young voices talking somewhere outside the room where they were sitting, and someone cajoling them to keep their voices down. Further away, they can hear the sounds of babies gurgling, and sometimes, a short cry filters back to them. Somewhere else, *Amazing Grace* is being softly sung. There is peace and harmony in the air, and they silently await Sister Agnes to reappear.

She eventually comes back with a heavy register and places the book on her knees.

"Which day did you say you were born?" she asks, and Husna replies, "30th June."

"Then I should look at the entries in September/October," she says. "Boy," she says as she goes down the register, then, "girl, but six months old...you were about three months old, you said? Boy again, boy again, girl, one year old. Ah, here, girl, three months old, adopted by Mr and Mrs Sudhir Nanda on 25th September 1980. This must be it."

Husna nearly jumps up in excitement, "Yes! It has to be, I am sure of it. Is there an address?"

"I need to check with Mother Superior before I give you the address," says Sister Agnes gently. "I really don't know who you are. Although many of the facts you have given me about yourself have led me to find this particular information. I have to be sure that you are the daughter. We can be in real trouble if we send you to the wrong address."

Husna's heart, which was soaring just a minute before, sinks. She knows she doesn't have a way to prove she is the girl that Mr and Mrs Sudhir Nanda adopted. She looks at Adam helplessly as Sister Agnes leaves the room again.

And then, a miracle! Sister Agnes comes rushing back a little time later.

"I am so sorry, but I missed it. Thank God Mother Superior saw it. Generally, when these entries are made, no name is given to the child, since the parents take them home and name the baby there. But here... look here," she pushes the register at Adam and Husna and points, "the name of the child 'Husna' has been given. They must have named you before they even got you! Hallelujah, thank the Lord," she says, making the sign of the cross. "I wanted to help you, child, and now I can."

With that, she gives them the address—Ocean View Apartments in Bandra—and Husna's face shines with happiness. The first hurdle has been overcome. In the cab heading to Bandra, Adam asks Husna, "How were you so sure that Sudhir Nanda was the one you were looking for?"

"I had heard that name before," she replies, "not once, but twice. When I was around ten years old, I walked into a heated conversation between my grandmother and mother, and I distinctly heard the name Sudhir. The minute they saw me, they fell silent. So, I asked them who Sudhir was. Granny just looked away, but my mother said that he was not anyone of consequence, just someone she knew in college. I asked her why she and Granny were so stressed over him, and she did not answer. Again, when I was around eighteen, the name cropped up in another argument between them. That is why, when that name came up, I was sure he was the person I was looking for."

The cabbie tells them that they are entering Bandra. It seems like a little town within a city, with sidewalk cafes and shops spilling onto the pavements. The streets are hilly, climbing up to apartment buildings or sloping down to the sea. It seems almost like a picturesque Italian seaside town.

When they reach Ocean View Apartments, they are stopped by the security guard, asking who they are there to meet. When they tell him Sudhir Nanda from 501, he immediately replies that they must have the wrong building, as no such person is there. When they insist that they are in the right building, he advises them to see the Society President, Mr Gaitonde, who is the administrative head of the building.

They are shown into a small reception room on the ground floor of the building, where they wait for Mr Gaitonde. Husna starts leafing through some magazines lying around without actually focusing on the pages. Realising that she is nervous, Adam stands behind her chair and presses her shoulders. A diminutive man enters the room and introduces himself as Gaitonde.

"So, what can I do for you?" he asks. "The security office told me that you were looking for someone who doesn't live here. Where are you from?" He looks at Adam, noticing that he is Caucasian.

"We are from America," Adam answers, "We are in Bombay looking for a gentleman who either still lives or used to live here."

"Ah, welcome, welcome! So you are from the United States of America? What a wonderful country... and from which city do you come?"

Husna, who is not at all interested in small talk, looks irritated. Adam, seeing her irritation, answers for her. "We are from Chicago. We really need some..."

"Oh, Chicago! My son lives in Chicago, too. He is a doctor and works in a very big hospital there! Very, very, big..."

"Please, can you help us?" Husna says, cutting him off. "We have come all the way from Chicago to find Mr Sudhir Nanda, and this is the address we have been given. He apparently lives in number 501."

"It can't be 501 as Mr Gandhi stays there and he has been in that flat for a long time," replies Mr Gaitonde. What did you say the name of the gentleman was? 'Sudhir Nanda', you said? Let me think... Do you remember which year it was when he lived here?"

"I know he lived in this apartment from 1980, or even before, and he was still living here in 1985."

"Let's ask Mr Gandhi. He used to work and live in Dubai, and he rented this apartment till he returned to India after his retirement in 1990. I came to live here in 1989, and I know that the owner was Mr Gandhi then. Come, let's go to his apartment. He will know more," Mr Gaitonde says kindly.

In the lift going up to the fifth floor, Husna holds Adam's hand nervously and whispers, "I'm going to the house where I lived the first four years of my life. It's unbelievable, Adam. But I cannot recall anything, this lift, this building, nothing."

"You won't, by the time you are ten years old, people find it difficult to retrieve memories of being a small child. But sometimes, a smell or a traumatic event can trigger something..." Adam says.

Husna is shaking as she steps out of the lift and waits for someone to open the door of 501.

The door leads straight into the living room, which has large windows overlooking the Arabian Sea. Without thinking, Husna walks to the windows and looks out.

"Isn't it so spectacular?" she says, to no one in particular.

Once Mr Gandhi has settled them down with a classic cup of tea (Indians drink tea all through the day), he talks about Sudhir. The room is warm, and a ceiling fan moves air sluggishly. There is an air conditioner, but it isn't switched on.

"Yes, I remember Sudhir very well," Gandhi says. "After I purchased this apartment in 1976, Sudhir and his wife were the first occupants, as I had leased it to his company. They were very good tenants, kept the place perfectly-maintained, and the company was never late with the rent payments, which is a perennial problem in Bombay, sorry Mumbai. It's such a problem to remember that the name of this city has changed, thanks to the Shiv Sena... But coming back to Sudhir, sometime in 1980, they adopted a girl—courageous of them, I wouldn't have done that. I remember this because I had come over from Dubai to meet them, and the house was very festive. That was the day they were bringing the little girl home."

He stops and goes to the large windows of the apartment that look out onto the Arabian Sea. He opens it to let the cool breeze in.

"That's better, we save on electricity this way. Anyway, a few years later, as I recall, Sudhir left the company rather hurriedly, and it cancelled the lease on this apartment. I lost money then, though they paid for the notice period. It takes time to get another good corporate client. You just can't give your apartment to anyone off the street in Mumbai, you know?"

"Do you remember the year in which Sudhir left this apartment?" Adam asks.

"1984 or 1985, I think. More like the middle of '85. I forgot to ask you, but why are you so interested in Sudhir?"

"I was the girl that they welcomed to this apartment the day you came from Dubai," says Husna. "I am his daughter."

"But, but... How can it be? Why are you looking for him? You should be with him!"

"It's a long story, and I wouldn't want to go into it. All I can say is that my mother and I left Bombay in 1985, and after that, we lost touch with my father. I have come to India to find him, and we got this address from the adoption agency."

Mr Gandhi jumps up and says enthusiastically, "I will help in whatever way I can. Now, let me think. I completely lost touch with Sudhir, but I do know that he left Mumbai when he vacated this apartment. His secretary, with whom I corresponded for the rent cheques, told me that. Yes! You should meet his secretary. I don't remember her name, but I am sure I have it somewhere in my files. I will search for it after you leave. I can give you the name of the company he worked for. For that, I don't have to look up my files. It's a famous multinational called International Products of India, and it has its offices in BKC. You could visit them. I am sure they will help you."

Adam and Husna thank Mr Gandhi and Mr Gaitonde for all their help and head back to their hotel. In the car, Husna says, "While Gandhi was talking, an image flashed through my mind. Right near the large windows, I felt I saw a man swinging a little girl on his knees as he lay on the carpet. It must be my imagination going wild, but it seemed so real."

Adam looks at her in astonishment.

Later that day, the helpful Mr Gandhi sends Husna a message with the name of her father's secretary, Monica Barreto. That evening, they decide to go to a famous Indian restaurant at the Taj Lands End, a hotel on the shores of the Arabian Sea.

The hotel lobby is beautiful, and since they are early, they relax at the lobby bar where a pianist is playing some soft music. Husna has heard many of these songs before; they are from old Indian movies. Tears well up in her eyes as she remembers some of them as being her mother's favourite songs. Sitting here in Mumbai, she is missing her mum so much. Luckily, the pianist switches to some more peppy numbers.

The emotions and the jet lag are making Husna despondent and doubtful.

"Do you think I am on a wild goose chase, Adam? I sometimes feel like giving up and heading back, but then finding the manuscript would have no meaning. I am so sorry that I have dragged you into this mess."

"Husna, I am so happy that I came with you. I wouldn't have ever missed this trip. Also, we have just started. I have a feeling that Bombay is our first stop, and we need all the courage and strength to continue this trip based on the clues and signs that we will get as we move forward. Once we reach a stage where we hit a wall, we will re-assess our moves. Until then, should we just keep moving?"

"I love you, Adam. You are the best thing that ever happened to me," replies Husna, smiling at him through her tears. "I think I fell in love with you when you were surreptitiously checking out my key card in the library back home. You looked so guilty, like a little boy caught with his hand in the cookie jar. Later, on the trail, it was so apparent that you were checking whether Feroz and I were sweet on each other. I noticed the disappointment on your face when I pounded Feroz's head. You didn't even wait to see what happened to me; you just ran from the hospital. Feroz and I had such a good laugh at that!"

Adam is overjoyed to see Husna's mood lifting.

"I know that you love me, my darling. It's funny that before I met you, I wasn't ready to commit myself. But the day I met you at the library, I was ready to swear myself to you forever, even though there were daggers in your eyes when you walked away from the table. I can hardly believe that someone like you could want someone like me."

They both laugh happily, gazing into each other's eyes while Adam's hands seek hers across the table.

Later, in the afterglow of their passionate lovemaking, Husna asks, "Do you think my dad loved my mom, or was it all just a sham?"

"What do you think, Husna?" Adam replies and then continues when she doesn't answer, "The love that your dad felt for your mom shines through in the manuscript. Who knows how the human mind works after it has been subjected to the kind of childhood trauma he had? He could have ended up doing drugs or being an abuser himself. But, no, he picked himself up, studied, tried to build his family, though his obsessive hunger for safety and comfort led him to other beds. But who are we to judge him?"

Husna is silent for a moment and then says, "I wonder how I will feel when I meet him. He has been such an obsession for me since my childhood. What will I say? How will I behave? Will I be able to forgive him for leaving us? I have so many questions to ask him."

The next morning, they decide to go for a run on Juhu Beach. It is full of runners or walkers, and the bracing morning air is exhilarating. They run without a care in the world. Both of them had been too long in the icy winds of the Midwest, and this sunny beach warms their happiness. After their run, they sit on the sand and savour the scent of the sea and the sweet morning air.

After breakfast, they leave in a cab for BKC (the Bandra Kurla Complex), Mumbai's financial centre. Husna had found the address of International Products of India on Google. After battling through traffic jams on the way, they are finally standing outside the shining blue building, housing the offices where her father once worked.

"Welcome to IPI! What can I do for you today?" the receptionist pleasantly enquires.

"We are here to see Monica Baretto," Husna replies.

"Oh, I am sorry to disappoint you, but Monica retired about two years back. She was the chairman's secretary when she retired. Do you want an appointment with the chairman?"

"No, we were here to see Monica on a personal matter. Is there some way we can contact her?" asks Husna.

"I knew Monica very well, but once she left office, as usually happens, we lost contact. Let me check with Ameeta, the chairman's current secretary; she may have her phone number or address."

The receptionist talks on the phone for a few seconds. She says that Ameeta has Monica's number, but she'd like to meet them first.

"Can you wait there?" She points to a sofa and chairs in the centre of the lobby. "She will come down once she is free."

After about half an hour, a young woman with a stern look comes up to Adam and Husna and says, "Hi, I am Ameeta. It seems you wanted to contact Monica? Can you let me know what this is about, as we are not allowed to give out the numbers of our employees, current or past, without knowing the reason for the request?"

"I am Husna, and I am looking for the whereabouts of Sudhir Nanda, who worked here many years back. Monica was his secretary then. We are hoping that she could give us his current address."

"Is it fine if I call Monica and explain this, since I haven't heard of Sudhir Nanda?" replies Ameeta.

Without waiting for an answer, she calls Monica on her cell phone and explains the reason for her call. Cupping the phone, she looks at Husna and says, "You say your name is Husna?" Then she speaks into the phone again. "She wants to speak to you," she says, handing the phone to her.

"Hello? This is Husna?"

"Husna? I cannot believe that it is you," Monica's voice comes over the line. "I saw you last when you were a baby. How are your mum and dad? And where do you all live now? I lost touch with your dad a long time back."

Husna's heart sinks.

"I live in Chicago now. I am here with my friend, Adam. My mom died a few months back, and my dad? I haven't seen him since I left India as a child."

"Oh, I am so sorry about your mom. She must have been so young. Was it cancer? I can't believe that you haven't seen your dad since you left India. It just doesn't seem possible. When Nanda Sir left for America, it was to bring you both back."

"No, no," replies Husna sadly, "it wasn't cancer but an accident." Her voice close to breaking as she says, "It is still so fresh, and I am coming to terms with it. Listen,

I am not aware that my father came to America. In fact, I am trying to locate him. Is it possible that we could meet?"

"Yes, we must meet. I was leaving for a family lunch, but I would love it if you came for dinner. It will just be us, my husband, and my niece. Although I have lost touch with your dad, I am sure that I can help you in some way."

"Oh! We would love to join you for dinner," says Husna, smiling.

Husna hangs up after getting the details of Monica's address and gives Ameeta her phone back. She thanks her profusely for her help.

In the cab back to the hotel, Husna tells Adam what Monica said to her on the phone.That evening, they take a cab to Andheri, where Monica lives. Both of them are getting used to cars being driven on the left side of the road. When they had first arrived, they were thoroughly disoriented in the cab that took them to the hotel.

"I am so excited to meet you, Husna," Monica says as she ushers them into her apartment. "And you are Adam? It was unbelievable to get that call this morning. Even in my wildest dreams, I couldn't imagine that I would hear from you. I have so many questions, but let's settle down first. Ah! Here is my husband, Savio. We both are retired and decided to stay put in Mumbai instead of going back to Mapusa, a town where we are from in Goa."

Monica is a petite lady with short hair and a round, cheerful face. She is wearing large, black-rimmed square glasses, which give her a studious look. Savio, her husband, is a slim man, thickening only at the waist, with a shock of grey hair. While Monica is dressed in a navy-blue skirt and a white blouse, Savio is wearing denim jeans with his T-shirt tucked in, which further accentuates his belly. Both are very welcoming, and Husna feels a warm glow as Monica hugs her, as if they had been family or friends for years. Their apartment is small, but the furniture is minimal, and with the curtains pulled back from the windows, there is a feeling of space.

Adam asks for a beer while Husna is offered a glass of white wine; both Savio and Monica have vodka soda. The table is set for five; obviously, their niece will soon be joining them.

Husna starts by telling Monica about their journey to Mumbai, what happened before they left, the discovery of the manuscript and the start of the search for her father. Monica is completely astonished that Husna has not seen her father since the ill-fated day that she and her mother left India.

"But Husna, I find it difficult to get my mind around this," she says. "After Nanda Sir left Mumbai, he initially remained in contact with me. Those were not the days of emails, so I used to send him his mail, like credit card statements, bank statements and any other personal mail. These were sent to his Dehradun address. In fact, we had hoped he would come back to the company... you wouldn't know about this, but some serious charges had been brought against your father by his executive assistant. Later, this person retracted his statement after he realised the impact that it had made on Nanda Sir's personal and professional life. He was very contrite, but was sacked all the same. The president of the company personally called Nanda Sir, but he refused to come back. Later, he called me and said he would never come back to Mumbai; that there were too many memories of Kalpana Ma'am and you. But what I don't understand is that after about nine months or a year after you both had left, he sent his passport to me. There was a problem with his US visa, which had been issued in Mumbai; I sorted it out for him. On the day he was leaving for America, he called me. I still remember his confident words, 'Monica, I am going to bring Kalpana and Husna back. Just you watch.' I don't know what happened after that, as we completely lost touch. I assumed he had returned with both of you and settled down in some other city, because he would definitely have called me if it had been Mumbai. Maybe he is still in Dehradun? Before you go, I will give you his Dehradun address. I know that the telephone that we use to talk on doesn't work, as I had tried to call him a few times on his birthdays..."

It is Husna's turn to look astonished. She turns to Adam and says, "That means he didn't abandon me? He tried to meet us, but for some reason, which only he can tell us, he couldn't. Tell me, Monica, what was my father like?"

"The kindest man that I have ever met," smiles Monica. "He was very handsome—all the girls in the typing pool wanted to be his secretary. I was thrilled when he chose me. He seldom lost his temper; he would arrive smiling every morning, and our moods would lift when we saw him. He used to joke a lot with all the secretaries. And he was very good at his work. I was so disappointed when he left us."

Then she picks up an album lying on the table between them and says, "Look what I have kept aside for you. This is the album of my sister's wedding in Goa, which your father attended."

Husna is completely overwhelmed. She clutches Adam's hands as they sit together on the sofa, and he can feel her shivering. She is going to see the man who has evaded her for so long, who has been kept away from her. Monica stands up and sits between the two of them, then opens the album.

The initial photographs are focused on the wedding ceremony, and as the pages flick by, Monica makes comments like, "Isn't she looking beautiful? That bridesmaid is my daughter..." and so forth. Finally, the photographs move on to the reception.

"I recall now! Nanda Sir could attend only the reception. Ah! Here he is."

Husna and Adam both look at the handsome man she points to. Sudhir is nattily dressed in a dark suit and is standing with the bride and bridegroom. The next photograph of him is more candid; the person next to him must have said something funny, and he is laughing gleefully. Then there is a close-up of him smiling into the camera. He looks so guileless. His smile reaches up to his eyes. It is such a happy face.

Husna asks, "How come my mother is not in any of the pictures?"

"If I recall," says Monica slowly, "it's been a long time now... Ah, yes! I think at the last moment you fell sick, so Kalpana Ma'am stayed back and Nanda Sir came alone."

There is another photograph where Sudhir has his arm over the shoulder of a foreigner, and they are both happily laughing into the camera. There is an amazing sense of togetherness between them.

"Who is this person?" Husna asks, immediately perturbed.

"Oh, that is Brian. He worked with the company in Australia and happened to be in Mumbai at the time, so

Nanda Sir brought him to the wedding. He and Nanda Sir were thick as thieves, as you can see."

"That must be Clive!" Husna whispers to Adam.

As they continue looking at the photographs, a young woman walks in.

"And here is the progeny of that wedding," says Monica with a big smile, "my niece, Tina."

Tina is a journalist working for a financial daily and is very passionate about India and its current progress. She regales them with her thoughts on India's economic reforms and growth; she is clearly proud of the direction the country is taking.

"It must be very exciting for a young person like you to be in the middle of such progress," Adam says.

Savio, who has been quiet all this time, pipes up, "Well, I have missed the bus, retiring before all this progress, but I am satisfied with what we have. Our children are well settled; our daughter and her family live in Toronto, and our son, though still a bachelor, is well settled in Lisbon."

Monica has laid a fantastic table for dinner, laden with exotic dishes like chicken cafreal and pork vindaloo, both of Portuguese origin, as well as a fiery Goan fish curry, fragrant and flavourful and eaten with thick brown rice.

"Goan food must be very different from the Indian fare that you get in America?" says Monica, then adds, "So, what are your plans now, Husna? I will give you Nanda Sir's address in Dehradun, but it is such a small town, and I don't see him still living there. There is no major industry in Dehradun, unless he started his own consultancy out there."

"Monica, when we came to India, I didn't even know my father's name. Since we have been here, we have made considerable progress: I know his name, I have seen him in your photographs, and I know that the last place he was confirmed to be was Dehradun. We could have gone to Dehradun in the first place, but I needed his name, which I somehow felt I would get to know from the orphanage. I haven't talked to Adam yet, but if he agrees," Husna glances at Adam, "we will go to Dehradun. Even if we don't find him there, we may be able to get further clues about where he is now. I just can't give up now."

"I have the phone number of the taxi service that Nanda Sir used to go to Dehradun," Monica tells her. "Let me call the owner and fix a driver and car to take you to Dehradun once you decide to leave Mumbai."

On the way back to the hotel, Husna seems tired. The excitement of seeing her father's photographs, coupled with the heat and jet lag, has taken its toll. Adam puts his arms around her and thinks of how their lives have changed over the last two months. From worrying about graduation and setting out in their respective careers, they have moved in a completely different direction, travelling to the other side of the globe on a convoluted quest to find her father.

Just before they fall asleep, Husna turns to Adam.

"The photograph of my dad with Brian, who I assume is Clive from the manuscript, seems to be imprinted in my mind. They looked so comfortable with each other, both of them so handsome and seemingly without a care in the world. My dad definitely did not look as if he was missing my mom at the wedding!"

***

Chapter 3
Dehradun

"I have driven Sudhir *sahib* many times to Dehradun, and I know the way to his house," says Prem, the driver. "It has been many years since I dropped him off at the airport in Delhi, after which I haven't met him again. This was nearly twenty years back. He was a very good person, always giving me extra money for my son. My son is now working in a good computer company, but at that time he was in school, and Sudhir *sahib* always asked about his studies whenever I drove him inside Delhi or to Dehradun."

It is a glorious day, and they are on the highway, driving to Dehradun. Monica, as promised, has made sure that the driver is the one Husna's father used for his trips to Dehradun. Prem is in his mid-fifties and still working with the same taxi service. Husna and Adam arrived from Mumbai that morning, and Prem was waiting to pick them up and drive them straight to Dehradun. While they know the chances of Husna's father being in Dehradun are minimal, it is the only place left where they can find out more about his whereabouts.

The highway is crowded, and Prem tells them this is usual at this hour. Around thirty kilometres out of Delhi, Prem swings the car off the highway and enters a narrower road that has a canal running parallel to it.

"Prem, is there a particular reason for this detour?" Adam asks.

"Don't worry, *sahib*. Even Sudhir *sahib* liked this road. There is very little traffic, and it takes much less time than the main highway, and you will also get to see how the farmers live in Indian villages," he says with a smile. "One does not take this route at night because of poor lighting, but during the day it's fine and safe. We call it the canal road, and after some hundred kilometres, we will meet the highway again and then take another canal road for another forty kilometres, after which we will be back on the highway, which gets us into Dehradun."

Sure enough, the road had very little traffic; it is dustier, but with the car windows closed and the air conditioner running, they are fine. The sun glints on the waters of the canal, scattering shining pearls on the surface. With the brown bulrushes poking out of the luscious green grass and pink heather growing alongside the road, the landscape is rustic and colourful. Occasionally, a tractor laden with sugarcane passes them. Prem explains that sugarcane is the main crop that is grown in the farmlands dotting either side of the road.

Once they get used to the rougher road surface, they start enjoying the picturesque journey. They pass many small villages. As their car passes, a group of young children run alongside and wave at them happily. They pass white-haired men sitting around a hookah sharing the smoke, and women sitting outside the doors of their huts gossiping away. Strange pancake-shaped mounds are sitting on the parapets lining the road, or are plastered on the walls of the small thatched dwellings, which Prem tells them are made from cattle manure for use as a substitute for firewood. The tranquil atmosphere is occasionally broken by the *phut-phut* of motorcycle-rickshaws, overloaded with villagers who stare curiously into their car. Husna dozes off to sleep from time to time, but Adam stays awake most of the time, fascinated by this country, which is made up of so many happy people, such vivid colours and such a cacophony.

As they near Dehradun, they enter a hilly region and are soon climbing a winding road that runs alongside a wide, dry riverbed. Prem explains to them that they are entering the forested area of Mohand, the national park and tiger reserve encompassing the Shivalik Hills, which lie in the foothills of the Himalayas. He opens the car windows, and a cool breeze smelling of pine fills the car; the fresh air is a tonic after the hours of conditioned air they had been breathing for the last few hours. This perks them up, and they decide that instead of going to the hotel where they are staying first, they will go straight to the house on Rajpur Road.

Dehradun is like any other place they passed by on the drive, except that, as soon as they hit the main road cutting through the town named Rajpur Road, they can see in the distance thousands and thousands of lights illuminating the sky. It is early evening, and the streets are crowded, but nothing can take away from the awesome scene in front of them. It is as if a shawl with twinkling diamonds has been thrown onto the hills to the north of Dehradun.

"That is Mussoorie, a small hill station just twenty kilometres away from Dehradun," says Prem, seeing their interest. "This was the place where the English would come from Delhi and the surrounding plains during the hot summers when India was under British rule. It is called the Queen of the Hills. I can take you there tomorrow if you want."

"We will see, Prem. First, let us go to Sudhir *sahib's* house, please?"

The road continues to climb from the centre of the town, and then they take a diversion off the main road, from where they can see the lights of Mussoorie on their right. Soon after, they leave this road and follow a narrower one, which passes tiny villages with their own corner teashops and grocery stores. After several turns on the winding road, the cab stops outside the gates of a bungalow covered with ivy.

"This is the house, madam," Prem says to Husna.

The gate has a sign that reads 'Beware of Dogs', so they start looking around for a call bell, but nothing is in sight. Prem pulls the gate. They could unlatch it, but hold back due to fear of the dogs; they stand there, wondering what to do.

"There is no one at home except the servant, and most probably he's taken the dogs for a walk. Are you looking for Rakesh?" a voice from behind takes them unawares.

They look around for the source of the voice and see a sprightly old ruddy-faced gentleman, wearing a tracksuit and holding a walking stick. He puts his hands on the walking stick and looks curiously at them.

"No, we are looking for Sudhir Nanda," says Husna. "He lived here once, but we are not sure if he still does?"

"Oh, Sudhir? He sold this house many years ago to Rakesh Vashist, who lives here with his family now. They have gone to Mussoorie for a few days and are expected to come back tomorrow morning."

"Did you know Sudhir?" Husna asks hopefully.

"No, I never knew him too well, but then nobody really knew him," sighed the old man. "It has been a long time, but I built that bungalow," he says as he points to a house a little further down the street. "When Sudhir's parents moved in. I knew them very well, but after their death, when Sudhir came to live here, he kept to himself most of the time. Apart from cursory greetings, we never spent any time together, unusual for this community. And who are you?"

"My mother is Sudhir's relative," replies Husna, knowing it sounds false and that the old man doesn't believe a word of it. "We were in India and thought of looking him up. Seems stupid though, that my mom didn't know he had moved away from here. Is there anyone here who might know where he is now?"

"Rakesh should know, as he bought the place from Sudhir. If I remember correctly, Rakesh mentioned to me that Sudhir had migrated abroad. Australia or New Zealand, I think. But Rakesh will be back tomorrow. Why don't you call on him tomorrow around noon? He normally returns from Mussoorie in the morning; it's just an hour and a half away from here."

Adam sees the shock on Husna's face when she hears the word 'migrated'. After thanking the old man, he quickly bundles her into the car, and they drive to the hotel.

"I can't take this anymore, Adam," she says in despair. "Where am I going to look for him? I can't think of chasing him to Australia or New Zealand. Let's go back, this just isn't working out." Seeing Husna so upset, Adam holds her close to calm her.

"Let's wait till tomorrow. Things will look a little different after a full night's sleep. We have been travelling all day, and we woke up at an unearthly hour in Mumbai."

Later, after a shower, they sit in the garden of the hotel drinking a beer while waiting for their dinner to be served. Husna looks at the lights shining on the Mussoorie Hills and says:

"Someday, I would love to come to Dehradun again and go up those hills, maybe like my father did, trekking all the way. At night, it looks like a fairyland high up in the sky, beckoning us to mysterious adventures. It really is startlingly beautiful, isn't it? Prem was telling me that both Dehradun and Mussoorie have many haunted houses. I love ghost stories!"

The next day, promptly at noon, they returned to the bungalow on Rajpur Road. Luckily, there is now a security guard at the gate who takes them into the house. As they enter, two golden retrievers come barking towards them with their tails wagging excitedly. They are extremely friendly and wouldn't have scared a cat, let alone strangers coming into the house for the first time. A middle-aged man is sitting in a chair on the lawn, and he invites Adam and Husna to join him for tea, which is steaming in a teapot next to him.

"I am Rakesh," he smiles. "I was expecting you. My neighbour, Mr Hoon, mentioned that he met you outside our house yesterday evening. Ah! Here is my wife, Nirmala, and my son, Nikhil. He studies in London and is here on his holidays. My daughter is around the house somewhere," he says, gesturing vaguely.

Nirmala is a slim woman who hardly reaches the shoulder of her son, who is a tall and well-built young man. They both join Adam and Husna at the table, and Nirmala starts pouring tea for everyone.

"It seems you came looking for Mr Nanda, from whom I bought this house more than twenty years back? I am surprised to know you were not aware that he had left Dehradun so many years back."

Husna looks at Adam, and he can see that she has decided to tell these people the truth. Over the next half an hour, she tells them the whole story and how they finally came looking for her father.

As had been Mr Gandhi's reaction in Mumbai, Mr Vashist is enthusiastic and eager to help them in any way he can. Adam is realising that Indians seem to be the most helpful people in the world.

"I met Mr Nanda when he had completed all the formalities to migrate to Sydney, where he was planning to settle down. At that time, he didn't know where he was going to live, so he gave us the address of his trusted servant... I think his name was Negi."

Then Nirmala speaks up, "No, his name was Rawat."

"Oh, yes, Rawat. In fact, he had many years of work left in him, and we wanted him to work for us, but he wasn't inclined to work for anyone else but the Nandas. So, your father gave him some money to set up a store in Kanatal, near a place in the Tehri Garhwal, up in the mountains. Most of the cooks in Dehradun and the surrounding areas come from villages located there. Before leaving, your dad gave us Rawat's father's address so that any mail coming for Mr Nanda could be sent to him. I don't even know whether I will have the address now, but Kanatal is a small place. I am sure you could find him if you go there."

"Dad, Rawat is such a common name in Tehri Garhwal; there is no way that they will find him without even knowing what he looks like. You surely must still have the address; knowing how organised you are, you would have filed it in the file containing the original documents of the house. Here, let me go and look for it," says Nikhil helpfully, and he goes into the house while Adam and Husna talk about their experiences in India since they arrived.

"Until yesterday, we could only see lights in the hills above your house, but now we can see the mountains and forests surrounding it. It is so peaceful…" Husna is saying dreamily.

"Here, I have found it!" comes an excited shout from Nikhil, who is carrying a dog-eared file. "And not just the file, I have found Rawat's address."

Excited, they all surround Nikhil, who pulls out the address:

Shyam Rawat,

c/o Basant Rawat

Main Chamba Mussoorie Road

Village Chaukhal

Kanatal 249145

Husna's face is suffused with hope. Looking at her, Adam knows that yesterday's sagging spirits are a thing of the past, and she is ready to continue the search. In the meantime, Rakesh has called Prem from outside the house and, after showing him the address, asks him how much time it will take to drive them there.

"Not more than four hours if I go through Dhanolti, and you can stay at the hermitage, which is on the main road and has a wonderful view of the surrounding hills," he replies.

After checking out of the hotel in Dehradun, they are soon on their way. Prem rushes so that they can be in Kanatal before five in the evening, as the night falls faster in the hills, and it is not safe to take the steep climb later than that.

As they get closer to Mussoorie, misty clouds affectionately play among the hilltops. Soon, they are inside the clouds, and the further they climb, the more the clouds start thinning. Prem diverts and heads towards

Dhanolti. Here, the climb is steeper, and below them, for miles and miles, are vertiginous drops to the undulating hills and valleys. Everywhere they look, birch and spruce trees are blanketing the hills that surround the winding road. The panorama is stupendous, and at times, heart-stopping. By the time they are about thirty miles away from Kanatal, dusk is upon them. It is so surprising how quickly the eerie twilight enshrouds them; just a few minutes earlier, it was daylight. The multi-faceted sounds of nocturnal insects and animals set up their orchestra, and the whole atmosphere changes. They are grateful and happy to reach the hermitage, whose lighted windows are warm and welcoming. They check in and are shown into a wood-panelled room. After a quick snack from room service, they are fast asleep.

The sun shines through the windows, even though it is very early in the morning, and Adam sees he is alone in bed. Pulling his tracks on, he looks for Husna and finds her sitting, sipping hot tea in the lounge. She looks serene and happy as she gazes out of the large windows into a small garden. He kisses her neck quietly, not wanting to disturb the peace of the moment, then sits next to her.

"Somehow, I am sure that this is where we will find all the answers after this long journey we've been on. I am so sure that once we find Rawat, we will know how to find my father," she says confidently.

"You do realise that your father is most probably in Australia?" Adam replies, playing devil's advocate, "and we may or may not need a visa if we want to go there to look for him, that is, if we get his address from Rawat."

"We don't need a visa, just an ETA, which we can apply for electronically and receive by email. I did my homework the minute I heard that Dad could be in Australia. Once we are back in Mumbai, we can apply for it, and then we need to wait for a couple of days to receive it. I know that you are not going to abandon me now, my darling?" She looks pleadingly at him when she says this.

"Never. I am with you wherever you go, now and forever," Adam says dramatically. "Come on, let's get ready and look for Rawat in his village."

They are told by the reception desk that Chaukhal village is within walking distance, and after taking directions, they begin.

"Remember to be back in time this evening. We have a bonfire for our guests with a special dinner!" the manager of the hotel calls out as they pass by his desk.

After some time, they leave the main road and move onto a bridle path leading down towards the village. The hills around are terraced with luscious green plants.

"They grow potatoes all the year round in the hills; it is their staple food," Prem explains as he is walking with them.

They enter the village, which is really a small hamlet made up of tiny one and two-roomed huts with thatched or tiled roofs, some of them precariously clinging to the rock faces of the hills. The houses are dotted all over the place, and as they walk into the village, little children with fierce-looking hill dogs have surrounded them. Prem speaks to them in Hindi and asks for the house of Shyam Rawat. One of the boys, with a sweet-looking girl, comes forward and tells Prem he will take them to his grandfather's house, who is called Shyam Rawat.

Shyam Rawat's house is bigger than most of the others. The little girl holds Husna's hand and whispers in Hindi that her name is Geeta and she studies in class four. The boy's name is Ajay; he proudly says he is in class eight, and that he doesn't want his sister hanging around him, but she just won't listen. Ajay says that they have the biggest house in the village, as their grandfather is the Headman.

"We have four rooms and a veranda in the house, and although I don't like it, I have to share my room with my dad while my sister sleeps in another room with my mother, and the biggest room is for my grandfather," he prattles on in Hindi.

The children's mother welcomes and seats them on rattan chairs, pulled from inside, before saying she will call her father-in-law. Rawat turns out to be a wizened old man who has some difficulty moving around. He later tells them that he is sixty years old, but years of smoking hookah and his rough life have aged him faster. He sits on a charpoy, which is already waiting for him with the inevitable hookah at its side.

Prem explains to him that they were looking for Sudhir Nanda. The minute Rawat hears that name, his face perks up and his eyes shine happily. Prem goes on to tell him that they are hoping he can help them find him.

"*Baba* has gone across many oceans to a land far, far away, and I miss him like I miss his father and mother," he says in Hindi, which Prem translates for Husna and Adam. "Sometimes he sends money to my bank account, but I don't have his address or phone number. In the beginning, I did send him his letters from our post office here, and I used the address he sent me... That was many, many years ago. I may have saved a letter as a keepsake."

With that, he sends his young grandson to get a box from his cupboard where he keeps his precious things. Obviously, the box is well-known and the boy quickly comes out with it. Rawat pulls out a key hanging from a chain around his neck and opens the box. It is full of various keepsakes: a locket and a ring, which he tells belonged to his dead wife, a photograph of Sudhir and his siblings with Rawat, and another one of Sudhir's parents with Rawat. Beneath the memorabilia is a letter that he pushes towards Husna. It is written in Hindi, but right on top is a partially legible address; they can make out the name of Brian Murphy, Cove Apartments, The Rocks, Sydney; the street name isn't readable anymore. Husna is startled when she reads the name Brian, the same person her father was with at the wedding of Monica's sister. Obviously, Sudhir connected with Brian once again in Australia.

By then, hot glasses of tea had been placed in their hands, and Rawat continues reminiscing in Hindi, with Prem translating,

"I joined Nanda *sahib w*hen I was fifteen years old; I couldn't study beyond eighth class, so my parents sent me to my uncle in Delhi, who got me the job. Who would have thought at the time that I would keep on working for them for so many years? *Baba* (Sudhir) was just five years old, Baby (Meena) was just a little older, and *Chota* Baba (Dev) was a toddler. *Bade sahib* (Manmohan) was always angry with everyone, but *memsahib* was a goddess. She treated me like a son, and whenever I was sick, she looked after me like a mother. I cried so much when she went to God. But I loved *Baba* the most; he was such a quiet boy, very kind to me, and he called me big brother. He was very scared of *Bade sahib*, and often when I was making the beds, I saw him run and hide under his bed when *Bade sahib* used to come home.

"When he left for college, I really missed him. He used to give me his colognes, saying, 'You will smell very nice, Shyam *Bhaiya*,' teasing me about my wife. Later, he came with his *Bibi* when *memsahib* died, and she was also very kind to me. They had a little daughter, but I never met her. Then, after *Bade sahib* died, *Baba* came alone to Dehradun and lived in the house for a year. Then he went away to America, saying he would bring back the *Choti memsahib* and the baby, but when he came back, they were not with him.

"After that, he became very quiet, and I used to see him crying. Later, when he became better and started joking with me again, he left for another country, far, far away. He told me that he will cross many oceans to get there. He never came back, but gave me money to start a store, which is now run by my son. *Baba* used to keep sending me money, and that really helped me. You know, I named this little girl Geeta because *Baba* used to read the *Bhagavad Gita* and told me to name my granddaughter Geeta."

As he spoke, tears welled up in his eyes now and then; he wiped them away with his gnarled hands.

When they get up to leave after writing down the address, Husna holds his hands and helps him get up, then hugs him tightly. It is funny that Rawat never asked them who they were; he just trusted them and somehow knew they were family.

Husna has unshed tears in her eyes as the three of them take leave of Rawat and his family. Husna hugs his daughter-in-law and Geeta, while Ajay stands diffidently to one side.

They could have left that day, but they decided to stay another night. The highly emotional, though fulfilling day, was magical. The air in this place is exhilarating, seeming to reflect the harmony inside them both. For the first time since Husna came to India, she feels at peace.

That night, they stepped out to join the other guests around the bonfire arranged by the hotel. All the guests are sitting around the fire, their faces glowing in the flame's blaze. The wood crackles, throwing showers of sparks into the air, and the whole atmosphere is cheerful and friendly. The hotel has set up an outdoor bar for drinks. Adam and Husna order a vodka and tonic. There is a sprinkling of foreigners: a couple of Germans, some Americans and a few Israelis, young with crew cuts, who tell them that after completing compulsory military service, many of them come to India's hills, where the supply of cannabis is plentiful. Soon, two of the foreigners start strumming on their guitars. Many of the guests begin making requests for their favourite songs, and they happily oblige.

The heat from the flames increases, so Adam and Husna move further away from the bonfire, from where they can see the whole scene spread out in front of them. It is all so beautiful: the glass windows of the hotel reflecting the flames, the happy faces and the sounds of the guitar resonating in the air, the lyrics of an emotional song touching their hearts. Husna's head is on Adam's shoulder, and she whispers:

"This reminds me of the magic of that evening in Goa when my father proposed to my mother. Then, too, it was so romantic," and then she sighs.

Adam lifts her chin to look her straight in the face and says, "I have been waiting for you to find your father before I ask you. But I cannot wait any longer. Will you marry me, my love?"

There is so much love in Husna's face when she says, "Yes, I will. I have been waiting so long for you to ask me. A few more days, and I would have asked you myself!"

The next day, they leave Kanatal and drive straight to Delhi. Prem has been their saviour, and it is with a heavy heart that they bid him goodbye at the airport. They promise him that they will come back to visit Mussoorie for a few days, and that *he* will take them there. Prem struggles to keep his emotions in check as he bids them goodbye.

When they arrive in Mumbai, they check into the same hotel, and the first thing that Adam does is to find a jeweller to buy a solitaire engagement ring for Husna. They call Adam's mother and give her the good news. The three of them agree that once they are back in Chicago, they will have the wedding as quickly as possible.

Husna goes online and applies for the ETA to Australia. In the meantime, they book Singapore Airlines for a flight to Sydney, which has a stopover in Singapore. The ETA soon arrives, and without much ado, they are on the flight that will hopefully be the final stop in their search.

***

Chapter 4
Sydney

As the flight comes in for landing, they can see the Sydney Harbour Bridge and, nestling next to it, is the gleaming white seashell, lit up from below—the Sydney Opera House. The beautiful scene reflected in the water makes an exquisite introduction to Australia. Adam and Husna's euphoria is soon rudely shaken by the high-handedness of the customs officers. They insist on searching Husna's bags, and on finding a wooden artefact that she had picked up in Mumbai, the customs officer goes ballistic.

"You want your mate's house eaten up by mites taking this into their house?" he shouts, wagging his finger under her chin. His Aussie accent is so strong that Husna barely makes out what he is saying.

"But this is varnished, so how can there be mites?" she asks.

"I should charge you for not declaring this item," he goes on, ignoring her.

Finally, they convince the officer that the artefact will not damage their friend's house. Arguing with authority is nerve-racking, they decide. It is late evening by the time they leave the airport and head for the serviced apartment in The Rocks, which Husna booked based on some good reviews online.

It is November, and the weather is balmy. There is a pleasant smell of the sea in the breeze blowing outside their cab, driven by a student from India. Guessing that

Husna is also Indian, he gets chatting about his hometown (Delhi) and the studies he is pursuing in Australia.

"Though I miss Delhi, I love this city and its friendly people," he says, adding, "though the people from Melbourne are far more snobbish."

Very early the next morning, they arrive at Brian Murphy's apartment on Harrington Street. The concierge calls up to the apartment, and they are allowed up. They are met by a young man at the door, who says cheerily:

"G'day! I just finished brekkie and was leaving for work, but how can I help you?" His voice has a gentle twang and is quite pleasing to listen to.

"We are looking for Brian. Doesn't he live here?" Husna asks.

"No, he doesn't. He lived here many years ago, but now he's rented out this apartment to me. He lives out at Mittagong, in the countryside. He's been there for a long time now."

"Wonderful!" Adam says, "Can you give us his address or his phone so that we can call him?"

"Sure, I'll call him. Does he know you?" the guy asks a little warily.

"No, but we need to talk to him about a friend of his," Husna says.

"Well, alright! Let me call him. You can talk to him, and if it's fine with him, I'll give you his address in Mittagong."

With that, he pulls out his phone and punches in a number. After a few moments, he hangs up and says, "Sorry, I think there is something wrong with the line. I keep getting a message saying the call cannot be connected. Listen, I am late for work, so I'll call again later and tell him I have given his address to you. What's your name again?"

They leave the apartment with the address and Brian's phone number in their pocket. After renting a car with a GPS, they are on the road to Mittagong. Initially, Adam feels awkward driving on the left side of the road, unlike in America. It takes him a little time to get acclimatised, but soon he can focus on the GPS voice. They reach the outskirts of Sydney.

Husna, sitting next to him, is quiet and lost in her thoughts. Adam puts some music on. It streams from the local radio station, but after some time, Husna bends forward and switches it off.

"Adam, do you think that I will finally get to know what happened to my father? It seems so surprising that he left India to come to Australia. He could have gone to America. All his family is there. Was it to be with Brian? There is more than just a friendship there, I'm sure. To me, it seems things are slowly falling into place. My mother was right not to trust him. I wonder how I will finally feel about him and Brian, once I finally meet him."

"Love, I am sure that we are coming to the end of our search and that Brian will know where your father is. I agree that there seems to be a deep friendship between them. You could see it in the photograph, but let's not jump to hasty conclusions."

"Ah!" she sighs. "Now that my wish of meeting my father is going to be fulfilled, I am beset by doubts. Will I hate him? What do I say to him? Will I sit there and judge him, his choices, and the fact that he deserted my mother? That he deserted *me*? I feel overwrought with all these questions. On one side, I have warm feelings for him after listening to those who knew and praised him, yet I see him as the sole cause of my family breaking up."

"You know quite well, Husna, that he didn't desert you and your mom. Okay, she had very good reasons for leaving him, but his story in the manuscript has made him more human. He is a person with as many foibles as the rest of us. Just as you and your nature were shaped by the fact that your father was not in your life when you needed him, his life was shaped by the terrible abuse he faced and the love he craved from his father. So let's not judge him. Go with the flow, my darling, be honest about your feelings after we meet him, and let him know how you feel. Don't hold back."

As they enter the streets of Mittagong, the craggy scenery of the highway is replaced with a lush landscape of trees and flowering bushes of startling colours. With the GPS guiding them, they pass through beautiful parks and lakes. The centre of the town has several charming small shops, open-air cafes and restaurants. Husna doesn't see all this. She is coiled up like a corkscrew and finds it difficult to hold on to her trembling emotions. Soon, they leave the town behind and turn onto a solitary road deep in a dense wood.

They can see homes with tiled roofs and large windows on both sides of the road. Most of the houses have long driveways through the lawns and immaculate gardens. The road they are travelling on soon curves into another, which traces the edge of a lake on one side. In the distance, they catch sight of a large English-style country house. As they come closer, they see the house nestled between manicured hedges with lawns flowing on either side of the driveway, and they can smell cut grass. A little further on, in the same compound, there is a picturesque cottage surrounded by daisies, white lilies, bottlebrushes with roses trailing on the trellis and climbing towards the roof. As they come to the gate, which is open and inviting, they see a nameplate with 'Brian Murphy' written on it and, above that, another board which says *M&N Consultants Pty Ltd.* The driveway ends at the main door.

Adam parks, and Husna is out of the car in a trice, like an uncoiled spring, and heads straight for the doorbell. She hears the tinkling of the bell inside, and then the door opens. Husna is stunned. Her father is standing there, easily recognisable from the pictures. Even after over twenty years, he looks as debonair as in the photographs, except his hair has turned grey at the temples and his face has lines around the eyes and the mouth.

Husna gasps. She hadn't expected to see her father in this house, and she couldn't believe her eyes. Before she can say anything, her father speaks.

"Husna? Is that you?" he says, "John just managed to get through to us, and I couldn't believe it when he said that a young woman called Husna was coming here to meet Brian..." Then he stops and looks at her in disbelief as she is actually in front of him. "Husna, my baby, my darling daughter." He moves forward to put his arms around her.

"No," she says, putting both her hands up to resist. "No."

Husna looks angrily at him but doesn't say another word.

"Hi, I am Adam, Husna's fiancé," Adam breaks the silence.

Just behind Sudhir, Brian looks at the scene in front of him. He is tanned and broad-shouldered, as handsome as he was in his photograph, with an infectious smile.

"I'm Brian. Come on in, let's sit down. I can see that the shock of seeing Sudhir has shaken Husna. Let me get you some water."

Sudhir stares at Husna and says, "You have grown so beautiful, just like your mother. Thank god, Kalpana finally told you about me. How is she?"

"She's dead. All because of people like you!" Husna says, her voice vehement and cold.

Sudhir looks as if he has been slapped. His face drains of colour.

"What... *what*? You cannot be serious! Oh, my Kalpana!" he cries, burying his head in his hands.

"Killed in a road accident by two homosexuals who couldn't keep their hands off each other even when driving. They killed my grandmother, too." Husna's voice breaks with anger and pain.

"What? Urvashi is also dead? Oh, my baby, this must be so terrible for you."

Once again, Sudhir makes a move to come to Husna, but she raises her hands again to push him away. It is then that the news that Husna has given Sudhir really hits him.

"Oh, no, no, it cannot be! I will never see Kalpana again. Oh, forgive me, Kalpana, please," he cries, and they can see his body shaking with sobs.

Sudhir eventually gets up and says, "Please give me some time, I need to be alone."

He makes to leave the room. Brian, who has placed small bottles of water in front of everyone, goes to him but is brushed away.

"Brian, give me some time. I need to be alone," Sudhir says and leaves the room.

"I am sorry, Husna and Adam. Sudhir has been hoping against hope for all these years that there will come a time when he will be with you and Kalpana again."

Husna got up and spoke, "Do you mind if Adam and I leave now? I didn't expect to see my father here, and the shock has greatly upset me. I am not in any frame of mind to continue sitting here. We'll go to the café in town and get something to eat. Hopefully, by the time we return, my father will be able to talk to me."

Brian seems perplexed, but without another word, lets them go. Adam can see him in the rear-view mirror of the car, standing on the porch, as they drive off. He stands there till Adam can't see him anymore. Adam knows that Husna will say something soon, so he lets the silence stretch till she speaks.

"I am so angry with my father. He was waiting for my mother to leave him so he could come running back to Brian, the love of his life, or so it seems. What more can I think when I see him living in the same house as Brian? I am sure the 'M&N' that we saw at the gate is Murphy and Nanda. Partners in business, and lovers in bed. Thank god, my mother is dead and doesn't have to learn that whatever she believed about this man was true. I felt sick when Brian dared to say that my father had been hoping to get back with my mother again. How can people be so shallow and deceitful? But I am not letting my father get away that easily. He will answer my questions, and after that, I will have nothing to do with him."

Adam keeps his counsel. The whole scenario is such that Husna's belief can't be contradicted without further explanation. He only knows that he needs to be there for her, even more so now.

Husna is preoccupied throughout lunch, and though the young lady who asks for their order is overtly friendly, Husna answers her questions in monosyllables. They take their time with the coffee after lunch. Adam does not want to rush Husna, who seems wary about facing her father again.

All of a sudden, Husna says, "Let's go. I can't wait any longer. Let me hear what he has to say and then let's go back home to our life together." She gives Adam a winsome smile. He hugs her, and they drive back to Brian's house.

This time, they take in the décor of the house after Brian lets them in. There are several Chinese ceramics placed around the sitting room, which is dominated by a large painting of the Sydney Harbour Bridge and the Opera House as seen at night. The sitting room leads to a sunken dining room, which has an open kitchen to the left. The dining room then leads to the bedrooms beyond. On the other side of the sitting room is a study, and they can see books neatly shelved in a panelled cabinet.

"My child, I know you have a lot of questions, and I will answer them. But what you believe about me and Brian is wrong. Before I tell you the rest of my story and how I got here, I am very interested to know how you found me."

Husna, impatient to understand her father's behaviour, grudgingly narrates the journey they've had from Chicago to Sydney. "It's been a long chase, and even here at Mittagong, I was expecting Brian to tell us how to find you. I was flabbergasted to see *you* in this house."

Sudhir, who is looking much more composed now, tells them his story from the time he left Bombay for Dehradun.

***

Chapter 5
Sudhir's Story

"After your mother left me, after the terrible happenings in the office, which you must have read in the manuscript, I settled all my affairs in Bombay. I went to Dehradun for my father's house, which he had bequeathed to me. After his death, I left Rawat as its caretaker, which was to be used on family holidays by all of us, not only by my family but also the families of my sister, Rachna, and my younger brother, Jayant. They were the ones I had called Meena and Dev in my manuscript. They both live in America, but they didn't want to lose their connection with India.

"Dehradun is a lovely valley, and in those days, the air was cleaner and the landscape far greener than what I hear it has become today. I haven't been to Dehradun since I sold the house, though I have been to Delhi for my cousin's wedding and a couple of times to Bangalore on work with Brian. Sorry, I am getting ahead of myself. Coming back to that period, it was the darkest time of my life. In Dehradun, I shunned my neighbours and stayed indoors, looking at photographs of Kalpana and you and weeping most of the time. My old fears and panic attacks returned with a vengeance, and sometimes I felt that I would lose my sanity. I hadn't told Rachna and Jayant about what had happened, so I had no one to talk to. My earlier experience with a psychiatrist had not been a happy one, so I didn't get any medical help.

"Every week, I would sit down and write long letters to Kalpana, imploring her to come back. I sent them to Urvashi's house, as that was the only address I had. Slowly, I started losing weight; I grew my beard, and I started drinking. Initially, it was a couple of times per week, but soon, it became every evening. Sometimes, after a bout of drinking, I would write angry and nasty letters to Kalpana, foolishly giving them to Rawat to post before I changed my mind. I also became dependent on anti-anxiety drugs, for which I had a prescription earlier. In India, chemists need to see a doctor's prescription, but they keep no record of how many pills you take under that prescription. I had reached rock bottom. No job, no family, nothing except the temporary relief from drinking and drugs."

Sudhir stops here to take a sip of water from the bottle, which Brian has placed in front of him. They are all silently listening, and Husna has her hands under her chin, staring straight at Sudhir, who is mostly talking directly to her.

"After a few months, I woke up one morning and looked at the tatters of my life spread around me. That is the day I decided that I would not go further down this terrible tunnel of self-pity. I cut back on my drinking, slowly weaned myself off the anti-anxiety pills and started running. Initially, it was difficult, but soon, I got into the rhythm of running. The area where I lived was very picturesque, so running in those hills was an absolute pleasure. I also started writing the manuscript that I had promised myself I would, and I painted the portrait of the little boy, Arvind, whose childhood had been snatched away.

"Though my savings had dwindled considerably, I booked a flight to New York. I felt that if I met Kalpana, then, after nearly a year, she would have forgiven me and return with me to India. I was sure that on returning, I would be able to get another job.

"After I reached New York, I went straight to Urvashi's house. She was surprised to see me, but Kalpana and you were not living with her anymore. Urvashi cursed me for destroying her daughter's life. She never really liked me because she had wanted Kalpana to marry Dhruv, her friend's son. Then she refused to give me Kalpana's address or phone number. Finally, when she couldn't deal with me anymore, she threatened to call the police. She softened when she saw the terrible impact our meeting had on me. When I was leaving, she promised to talk to Kalpana and call me at the hotel the next morning to inform me if she would agree to see me.

"The next morning, true to her word, she called me. 'Kalpana has sent a message for you,' she said. 'Get lost! Husna is happy and has forgotten you, and the best possible way for you is to carry on your miserable life as before. You cannot be forgiven, and if you send me any more of those nasty letters, I will file a case of harassment against you in an American court.' I wept then, begging Urvashi to give me one chance to meet with Kalpana. But Urvashi wouldn't agree to it. She said, 'I can't help it; Kalpana does not want to see you.' Finally, she was moved enough to say she would keep talking to Kalpana, at least to allow me to see Husna sometimes. I thought of going to a solicitor to ask the courts for visiting rights, but I knew I wouldn't go through with it, even if I could afford it. I wasn't ready to create confusion in your childhood for my selfish reasons, especially as Kalpana would have fought it tooth and nail."

Husna speaks, "I guess Grandma did try to talk to my mom, but she wouldn't agree. I have recollections of your name being mentioned between them when they thought I was out of earshot. On my eighteenth birthday, I definitely heard them arguing about you."

Sudhir continues, "On that trip, I couldn't see both Rachna and Jayant as they were on the West Coast, but I called them and, for the first time, I told them about Kalpana leaving me and not allowing me to see you. Jayant said he would find out if anything could be done through the American courts, but I think he knew from my reaction that I wasn't going to pursue a legal option. I called Brian, who had gone through a messy divorce some months earlier, and although he knew from the grapevine what had happened at my old job, he wasn't aware that Kalpana had left me.

"I came back to Dehradun, and all the hopes that I had about bringing Kalpana and you back were completely crushed. I didn't feel like facing up to life as it existed. I was listless and in a terrible funk. I was in danger of slipping back to an aimless life of self-pity and drinking. I knew I needed to get back to work; I was coming to the end of my savings and would have to dip into the funds that our dad had shared among the siblings. But the effort to go back to work seemed enormous. Luckily, there was a yoga and meditation teacher giving classes in an *ashram* not far from my house, so I decided to join them. That changed my life completely. After I finished the course, I continued practising yoga on my own, and as time went by, I started enjoying the solitude of meditation. When I would sit in meditation on my veranda each morning and evening, the silence would envelop me in its embrace. It would flow around me in harmony, slowing my thoughts and mind and making me forget my body and treacherous thoughts. It was beautiful, and every time I came out of the trance, I would be refreshed and energetic. I decided to take control of my life and started applying for jobs.

"And then I got a call from Brian."

Brian speaks up then.

"A few months after my divorce, I decided to try to go back to Australia, the country I was working in earlier. I knew many recruitment firms and got in touch with them. At that time, Australia made it very easy for English-speaking professionals to migrate here. I was recruited by this company directly from America, and I moved to Sydney some eighteen years back. I settled down at The Rocks, the same apartment I bought later. I also knew that Sudhir was now getting his life together after he returned from America and was looking for a job, preferably in the UAE. He said he wanted to work abroad, given the circumstances for quitting his last job. Even though it was later proved that the accusation was false, in the small world of corporate India, that kind of muck doesn't drop off someone easily. When I learnt from HR in my company that they were looking for someone with the kind of experience that Sudhir had, I called him."

"Brian's call came out of the blue and was the answer to all my prayers," continues Sudhir. "Brian and I had always got along famously, and working with him again was a dream. As Brian mentioned, I needed to get away from corporate life in India and from my memories of Kalpana and you, Husna. So, I decided to interview for the job and was accepted.

"Initially, I stayed with Brian, but then rented an apartment in Sydney. Work in the company was challenging and had its own share of prejudice for non-Australians, especially someone brown like me. Even Brian didn't miss out on the prejudice, though he was white. There was a lot of travel, which compensated for the tougher parts, and we both had each other.

"We worked in that company for about thirteen years, and then Brian decided to quit and set up his own consultancy company with a focus on clients in the Far

East and India. He had bought land in Mittagong and built this house. He asked me to partner with him, and M&N Consultancy Services was born. We both moved out of Sydney and came here to Mittagong. No, Brian came first, and I moved in a year later. Brian, being the outdoor type, found city life too restrictive and claustrophobic, and with computers, we can work from anywhere."

"Are you lovers?" This comes like a shot out of the blue from Husna.

"No, absolutely not!" says Brian, colouring under his tan.

"No, we are not lovers," adds Sudhir, "Brian is someone I love as a friend."

"Then how come you live together?" asks Husna disbelievingly.

Brian is about to speak, but Sudhir puts up his hand.

"I think Husna deserves an explanation," he says calmly.

"Before I moved in here, I asked Brian if I could build a cottage on his land so that I could be closer to him and our place of work. The cottage that you see when you enter the property is mine. I live there. I know you have many questions, Husna, so let me try to address them in a more detailed way.

"When I came out to Sydney, I came with all the baggage of my past. I was still full of irrational fears, was dependent on anti-anxiety pills for my panic attacks and had a low sense of self-worth. Brian knew about my childhood, and we had talked about everything that happened to me until Kalpana left me. He also knew that I had fought with drug addiction and alcoholism, and he knew that with yoga and meditation, I was feeling less guilt-ridden and more in control of my life. He decided to shore up my confidence, something I have lacked since my childhood. His theory was to push my physical limits to great lengths—it would automatically generate so much inner strength that I would feel more powerful in facing the world.

"So that is what he did. He pushed me to take up physical challenges that came so easily to him. He made me look at my fears straight in the face and learn to kick them. He made me go white-water rafting on the Kaituna River in New Zealand at a time when I was afraid of swimming and bungee jumping, when I couldn't face a roller coaster in my childhood. He made me climb Mount Kilimanjaro and walk the Camino de Santiago in Spain. He was like my brother, and he also supported me like a father and made me slowly give up all my irrational fears."

Then Brian interjects, "Sudhir was someone whom I respected for his professionalism. It was sad that his past had played so much havoc in his life that he had forgotten what it was to wake up in the morning without thoughts of impending tragedy. I saw that running and meditation had given him a better sense of balance, but he had a self-defeating attitude to everything. I love Sudhir as a friend, and he had this terrific way of always getting into my head, knowing what I was thinking even before I could articulate it. I knew he was a fighter, but the spark went out when Kalpana left him. When I met him upon first coming to Sydney, he was defeated inside, but was doing everything to cope. As I came to understand and love him more, I knew that I had to inspire him to challenge himself. I was also careful that I did not become another crutch for him. He had to get up and run under his own steam. He was difficult, often refusing to push himself, and I had to threaten him with dire consequences..."

Sudhir adds to this by saying, "But he always had my back. You must understand that Brian made me whole again. I love him more than I have loved any other man in my life, not even Jayant."

Husna begins to see that Sudhir has come to terms with himself and that Brian has understood and respected this. A beautiful friendship is being revealed to them, nothing more. She finds her anger melting and her confusion dissipating.

"But the deep hole left inside me when your mother left was yet to be filled. My search for Kalpana and you never ended. Each year after Google and Facebook came into being, I would search for both your names. Surprisingly, you were never on Facebook. I tried all the possible surnames you could have been given: Chatterjee, Nanda, even Bhasin, your grandmother's name, but there was no trace of you on social media.

"This was until one month ago. As I always did, I entered Husna Chatterjee in Google and up popped an article in the Moda Magazine of the Wisconsin Union. It was a review of a production of *A Streetcar Named Desire*, and you were the author of the piece."

"I remember that day so well," continues Brian. "I heard a shout from his office, and when I ran across there, Sudhir showed me the article. He was ready to leave, right then and there, to search for you in Wisconsin, but we had been working with a critical Chinese client and Sudhir had scheduled a visit to China that couldn't be cancelled. We both agreed that once we had bagged the client, we would both fly to Wisconsin and look for you, even if we had to bribe the college to part with your address. But then John called us this morning and, miracle of miracles, you were here."

They have all been talking for a long time now, and it is time for Adam and Husna to return to Sydney. Husna gets up to go, but Sudhir stops her.

"Why don't you both stay with me at the cottage? I have to make up for so much lost time, and I hardly know anything about either of you."

Husna has softened by now.

"I promise we will check out of the apartment tomorrow and come and spend whatever time we have left in Australia with both of you," she says, tears shining in her eyes.

On the drive back to Sydney, Husna's thoughts are swirling around in her head. She has spontaneously agreed with her father to move into his cottage the next day, but this does not mean that she has suddenly forgotten the pain of having lived without her father, who had cheated on her mother more than once. But she also realises that there are no more secrets about her father. In his manuscript—and today—he has opened himself to them completely. It is now up to her to find within herself the means to forgive him and learn to love him. She also knows that only she can find this within her. She cannot ask Adam to help resolve her mind. She is sure that her spontaneous acceptance of her father's invitation is the right step towards healing.

The next day, they move in with Sudhir. His cottage is charming and full of artefacts, both Indian and Aboriginal, with a beautiful lithograph of horses on the main wall in the sitting room. Sudhir tells them that the original had been painted by a famous Indian artist, Hussain. The cottage has a beautiful lived-in appearance, and the garden is colourful, with butterflies fervently flying between the sweet peas and hollyhocks and many other English country flowers.

"When I was growing up, I always saw myself living in an English cottage with French windows opening out to a garden with honeysuckle and morning glory creepers hanging on the gates, and wild roses trailing all over the place. I got my wish once I came here to Brian's place. Now I am so happy to have you with me, Husna; I feel at peace."

Husna and her father spent the next few days just getting to know each other during the day and travelling to Canberra or Sydney for dinner in the evenings. One day, Sudhir pulls out an old album with photographs of Kalpana right after they married and Husna from the day she came to live with them. For the first time, Husna sees pictures of herself as a baby and a toddler, and quite a few of her birthday celebrations before Kalpana left Sudhir. There are other photographs of their friends, Sudhir's sister and brother, and his parents. Husna is exhilarated and overwhelmed to learn that she has uncles, aunts and cousins, all in America. In the evenings, when they sometimes visit Sydney, Husna loves the scintillating atmosphere of Darling Harbour and the buzz of the quayside's restaurants, where they go for dinner. On most evenings, Brian's girlfriend Cathy joins them, and there is a great deal of good-natured banter between Sudhir and Brian.

"Brian is a bigger kidder than the Aussies themselves," is Sudhir's oft-repeated refrain, and then Brian starts his clowning around, aping the accent of the Aussies, dropping his r's and g's and saying "good aye mate" to everyone who passes by. Once, when Cathy goes to the restroom, Sudhir wonders how long this relationship will last, given Brian's penchant for playing the field.

Brian says, "Cathy is a lovely woman, and we have a great relationship. Hey, mate, all of us can't live life like a monk like you!" and he elbows Sudhir playfully.

The next few days pass like a whirlwind with trips to Bondi Beach, where Brian shows off his tanned body and muscles, and the Sydney Opera House, where they go for a show, and The Rocks for souvenir-hunting and bargaining for opals.

Sudhir recalls anecdotes from his days in college with Kalpana and the rest of the gang; he also talks about Jayant and his wife Pamela and their two daughters, who live in Los Angeles, and Rachna, her husband Jakub and their son and daughter. Sudhir promises to email them, telling them about everything that has happened and about Husna.

"You can be sure that they will call you once they have heard from me," he says, laughing happily.

There are days when Brian goes to work, and Adam takes a book from Sudhir's considerable library and relaxes outside in the hammock in the garden, while Sudhir and Husna cook together. Sometimes they go for long walks around Brian's substantial property and talk. Sudhir tells Husna again of his continuing anguish in having cheated on her mother and the deep love he feels for her. He tells her about his guilt, due to what happened in his childhood and the love he holds for his mother and the hopelessness he feels about his father, who never gave him any loving attention until right at the very end. Husna talks about her childhood, about the silences from both her mother and grandmother whenever she tried to talk about him, and about the source of her strong feelings against gay men.

One day, out of the blue, she asks her father, "Are you in denial about being gay?"

"I... honestly don't know. I was never given a chance to naturally discover my sexuality," he replies, but then adds, "Maybe, but that is a path I do not want to go down anymore."

"What about Brian? Does your love for him go beyond a deep friendship?" Husna prods.

Sudhir is quiet for a while, and then he says softly, as if to himself, "You are correct. For a long time, I have hidden within myself a love for Brian, which hasn't excluded the physical. But I will not let it destroy my beautiful friendship with him by making a wrong move. I believe that in his heart, Brian knows about my struggle, but nothing is ever said, not even in a lighter vein."

So that is where Husna is concerned.

She often talks about her deep love for Adam and her anxiety as to whether she is worthy of him.

"He just upped and left everything to help me reach you, and I feel that I have been so obsessed with this search that I haven't cared enough for his feelings during these days."

"He adores you, Husna, and why wouldn't he? You both have your life ahead of you to love and stay loved. It must have been amazing for him to propose to you surrounded by the beauty of Kanatal," Sudhir says.

There is a lot of excitement about their upcoming wedding. Husna and Adam announce that the wedding will neither follow Hindu nor Jewish rituals, even though Adam still has to convince his mother of this decision. They want a simple ceremony which emphasises love, friendship, trust and giving. Brian and Sudhir are as excited as kids when making plans to travel to Chicago for the wedding. It is then that Husna asks Sudhir shyly, "Will you give me away?"

"Oh, my darling girl. I dare anyone to stop me!"

Finally, the day comes for them to leave for the US. Brian drives them to the airport in Sydney. Adam sits next to Brian while Sudhir and Husna sit in the back. Sudhir is fretting like a mother. "Have you checked your ticket? Did you reserve your seat? Do you have enough leg space in front? Why don't you let me use my miles to get you an upgrade to business? Have you checked your passport?" And so on, till Husna says, "Stop it, Dad! We are fine."

There is a shocked silence. Sudhir and Brian both speak at the same time, "You said Dad for the first time..."

Husna smiles, and Sudhir wipes the tears from his eyes.

Then it comes time to say goodbye. Sudhir opens his arms to Husna, and she effortlessly slips into his embrace. Brian puts his arms around both of them, and Sudhir pulls Adam into the group hug. They look like a football team in a huddle.

"I came here looking for a father," Husna says, tearfully pulling herself from the embrace, "but I got so much more. I grew up without a father, but I was loved by my mother and grandmother, sheltered from any trauma or an identity crisis. I met a person—you, my dad—buffeted with intense trauma since childhood, insecure in facing the world and misunderstood by so many. You fought your battles, sometimes faltered and failed, but got up again and again to face whatever hand life was going to deal you. You loved and lost, but you never forgot. From you, I have now learnt to forgive and to accept that people develop in their own way, as a result of the sum of their experiences and being different is perfectly fine! I love you, Dad, and you, Brian, for your beautiful friendship with my father."

Sudhir breaks down in tears as Husna speaks. All his wounds, that had once torn apart his family, come to be stitched one by one by his daughter's words. He realises that he has finally found his place in this world, the *home* he always dreamt of.

For possibly the first time in his life, Sudhir feels weightless—absolved.

***

Glossary

Abba: Father in Hebrew
Angrezi: English/ Westerner
Anars: Firecracker (Flower pot)
Arya Samaj: Hindu society
Bade Sahib: Elder master
Baraat: Bridegroom's procession
Bauji: Grandfather
Beta: Son
Beti: Daughter
Bhabi: Sister-in-law
Bhabiji: Grandmother
Bhapaji: Elder brother
Bhaiya: Brother
Bheji: Grandmother
Bibi: Wife
Burqa: Outer garment worn by Muslim women
Chakka: Homosexual
Chawl: A tenement building in Bombay
Chokri: A young girl
Choti Memsahib: Younger mistress
Chowkidar: A guard
Dadi: Paternal grandmother

Darshan:	Hindu word for vision of the divine
Dhoop:	Indian incense
Didi:	Elder sister
Diya:	Oil lamp
Eema:	Mother in Hebrew
Femmenella:	Effeminate man
Ghar Jamai:	A son-in-law who lives in his wife's family home
Gulab Jamun:	An Indian sweetmeat
Hammam:	A large container in which water is heated
Halwai:	Vendor of Indian sweetmeats
Jai Mata Di:	A salutation to the divine deity of Vaishno Devi
Jalebi:	An Indian sweetmeat
Jeejaji:	Sister's husband
Jolawala:	A student in Delhi with socialist leanings
Karma:	Law of cause and effect
Khukrain Biradari:	A particular sect from the Punjab
Kulta:	Downtrodden woman/ prostitute
Kurta Pyjama:	Traditional Indian dress worn by men
Lalaji:	Respectable term used for an elder
Laxmi Puja:	Prayers for the goddess of wealth

Manglik:	An astrological combination not favourable for marriage; no scientific basis
Mamu:	Mother's brother
Marathis:	People belonging to the state of Maharashtra
Memsahib:	Mistress of the house
Mohalla:	The neighbourhood.
Mussalman:	A Muslim
Nani-ma:	Maternal grandmother
Om:	A mystical sound of Hindu origin, used as an invocation
Paan:	Betel leaf eaten as a digestive.
Pakoda:	An Indian snack made of chickpea powder
Pallu:	The loose end of a *sari*, the garment worn by Indian women
Parsi:	Emigrants in India descended from the Persians
Pindies:	The rock formations in Vaishno Devi, representing the trinity of Hindu goddesses: Saraswati, Laxmi and Parvati
Pittu:	Game of seven stones
Puja:	Hindu prayers
Punjabi Sabha:	A society dedicated to Punjabis

Purdah:	A covering made for a woman's face so they cannot be seen
Raga Bhageshri:	A Hindustani classical Raga
Rasam Pagri:	A ritual carried out on the 4th or 13th day after the death of a parent
Sahib:	Master
Sala:	Mild abuse
Samosa:	A North Indian savoury snack, stuffed and deep-fried
Sardarji:	Respectable form of greeting a Sikh
Sari:	A long wrap-around garment worn by Indian women
Sethji:	A respected name given to a trader
Shalwar Kameez:	Dress worn by women in South Asia
Shlokas:	A poetic form of Sanskrit
Shiva:	The week-long mourning period (Judaism)
Shura:	A council (Hebrew/Arabic)
Swami:	A Hindu priest
Teen patti:	A game of chance played with three cards

Thali:	A plate that carries the items required for prayers
Topi:	Light hard hat
Tongawallah:	Driver of a tonga, an old form of transport in India
Vaishnavi:	The goddess of Vaishno Devi
Wie geht es dir:	How's it going? (German)

About the Author

Sunil Sethy is a retired chartered accountant who has worked in various companies in India before retiring in 2020 as CEO of two large Indian corporations. His work has led him to travel to many countries over the years, and this has helped him to authentically locate this book in countries such as Australia and the USA. His parents came to divided India as refugees from Pakistan, though he was born after Partition, in 1951. All the events relating to displaced families and their nomadic existence in the early chapters of the book are based on stories he heard during his childhood. When Sunil Sethy was a child, he was, for many years, subjected to sexual abuse. The aftermath of this abuse and his survival to come out stronger inspired him to write this book, though the story is fictional. This is his first full-length novel, although he has written poetry (unpublished) for many years. He lives with his wife in Goa, India and has a son and a daughter.